Claiming
by Y

"I don't know

"Ah, that's where you are wrong, my beautiful wife. You know me. Intimately."

With that he bent down. She was momentarily aware of the almost driven expression on his face before the distance between them closed and the coolness of his firm lips captured hers. She bunched her hands into fists to stop herself from lifting her arms, from curling them around his shoulders and pressing her body against his to ease the ache.

Abruptly Luc pulled away.

"See, we're not such strangers after all." His eyes glittered, daring her to deny the way her body had awakened in response to his kiss.

Claiming His Runaway Bride
by Yvonne Lindsay

"I don't know you,"

High-Stakes Passion
by Juliet Burns

"I'll see your ten and raise you, um, this whole stack of money," Audrey said triumphantly.

"I don't have any money left," Mark said.

"Well, I guess you could bet something besides money."

"Like what?"

Audrey stopped smiling and looked directly into Mark's brooding blue eyes. "If I win...you stop drinking," she said, "and you shave that awful beard!"

"What the hell kind of bet is that?"

"If you don't think you can do it – "

"OK, Ms High-Stakes Player, let's say we up the ante."

"What do you mean?"

It was Mark's turn to look smug as he clasped his hands behind his head. "I'll see your bet by shaving my beard and I raise it by getting off the booze. Now, see my raise by wagering something *I* want, or fold."

Surely he didn't want... "Um, what do you have in mind?"

His smouldering gaze slid down her body. "I think you know exactly what *I* want. Now, do you fold, or play?"

Available in October 2009
from Mills & Boon® Desire™

High-Society Secret Pregnancy
by Maureen Child

&

Front Page Engagement
by Laura Wright

Spaniard's Seduction
by Tessa Radley

&

Cole's Red-Hot Pursuit
by Brenda Jackson

Claiming His Runaway Bride
by Yvonne Lindsay

&

High-Stakes Passion
by Juliet Burns

CLAIMING HIS RUNAWAY BRIDE

BY
YVONNE LINDSAY

HIGH-STAKES PASSION

BY
JULIET BURNS

⊚™ MILLS & BOON®

First published in Great Britain 2009
Harlequin Mills & Boon Limited,
Eton House, 18-24 Paradise Road, Richmond, Surrey TW9 1SR

The publisher acknowledges the copyright holders of the
individual works as follows:

Claiming His Runaway Bride © Dolce Vita Trust 2008
High-Stakes Passion © Juliet L Burns 2005

ISBN: 978 0 263 87115 9

51-1009

Harlequin Mills & Boon policy is to use papers that are natural, renewable and recyclable products and made from wood grown in sustainable forests. The logging and manufacturing processes conform to the legal environmental regulations of the country of origin.

Printed and bound in Spain
by Litografia Rosés S.A., Barcelona

CLAIMING HIS RUNAWAY BRIDE

BY
YVONNE LINDSAY

New Zealand born, to Dutch immigrant parents, **Yvonne Lindsay** became an avid romance reader at the age of thirteen. Now, married to her blind date and with two surprisingly amenable teenagers, she remains a firm believer in the power of romance. Yvonne feels privileged to be able to bring to her readers the stories of her heart. In her spare time, when not writing, she can be found with her nose firmly in a book, reliving the power of love in all walks of life. She can be contacted via her website, www.yvonnelindsay.com.

Dear Reader,

As a child I always loved fairy tales – in fact, I never tired of reading them over and over again. Having children of my own was a chance to relive those tales of wonder – of the course of true love never running smooth, of happy ever after. One story that always spoke to my heart, as a child and as an adult, was *Beauty and the Beast*. I think it's the whole "Love Conquers All" that just gets to me – the unwavering belief that true love can break the wickedest of spells and redeem the hardest of hearts. Anyway, suffice it to say that I've always been a bit of a romantic, and when I first started thinking about *Claiming His Runaway Bride* it was a simple matter to go for a *Beauty and the Beast* theme. My convoluted mind just couldn't help but add an amnesiac runaway bride to the mix.

When I start my romance novels I always think very hard about the setting, and in all the beauty that is New Zealand I'm spoiled for choice. A part of the North Island I've always loved has been the Taupo district. Lake Taupo is the largest lake in the country, and the scenery around the area is exquisite in its beauty and diversity. Tourists travel from far and wide to appreciate the splendour of the countryside – especially those who enjoy outdoor pursuits. My "Beast" needed his own castle and domain, and what better area than the rugged strength and power of the hills to the southeast of Lake Taupo, where hunting, fishing and tramping reign supreme. And so Luc's Tautara Lodge was created as an exclusive luxury adventure-holiday empire.

I hope you enjoy my own version of a modern fairy tale.

Best wishes,

Yvonne

This one is for my beautiful girls, Morgan and Tegan.
One day your prince/s will come... :)

One

HIS *wife?*

How could she have forgotten something like that? Someone like him?

Belinda eyed the silent stranger standing beside her father at the foot of her hospital bed. Tall, and looking as if his designer clothes were just a little too large on his frame, the stranger stood with his left hand in his trouser pocket, his right hand resting on the knob of a shiny black cane.

She didn't even know his name. How could she be married to him and have no knowledge of it? Fear choked her throat.

His glittering green eyes never left her face. An intangible thread of something—was it anger?—burned just below the surface. His expression remained in-

scrutable. The hard lines of his face spoke of an iron
will—this was not a man who tolerated fools.

Her breath hitched. She didn't know him—how
could they expect her to go home with a total stranger?
Belinda cast a frightened look at her father. The smile
he returned seemed strained; the lines on his face
deeper than usual. Suddenly her desire to be released
from her room here at Auckland City Hospital fled,
and the place she'd itched to be free of assumed proportions more in line with a much-sought-after sanctuary.

A disturbing thought occurred to her.

"If you're my husband why haven't you been here
at my side, like my parents have? It's two weeks since
I came out of the coma." Her challenge rang hollowly
across the room.

Belinda intercepted a glance between her father and
the man who claimed to be her husband, saw the im-
perceptible nod her father gave.

"Well?" she demanded, her hands fisting in the
bedclothes.

"The accident that took your memory also caused
me injury. I am fit to return home now. With you."

There was a great deal he wasn't saying, and what
he left unsaid caused her more anxiety than the realisation he too had been hospitalised. She'd been treated
with kid gloves by the medical staff and her parents
since she'd regained consciousness, everyone prepared
to give her medical answers but nothing else. Not even
the details of the accident that had left her in a coma
for four weeks. Throughout the past two weeks of tests
and examinations, her doctors had tried to find the

cause of her amnesia and had come to the conclusion it was not a direct result of the blow to her head that she'd sustained in a car accident. She'd overheard the words "traumatic amnesia" and "hysterical amnesia" being discussed in low tones.

The last had made her shudder. Did that make her crazy, she wondered, that she chose to forget a part of her life that for anyone should have been full of excitement, fun and passion? Or did she have good reason to want to forget?

She looked again at the stranger. The slightly less-than-perfect fit of his clothing now made sense if he had been stuck in hospital. Had he been too incapacitated to see her? Did a lengthy stay in bed explain his gauntness? She had no doubt that he was the type of man who paid attention to every detail, and that under normal circumstances his clothing would conform to his body as if tailor-made.

Another thought skittered through her mind. Had they timed her release to coincide with his? Protest flared inside.

She'd been railroaded.

"No, I won't do it. I won't go home with you. I don't even know you!" Her voice sounded shrill, panicked.

The stranger's eyes narrowed, a muscle worked in the side of his jaw.

"I'm Luc Tanner, you are Belinda Tanner—my wife. Of course you'll come home with me." He nodded in her father's direction. "Do you think your father would allow you out of his sight if I was a threat to his precious child? Rest assured, you know me well."

There was an undercurrent in his tone she couldn't

quite nail, but it was enough to send a shiver down her spine. She shook her head slightly to rid herself of the sensation. What the stranger—Luc, she corrected herself—said made sense but a cautionary niggle played at the back of her mind.

"Why can't I go home with Dad? At least until my memory returns." She was grasping at straws, and she knew it.

"And if your memory never returns? Are we to forever forget our marriage? Our vows to each other?"

There was a thread of steel in his tone that sent a chill through her. It was a good question. What if she didn't get her lost months back? And why, when she could remember so much else, could she remember nothing of their courtship, their marriage? The love they'd supposedly shared.

A spear of something else shot through her body. Had they been intimate? They must have been, even now her body warmed to his with a physical recognition her mind refused to accept. He was a very attractive man despite that air of aloofness he wore like a warrior's mantle. A flush of heat suffused her cheeks as she studied his features—the slightly shadowed line between cheekbone and jaw bisected by a thin pink scar, the straight blade of his nose, the sensual curve of his lips. Had they lain together, delighted in each other's scents, reactions, pleasure? Had she clutched that short-cropped sable-coloured hair as she'd held him to her body?

The stranger's voice was like the sensual stroke of velvet across her skin as he changed tactics in the face of her refusal to go with him. "Belinda, I know you're afraid, but I'm your husband. If you can't trust me who can you trust? We will work through this," he cajoled gently. "And if your memory never returns, we will make new memories."

New memories. Why did the very thought strike dread into her heart?

She shot an imploring look at her father. "Dad?"

"You'll be fine, my sweet. Besides, you know your mother and I had planned to travel for a bit. We postponed the trip because of the accident. Now that you and Luc are well again we can set our plans back on track. Go home with Luc, honey. Everything will be all right."

Was it her imagination or were her father's words just a little too emphatic?

"The doctor has seen fit to discharge you. It's time for you to come home." Luc held out his left hand to her, a hand that bore a glint of gold on his ring finger. A ring she'd supposedly put on him while declaring her love for him before witnesses.

Belinda was suddenly aware of her own naked hand. There wasn't even so much as a dent in her skin to show where a ring had encircled her finger.

"Ah, yes, of course. Your rings." Luc slid his hand inside the breast pocket of his jacket and extracted two rings. He limped forward to the side of her bed. "Let me."

His fingers were surprisingly warm to the touch. They curled about her hand in a gentle, yet undeniably possessive grip. Something perverse inside her encouraged her to pull from his touch. As if he anticipated her action his fingers tightened as he helped her to her feet—his grip holding her hand captive.

He slid the platinum band, inlaid with baguette-cut white diamonds, onto her ring finger. As the overhead light caught the sparkle and fire in the stones, Belinda fought to control the tremor that quaked through her body, the sensation of having been branded Luc Tanner's property. A shocking sense of déjà vu swamped her as the image of Luc placing the ring on her finger in another time and place filled her mind. A remembered thrill of excitement and anticipation surged through her.

She fought to hold on to the impression, the fleeting consciousness of her lost months, but it dissipated as quickly as it had come, leaving her feeling empty and alone.

Belinda became aware of Luc's long fingers sliding another ring on her finger, bringing it up over her knuckle to nestle against the wedding band. The radiant-cut blue-grey diamond burned with cold fire, the shoulders of its setting decorated with smaller baguette-cut white diamonds. She gasped aloud at the size and beauty of the stone.

"Did…did I choose this?"

Luc's dark brows pulled together, making him appear even more formidable than before. "You don't remember this, either? For a moment I thought you did."

Somehow he'd sensed her flash of memory when he'd put on her wedding band. The implication of how well he understood her was unnerving, more unnerving perhaps than even the knowledge that she couldn't remember a single thing about him.

"No," she replied on a whisper. "I remember nothing."

"I commissioned the ring for you the day I met you."

"The day we met? But how...?" Belinda looked up at him in surprise.

Luc's gaze held hers. "I knew from that day you would be my wife."

Her laugh sounded forced, even to her ears. "And did I have any say in the matter?"

"Belinda." He pronounced each syllable of her name with care, making it sound like a caress. "You loved me before. You will love me again."

He lifted her hand to his lips, and pressed a kiss against her knuckles. His lips were surprisingly cool and an unexpected quiver of longing spread through her. What would it feel like if he kissed her? Would that unlock their past, the memories entrapped within her mind?

Luc drew her to his side, the imprint of his body heat seeped through her light clothing and deeper, to her skin. She pulled away, just enough to break the unnerving contact that had already sent her pulse into an erratic beat. His body felt unfamiliar, yet she was drawn to him at the same time. Surely if they had been married, been intimate together, she would have some physical memory imprinted in her psyche?

"The helicopter is waiting. We can't obstruct the hospital helipad for any longer than absolutely necessary."

"Helicopter? We aren't driving? Just how far are we going?"

"Tautara Estate is southeast of Lake Taupo. Perhaps being back there will assist in triggering a memory for you."

"Lake Taupo, but that's almost a four-hour drive from here. What if...?" Her voice trailed away helplessly. What if, indeed? There'd be no one there to help her if the fears that plagued the edge of her consciousness became more than she could bear.

"What if…?" Luc prompted, his lips a thin implacable line across his face.

"Nothing." Belinda dropped her head slightly, allowing the fullness of her hair to cover her face, to hide the sudden tears that stung her eyes. Everything inside her screamed that this was wrong, but she couldn't, for the life of her, remember why. The doctors had told her her memory should return in time, that she should stop trying to force things, but right now the black void in her mind threatened to overwhelm her.

"Then let's go."

Belinda walked two steps with Luc then halted, her sudden stop sending him slightly off balance. She noticed he used the cane to regain his stability. Was he fully recovered himself? She already sensed it was a question she couldn't ask, sensed he was too proud to admit to physical failure or weakness. Pulling from Luc's hold, she turned to her father, holding her arms out for a hug.

"I'll see you later, then, Dad. You'll give my love to Mum?" She searched his face once more for any inkling of why she felt as if she'd been shucked off like last year's haute couture, but he refused to fully meet her gaze. Instead he wrapped her in his arms and held her as if he'd never let her go.

"Yes, I will. She wasn't up to today's visit but we will see you soon," Baxter Wallace said, his voice thick.

"Baxter." Luc's voice cut through the air with the precision of fine steel, and her father's arms dropped to his side.

"Go on, darling, everything will be all right. Just wait and see," he urged.

"Of course everything will be all right. Why wouldn't it be?" Luc tucked Belinda's arm in the crook of his and guided her out the door.

Later, as the helicopter lifted from the pad, Belinda tried to remember why she'd been so excited when the doctor had told her she'd be discharged this afternoon. Now she felt anything but. She had nothing with her but the clothes on her back and the rings on her finger—rings that felt as foreign to her as the man who was her husband. She didn't even have so much as a pair of sunglasses to ward off the sharp late-summer-afternoon light.

She cast a glance forward to her husband who sat next to the pilot in the cockpit. Her husband. No matter what they said, he was a stranger, and deep in her heart she knew he'd remain that way for a long, long time.

You loved me before. You will love me again.

His words echoed in her mind and as they did it occurred to her he'd said nothing of his feelings for her. Not one word of love had passed his lips from the moment she'd set eyes on him. The realisation sat like a cold ball of lead in the pit of stomach.

Relief poured through Luc's aching bones as his Eurocopter Squirrel neared Tautara Estate—so named because of its position on the hilltop overlooking a small tributary river to New Zealand's largest lake. He consciously fought to stop himself from rubbing his hip to ease the ache of sitting in the confines of the cockpit of the helicopter. He'd accepted he was unable, at this time anyway, to pilot the craft himself. His recovery from the broken hip and torn spleen had taken longer than expected when a bone infection had delayed his rehabilitation.

The knowledge that his wife lay only a couple of floors away from him, locked in a coma that had baffled her doctors, had done much to hasten his recuperation. Her emergence from the coma had come just as he commenced intensive physical therapy and had begun to welcome the challenge of restoring his body to its customary strength. He'd had no desire to appear as a cripple the first time she saw him after the accident. He'd pushed himself hard this past fortnight, but it had been worth it. He was nearly home.

With her.

The chopper followed the path of one of the lake's tributaries, where he often hosted trout fishing expeditions for his celebrity guests, and Luc took comfort in the familiar landscape, the energy of the land below reaching out to him. Yes, he'd heal more quickly here, in charge of his own progress. In charge of his life. The way it should be.

He cast a look backward to where Belinda sat staring out the side window. A fierce wave of possession swept through him. She was his. Lost memory or not, things would return to the way they should have been all along—before the accident.

Her misty blue-grey eyes were serious as she gazed at her surroundings, her face pale, her hands curled into tight fists in her lap. She'd barely moved for the duration of the flight. Frozen in the past he supposed. She didn't remember meeting him, their courtship or their wedding. She didn't remember the crash. A part of him hoped she never would.

As the helicopter gained height, then circled over Tautara Estate, Luc allowed a smile of satisfaction to play across his lips. The estate was a monument to his success and power and was renowned worldwide amongst the wealthy, the famous—even royalty—for its facilities and attractions. And it was home in a way he'd never had a home before. The words his father had beaten into him on a regular basis—"You'll never amount to anything. Nothing you have will stay yours."—echoed in his head.

"You were wrong, old man," he swore silently. "I *am* and I *have* everything you never were or ever had."

Yes, now they were back all would be well again.

The pilot set the chopper down on the designated pad and Luc disembarked, turning to help Belinda from the cabin. They walked in silence toward the main house, which sprawled before them. Belinda halted beside him.

"Is something wrong?" Luc asked, forcing himself not to scoop her up in his arms and carry her to the front door through his sheer will.

"I've been here before?" she asked, her voice tentative.

"Of course. Many times before our wedding."

"I should remember something, but I don't. There's…nothing there."

Luc sensed the frustration that held her in its grip and

unbidden, felt a brief but undeniable pull of sympathy for her. The feeling left him as quickly as it had come.

"Come into the house, perhaps something there will jog your memory."

He took her hand in his and felt a measure of relief when her slender fingers curled around his, almost as if she was frightened to take the next step without him at her side. A grim smile settled on his face, and the fingers of his other hand gripped the head of his custom-made cane, its solid weight against the palm of his hand a reminder of the disability that would forever remain a legacy of their short marriage.

Whether she remembered again or not, he had her back at Tautara Lodge, where she belonged. As they crossed the threshold onto the New Zealand native parquet floor in the imposing cathedral-ceilinged entrance, Luc fought to hold back a roar of triumph. Nothing would interfere with his plans now.

No one reneged on Luc Tanner and got away with it—least of all his beautiful wife.

Two

Belinda stared around her. She felt as if she'd been totally displaced in her world. Nothing about the ornate stained-glass and rimu wood-framed doors at the front entrance felt familiar, and as her heels clicked on the highly polished wooden floor the faint echo rang out as a taunting reminder of the echoes in her mind. Fleeting. Intangible. Lost in a moment.

"Let me show you our suite."

"Our suite?"

"Yes, I run Tautara Estate as a luxury lodge for overseas visitors. They pay handsomely for their privacy, I demand mine. Our rooms are to this side."

Luc led her through another set of panelled rimu doors and down a wide, high-ceilinged, carpeted corridor. To her left was a panel of floor-to-ceiling glass windows giving an exquisite view down through the valley, with Lake Taupo, sunlight glinting off its surface, far in the distance. The tranquil beauty of the scene lay in direct contrast to the nerves leaping and dancing in her stomach.

At the end of the corridor Luc swiped a key card and thrust open the door. Belinda stifled a gasp at the step-down lounge that spread before her. It was twice the size of her parents' formal sitting room at their palatial St. Helier's Bay home in Auckland. Twice the size and, by the looks of it, twice as expensively comfortable.

She walked down the stairs ahead of Luc. Her hand stroked the fronds of the potted palms that guarded the base of the shallow stairs and trailed over the surface of the baby grand piano nestled in an alcove of the room to her left.

"You play?" she asked.

Her fingers grazed the cool ivory of the keys, sending a single discordant note to hover on the air.

"After a fashion," Luc answered noncommittally.

Belinda lifted her head and met his gaze fully for the first time since they'd left the hospital.

"Did you play for me?"

Suddenly she needed to know. The piano was a beautiful instrument—an instrument of passion, capable of expressing deepest desires and yearnings even when words failed. As she waited for Luc's response his eyes changed, deepening in colour, becoming the stormy green of a storm-tossed lake. The scar across his cheek paled and she noted the tension in the set of his jaw.

"Luc?" she prompted.

"Yes. I played for you," he finally ground out.

The light in his eyes changed again, reflecting a heat that flared to unexpected life from deep within her body. She saw the muscles working in his throat, the twin spots of colour that marked the slant of his cheekbones—sensed the unleashed power of his body. Had he wooed her with music? Had she been seduced by the power of his long-fingered hands as they'd coaxed perfection from the keys of the baby grand? Had he then coaxed perfection from her?

A shiver of longing played down her spine, and she felt her breathing slow, her blood thicken languidly in her veins.

Belinda forced herself to break eye contact, to step further into the room with its luxurious fittings and deeply comfortable furnishings. Despite the value of each piece it was obviously a room that was used and enjoyed. Or at least it had been until they'd been hospitalised.

"I'll show you the rest of the suite." Luc's voice cut sharply across her thoughts.

"Yes, that's a good idea," she replied as she followed him up the shallow stairs on the other side of the lounge, to the informal dining area and small but functional kitchen. "So you're completely self-contained here," Belinda observed as they passed through to another corridor.

"We are."

Belinda couldn't help but notice his subtle emphasis on the word "we."

Luc continued. "The lodge has its own gym and indoor pool, and you can see the tennis court through there." He indicated a deep-set window that framed a vista out toward the back of the main section of the lodge where a full-size tennis court stood in readiness. "My office is located in the main section of the lodge."

"Do you have any guests here at the moment?"

"No. Not since the accident."

Belinda furrowed her brow in confusion. "Is it your off season or something? Couldn't your staff still have been able to provide their services and the full range of your facilities even while you were in hospital?"

"Certainly they could. I wouldn't employ them otherwise."

"Then why?"

"This time had been booked up for personal reasons."

She hesitated, noting how his hand had tightened on the head of his cane. His limp seemed more pronounced.

"Personal reasons?" she probed.

"Our honeymoon, to be precise."

He bit the words out as if they were poison past his lips and Belinda flinched at his tone.

Their honeymoon?

"Just how long have we been married?" Her voice shook as she asked the question.

"Not long."

"Luc? Tell me." Belinda pushed her back against the wall behind her, certain she'd need its support.

"Belinda, the doctors said you need time. You must take things slowly."

"How long have we been married?" she insisted, enunciating each word as clearly as she could through a mouth that felt as if it was stuffed with cotton wool.

"Just over six weeks."

"Six weeks? But then that means…" Her voice trailed away weakly. Her legs threatened to give way on her, and she braced her hands against the solid strength of the wall behind her.

"I shouldn't have told you."

Luc stepped toward her, but Belinda threw up one hand in protest as he leaned forward to touch her.

"No! Don't. I'm okay. I'll be okay. It was just…unexpected, that's all."

Six weeks? That meant they'd been involved in the accident shortly after their wedding. But then why would no one give her any details about it? Why couldn't she remember?

Luc remained silent, his eyes flicking over her, searching for proof of her affirmation that she was indeed all right. He took a step away and turned to throw open double doors that led into a sumptuous bedroom. Her eyes were inexorably drawn to the king-size pedestal bed that dominated the room, dwarfing the exquisite outlook from the French doors that lined the outside wall.

Despite the generous proportions of the room and the bank of glass that allowed the crisp sunlight to warm the air, she felt the walls close in on her as the tension between them tautened like a drawn bow. Belinda could barely tear her eyes from the expanse of fine linen, the teals and blues of the damask duvet cover mirroring the tones and textures of the water in the far distance and the flora outside. She hadn't stopped to think about their arrangements once they arrived here. What if he expected to sleep with her?

An image imprinted in her mind of her body entwined with Luc's. Her throat dried, making it difficult to formulate her next words.

"Is this the only bedroom?"

"Yes. When we start our family we will extend this part of the lodge. I already have the plans drawn up."

"I would prefer to sleep somewhere else."

"Impossible."

"What?"

"You're my wife. You sleep with me."

"But—"

"Are you afraid of me, Belinda?"

Luc stepped close enough to her that she could smell the subtle tang of his cologne, the lime and spice intertwined into something that sent her pulse skittering through her veins. He lifted a hand to stroke a tendril of her hair back behind her ears. She tilted her head slightly, breaking the tenuous contact even as it began, but not soon enough to halt the heated tingle that danced across the surface of her skin.

"Afraid? No. Not at all," she lied. Afraid? She was terrified. As far as she was aware, their acquaintance, their *knowledge* of each other—be it physical or mental—had started from the moment he'd walked into her hospital room only a scant few hours ago.

"Then you think I would force my attention on you?" He cupped the back of her head, stroking her hair, forcing her to meet his gaze.

"I—I don't know," she stammered. "I don't know you."

"Ah, that's where you are wrong, my beautiful wife. You know me. Intimately."

With that he bent down. She was momentarily aware of the almost driven expression on his face before the distance between them closed and the coolness of his firm lips captured hers. She went rigid at the contact and felt his fingers tighten imperceptibly at the nape of her neck. Her lips parted on a gasp of shock and despite her determination not to return his caress she found herself unable to halt the answer of her body to his. The pressure of his kiss firmed, demanded more, and like an automaton she gave it.

She bunched her hands into fists to stop herself from lifting her arms, from curling them around his shoulders and pressing her body against his to ease the ache that made her breasts throb with need. Luc deepened the kiss, his tongue probing past her lips to gently stroke the soft inner recess of her mouth. A spear of desire drove through her from deep within her core. She fought the near overwhelming craving to be touched by him. To be dragged from the fugue of not knowing, to full aching awareness of Luc—of his taste, of his touch.

Abruptly Luc pulled away.

"See, we're not such strangers after all." His eyes glittered like chips of aventurine as he pinned her with his unblinking stare. Daring her to deny the way her body had awakened in response to his kiss. "There will be no force, I can assure you."

He limped toward the door, leaving Belinda standing there, alone.

"Where are you going?" she blurted. As unsettling as she found his presence, and her reaction to it, the prospect of being left alone was even more so. He was the only thing even vaguely familiar to her.

"Missing me already?" His lips fleetingly curved into an approximation of a smile. "I have business to attend to."

"Business? But surely it can wait. You must be tired. You're limping worse than before."

As soon as the words escaped her lips she knew she'd made a mistake. Luc Tanner was not the sort of man who liked to be reminded of his all-too-human frailty.

"Why, Belinda, you sound just like a concerned wife." He flashed her a smile that had nothing to do with humor. "My business has waited too long already. I suggest you rest until dinnertime."

He wheeled around on his good leg and left the room, leaning heavily on the cane she instinctively knew he had come to hate with all the seething passion she sensed beneath the cool surface he projected to the world. The seething passion he'd held in check while provoking a clamour in her that she knew already only he could answer.

Who was this man who was her husband? What had drawn her to him? And what on earth about her had drawn him in return?

She pressed shaking fingers against her lips. Had their attraction been purely physical? If her incendiary reaction to his kiss had been any indicator, she could certainly have believed that. But she'd never been overtly sexual. Her relationships had always been…civilised, for want of a better word. She had the feeling that any pretension to civilised behaviour from Luc was a mask. Beneath the surface, at grassroots level, he was indomitably feral.

So what was it, then? Had she been so drawn to the wildness in him, been so desperate to escape the confines of her "safe" world? She'd worked darned hard being the perfect hostess for her father in recent years, years in which her mother's health had steadily declined. She'd sublimated her own burgeoning career as a landscape designer, settling for the occasional showpiece job for her father's wealthy cronies. Jobs that had left her feeling as if she'd been appeased, like a fractious child. No matter how many magazines her gardens had been featured in, her family, including her two older sisters, had continued to condescendingly treat it as her little hobby.

Belinda sank down onto the comfortable two-seater couch, positioned to make the most of the expansive view across the valley. She knew everything about her life up until the point where she'd met him. Why couldn't she remember anything about that time?

Couldn't remember, or wouldn't?

The question chilled her to her bones.

She pushed herself up and out of the seat, determined to find something that would trigger a memory. He said she'd been here before, many times. Surely she'd left a piece of herself here. Something familiar.

She hesitated a moment before pulling open a door, almost fearful of what she would find behind it. It was one thing to want to know what had happened in the past, it was quite another to discover it.

A sigh of relief rushed past her lips as she viewed the luxuriously appointed bathroom. A massive spa bath lay along one glassed wall, a double vanity lined another, and set into an alcove was a large shower stall with multiple showerheads. Clearly, everything here was designed with two in mind.

She smiled as she identified her Chanel products in the shower stall, on the bathroom vanity. Her favourite fragrance and lotion nestled side by side as if they had done so forever. She reached out and grabbed the lotion, squeezing out a small blob and smoothing it over her bare arms, taking comfort in the familiarity of its scent.

Inside a drawer she recognised makeup and personal effects. All undeniably hers. Bit by bit the tension inside her started to ease away. As strange as Luc felt to her, this was her home. These were her things.

Emboldened by her discovery, Belinda went to investigate what lay behind the other door from their room. She laughed quietly. Already she was calling it theirs. It must be right.

A spacious dressing room with his and hers large wardrobes set on either side revealed an extensive array of clothing—for both of them. Formal wear, casual wear, in between. Belinda's fingers lingered over the array of fabrics and designs, hoping for a "ping" of memory. An image to hold on to.

A tremor ran through her as she reached for a garment, still shrouded in the cheap plastic dry cleaner's bag, and pulled it away from the rest. Even through the protective covering the myriad of crystal beads sparkled like tears embroidered against the cross-over bodice of the ivory satin bridal gown.

Belinda dragged the cover off. Her wedding dress. She should feel something, anything but this emptiness. Surely some sensation, some remembrance should linger in her mind. She shook out the full train

of the dress and held the gown to her and studied herself
in the full-length mirror. She tried to imagine herself in
it, walking toward Luc, ready to pledge her love and her
life to him.

Nothing.

A frown furrowed her brow and she felt the beginnings of a headache start to pound. In frustration she
haphazardly shoved the bag back over the dress and
pushed the hanger back onto the rail. As she did so her
hand caught on the dry cleaner's ticket, attached to the
bag. She pulled it off and her stomach lurched as she
saw the box that had been ticked for special attention—
remove bloodstains—and the handwritten note saying
the removal of stains was successful.

Blood. Had it been hers or Luc's?

She rubbed her forehead and gave a hard mental
push through her mind, but all it elicited was a sharper
edge to what had started as a dull pain behind her eyes.
Whatever she'd locked in the past determinedly
remained there.

It wasn't until she had gone through a few drawers
of underwear and other clothing that she found a dis-
reputable pair of jeans and a handful of T-shirts that,
despite being laundered, were streaked with green
stains. She sank to her knees as she pulled them from
the drawer and unfolded them.

Her gardening gear. Her heart began to race. Finally
she recognised something. Her hands shook as she
kicked off her shoes and peeled away the clothes she'd
worn home from the hospital—clothes her parents had
brought up to her the night before—and stepped into the
jeans. They fit. A little on the loose side, but that was

only to be expected after her stay in hospital. She searched for a belt and put it through the loops, adjusting it a couple of notches tighter than the wear on the belt suggested was usual. A smile pulled at her lips as she pulled on one of the T-shirts. Yes, this felt right, and if she could get into the garden maybe she'd remember more.

Leaving her discarded clothing on the floor, Belinda slipped on a pair of rubber-soled flat shoes from the shoe rack and headed for the French doors across the bedroom. She flung them open, stepping out onto the private deck, and inhaled the herbaceous scents on the air.

Stairs led off the deck from the right-hand side, down into the impeccably landscaped gardens. As she danced down them, she cast her eyes around, waiting for that same spark of recognition that had struck when she'd found the gardening wear, but it continued to elude her.

The grounds were extensive and the sun was low in the sky when she found the herb garden. Crushed-shell pathways, edged with old bricks, formed a complex Celtic knot pattern, with lush foliage of a variety of herbs—their scents rich in the evening air—filling the spaces in between. At its central point a sundial was mounted, casting long shadows into the boxed rosemary nearby.

Rosemary—for remembrance. She'd have laughed out loud if the irony hadn't been so painful. Yet of all the places she'd explored in the garden this was the one area she felt most at home. Absently Belinda snapped off a sprig of rosemary and, rubbing it between her fingers, brought the fragrant herb to her nose and inhaled deeply.

Suddenly she knew. This was *her* garden. She'd planned and painstakingly directed the position of each plant in its place. The parsley she'd planted herself— she remembered that much—laughing at the time at something her sisters had said about how each time they'd planted parsley they'd fallen pregnant. The hope she'd felt that the old wives' tale would come true for her struck her square at her centre, and she staggered to the bench seat positioned to make the most of the final rays of the sun.

She remembered. Oh, God, she remembered the garden. It had taken months to get it to this state, but what of the rest? What of the time she must have spent here with Luc, of their growing relationship and their plans for a future together—their love?

The pounding behind her eyes changed in tempo, sharpening to a vicious stab that made her flinch. As her eyes uncontrollably slid closed and Belinda began to lose her grip on consciousness, a question echoed in her head: was this the pain of remembrance or the pain of regret?

Three

Luc threw his Mont Blanc pen on his desk with scant regard to the limited-edition, eighteen-karat-gold masterpiece. He pushed his chair back from the desk. Damned if he could think straight today, and he knew whose fault that was.

Belinda.

A fierce sense of possession swirled deep inside him. He'd had to force himself to walk away from her earlier, to give her space, when all he'd wanted to do was imprint himself back into her mind, her body. He could have done it. She'd welcomed his kiss, participated fully in the duel of senses. But some perverse sense of honour embedded in his psyche insisted she come to him again willingly.

He pushed himself up and out of his chair and

crossed his expansive office to the window overlooking the gardens. His first thought on seeing the young woman in tattered jeans and a T-shirt was that they had a trespasser on the property, but the quickening inside him told him exactly who it was. He'd had the same visceral reaction the first time he'd laid eyes on her and decided she'd be his. He smiled.

Expanding the existing kitchen garden had been the impetus to orchestrate her arrival at Tautara Estate. He'd done his research and known she would never be able to resist the opportunity to create an herb garden to rival any other in the country. Didier, the chef he'd unabashedly poached from a Côte D'Azur five-star hotel, had long bemoaned the lack of an extensive array of fresh herbs to use in his sumptuous cuisine and had theatrically fallen to the ground to kiss Belinda's feet once the garden had been planted.

Her lengthy stay at Tautara, punctuated by trips back to Auckland to act as hostess for her father's enumerable functions, had set the scene for his successful campaign. She had been away often enough to miss him—enough to realise she loved him and belonged here, at his side. It had taken time, but he'd achieved his goal.

But then Luc Tanner was the kind of man who always got what he wanted and he'd wanted Belinda with a gut-deep need that surpassed anything he'd known before. He thought back to the first time he'd seen Belinda, at a boutique hoteliers' function hosted by her father.

Rather than approach her directly, Luc had gone instead to her father, Baxter Wallace, who'd laughed in

Luc's face at his request for an introduction to his precious youngest daughter and turned him down flat. Undeterred, Luc had bided his time, always watching from afar, knowing, eventually, he would succeed in his quest. And the time came, as it always did.

When, several months later, Baxter was fleeced to the tune of several hundreds of thousands of dollars in a credit-card scam targeting boutique hotels and chains, his bank had happily entered into extensive loans to rectify the situation. But by the time Baxter's wife had been diagnosed with a rare form of cancer, requiring expensive treatment overseas not covered by their insurance company, the banks had already capped their financial well. So to whom had a desperate Baxter turned?

Luc Tanner.

No one else had the resources, or the motivation, to help. And much as it had obviously galled Baxter Wallace to turn to the one man he'd spurned, he'd succumbed in the end.

They'd come to an agreement, one that had suited them both. One that now hung on whether or not Belinda regained her memory.

Luc's eyes narrowed as he saw Belinda drop to the surface of a bench seat in the garden, one hand pressed to her head. Something was very wrong. He propelled himself toward the door, calling to Manu, his major-domo, for assistance even as she slid to the ground.

Manu reached her first. Luc's hand ached from his grip on the head of his walking cane and he silently and vehemently cursed the disability that had prevented him from being at his wife's side when she needed him.

"What do you think? Is she okay?" Luc asked, as the

one man he trusted above all others checked Belinda's vital signs.

"She's coming round, it's just a faint, I reckon."

Luc clumsily dropped to his knees, ignoring the shaft of pain that speared through his hip, and brushed the hair from Belinda's face just as her eyes fluttered open.

"Luc?" Her voice was weak, her eyes unfocused.

"You fainted. Manu's checking you over to make sure you haven't hurt yourself. Don't worry. I trust him with my life."

"She looks fine, Luc. No sign of any bumps on her head. No grazes anywhere."

"How do you feel?" Luc wrapped his arm around Belinda's shoulders as she struggled to sit up.

"I…I don't know what happened. One minute I was okay, with a bit of a headache, the next it was excruciating pain. Then you guys were here."

"And now? The headache. Has it gone?" As soon as he had her back inside the house he would call her neurologist. He didn't like the sound of this headache. Not if it had the capacity to render her unconscious.

"It's going away. I'll be fine in a minute."

Her pale face belied her words. Between them, the two men helped Belinda to her feet. Luc felt frustrated that he had to defer to Manu's unencumbered strength in this situation. Before the accident he would simply have lifted Belinda into his arms and carried her to their suite, but now even such a responsibility was denied him. They walked slowly to the lower entry to the house where an elevator door stood open and waiting. It was a short ride to the next level, where they made their way to Luc and Belinda's private suite.

"I'll arrange for your evening meal to be sent through to you," Manu said as he left them at the door to their rooms.

"Thank you—" Luc clasped his seneschal's hand "—for everything."

"Not a problem, Luc. You know I'm here for you, man."

Luc gave a sharp, brief nod. He and Manu went back further than either of them wanted to admit. The bond they'd formed in their preteens, occasionally tripping on the wrong side of the law in a vain attempt to shake off their respective parents' unsavoury influence, was immutable.

Belinda dropped into one of the deep leather couches in the sunken living room with an audible sigh.

"I'm calling your doctor." Luc crossed the room and lifted a cordless handset from a side table. He punched in the private number of her specialist without once referring to the card the man had given him prior to Belinda's release from hospital.

"No, please. Don't. I'll be okay. I probably just overdid things is all. I was trying to force myself to remember. Doing everything I'd been told not to do." She rose and took the phone from him, firmly replacing it on its station. "Honestly, I'll be fine."

"You will tell me immediately if you suffer another of these headaches," he insisted.

"Yes, of course." Her eyes briefly met his before fluttering away.

Would she? Her body language told him differently, but he had to give her the benefit of the doubt.

"Until I'm satisfied you won't have a recurrence of

today's episode I don't want you out of my sight." It was a vow as much as a statement, and he saw her stiffen at his words.

"Surely that won't be necessary, besides being totally impractical," she argued gently.

"Let me be the judge of that. I will at least need to know where you are at all times." He took her hand and drew her toward him, placing her hand over his heart. The air between them heated with the warmth of their bodies. "I nearly lost you once already. I'm not prepared to take any more chances."

He saw the shiver run down her spine, the flare of her nostrils, the widening of her eyes as the impact of his words sank in. On the surface he knew they appeared to be little more than what one would expect from a newly wed groom to his bride. Only he knew the difference.

Belinda allowed his words to penetrate into the dark recesses of her mind. She should feel comforted, reassured by his protectiveness, but instead she felt only trepidation. He still held her hand against his chest, and she tried not to focus on the strong, steady beat of his heart, the breadth of muscle she felt beneath her fingertips.

Or the overwhelming desire she had to flex her hand against his strength, to imprint the shape and feel of him against her palm. Her heart picked up a beat and skittered in her chest as her eyes met his.

His gaze was unbreakable, and she was drawn even closer to him as she returned his stare. Now there was no air between them, her body was against his, length to length. Had he pulled her closer, or had she crossed that final barrier of distance without realising it herself? The long, strong muscles of his thighs pressed against hers, her pelvis cradled his slightly narrower hips, the soft curve of her belly moulded against the washboard hardness of his.

His pupils dilated and she felt his indrawn breath as if it had come from deep inside her own chest. Maybe it had. Already the lines between where she began and ended were blurred as she parted her lips, moistening their suddenly dry surface with the tip of her tongue. His own lips were set in a firm line, his brows drawn together slightly.

"Luc?" Her voice broke from her throat as more of a plea than a reassurance, and she felt the tension in him break as he lowered his head and caught her lips in a kiss that threatened to knock her hard-fought equilibrium six ways from Sunday.

If anything she felt more light-headed than she had in the garden when she'd regained consciousness, yet something still held her back, prevented her from committing fully to his touch. She drew back, feeling the loss of him like a physical ache as he let go her hand and she no longer absorbed his heartbeat or his heat.

He turned away from her and tunnelled one hand through his short-cropped hair in a gesture that told her more than any of his carefully calculated words. So, her cool, calm and collected husband could be rattled. Somehow the knowledge didn't give her the power she had hoped.

"I'm going to shower before our dinner arrives. Join me."

His invitation—or was it more of a command?—

hung on the air between them as he limped up the shallow stairs toward their bedroom, his cane stabbing at the thickly carpeted surface like some kind of weapon.

Belinda's throat constricted on her words of denial. They were husband and wife, no matter how foreign the words felt to her. Dare she bare herself to a man who was essentially unknown to her? Would she find familiarity in his touch? She took a tentative step toward him, then halted as fear overtook her need for the truth.

"Belinda. I meant what I said about you not being out of my sight." Luc paused at the top of the stairs, his body vibrating with a tension that was almost palpable. "You don't need to shower with me if it makes you uncomfortable, but I want you there. In the room with me."

A thrill of something charged through her veins. Was this a test of some sort?

"Fine," she answered unsteadily. "But I think I'd rather have a bath."

"I'll draw it for you."

"I can manage myself."

"Of course you can." His voice was conciliatory. "But let me do this for you. For my wife. I've been able to do little else for you in the past six weeks."

She sensed a hidden message in his last words and it left a prickle of discomfort running across her scalp. She shook her head lightly to rid herself of the sensation. She was being overly sensitive. Not surprising really when only this morning she'd been safely ensconced in a private room in hospital. Suddenly she couldn't wait to immerse herself in clean, soft water, to rid herself of the remnants of any lingering scent from her stay in hospital.

As she entered the bedroom she saw his jacket already casually thrown onto the bed. She could hear the thunder of water in the voluminous spa bath.

A shudder ran through her. What if he changed his mind and decided to join her in the bath? A throb pulled deep inside her womb at the thought, even as her mind insisted its denial. She forced her feet toward the bathroom. Luc was bent over the bath, pouring a splash of perfumed bath foam into the water and swirling it with a sweep of his hand. She watched as he inhaled the fragrance, the expression of sheer longing on his face striking hard to her core.

She hadn't stopped to think how this had all been for him. To be married and then to have lost her to this frozen wasteland of not remembering even the smallest thing about their life together.

"I've missed this," he said as she entered the spacious room. His voice dropped an octave. "I've missed you."

"I…I'm sorry, Luc. I'm trying to remember." Her hands fisted in frustration at her sides and her voice became more insistent. "And I did! I remembered the garden. That's when the headache became unbearable."

"Don't force it, Belinda. We don't want a recurrence of your blackout. Let it come back to you in its own time." He reached down and turned off the faucet, his movements fluid—just hinting at the muscled strength beneath his clothes. "There, your bath is ready."

Without a second glance he turned away from her, pulling his shirt free of his trousers and unbuttoning it.

She couldn't tear her eyes away as he shrugged the fine cotton off his shoulders exposing the long lean line of his back. His skin still held a warm golden tan. As he unbuckled his belt and unsnapped his trousers she felt a deep longing rise within her, right up until the moment he exposed the long angry scar that laid an undeniable stripe from his hip down his right leg.

She couldn't hold back the cry that broke from her lips.

"Ugly, isn't it?" Luc half turned toward her, a flash of anger sparking in his eyes. "I'm told it will fade, and this one, too—" he gestured to the surgical scar on his abdomen "—in time. But I'll always have a limp."

"Is it still painful?" Belinda managed to ask, her gaze still riveted to the wound site. A stab of guilt lanced through her. So wrapped up in her own problems, she hadn't considered what he'd physically been through.

"Sometimes it's worse than others," he admitted flatly before reaching into the shower to turn on the water. "Go on. Enjoy your bath."

He stepped into the large shower cubicle, and she watched as the water cascaded over his body, rivulets running through the light dusting of hair on his chest and arrowing down lower, past his taut stomach. Even though he'd obviously lost some weight in hospital, he still had a commandingly powerful build. As he lathered shower gel over his skin, she suddenly wished she'd had the courage to join him in the shower. To be the one stroking the glistening liquid soap down his chest and across the ridged hardness of his abdomen, and lower.

A flush of heat suffused her body. What was she

thinking? Only hours ago she'd been terrified at the prospect of travelling with him, of leaving the virtual safety of her hospital room. Now here she was, little more than an opportunistic voyeur as he luxuriated under the pounding water of his shower.

She wheeled about and focused instead on the bath he'd drawn for her. She needed to twist her hair up, and unerringly she opened the correct drawer where her hair accessories were lined up. It should give her some comfort, she decided, that she instinctively knew where such things were. With a modicum of movement she pinned her hair up, undressed and lowered herself into the warm fragrant water. As the foaming bubbles closed over her body, she relaxed. They offered her some privacy for when Luc came out of the shower, but something inside her begged to attract his attention, something she couldn't control.

And that, right now, was her greatest fear. She didn't recognise the woman who'd fallen in love with Luc Tanner and agreed to marry him. Clearly it wasn't the Belinda Wallace she believed herself to be.

Something within her had changed in the past several months. Something drastic. It had seen her uplift herself from her home in Auckland, from her family and from her career. To give all that up for him.

She sank lower in the bath, covering her shoulders and stretching her long legs out before her. As she looked out the window over the valley, bathed in the start of a glorious sunset with swaths of red and purple creeping across the sky, she acknowledged she owed it to herself, and to Luc, to remember what that was.

Four

Despite the misgivings that plagued her about how she'd handle Luc's exit from the shower, she was surprised to find that it all felt almost impossibly familiar. Even so, tension gripped her shoulders and she pushed her head back against the built-in cushion on the side of the bath, closing her eyes the moment she'd heard him snap off the water and push open the shower door.

Her active imagination painted a very clear picture of how he looked as she heard him drag one of the thick white bath towels from the heated rail and cast it across his body to dry himself. She counted to one hundred, very slowly, before she opened her eyes again.

Luc stood at the vanity, the towel riding low on his hips, his cane resting against the blush-coloured marble countertop. She watched as he smoothed shaving cream across the hard angles of his shadowed jaw and picked up his razor. There was something incredibly sexy about watching a man shave, Belinda decided as she found herself captured by his every movement.

She must have stirred because suddenly he turned and caught her watching him. A slow smile pulled at his lips, a smile that melted her right through to her core.

"Enjoying the bath?" His eyes glowed as he took in the curve of her shoulder, the sweep of her arm as it rested along the edge of the tub and back up again to her throat where her pulse beat rapidly in the slender column of her neck.

If he'd have traced his fingertips along the same path she couldn't have felt it more distinctly. Beneath the froth her breasts ached, her nipples tightened and her inner muscles clenched in response.

"Mmm, wonderful," she managed, but as she gazed at him she found herself referring more to the vision of male than the silky-soft environment in which she reclined.

"Hungry?" he asked, sending her mind into over-drive before she realised that she was, indeed, starving.

"Yes, I suppose I'd better get out."

"No, don't bother. I'll check first to see if dinner's ready yet." He swiped at his face with a small towel and dropped it into a laundry hamper on his way out of the bathroom.

When he returned he pushed a small wheeled trolley with one hand. As he drew closer to the bath, Belinda spied a large ceramic platter and an ice bucket containing a bottle of one of the Hawke's Bay region's finest sauvignon blancs. Two elegantly cut crystal wine-glasses stood beside the ice bucket.

"You look like you've done this before," Belinda commented as Luc extracted the bottle from the ice and deftly wiped it with a crisp white serviette.

"I've done some waiting in my time," Luc replied guardedly.

He poured two glasses of wine and handed one to her, then pulled up the vanity stool next to the bath and sat down. His towel dropped away at the side, revealing the length of his right leg—exposing the angry scar. She averted her gaze to stare out the window and past the darkening valley to where the final remnants of the sun slipped beyond the last hill. His very nearness, and nakedness, played havoc with her heart rate. Even the warmth emanating from his body tempted and tormented her.

Belinda focussed on taking a sip of the pale straw-coloured wine, letting the perfectly chilled tropical fruit flavours roll over her tongue and down her throat. She knew from what memory she still clung to with an iron grip that no one else had ever elicited such a powerful reaction from her before.

Was this what had bound her to Luc? The overwhelming physical awareness that simmered constantly beneath the surface?

"Here, try this," Luc said, interrupting her thoughts.

Belinda turned her head toward him, to the morsel of provolone cheese encased in a sliver of prosciutto he offered. Obediently she opened her mouth. If she'd thought for even a minute that she'd regained control of her equilibrium around Luc it was shattered the instant his fingertips touched her lips. Tiny shocks buzzed across her skin at the fleeting contact as the flavours exploded in her mouth.

"Good?" he asked.

"Mmm, delicious. But, Luc, you don't need to wait on me," she protested.

"I know," he answered simply. "Indulge me." He dipped a slice of crusty bread in aioli. "Here, try this. It's Didier's own recipe and made with product sourced solely from Tautara Estate."

As he brought the morsel to her mouth a drop of oil fell and pooled in the curve of her collarbone right where it met her shoulder.

"Ah, we can't have that," Luc murmured.

He leaned forward, his tongue darting across her skin to lick up the single drop. Every muscle in her body coiled tight and she nearly shot out the water at the exquisitely brief caress. Her fingers curled tight around the stem of her wineglass, and she had to consciously stop the reflexive jerk that threatened to snap the delicate stem.

"More?" His lips were by her ear, his breath fanning the suddenly hyperresponsive skin of her neck.

"M-more?" She could barely get the single syllable past her tightened throat.

"Antipasto." Again his breath was a stroke of heated air over her skin.

"I—"

"Try this."

Helpless to do anything but open her mouth, she accepted the slice of marinated artichoke heart. Slowly he offered more bite-size delectable delights interspersed only with sips of wine.

Luc carried their conversation, keeping things general. Aside from that one time he'd licked the oil from her skin he didn't touch her again and, she was shocked to realise, she wanted him to. Oh, how she wanted him to.

When her glass was empty he took it from her and replaced it on the trolley, then leaning heavily on his cane he rose to his feet.

"Our main meal will be ready now. I'll leave you to get dried and dressed, unless you'd like some help."

Luc looked down upon her in the cooling water of the tub. A pulse throbbed at the side of his neck. A fine sheen of perspiration glistened on his brow. It gave her some relief to know that he was as similarly affected as she by the intimacy of their situation.

"No, I can manage. Thanks."

"Good. Don't be too long. I meant what I said about you not being out of my sight."

"Within reason, of course," Belinda felt compelled to add, suddenly desperate for some control of her racing pulse and the heady sense of seduction he'd transfused through her.

"Belinda, when it comes to you I'm not a reasonable man. Don't keep me waiting." His green eyes flared with heat and a self-deprecating smile pulled at his lips.

She stared at the door for several minutes after it closed behind him. His words carried more than a warning. There was an implied threat underwriting his statement, a threat that made her near uncontrollable physical reaction to him a risk to her precarious equilibrium.

He was a conundrum, sending conflicting messages

that alternately confused and calmed her. The man who'd shared the antipasto with her was completely inverse to the man who'd brought her home from the hospital today, or the one who'd been at her side when she'd fainted in the herb garden. But which one was the real Luc Tanner? Which one was the man she'd fallen in love with?

By the time Belinda had dried herself and slipped through to the dressing room to select some clothes, Luc was waiting for her in the bedroom. He'd dressed casually in black jeans and a black polo shirt, and the colour made his eyes appear even greener than usual. Her breath caught in her throat at the sight of him. Starkly handsome, he was both beautiful and terrifying to behold.

She nervously smoothed her hands over the caramel-coloured linen trousers she'd teamed with the cream silk top she'd chosen.

"Will this do?" she asked, uncomfortable under his silent scrutiny.

"You look beautiful in anything. Come. Manu has set the table for us on our deck so we can enjoy the summer evening while it lasts."

Belinda followed him through to the living room and out the open French doors. Burning tapers attached to the deck lit a table set with white linen and gleaming silverware. Heated chafing dishes sat on a smaller table to one side, alongside them a colourful tossed salad. For a moment she felt as though she'd stepped into a fairy tale.

Everything was magically perfect—the setting, the darkened valley with the peppering of lights from the far distant Taupo township on its periphery. Even the gentle strains of her favourite opera piped through the ceiling-mounted speakers in the eaves over the deck. It was almost surreal, but the aromas from the chafing dishes gave her a reality check. Not even in her dreams had she smelled anything so divine.

"I told Manu we'd serve ourselves tonight," Luc said, slipping back the cover on one of the dishes to expose tiny gourmet potatoes garnished with fresh chopped chives and handing Belinda a gold-rimmed plate.

Her experienced eye recognised the pattern of the fine imported china. Was it one they'd chosen together, or was it just a normal part of Luc's everyday life?

"You're frowning. Trying to remember again?" Luc's voice cut across her thoughts.

"I recognise this china. Did we choose it?"

Surprise flitted through his eyes, but was swiftly veiled before he spoke. "Yes, we did. You helped me outfit most of our suite before the wedding. It was important to you."

And he'd encouraged her, she was sure of it. She had a sense that he'd been prepared to do anything to keep her here—to make Tautara Estate her home as much as it was indelibly his.

"I know." She hesitated a moment, then continued. "I don't remember, but in here—" she pressed her hand against her chest "—I know."

Luc didn't speak straightaway, but Belinda couldn't help but notice the sudden tension in his shoulders or the way his eyebrows drew together. Eventually he spoke. "That's excellent. You're making great progress."

Did his hand shake ever so slightly as he dished up for them both? Chiding herself for being fanciful, she applied herself to savouring the grilled trout fillets drizzled with a subtly herbed sauce, baby potatoes and fresh salad greens with the rest of their bottle of wine. It had been so long since she'd had anything with such delicate flavour. If she never tasted a bite of hospital food again it would be too soon. They ate in comparative silence, a silence that could have been awkward but for the beauty of the velvet-dark vista spread out before them.

"It's so beautiful here." She sighed. "How do you ever tear yourself away?"

"Sometimes business requires it. For the most part I'm more than happy to remain here. Tautara Estate comprises 6,500 hectares. There's always plenty to do." He smiled as Belinda fought back a yawn. "Why don't we call it a night? You've had a tiring day, and I have to admit I could use the rest myself."

"Your leg is sore?" Belinda felt a sudden surge of guilt.

"No more than usual," Luc replied with a wave of his hand, dismissing her care.

"Is there anything I can do for you?"

Luc's lips firmed into a straight line and she sensed rather than heard his sigh.

"No. Just be yourself," he replied enigmatically.

What did he mean by that, she wondered, catching the inside of her lip between her teeth as she bit back the words that would ask him precisely that. Be herself. Right now she'd give anything to know what version of "herself" he meant.

Luc leaned heavily on his cane as he stood to get up from the table. She caught the fleeting grimace of pain he swiftly tried to mask.

Was this the way it had always been between them? Him hiding his true feelings and thoughts? She couldn't imagine that she'd have fallen in love with or married a man who was so closed to her emotionally. It just wasn't her style. Her family had always been demonstrative, affectionate. They shared their worries and concerns between them—a problem shared is halved, her father always said.

Did she and Luc have that kind of marriage? Something inside her whispered to the contrary, and the inner voice was distinctly unsettling.

Five

When they returned to their private suite, Belinda's nerves were strung out to screaming point. Inside the bedroom the drapes had been drawn, and the bedside lamps cast a warm inviting glow over the expansive bed. A bed she was now about to share with her husband. Someone had been in the room and dispensed with the throw pillows adorning the head of the bed and had turned down the sheets. A single perfect deep-pink rose stood in a bud vase on the bedside table.

The reality of sleeping with Luc bore down on her with terrifying pressure. Her heart jumped erratically in her chest and she fought to keep her breathing measured. Could she do this? Lord, she didn't even know which side of the bed he slept on. As if he read her thoughts, Luc gave her a small smile.

"You usually sleep there." He indicated the side of the bed where the vase stood. "Although I'm happy to change if it makes you feel more comfortable."

Twin beds would make her feel more comfortable right now, Belinda decided. Even separate rooms. She drew in a levelling breath and forced herself to meet his gaze.

"No, that will be fine. If that's the way we've always done it."

Luc's smile froze on his face for the briefest moment before he nodded.

"Belinda—" The chime of his cell phone interrupted what he'd been about to say. He flicked a glance at the caller ID. "Excuse me. I need to take this. I might be a while."

Belinda watched as he left the room, his murmured tones disappearing behind the closed door. She hurried to the dressing room and grabbed a ruby-coloured nightgown from one of her drawers. With more haste than care she shucked off her clothing and pulled it on. The gown was a filmy piece of next to nothing, with a soft stretch lace bodice that hugged her breasts like a lover's caress.

She smoothed her hand down over the gossamer-fine material and wondered if she had bought the nightgown as part of her trousseau or whether it had been a gift from Luc. The very idea of his hands caressing the fabric the way her own did now sent a perverse thrill of longing through her body.

What was wrong with her? Inside her mind she reacted like a frightened virgin, yet physically her body yearned for Luc's touch. Belinda shook her head and hurried to the bathroom. Every step of today had brought her nothing but more questions. She was weary of it all. Bone weary. Suddenly that big, softly lit bed was very inviting indeed.

Catching her reflection in the bathroom mirror, Belinda wondered whether she shouldn't have simply chosen a T-shirt to sleep in instead. The tiny spaghetti straps looped over her shoulders lent an impression of wanton fragility, and the warmth of the red fabric made her skin glow like that of a woman welcoming her lover. Belinda huffed in frustration. She was driving herself crazy and it had to stop.

She seated herself at the vanity and grabbed a hairbrush from the drawer and started to brush her long dark hair with punishing strokes.

A movement in the doorway stilled her hand. Luc stepped forward and took her hairbrush from her fingers. "Are you trying to rip it all out?" His censure was as gentle as his touch as he took over from where she'd begun.

"I thought you might have been in bed already," he commented, his eyes meeting hers in the mirror.

So he'd recognised her sudden fear. He knew her better than she gave him credit for, but then, of course he would. Right now he knew her better than she knew herself. Sudden tears of frustration sprang to her eyes.

Luc stopped brushing, his hands settling on her shoulders.

"Belinda?"

She blinked away the burning moisture, breaking eye contact with him. He saw far too much.

"I'm okay. Just tired, that's all."

"Understandable. It's been a full day, for both of us." He took her hand and helped her to her feet. "Go to bed. I'll be along in a while."

She couldn't decide whether she was relieved or disappointed that he wasn't coming to bed now.

"Aren't you tired, too?" she asked.

"Yes, but something's come up. Guests we weren't expecting until late next week have brought their trip forward to the day after tomorrow. Manu and I have some contingency plans to lay in place."

"Guests? Already?"

"It's not ideal, but they can't be put off. They should only be here a couple of nights."

"They're regulars?"

"After a fashion, yes."

"Then they'll have certain expectations. We must meet them. You can't give them less than that. You wouldn't under normal circumstances," she said carefully.

Right now Belinda couldn't think of anything worse, but this was Luc's business. The fact he'd cancelled out six weeks of patronage for their honeymoon—six weeks they'd lost—meant he would have to get back to business. Besides, the sooner she resumed life as she'd known it, the sooner she might start to remember.

"Spoken like a true hotelier's daughter. We'll worry about it in the morning. Now, go to bed."

He dropped a fleeting kiss on her forehead and turned her toward the bedroom, following close on her heels. When she was settled in the bed, he switched off the lamp nearest her. Belinda suddenly reached out and held his arm.

"Please, leave the other light on until you come to bed?"

"It won't disturb you?"

"No. I grew used to a light in the hospital." She stifled a yawn. "Besides, I doubt anything could keep me awake now."

Challenging heat flared in Luc's eyes and Belinda felt an answering response in her body. The elasticized bodice of her nightwear felt too small as her nipples hardened and pressed against the fabric.

Well, maybe there was one thing. As wrong as this all felt to her she couldn't deny there was a powerful magnetic pull between them. Luc straightened and trailed his hand over her shoulder and down her arm, leaving her skin tingling beneath his fleeting touch.

She barely heard the click of the door as it closed behind him. A near overwhelming desire to call him back choked in her throat as Belinda silently admitted she'd never felt so completely lost and alone in her entire life.

The meeting with Manu had been productive, and Luc let himself back into their suite with a tired sigh of relief. Their guests would arrive the day after tomorrow around lunchtime, in time for drinks followed by an al fresco luncheon on the deck. Then, if Belinda was up to it, she'd accompany the female member of the party to Taupo by helicopter for a couple of hours' shopping while he and Manu took her husband fly-fishing in one of the rivers that ran through the property.

The female member.

Luc clenched his jaw against the curse that fought to rip from his throat. He had no doubt that Demi Le Clerc had trouble up her sleeve when she'd had her assistant phone the estate to change her booking. His unease had magnified when Manu reported he'd tried to contact the award-winning jazz singer to inform her that the booking couldn't be altered but apparently she and her new fiancé were "in transit" and therefore unavailable. With modern communication being what it was, Luc very much doubted she was unreachable, rather that she'd informed her staff of her intention to be that way. How she'd found out so quickly that he'd returned home said a great deal for her spy network.

Manu had already agreed to check amongst the staff to find out if that particular spy network had been fed by one of their own. Confidentiality and loyalty were sacrosanct. If anyone had abused either, they were in breach of their employment contract and would be dispensed with immediately.

Luc swallowed against the bitter taste in his mouth when he thought of Demi and Belinda meeting. He was reluctant to expose her to Belinda while his wife was still in such a vulnerable position, but then, it may well work to his advantage. What harm could Demi possibly do when Belinda remembered nothing of their time together? Belinda had no idea their marriage had been the catalyst that had seen Demi break tabloid records with the speed of her engagement to aging billionaire oilman Hank Walker.

He'd been a fool to ever let Demi think there was more to their relationship than casual friendship. He'd never once entertained the idea of marrying her, despite her attempts to entice him into commitment. They'd made love just the once—a coupling that provided physical release only, with little else to recommend it.

Luc moved restlessly toward his piano in the dimly lit room. He was too wound up to sleep. He closed his eyes and let his fingers drift gently across the keys, the haunting quality of the music he played flowed over him—relaxing his muscles and his mind.

Playing had always had that effect on him, even back in his teens, although he was never the kind of teenager who'd have admitted to this particular skill. No, hotwiring cars and breaking and entering were more his style then. It had been during a B&E that he'd been sprung by the owner of the house—an elderly gentleman who'd seen right through Luc's attitude and invited him back, through the front door next time. It had taken six weeks but Luc had found his feet retracing the path to Mr. Hensen's home. The retired pianist had sensed Luc needed an outlet, a change of direction in his path of self-destruction. He'd insisted on giving Luc lessons— lessons that had been emphatically refused until the threat of going to the police was coolly raised.

It had been ages since Luc had thought about Mr. Hensen. Ages since he'd allowed himself to miss the old man in a way he'd never missed his parents after their deaths.

As the final note hung on the air, Luc let his eyes open again. Belinda sat opposite him on one of the large cream sofas, her feet curled under her. His eyes raked over her barely clad body, his pulse leaping to instant life. It had been torture to leave her in bed, her body gilded by the bedside lamp, her hair a glorious fan across the fine linen of her pillowcase. He'd wanted to make love with her with a physical ache that had almost driven him to his knees—to imprint himself back in her mind and her body in a way she would never forget again.

He dragged his wayward thoughts under disciplined restraint. Luc Tanner hadn't gotten where he was today by giving in to impulse. No, everything about his life was about control. He'd learned the hard way what a lack of power did to a person, how it demeaned them— rendered them helpless victims. The helpless had no respect in this world. Pity, yes. But he'd had his fill of pity and well-meaning intentions. Now he commanded respect in all walks of his life.

"You play beautifully," Belinda said, her voice hesitant, as if she sensed the power play going on inside him.

"I didn't mean to wake you."

"You didn't. I guess I'm too used to the disruptions and noise of the hospital. The quiet, of all things, woke me. A bit later I heard you on the piano. Did your meeting with Manu go well?"

"Yes, everything's organised. Are you sure you're okay with this? I can have them rerouted to another property if necessary."

"Luc, when I couldn't get back to sleep I started to think about a few things, and to be honest, as terrifying as it is, I have to get back into my old life if I'm going to move forward. I can't turn back time and see what happened before, but I can't stay stagnant like this, either. It's driving me crazy. Everything around me—" she waved her arm to encapsulate the room "—it's all

new, yet sometimes familiar at the same time. Even the
music you played. I know you've played it for me
before, haven't you?"

"I have."

Luc swallowed. Yes, he'd played it for her before.
The last time had been the night he'd proposed. They'd
spent a day out on the estate together, made love
together for the first time on the riverbank during a
picnic—his body tightened in remembrance of her welcoming embrace, at how she'd uninhibitedly given
herself fully to him. He'd instantly become addicted to
her in a way he'd never imagined possible.

He'd never wanted anyone or anything in his life as
much as he wanted her. The truth had frightened him
until he'd persuaded himself it was because she was the
perfect accompaniment to the world he'd built. He
couldn't have been thinking of anything else. By the
time they'd driven back to the house, he'd decided to
step up his plans and propose to her earlier than he'd
anticipated. He still remembered the surge of triumph
when she'd said yes.

They'd fallen to the floor, right here in this sitting
room, and made love again to seal their betrothal. All
she'd worn for the next twenty-four hours had been the
blue diamond engagement ring he'd had made for her
months earlier.

"Will you play something else for me now?"
Belinda's voice dragged him back from the past.

"Another time," he said, rising from the piano bench
and grabbing his cane.

He offered her his hand to pull her to her feet, and
they went through to the bedroom together. By the time

he'd undressed and was ready for bed she was curled on her side of the bed, her eyes closed, her breathing even.

She'd fallen asleep after all. But as he slid between the cool cotton of the sheets, she rolled over to face him, her blue-grey eyes massive in her heart-shaped face.

"Luc?"

He lifted a hand to smooth away a strand of her hair that fell across her cheek. "Hmmm?"

"What I said before…" She closed her eyes and took in a deep breath. "What I said before about getting back into my old life—I meant *every* aspect of my old life. Obviously we're not strangers to each other. Whenever I look at you my body tells me that."

So she still felt the same inexorable pull between them. Luc suppressed the smile of satisfaction that threatened to spread across his face at her words.

He watched as she moistened her lips with the tip of her tongue, clearly choosing her next words carefully.

"Well, what I mean is…if you want to…y'know. Maybe it'll help." Her words faded away into the expanding silence of the room.

Luc traced the curve of her brow, then the sweep of her cheekbone with one finger, before bringing it to rest at the cupid's bow of her lips. He'd wanted her to come to him willingly and now she had. Something foreign warmed and bloomed deep inside him.

"No," he said quietly, his negative response surprising even himself.

"You don't want me?" She sounded hurt and relieved at the same time.

"Oh, I want you. When the time is right we will make love again. But tonight isn't that time. When we make love it won't be because you want to remember, but because you do."

Was that relief in her eyes or disappointment? He leaned forward and took her lips gently with his own, holding back the beast that clawed within him to plunder their generous softness. As much as it tormented him, he would wait.

She sighed softly against his lips. "Good night, Luc."

She rolled over to her other side, and Luc curved his arm around her, pulling her in close against the hardness of his body. He felt her stiffen as the evidence of his arousal nestled along the crease of her buttocks, then felt her relax into him as the truth of his obvious desire for her sank in, secure in the knowledge his rejection of her wasn't because he didn't want her.

He lay there for hours, his eyes burning in the dark as she slid into a deep sleep. Her body shaped to his. His instincts screamed to take her and brand her his once more. It would be the ultimate satisfaction, when she remembered everything, for her to know she hadn't been able to resist him. But he'd meant what he'd said before. When she made love with him again it would be because she remembered what their lovemaking had been like, how it had become a compulsion neither of them could deny. How they'd both resented everything that had come between their opportunities to be alone together. If he could do anything in his power to encourage that memory, he would.

The intense satisfying physicality of their relationship had been an unexpected bonus. An indicator, of sorts, that he'd been right all along when he'd decided to make Belinda Wallace his wife and mistress of Tautara Lodge.

His life—his plan—would carry on as before. The hiccup of their accident would fade into a minor blip on the radar of his success.

Six

The next morning Belinda awoke feeling more rested than she had in ages. But with the fresh light of the morning, and the cool empty sheets beside her, anxiety had reasserted itself once more.

Where had the trepidation she'd felt when she'd first seen him at the hospital gone? She'd been forced into close contact with him yesterday—a close contact she hadn't questioned and which, to be totally honest, had felt right. Was this how victims of Stockholm Syndrome felt? Had that been Luc's intention all along—to make her completely reliant on him so far away from what little familiarity she had?

Aside from the obvious, the fact she couldn't remember what was a very important part of her life, why did she still feel as though there was something more overshadowing her mind's refusal to recall her memories. Even now, as she approached Luc at the dining table, where he sat reading a paper over breakfast, she sensed a closed door deep inside of him, a part of him that lay deep in shadow, and she wanted to know what was behind that door.

The only way she would find out was to keep going. He was her husband. She owed it to them both. Belinda painted a smile on her face and forced herself not to smooth the short-sleeved top she'd pulled on over designer jeans one more time as Luc looked up.

"Good morning," Luc said, folding his paper neatly and putting it to one side. "You slept well?"

"Very well." A faint rush of heat bloomed across her cheeks as she recalled how his enveloping arms had held her against him, how her body had reacted to his touch.

"Good." Luc gave a nod of satisfaction. "Since we're technically working from tomorrow, I've planned some fun for us today."

"Fun? That sounds intriguing. What have you got in mind?"

Belinda reached for the coffee carafe and poured Luc another cup. She was halfway through pouring when her hand suddenly shook.

"I'm sorry, I didn't ask if you wanted another." She stopped pouring and rested the carafe on a place mat on the table.

Luc gave her a searching look. "I always have two cups at breakfast."

The ramifications of Luc's reply echoed through her mind. She instinctively remembered that, but she didn't remember him? How labyrinthine could the mind get?

Her neurologist had spoken to her at length about the voids in her memory and how simple everyday matters could appear, as this one had this morning. Being here—being with Luc—obviously stimulated the part of her mind that held her memory captive.

Luc placed his hand over hers, where it rested on the handle of the carafe. She fought not to flinch from his touch, from the spark of physical recognition that relentlessly spiralled through her every time he was near.

"You remembered that without trying. Don't over analyse it. Just let it come."

"How can I do that when I don't know the difference between remembering and not?" Her voice shook slightly.

"We'll find a balance. Don't worry. Who knows what might happen today."

He let go of her hand, took a swig of his coffee, then rose from the table.

"Where are we going?"

"I thought we'd take a trip around parts of the estate today. Play hooky." He gave her a smile. "Are you up for it?"

A sensation, not unlike fear, snaked along her spine. She couldn't help but feel he had a hidden agenda to his suggestion.

"Just the two of us?" she asked.

"Does that bother you?"

"No, it doesn't bother me. Should it?" She forced her lips into a smile.

Luc's eyes narrowed as her question hung on the air. "If you'd rather stay here at the lodge today, that's okay."

"No, no! Going out today would be fabulous."

"Well, if it assuages your fears any, Manu will be driving us." He rose to his feet and snatched his cane up from by the table.

"I could drive," Belinda offered.

Luc halted midstride. His face paled measurably and he gave her a searching look that made her heart stutter in her chest. What had she said wrong?

"Or not." She attempted to lighten the air that had suddenly frozen between them with glacial coolness.

"I think not. Not yet, anyway." Luc appeared to have recovered his equilibrium and his skin recovered its usual hue. "How soon can you be ready?"

Belinda flicked a glance at the clock above the kitchen stove. "Give me ten minutes, then I'm all yours."

"*All* mine?" Luc's voice deepened and Belinda was suddenly swept with an uneasy sense of déjà vu.

She put out a hand and grasped a chair back to steady herself. Tiny black dots danced before her eyes. She forced herself to breathe, drawing air into her lungs and expelling it again with careful deliberation. She felt Luc's hand at her back—a reassurance that lent her much-needed strength.

"You okay?" His breath stirred the hair at her nape.

"Yeah," she said on shaky breath. "I'll be fine. I'll go and get ready."

"Make sure you grab a jacket in case it gets cool later, and wear comfortable walking shoes, okay?"

"We'll be out all day?"

"If you're up for it."

She let go of the chair and stepped out of his reach. "I'm up for it."

"I'll meet you out front."

By the time she'd splashed her face and reapplied her makeup, she was heading closer to fifteen minutes than the ten she'd promised, but as she joined Luc at the front door she had at least regained most of her equilibrium. It niggled at her that he hadn't been keen for her to drive. She'd held her licence since her late teens and had always been a good driver, but he'd looked sick to his stomach at the prospect.

Ah, well, she sighed, at least this way she'd get to enjoy the countryside a bit more than if she had to concentrate on the roads.

She was surprised when Luc sat in the back beside her as they headed off, and said as much. Luc responded by linking his fingers through hers and answering, "I've been forced to be apart from you for too long already. Why wouldn't I want to be by my wife's side?"

There was an intensity to his words that both soothed and unnerved her. She gave herself an internal shake. What was wrong with her? Everything she felt at the moment was a contradiction to what she'd felt only a moment ago. And underlying it all was the insidious awareness that something wasn't right, that somehow she was living the wrong life. Maybe she should have let Luc call the doctor yesterday. This weird sense of displacement, the inherent sense of wrongness couldn't be normal.

Luc dragged her attention to the land that spread out before them and described the extent of the estate's farming and forestry operations, as they followed the road down the side of the hill, going deeper into the valley with every kilometre. As far as she could see in any direction the land was entailed in Tautara Estate. She started to get a new appreciation of how vast her husband's business interest here was and how many staff he employed.

"And Luc is being modest," Manu interrupted as he negotiated a hairpin bend in the road. "We offer some of the best fishing and hunting grounds in the whole of New Zealand, and for the adventurous they can go rafting, too."

"Sounds like you offer it all," Belinda commented.

"Yeah, well, we aim to please, don't we, mate?" Manu's gaze flicked to the rearview mirror, his eyes crinkled with the smile that wreathed his face.

"We do at that," Luc answered enigmatically, and gave Belinda's hand a gentle squeeze.

After just over an hour they reached a clearing and Manu pulled the four-wheel-drive vehicle in and parked, leaping down to open Belinda's door for her before she could alight.

"Here you are. I'll head on as we discussed this morning, okay?"

"Thanks, Manu," Luc answered.

"Are you sure you'll be okay?" There was a note of concern in the other man's voice that alerted Belinda he was not entirely happy to be leaving them here.

"I'll be fine. Don't worry. Besides, I've got this and I've got the two-way." Luc lifted his cane slightly with one hand and patted the small radio clipped to his belt with the other. "I'll call you if I need you."

"Make sure he does." Manu turned to Belinda, the serious light in his eyes telling her unreservedly that he wasn't kidding. "I mean it, if he looks like he's in any pain at all, call me."

"Stop fussing, Manu." Irritation laced Luc's words with acerbity.

"You call being sensible, fussing? Her with her blackout yesterday, you with your hip, both of you just out of hospital and now me leaving you both in the wilderness. I need my head read is what."

Though he tried to inject some humour into his voice Belinda could see he was genuinely worried. She put her hand out to him, gripping his forearm and meeting his worried gaze full-on.

"I will look after him, don't worry. And if I feel like I can't manage, either him or myself, Luc will call you. Okay?"

"S'pose it'll have to be. Right, then, catch you later."

Still muttering, Manu climbed back into the four-by-four and wheeled back out onto the private road, heading off in the same direction they'd been travelling.

"He has a point." Belinda turned to Luc. "We pretty much are the walking wounded."

"Are you worried?" He gave her a searching look.

"No, not at all. In fact it's great to be out in the fresh air. Away from walls."

"I know what you mean. If you want to head back at any stage just tell me."

"I'll be fine," she said with emphasis on the "I," and left unsaid the query as to whether he could manage. It was clear his strength was an issue of pride; she didn't want to aggravate him with her concern any more than Manu already had.

"We'll both be fine. The walk is level and there are plenty of rest stops on the way. C'mon."

Luc took her by the hand and led her along a well-trodden trail that wound alongside a bubbling river. All around them the sounds of bird life and the ever-present hum of cicadas filled the air. The air was warm and a soft breeze played in the trees. She was glad they'd left their jackets in the car. Despite her earlier fears, Belinda felt herself begin to relax. They took their time, and Luc paused every fifteen minutes or so to point out items of interest—a particular indigenous plant he knew she'd delight in, or the movement of fish in the water.

At one point Luc pulled her down to sit with him on a large fallen tree.

"Let's rest awhile," Luc said, rubbing absently at his hip as he propped his cane beside him.

"Is your leg bothering you?" Belinda wondered just how much pain he was in.

"A little," he admitted. "I'll be fine after a bit of a rest."

"Are you sure?"

"Of course I'm sure. Besides, it never hurts to stop and just enjoy the scenery from time to time."

Belinda's cheeks flushed under the heat in his gaze. Judging by his intensely focused look, he wasn't talking about the riverbank or its surroundings. Luc lifted a hand to smooth her hair away from her face, and his fingers slid along her scalp to cup the back of her head.

"Tell me you don't want me to do this."

His face drew closer, his lips parted ever so slightly. The air around them thickened. Sound retreated. The distance between them closed. Even if she'd been capable of denying him she very much doubted she would.

Without conscious thought she closed the distance between them. His lips were firm and dry as they captured hers, and her senses leaped to sudden and demanding life. When Luc's fingers tightened on the back of her head, she sank into him, her arms snaking around his waist, her breasts pressing against the hard wall of his chest.

Whatever uncertainties plagued her she couldn't deny the absolute synchronicity of their physical sense of belonging. Belinda gave herself over to sensation as Luc deepened their kiss. A flame of want kindled deep inside her, pressing her closer against him, welcoming his touch and taste with a sense of homecoming that was as fundamental in its origin as the rising sun each morning.

When Luc pulled away, his breathing was rapid and his eyes shone with the burning clarity of desire. She should feel intimidated by that look, Belinda told herself. She should be telling him "no more." Instead, her body clamored for his touch, her lips ached for more of the fierce pressure of his lips. She was surprised when he pushed up to his feet and stood, with his hands planted on his hips, and looked out over the river, away from her.

When he turned he was back under control. The light in his eyes had dulled, his breathing returned to normal.

"Shall we go on?"

Confused, Belinda stood and brushed the remnants of bark from the seat of her jeans before answering. "Sure. Let's go." What had made him pull back like that? She could have sworn he was as lost in their kiss as she'd been.

Again Luc took her hand, and as they continued on the path, she noticed he leaned more heavily on the cane than he had before.

"Is it much further?" she asked.

"Just around the next bend in the river," Luc replied, his words clipped.

Belinda stopped in her tracks. "What is it? Why are you angry?" She was talking to his back as he doggedly kept walking.

"It's nothing. Let's carry on."

"Is it your leg? Because I don't mind resting a bit longer before we carry on. It's been a long time since I've exerted myself this much, and I could do with the rest."

He stopped and turned to face her, his expression raw with something she couldn't quite define.

"No, it's not my leg."

"Then what is it? Was it the kiss? Did you want me to say no?"

"It wasn't that. It's nothing you can do anything about in your current state. Just leave it." He turned back and started walking again.

Belinda huffed in exasperation. He'd closed up as effectively as a bank vault under siege. There was nothing else for it but to follow him, but instead she stayed right where she was, chewing over his words as she did so. "In her current state." What the heck had he meant by that? Obviously her amnesia was as frustrating to him as to her, but he had the advantage of remembering their life together—of remembering their love.

For her the only thing she knew was that she desired him, and that was terrifying enough. She'd never been the type to embark on a frivolous relationship, and took the physical side of a relationship very seriously.

If she listened to her body, they would already be lovers again—even though he was a stranger to her. It went against everything she believed in, but she couldn't deny the truth—not when her blood raced hot and demanding through her body and her core ached with an emptiness she knew only he could fill.

Her cheeks coloured as she remembered again his rejection of last night. She kicked a stone off the path and watched it tumble down the bank and into the river and sighed helplessly.

"I'm sorry."

Luc's voice from close behind her made her jump and turn. He placed his forefinger on her lips, preventing her from speaking.

"Yes, I am sore. Yes, it was that kiss. And yes, I want you more than I've ever wanted you before. But I know what our marriage meant to you. I want that back. I want it all back before I make love with you again. That's why I'm in a foul mood."

Belinda's anger melted in the face of his honesty. It was clear how much it had cost him to bare his emotions like that. Sharp lines bracketed his mouth, his eyebrows were drawn in a harsh straight line, his fist clenched on the top of his cane.

"I'm sorry, too. I forget that I'm not the only one who's lost something here," she said, her voice shaking slightly.

She slipped an arm around his waist and together they strolled in silence along the path. As they came into another clearing Belinda gasped in surprise. Ahead of them a green-and-white-striped canvas canopy had been erected over a wooden table and two matching chairs. An ice bucket, with a bottle of champagne cooling within it, sat in the centre and was surrounded by a series of covered dishes. A long-stemmed rosebud, this time an intense coral colour, stood in a bud vase next to the ice bucket. Beside the table a sumptuous collection of pillows and fine cotton throws adorned the grass.

"You planned this all along?"

"You like it?"

"I love it. It seems so...decadent."

"It's what we specialise in. Decadence. Privacy."

Luc watched Belinda carefully. Walking away from her earlier, knowing exactly what awaited them around the corner, had been one of the hardest things he'd had to do since he'd collected her from the hospital yesterday. While he'd recuperated in hospital, he'd thought waiting patiently for her memories to return would be easy, but he was not in the mood to be patient anymore. With luck, this planned seduction, the mirror of their first time together, would be the trigger that would restore his life to the way it should have been all along. Perhaps, he dared hope, even better than before.

Seven

Belinda turned to face him. A smile of pure joy slowly wreathed her beautiful face and put a light in her blue eyes. He'd pleased her, and that pleased him. The realisation was a cold, sharp shock that sat at odds with his agenda. As did the sudden pull in the region of his chest—an expansion of warmth he'd instinctively learned to suppress as a child. A feeling he'd trained himself never to acknowledge.

"This is spectacular. Thank you." She reached up and kissed him on the cheek.

It was a peck, nothing more, yet with its innocence it stoked the fire that constantly simmered inside him. He watched as she sank down onto the bed of pillows, her hair spreading about her like a silken web of enticement.

Her T-shirt lifted slightly above her waist to expose a band of smooth creamy skin. His fingers itched to trace the inviting line. Down low his blood pooled, his body throbbed with a primal beat that threatened to dominate his careful strategy. He had to remember what had brought them together, and what had torn them apart. He had to preserve the former whatever it took.

He poured a glass of champagne, then lifted the rosebud from its vase before carefully lowering himself by her side.

"Some wine?"

He held the flute to her lips as she propped herself up a little, then took a sip of the bubbling liquid himself.

"Mmm, you said we specialise in decadence, I can't think of anything more decadent than this right now." She sighed.

Luc raised an eyebrow and pinned her with his stare. "Really? Nothing else more decadent?"

Her laughter was unexpected, a rich cascade of joy that penetrated deep inside. And there it was again, that glimmer of warmth from within his chest, a sense of rightness. His throat dried and words failed him as he looked down at her. He couldn't help but remember the last time they'd been here. Couldn't help but want to draw that memory from deep within its prison in her mind.

He casually trailed the rosebud back and forth across the exposed skin of her belly and watched her skin twitch and contract beneath the intensely coloured petals. The contrast between the pearl-like incandescence of her skin and the vibrance of the rosebud was wickedly appealing. What would it take, he wondered, to provoke her mind? To provoke the memories of physical pleasure the touch of the rose should invoke. After their first time here she'd barely been able to look at a rosebud without a flush of desire staining her cheeks, her throat, her chest.

Under the light touch of a flower such as this, she'd revealed a sensual side of her he'd only dreamed about. It was something he'd been prepared to forgo when he'd planned to make her his wife, knowing that in every other aspect she'd be the perfect complement to his perfectly created personal sphere. Sex, to him, had always been enjoyable but never the driving force of his world—until he'd made love with Belinda for the first time, right here in this clearing.

He would coerce her into remembering. One exquisite tingling sensation at a time.

He knew it was a risk, a huge risk, but the doctors had said several times that while her memory could return at any time, it was unlikely she would remember the details of what happened immediately prior to the accident that had led to her brain injury.

Luc had built his life on risk. Today was no different.

He offered her another sip of champagne.

"To new beginnings," he toasted.

"To new beginnings," Belinda repeated and put her lips to the tilted glass, putting her hand over his as she did so.

As she tipped the glass back up and swallowed, Luc softly trailed the rosebud down over the muscles in her throat, dipping into the hollow at its base before tracing a line along her collarbone. A flush of colour stained her cheeks, and her breathing became a little uneven. She relinquished her hold over his hand and let her hand drop to her side. A shudder ran through her as he let the rose drift down to the vee of her T-shirt, to the shadowed valley of her breasts.

She drew in a sudden sharp breath, her eyes flying to his, a stricken expression in them that made him stop what he was doing immediately and toss the rose to the blanket.

"Luc?" Her voice was unsteady.

"What is it? Are you feeling unwell?"

He dropped the flute on the grass, unheeding of the liquid as it drained into the ground, and wrapped his fingers around her hand as she reached for him. He was shocked to discover her skin was cold and clammy.

"Not unwell, exactly, just strange. Like we've done this before. It's sort of like how I felt yesterday, when I remembered about the garden, but different."

"Tell me, what do you remember?"

"I'm not sure exactly. I...I think we'd been swimming, yes, the water was freezing and you teased me about the goose bumps on my skin. Told me I was soft."

"Go on," he coaxed. Would she remember the rest? How he'd helped her from the water hole at the edge of the glade where they were now. How he'd wrapped her in a thick fluffy towel and dried her body, chafing her skin until her circulation had returned—until the light in her eyes had changed and he'd let the towel drop to the grass at their feet and lifted her into his arms and carried her to the bed of blankets and pillows just like the one they now lay on. How he'd traced every delectable line of her body with a rosebud, a yellow one that time, teasing her to a peak of aching trembling need before bringing her to the pinnacle of satisfaction with its soft-petalled touch.

Belinda remained silent. Her gazed locked on a faraway place. He watched the expressions flit across her face, the struggle as she fought to draw together the elusive threads that hovered on the periphery of her mind, then the change in her eyes, the blush of heat across her cheeks, down her throat.

She'd remembered. He'd wager the deed to Tautara Estate that she remembered that day and what had happened next.

A fine tremor ran through her body and she turned her gaze upon him.

"It's coming back to me, Luc. I remember that day."

Luc felt the warmth begin to return to her fingers, felt them shift beneath his touch. She pulled his hand toward her and drew it to her chest.

"Can you feel my heartbeat? It's racing a million miles a minute. Luc, can you believe it? My memory is coming back."

His hand flexed beneath hers, against the softness of the fine cotton of her T-shirt, against the curve of her breast. Through the lace of her bra he felt her response to the memories, to his touch.

"Was that why you planned today like this?" she asked, leaning into the strength of his hand, allowing his palm to shape around the fullness of her breast, to feel the hardness of her nipple as it firmed and crested.

"I had to do whatever I could to get you back. I know I've been telling you not to force it, but—"

"Shh." Belinda pressed her fingers against his lips. "Don't say any more. It's okay. I know what I'm remembering now isn't everything, there are still huge gaps there. But of all the memories I've lost, this one is probably the most precious. I even remember how I felt that day, how excited I was that you'd taken the whole day off work to spend with me. How much fun we had in the water until I got too cold to stay in there any longer. Then you dried me off…"

Luc nodded slowly. Would she remember what had happened next? He wasn't disappointed.

"You…you picked me up and brought me here, laid me down on the blankets and—" She gestured to the rose on the blankets. "You made love to me, first with the rose and then you covered me with your body."

Luc shifted across the distance between them, lowering her onto her back and sliding over her until her hips cradled his.

"Like this?"

"Yes." She sighed. "Just like that."

Beneath him she flexed her hips, pushing her mound against his now-straining erection, forcing him to swallow a groan of need.

Belinda let her eyes slide closed and shook as memories cascaded through her mind, memories and sensations that wound her body tight with need, playing like an erotic dance against the background of her consciousness. She lifted her hands to cup Luc's face between them, to draw his mouth to hers, to take his lips and delve beyond them with her questing tongue. Another shudder shook her as his tongue grazed against hers, and she relished the taste and texture of him. Relished and, she realised with a thrill of sheer pleasure, *remembered* the way he made her feel. She drove her hands up into his hair, holding him to her—terrified that if she let go, or if he broke contact, the exquisitely precious memories that flooded her mind would become as ephemeral as the gentle breeze that caressed their bodies.

Sunlight dappled against her closed lids, sending a kaleidoscope of sensuous rich reds to imprint on her retinas. Luc shifted slightly, and she moaned with pleasure as his lips trailed along her jaw, to her earlobe where he took the unadorned piece of flesh between his teeth, letting them graze softly over the surface. Then his tongue dipped into the hollow behind her ear, and her nerves jumped with pleasure.

For everything she'd forgotten it was clear he remembered it all. Remembered every tiny part of her that could send pleasure cascading through her body.

"Luc." His name was a sigh across her lips as his hands pushed up under her T-shirt, skimming the surface of her skin with a gentleness she wanted to drive to the next level. She didn't want gentle from him, not now. Not when her memory burned with the remembrance of the first time they'd made love here in this enchanted glade. Where he'd driven her body to heights she'd never dreamed possible, leaving her spent and weak in his arms before doing it all over again.

She shifted slightly as he clenched the fabric of her top in fisted hands, dragging the material up her torso and over her head, dropping it somewhere. She was beyond caring as the soft breeze stroked her skin.

"Open your eyes," his voice commanded, thick with the desire she felt surging through him like the inexorable journey of the river beside them.

She forced her heavy lids open, met his green-eyed gaze and felt the instant buzz of connection she now knew had been missing in the past twenty-four hours.

"You're mine. All mine." The words ground past his lips and she nodded.

"All yours," she whispered as he bent his head to her breasts, his teeth pulling aside the lacy cup of her bra and exposing her aching nipple to the caress of his tongue, the rasp of his teeth. A spear of pleasure shot straight to her core, and she clenched her inner muscles reflexively against the sensation, the movement setting up a ripple of smaller bursts of pleasure to thrill through her body.

Now she understood why those words had given her that shocking sense of déjà vu this morning. Why it had left her feeling as if she was a boat adrift from its moorings. He'd uttered the same words to her only months ago as he'd worshipped her body on these very blankets. But she no longer felt as if she was adrift. No, she was where she belonged, with the man to whom she belonged. Their reunion felt right on every level, and while she wanted him to hasten, to race her to the completion she knew lay on the periphery of his touch, she also wanted to savour every exquisite second.

She traced the shape of his head with her hands, stroked the cords of his neck, gripped the hard-muscled strength of his shoulders.

She was his. He was hers. How could she have forgotten such a simple truth?

Luc moved lower, his hands now splayed across her rib cage, his tongue tracing tiny circles around her belly button. She ached to feel him inside her again, to feel him fill her, complete her the way she now gloriously remembered. When his hands skimmed down to the waistband of her jeans she sighed in relief. He unsnapped her fly and pushed the denim away from her hips and down her legs.

He dipped his head lower again, his tongue dancing a tantalising line across the waistband of her panties, his hands now sliding beneath her buttocks, kneading the globes of flesh as he tilted her hips up. The contrast between the firmness of his hands and the enticing featherlight touch of his tongue as he tormented her with tiny touches sent her wild. At the tiny hollow at the top of her thighs, in the curve of her hips—everywhere but where she craved him most.

Then, gloriously, his mouth was suddenly, hotly against her. The warmth of his breath through her panties made her arch her back as sensation roared through her. She pressed against his mouth, her head thrashing from side to side, words tumbling from her lips begging him for more. His hand twisted in her underwear, tearing the fabric away from her body, baring her to his touch.

The contrast in sensation between the breeze that swept around them and the heat of his mouth as he closed over her sent a piercing shaft of desire through her. As his tongue swirled over her, at first softly then with increasing pressure, she clutched at the blankets beneath her. Her thighs trembled, and her inner muscles clenched in rhythm with his onslaught until, with a scream that tore from her throat, she went hurtling over the edge.

Luc shifted and Belinda, too boneless to do anything but watch, lay before him—her legs splayed, her skin flushed with orgasm—as he pulled off his shirt and shucked off his jeans and briefs. There was a light in his eyes that hadn't been there before. Framed by his short dark lashes, they gleamed with the heat of his need for her. A need that spiralled again within her, within seconds, as if she hadn't just climaxed moments before. As he positioned himself between her thighs again, a tremor of anticipation shivered along her spine.

"My wife." His voice was low pitched, almost guttural.

She could feel the heat of him, his blunt tip teasing her as he hesitated at her entrance.

"Luc, please," she begged, "please!"

He plunged inside her, driving himself to the hilt, and she hooked her legs around his waist, tilting her hips higher to take him in more deeply. She clung to his shoulders, near mindless with bliss as he slowly withdrew then entered her again, repeating the motion with increasing urgency until she felt him tense and shake, every muscle straining, holding back his climax. He slid one hand between them, where they were joined, before sliding his thumb across her hooded bundle of nerve endings. At his touch she felt the ripple begin within her again, this time with an even more urgent edge than before, and she clenched against him, her hips rising to meet his, forcing him to increase the pressure against her until she fractured apart. As the waves of pleasure undulated through her body, she felt his muscles bunch beneath her hands, heard his raw groan of completion as he shuddered against her over and over as the paroxysms of his pleasure rocked his body.

When he collapsed against her, Belinda could barely breathe, but she welcomed his weight, his total possession. This was how it had been between them—she knew it at a level that was soul deep. She could begin to thank her lucky stars that her memory of this link between them had returned, and from here who knew what would come to her next.

But for now, she decided as she stroked her hand down the line of Luc's spine and over his buttocks, she'd relish every second of this reunion.

Luc waited for the racing beat of his heart to slow, for clarity to return to his brain. He'd been so overwhelmed by the power of his response to her he'd barely been able to think, but now he realised he was crushing Belinda. He rolled off her and wrapped his arm about her slender waist, dragging her half over his body as he did so. Her long dark hair spread like a silken cloak across his chest. He inhaled deeply, relishing their comingled scents.

This had turned out far better than he'd anticipated. He'd expected some flashes of memory, some insights into their past, but he'd never expected her to remember their lovemaking so vividly. He'd been prepared to do whatever it took to get his wife back into his life—the life he'd carved out of nothing, the life he'd vowed would be his one day—and he'd succeeded. It didn't matter to him now if she remembered nothing else. If anything it would probably make life easier for them both.

He listened as Belinda's breathing deepened, as she slid into sleep and he smiled—a grim smile of satisfaction. Their accident had been a short-term derailment of his plan. He was back on track, better than before.

Eight

Belinda stood nervously at Luc's side near the helipad as the Tautara Estate helicopter came up through the valley. After their rediscovery of each other yesterday—a journey that had taken a sultry afternoon of food, wine and making love to complete—she felt almost resentful of this intrusion on their time together. After all, it wasn't as if they'd had a honeymoon—at least not one she remembered, and she still sensed Luc was holding back from her. If not physically, then certainly mentally. She wanted to push past that barrier more than anything. She wanted it all.

Luc still steadfastly refused to disclose any details to her of their past together, or of the accident. The gaps that remained, like yawning black holes in her memory, were increasingly frustrating. She edged closer to her husband and linked her fingers through his. She might not have it all back, she thought, relishing the warm, solid strength of him beside her, but what she did remember was like a gift.

Over breakfast he'd outlined the plans they had for today, that after a light lunch on the patio outside the main living room she and Demi Le Clerc would ride in the chopper to Taupo where they'd do a little shopping while Luc took her fiancé, Hank Walker, to the river for some fly-fishing. As daylight saving hadn't yet finished there'd still be time for Hank to enjoy dangling a few flies for the fish in the river. Tomorrow they'd all travel, again by helicopter, to Hawke's Bay for a vineyard trail ending the day with Demi singing at a concert at one of the vineyard estates.

Under any other circumstances Belinda was certain she'd have enjoyed the coming days entertaining their guests. Under any circumstances other than the fact that in the past twenty four hours she'd rediscovered how hopelessly and passionately she was in love with her husband.

As if he read her thoughts, Luc squeezed gently on her fingers before lifting them to his lips. As the helicopter set down in front of them, Luc turned her away from the buffeting wind, sheltering her with his body. She felt his answering surge of awareness to her proximity, and she deliberately leaned against him, imprinting the evidence of his desire against her. Something she could hold to herself during the next few hours.

"Minx," Luc growled in her ear as the turbines began to wind down and they heard the door open on the chopper. "How am I supposed to greet our guests like this?"

He flexed against her, leaving her in no doubt that, given the chance, they'd be on their way back to their suite.

"Try not to think about it—" she smiled back "—and try not to think about what I have planned for you tonight."

His pupils flared, their darkness all but consuming the pale green of his eyes.

"I'll deal with you later." While his voice was grim, the belying twinkle in his eyes made her look forward to the night ahead of them with even more urgency than she already possessed. "Now, smile nicely and greet our guests."

Together, hands still linked, they waited for Demi and Hank to come over to them. Belinda didn't miss the hungry rake of Demi's gaze as she kept her heavily made up eyes firmly on Luc, nor did she miss the brief twist of the other woman's lips as her gaze dropped to see their entwined fingers.

Every feminine instinct in Belinda's body went on full alert. If she wasn't mistaken there was a past between these two. A past that went deeper than old friends. She threw a look at Luc but his attention remained on their guests. She'd have given anything for some hint of reassurance from him right now. Some hint that she'd been wrong in her intuitively defensive response to Demi Le Clerc.

The jazz singer was everything Belinda was not. Her short-cropped white-blond hair spiked in an elfin-style cut around her delicate face. Although she was petite, standing no more than about five feet two, and was lightly built, Belinda had the distinct impression that the air of fragility Demi projected was a front for a far, far stronger personality than most people expected.

Belinda pulled her lips back in a smile, hoping against hope itself that Demi Le Clerc would prefer to rest at the Lodge today rather than head out shopping.

Hank Walker was a bit of a surprise. White-haired and stoop-shouldered, he exuded the world-weary air of someone who'd seen it and done it all and was not terribly impressed. Belinda fought down a swell of disquiet. The next few days looked as if they could be hard work.

"Dar-ling!"

Belinda stiffened as Demi launched herself at Luc, forcing him to drop her hand and accept the exuberant embrace from the other woman.

"It's *so* good to see you again. I was thrilled to bits when Hank agreed to include a stop here on our trip. Mind you—" she leaned back a little and gave Luc a lascivious wink "—he did take some convincing."

Belinda fought back a grimace at Demi's saccharine-sweet tone and the allusion she'd made. If she was trying to make Luc jealous, and Belinda suspected that was her intent, it certainly didn't seem to be working. She felt a surge of satisfaction as Luc disengaged Demi's painfully slender arms from around his neck and stepped forward, hand out, to introduce himself to Hank.

The two men appeared to size each other up for a split second before Hank took Luc's hand.

"Welcome to Tautara Estate, Hank. I'm Luc Tanner."

He gestured toward Belinda. "Hank, Demi, this is my wife, Belinda."

Was it her imagination or had he placed unnecessary emphasis on the word *wife?* Belinda stepped forward and shook Walker's hand. Demi gave her a swift once-over and a smile that was as fleeting as it was insincere.

"I've heard a lot about you, Luc," Hank drawled with his rich Texas accent. "Read a lot about you, too. Seems there are some rumors about how you got this place."

"There will always be rumors," Luc replied noncommittally.

"So are you saying they're not true? And here I was hoping you were a gambling man after all."

"I've been known to take a gamble, but only when the odds are very firmly on my side."

"Come on, Hank," Demi said in a faux conspiratorial tone, "I told you not to ask him about how he won this place in that poker game."

Belinda fought back a fresh surge of irritation. The woman's words highlighted yet again the gaps in her mind. She should know how Luc came to own Tautara, but it was locked somewhere deep inside. Accepting that, at the moment, Demi Le Clerc knew Luc better than she did herself was a bitter pill to swallow.

Luc gestured toward the house. "Come on inside. Manu has lunch waiting for us on the deck, then we can discuss what we have planned for you both while you're our guests."

"Guests?" Demi hooked one arm through Luc's and the other through that of her fiancé, effectively shutting Belinda completely out. "I think we go back far enough that you should say we're friends—very *good* friends—wouldn't you?"

The woman had all but purred, as she unequivocally staked her claim. Belinda took in a deep breath and forced her shoulders to relax and her hands to unclench before following the trio toward the house. The fact that Demi had in all probability been here before, had, perhaps, even shared Luc's private suite on her previous visits, rankled. As did the thought that she was more familiar with the lodge and its amenities—including its host—than Belinda was.

Well, there was nothing for it but to assert her position as Luc's wife and cohost. As they made their way through the entrance and veered left and through the expansive visitors' lounge room that led to a large deck area she made it her mission to ensure that her "guests" were made to feel as comfortable, and as welcomed, as she could possibly manage. After all, she was the one Luc would sleep with at night.

Manu had clearly done his research well, as the dry martini that Demi obviously preferred, along with the single-malt scotch that was Hank's favourite, were poured as they were ushered into comfortable wicker chairs under the large cantilevered umbrella that shaded this side of the deck. Belinda glided forward to take the drinks from Manu and personally delivered them to their guests with a smile. The glow of approval in Luc's eyes told her she'd done the right thing.

But then, doing the right thing had always been second nature to her. She'd acted as her father's hostess since she'd left school at eighteen—stepping into her mother's shoes as her health had weakened. She'd been so effective in the role she'd almost completely lost her own identity.

It had been frightening how easily she'd been absorbed into her role as effectively as a piece of fine antique furniture in any one of the chain of boutique hotels her father owned and operated. Her gardening, which had started out as a respite from her duties and her father's expectations, had sprung from her desire to break free of her anonymity. Of her need to be someone other than Baxter Wallace's sometime daughter and full-time hostess.

A whisper of something tickled at the back of her mind, triggered by her desire to be her own person, but it disappeared before it could take form.

"Belinda, what can I get you to drink." Manu's voice jolted her from her reverie.

"Just a mineral water, thanks. I think I need to keep my wits about me this afternoon."

Manu gave her a wide grin and said in a low voice that wouldn't reach the others as they sat in their chairs, "I reckon you can hold your own. Don't let that bit of fluff bother you."

"Don't worry, I won't." She smiled back.

It was ridiculous, but suddenly Belinda felt freer, lighter. As if she had an ally. She leaned against the deck railing and took a sip of her mineral water, enjoying the soft fizz against her tongue and its refreshing path as it travelled down her throat. She could do this. Memory or not.

"I hear you have one of the best herb gardens in the Southern Hemisphere." Hank's deep drawl made Belinda stand upright. "Care to show me around? I'm thinking of getting something along those lines set up at my place. I sure know the cook would be happy if I did."

"I'd be delighted to show you. Luc? Demi? Would you care to join us?" Belinda offered. She was reluctant to leave the other woman in Luc's sole company, but then again, maybe she could give her a dose of her own medicine.

When Demi refused, claiming weariness from travel, Belinda slipped her hand in the crook of Hank's arm and led him away. She didn't miss the twinkle in the older man's grey eyes as they walked back through the house to the elevator that would take them to the lower level and out onto the path leading to the herb garden. Perhaps she hadn't been subtle enough.

"You know you don't have anything to worry about with Demi," Hank said.

"I beg your pardon?"

"Once she realises that whatever she and Luc had before is well and truly gone, she'll back off. It's part of why I agreed to come here. I know she said 'yes' to me on the rebound but, for all her faults, I love her. And she will love me, too. Besides, any fool can see Luc loves you. He can't keep his eyes off you, no matter where you are. Did you catch that glare he gave me as we left? I've seen mountain lions less territorial than he is." He laughed, a rich barrel laugh that forced a smile to Belinda's lips. "Now, show me this garden of yours, and if I like it, you can pay me a visit to design something for me."

By the time they returned to the others, Hank was trying to convince Belinda to visit his home in Texas to draw up plans for an herb garden on his main residential property. Belinda was laughing at something he'd said as they walked through the large open doors and onto the deck. The look sent her way by Demi was positively wild, and Belinda hoarded the inner victory.

Belinda was surprised when Luc effectively stonewalled Hank's suggestion that they travel up to the States soon so she could choose for herself the best position to put in the garden he was so dead set on having. His deliberate move to change the subject away from her work niggled at the back of her mind, as if he'd done it before. Belinda shook her head slightly. That couldn't be right. Surely he wouldn't stand in her way when it came to doing something she loved so much?

Manu served lunch as they took their seats at the large round table, positioned out of the sun and in such a way as to make the most of the view. When lunch was over, the couples left to change and freshen up, all agreeing to meet at the front entrance in twenty minutes before heading out for their afternoon's activities.

Belinda dallied over reapplying her lipstick; she knew she'd only chew it all off again. Demi had a way about her that constantly kept Belinda on edge, and she wasn't looking forward to their shopping trip one little bit.

Luc's image appeared beside hers in the mirror.

"Are you up for this? No headaches?"

He snaked his hand under her hair and up along the back of her neck. She dropped her head back against his fingers, loving the strength of them as he massaged the tension that had knotted there.

"I'll be okay. After all, we're going shopping, what could possibly go wrong?"

Luc laughed, but his eyes remained serious.

"I'll get Manu to give you a cell phone to use in case you need to come back earlier."

"No, seriously, we'll be fine. *I'll* be fine, even though there's nothing I'd like better than to be home alone with you."

She turned and kissed him on the chin. His fingers tightened at the back of her head, and he tilted her face up toward his before bending slightly to kiss her. Desire flamed, instant and demanding, sending flickers of heat dancing along her nerves. When Luc broke away, she mourned his touch instantly.

"That's for what you did to me before," he growled against her lips, "and for what it's worth, you know I don't want to let you out of my sight, ever. I've suggested a change of plan to Hank, and he's agreed. Instead of coming back here tomorrow night after the concert, they're heading off to one of my other properties near Queenstown. But I'm serious, if you have any doubts about this afternoon, I'll call it off. You can stay here."

"You'd do that for me?" Belinda lifted a hand to trail her fingers over the scar that marked his jaw. A frisson of something unpleasant tickled at the back of her mind as she touched the smooth skin. She resolutely pushed the sensation away.

"You're my wife. There's no question."

"You say that like it's carved in stone, like *we're* carved in stone."

"Belinda, I hold on to what's mine."

"Was Demi ever yours?"

His face grew rigid under her fingertips. "What has she said to you?"

"She hasn't said a thing, yet. In fact, you might have noticed, she barely acknowledges I exist." Belinda forced a laugh so her comment wouldn't sound too catty. "But you haven't answered my question. Honestly, Luc, while I don't necessarily like it, I can accept that she may have been one of your past lovers, but I'd prefer to be forewarned before I spend the afternoon in her company."

"What Demi and I had was brief. A mistake she refused to let go of. And that—" he cupped her face with both his hands "—is all I will say on the matter. You have nothing to fear from her. Nothing."

Luc pressed his lips to hers again, as if underscoring what he'd said about Demi Le Clerc being a mistake, as if he could allay Belinda's fears with sheer determination. Helpless to resist him, Belinda opened her lips to his caress, welcomed the invasion of his taste, his tongue, his will.

When Luc made to pull away again she wrapped her arms around his shoulders, refusing to relinquish him. The other woman had made her feel insecure and right now, after the events of the past two days, she needed Luc to be her anchor. Needed him to use more than words to put her mind at ease.

She leaned back against the bathroom vanity, the cool marble imprinting through the silk of her dress in stark contrast to the heat that flamed deep within her body.

"Make love to me, Luc. Here. Now." Her voice was a harsh demand, a plea from her woman's heart, her vulnerability.

In response Luc skimmed his hands down over her

shoulders, and lower to fondle her breasts through the fabric of her dress. He bent his head and suckled, through the silk, the moisture of his mouth making the material cling to her aching nipples. She arched her back, thrusting her breasts forward to his mouth, to the pull and release of his lips and tongue.

Her hands fluttered over his shoulders, pushing aside the jacket he wore, then fumbled the buttons of his shirt open. She shoved his shirt down, off his shoulders and free of his arms, then raked her nails lightly across his chest, across the hard flat disks of his nipples. When he groaned in response, the vibration of the sound rippled through, making her nipples tighten even harder.

She pushed the palms of her hands flat, pressing them against the muscles of his chest and dragged them down, over his ribs to the top of his hip, where the shadowed line of his groin began. Getting rid of his belt and the fastenings on his trousers took only a second. Already she could feel his erection pressing against the zipper. She ached to free him, to hold his satin hard length in her hand, to stroke him, feel him, then guide him into the part of her that throbbed for his possession.

His briefs clung to him like a second skin, and she forced herself to slow down as she eased the waistband over his straining flesh and down his legs.

He lifted her to the vanity top, their movement drawing her gaze to the side mirror—their image sent a shocking thrill of excitement through her. There she was, perched on the edge of the rose-tinted marble, her hair in disarray, her eyes bright and gleaming with desire. The fabric of her dress showed dark and wet where Luc had suckled her, her nipples clearly delineated. The skirt was bunched up around her thighs where Luc's hands now slid, his naked torso a direct contrast to her clothed form.

Luc sensed the thrill of desire that rippled through Belinda as she watched their reflection in the side mirror. He lifted her slightly and eased her panties away from her, stepping away from the vee of her legs only long enough to discard the scrap of lace before he settled between her legs again. He was impossibly hard and he needed to be inside her—soon, very soon. She'd become as necessary to him as every breath he took. Necessary in a way that surpassed physical need. He shifted his weight to his good leg, ignoring the nagging pain he'd borne for the better part of the morning—no doubt a result of yesterday's activities. But it had been worth every second of it, as would this time and every time hereafter.

He pulled Belinda forward and she gasped as her backside slid along the cold marble.

He bent his head to the side of her neck, kissing, sucking and gently biting his way down to the curve of her shoulders.

He nestled his hips between her thighs, his erection probing at the hot, honeyed moisture at her entrance. He slid his hands up her arms, to the tiny cap sleeves of her dress and thanked the designer whose deep vee-cut neck and backline had decreed wearing a bra with this dress nigh on impossible. He slid the sleeves of her dress down, trapping her elbows at her sides and exposing the lush fullness of her breasts. The deep rose crests were tight buds, and he drew first one then the other into his mouth. Her shuddering sigh of pleasure was almost his undoing and he lifted her skirt higher, exposing her hips and the curve of her thighs to their view.

Slowly he pushed inside her, fighting the urge to sink himself in her as hard and fast as he could. He watched her expression, saw her eyes glaze and colour spread across her throat and chest. She'd wedged her hands on either side of her hips to keep her balance, using what leverage she had to flex against him, driving him in deeper. She moaned in response, and, now helpless to control his movements, he gave in to the rhythm his body demanded, his hips pumping hard and fast until her cries filled the room and her inner muscles spasmed around him. Pleasure surged through his body in response and he buried his face in her neck, muffling his shout of triumph as his climax ripped through his body and left him trembling against her.

"Now do you believe me?" he growled against her skin. "There is only you in my life. Now and forever."

"Forever," she whispered.

The word bounced softly off the marble of the room, almost as if it was captive, but Belinda remained deaf to its significance.

Nine

They stayed locked together for several minutes, their heartbeats slowly returning to normal, the perspiration on their skin drying. Eventually Luc forced himself to withdraw from her and helped her from the vanity top.

"We're going to have to hurry. Do you want to shower first?"

"There's room for us both, isn't there?" Belinda's tone and flirtatious glance was a far cry from the woman he'd come face-to-face with in her hospital room.

"There is, but not time enough for what we'll end up doing together." He undid the side zipper on Belinda's dress and tugged the garment off her body before turning her toward the shower with a gentle pat on her rear. "Go on."

When they eventually met their guests in the front

vestibule, Belinda warded off a sharp glare from Demi. Clearly she was far less than impressed about being kept waiting and didn't hesitate to voice her disapproval.

"Just how long before the shops close? It'll hardly be worth going soon." Her voice was petulant, her eyes cloudy with irritation.

"Don't be ridiculous, honey," Hank placated her. "There'll be plenty for you to see and buy. And why don't you girls stay in Taupo for dinner—it's on me. We'll be fishing until dark. You two may as well stay out and have a bit of fun."

After an hour in Demi's company, Belinda was distinctly weary. It wasn't that Demi was outright rude. But the constant niggles and comparative references to *her* time with Luc, at previous times and during this visit, told Belinda in no uncertain terms that despite what Luc thought, Demi was in no way "over him" just yet. And by the time Demi had turned her nose up yet again at another fashion boutique, Belinda began to despair of being able to keep her temper.

She was on the verge of suggesting they call their driver to take them back to the airfield for the chopper ride home when Demi's eyes suddenly lit on a car rental office.

"Look," she said, pointing. "They hire out luxury cars. Let's ditch the shopping thing and go for a drive around the lake."

"Are you sure you want to do that? It'd take a couple of hours to get around the whole lake, maybe longer," Belinda said.

"Well, let's head north then, what's that place? Oh,

yeah, Huka Falls. I heard there was a winery near there."

Before Belinda could stop her, Demi was off across the street and in the office of the rental place. All she could do was sigh and follow her. Demi was pointing to the car she wanted in the catalogue and negotiating pickup from Tautara Estate tomorrow as Belinda walked in the door.

"I thought we could send the chopper back and drive home ourselves after visiting Huka Falls and the winery. The guys won't be back until late, so it's not as if they'll miss us. Give me your phone and I'll let the pilot know."

Surprised, and a little uneasy at Demi's plan, Belinda handed over her cell phone after pulling up the number of their pilot on the screen.

"There." Demi snapped the phone shut. "All settled."

Once the paperwork was complete the two women were taken out the back of the building to where the car had been brought round. Belinda eyed the low slung, blood-red Porsche with some trepidation.

"Are you sure you want this one?" she asked.

"Oh, yes, definitely. Only this one will do. It's almost as flashy as Luc's one was." Demi gave her a piercing look. "You do still drive, don't you?"

"Of course I do," Belinda replied.

At least she thought she did. She'd always had her own car up in Auckland and assumed that that hadn't changed during her time with Luc. But even so, a sense of dread trickled cold and slow down her spine. The fine hairs on her arms stood up against her skin, and she rubbed her arms to ward off the sudden chill that invaded her body.

Demi had already settled herself in the driver's seat and had turned on the ignition before Belinda could force herself forward and into the car. She settled into the deep leather seat and clipped her seat belt on.

"Here." Demi tossed a map on her lap. "You can navigate this section."

Glad for something to do, anything that might distract her from the heavy ball of lead that had settled low in her stomach, Belinda studied the map and gave Demi instructions on how to head out of town. By the time they reached the winery, she'd almost convinced herself that her reaction back at the rental place was just part of the readjustment to normal life. She'd been out of circulation for some time. She'd incurred her head injury in a car accident. No wonder she'd been a little nervous. But Demi was a competent and confident driver, and Belinda had soon relaxed in her seat and enjoyed the countryside as it had swept by them.

The vineyard specialised in a boutique pinot noir, which Belinda really enjoyed. The French barrique-aged wine had a delightful flavour, and even though it was still a young wine she decided to have several cases sent to Tautara Estate to add to Luc's cellar.

It was as they were relaxing over a latte at the adjacent restaurant that Belinda found herself back on full alert.

"I have to say I was surprised to find you and Luc still together when Hank and I arrived," Demi commented as she swept sugar into her coffee and swirled it about with her spoon.

Belinda stiffened in her chair. Her hand arrested midway as she brought her cup to her lips. Without taking a sip of the fragrant coffee, she carefully set the cup back on its saucer.

"Why do you say that?" she replied cautiously.

"Well, because of the accident, of course. I've never understood Luc to be a particularly forgiving man. It just seemed out of character for him, is all." Demi waved a hand airily. "Don't let it bother you. Obviously, it doesn't bother him."

"What doesn't bother him?"

"Well, you were there. Of course you know."

"Actually, no, I don't. I have gaps in my memory. Our accident is one."

For some reason, probably self-preservation, Belinda didn't want to admit to the other massive holes in her mind. She had the distinct feeling that Demi wouldn't hesitate to use the knowledge to her advantage one way or another.

"I've heard that's quite common after a knock on the head. Didn't anyone tell you about it, then?"

"No. The doctors were emphatic that no one tell me what happened. I remember bits here and there, but not the whole picture. Yet."

"Not even Luc? How interesting."

Demi sat back in her chair and gave Belinda an assessing look. Whether she meant it to or not, it made Belinda very uncomfortable, and she wondered what would come next. It was a surprise when Demi did nothing more than turn the conversation back to her upcoming concert tomorrow evening. They lingered over a second coffee, then decided they should head back toward Taupo for a meal and then home. To Belinda's mild relief, Demi automatically slid behind the wheel to drive back.

They took a short detour to the Huka Falls, where they joined a group of tourists who stood on the over bridge marvelling at the power of the water tumbling at a massive rate beneath their feet. The surge and force of the foaming white water left Belinda feeling a little shaky. Its channelled yet uncontrolled flow was not unlike how she felt in her world at present: guided by the canyon banks, carved out by an ancient eruption, and pushed at an incredible rate to a plummeting fall.

Her fingers gripped the railing in front of her so tight she could feel them burn, but despite that, couldn't bring herself to let go. It was as if the physical act of letting go might actually tumble her over the edge and down through those canyon walls to plunge uncontrollably to an uncertain fate.

As the tourist group moved on to another viewing area, Belinda slowly peeled her hands from the railing.

"I think I'll go and wait by the car, unless you're ready to head off now?" she said as she started to walk off the bridge.

"Sure, we can head off now. Are you feeling okay? You've gone a bit pale."

Solicitous words from Demi? If Belinda hadn't felt so unbalanced right now she'd have laughed out loud.

"Just a bit of a headache, that's all. Must have been the noise of all that water."

Even as she brushed off the beginnings of another headache, Belinda knew it had nothing to do with the thunderous foaming mass of water. It was as if a dark shadow lingered in the back of her mind. A shadow that demanded acknowledgment. She shook her head slightly, as if she could dislodge the unsettling sensation, and reached in her bag for some painkillers.

She wished Luc was here with her. He would ground her. Make her feel safe and secure.

She would have laughed at herself if she could've summoned the energy. Only days ago she'd refused to leave the hospital with him and now she wanted to be with him more than anything else. She had to hold on to the fact that in another day they'd be alone again. Rediscovering their marriage together.

Her body warmed instantly at the thought, and she hugged the knowledge tightly to her that, while her mind refused to disclose much about their past, her body knew him. In itself that fact gave her a huge amount of security. Their physical union was a connection that could only have been forged, on her part at least, after building a great deal of trust and commitment. As far as she was concerned they couldn't get home soon enough, but she knew she had a duty to perform, as hostess to her guest, and duty was something she took very seriously—no matter the cost.

They chose a hotel near the Taupo waterfront that boasted an award-winning restaurant with picturesque views across the lake. As they swept into the forecourt and a parking valet came forward Belinda was struck by the sense of familiarity the hotel evoked.

The look of shock, hastily disguised by a welcoming smile, on the face of the maître d' momentarily rattled her, but by the time they'd been seated she'd convinced herself she'd been overreacting. The headache that had begun earlier had been effectively dispatched by the tablets she'd taken and she perused her menu with enthusiasm.

"Would you like to see the wine list, madam?" The wine waiter interrupted.

Belinda looked up to Demi who took the proffered list with enthusiasm.

"You go ahead," she said to Demi, "I'll stick with mineral water for now."

"Oh, good. You can drive back to the lodge then. And if you don't remember the way I'll navigate for you!"

Demi's laugh had a harsh edge to it that Belinda didn't like. She smiled back, but inside she was uncomfortable. By the time their entrees arrived, the other woman had worked her way through the better part of a bottle of wine and was laughing at the slightest thing. She barely touched her main meal, doing little more than push her rack of lamb about her plate.

When the maître d' came by their table to check on their enjoyment of the meals, Belinda was surprised to see the man step away from their table then hesitate before turning back.

"Mrs. Tanner?" he asked.

Belinda started. He knew her by name?

"Yes, I'm Mrs Tanner."

"I just wanted to say how relieved I am to see you're fully recovered from your accident. And your husband—is he well again, too?"

"Yes, thank you. We're both doing fine now." Belinda took a sip of her mineral water before continuing. "May I ask you how you know us?"

The expression on the man's face would have been laughable if he hadn't looked quite so stricken.

"Mrs. Tanner, don't you remember? You had your wedding reception here."

"We did? I'm sorry, there's still so much I don't remember before the accident."

"I'm not surprised. We were all horrified when we heard the crash outside."

"Outside?" Belinda's blood chilled in her veins. "Outside here?"

This was where it had all happened? How could she not have known, not have recognised the place as Demi had driven up into the forecourt?

"Yes, Mrs Tanner, straight after the reception. Are…are you all right, Mrs Tanner? I apologise if I've said anything I shouldn't have. Can I get you anything else?"

"No, no. There's nothing." She forced back the numbing fog of shock to remember her duties as Demi's hostess. "Unless there's something else you'd like?"

Demi just gave her a peculiar look and shook her head.

"Well, if you don't mind I think we'll settle the bill and head back to Tautara." Belinda tried to smile but her lips felt wooden, her face as if it was set in stone.

As they waited in the front portico of the hotel for the parking valet to bring the car around, the cell phone Manu had given her earlier started to trill. She'd no sooner flipped it open when she could hear Luc's baritone.

"Where are you? Why did you send the chopper back?"

"Luc! How was the fishing?"

"Fine. We've just come back to the house. Where are you?"

"We're at—" Belinda looked around and spied the

name of the hotel in gold lettering over the front door. She told him the name only to be met with stony silence. "Luc? Are you still there?"

"Why are you there?"

"We stopped here for dinner. Demi thought it would be a good place." She took a deep breath. "I didn't know it was where we had our reception or...or the accident."

"Are you okay? You sound shaky."

Just then the valet drove their rental car onto the forecourt and swung it to a halt in front of the two women.

"Here, give me that." Demi stepped forward and took the cell phone from Belinda's suddenly nerveless fingers. "Luc, it's Demi. Look, our car's just been brought round so we're on our way back."

Belinda heard Luc's voice resonate through the phone's tiny speaker.

"Car? What car?"

"The car I hired when we sent the helicopter back. You should see it. It's a Porsche Carrera, a lot like your old one, really."

"Stay there, I'll come and get you."

"Get us? Don't be silly. We'll be fine. We should be back in about half an hour to forty minutes."

"Demi—"

Demi snapped the phone closed and handed it back to Belinda with a smile.

"Men. They're always trying to order us women about. It has its uses, but Luc always did overdo it. Come on, let's head back."

She slipped into the passenger seat and settled

herself, giving the valet a smile as he closed her door.
Belinda had no option but to get behind the wheel of
the low-slung sports car.

Demi gave her a strange, almost challenging look as
she clipped her seat belt.

"You have driven a stick shift before, haven't you?"

"Yes, of course. But it was ages ago."

Belinda swallowed against the bile that suddenly
rose in her throat as she settled one hand on the steering
wheel and rested the other on the gearshift. Her skin had
turned cold and clammy and she wanted nothing better
right now than to pull at her clothing, which suddenly
stuck to her body as if she was bathed in perspiration.
She could do this. She'd driven a car for years. But then,
why was she suddenly, sickeningly, filled with dread?

She put in the clutch and selected first gear when the
blinding shaft of pain hit behind her eyes. Her foot slid
off the pedal and the car lurched away from the portico
to stall ignominiously on the drive. A small frightened
cry fought past her tightly pressed-together lips.

Belinda closed her eyes tight and pressed the heels
of her palms against them as visceral visual memories
blasted past the blocks of her mind. Pictures of her
behind the wheel of a car similar to this one, except its
paintwork was as dark as midnight—the lights of the
forecourt gleaming on its pristine surface.

An overwhelming sense of fear mixed with anger
and, yes, betrayal, made her breathing tighten in her
chest. She'd been alone in the car and in the driver's
seat—her wedding dress, a foam of white organza in the
leg bay. Tears blinded her eyes as she'd put the car in
gear and applied her foot vigorously to the accelerator.

Everything in her focused on only one thing—to get away.

Then suddenly, in front of her, Luc tore across her path. And she was too late. Too late to stop.

She relived again the horrified sob that wrenched from her throat as she'd swerved, the car slewing to the left as she tried unsuccessfully to avoid him. Then the terror as his body crumpled to the gravelled driveway before her as her ears were filled with a deafening crunch of metal and glass and everything went mercifully black.

"What the hell do you think you were doing?"

Luc's furious voice penetrated the darkness, followed immediately by Hank's protestation.

"Now quieten down, boy. It's not Demi's fault. Your wife shouldn't have been behind the wheel of that car, and you know it."

Belinda fought to raise her eyelids as the voices swirled around her.

"Yes, I do know it. That's precisely why I'd arranged the helicopter and a driver for them in Taupo. Whose idea was it to hire the Porsche?"

"Mine, it was mine." Demi's voice was defensive. "Someone had to do something. You weren't prepared to do anything about her memory loss."

"On instructions from her medical team. Instructions I made clear to you. You had no right to do what you did."

"I thought she was faking it. That's why I did it. For God's sake, Luc, she nearly killed you, and you still brought her home!"

"That was my choice to make. She's my wife."

Belinda sensed a tension between Luc and Demi that threatened to boil over into a full-blown conflagration. She had to stop it, stop them.

"Luc?" Her voice was thready.

He was at her side immediately, his strong arm a secure comfort as it snaked around her shoulders, helping her as she struggled upright.

"What's going on? Where are we?"

Belinda looked around the room. Nothing was familiar to her.

"We're at the hospital, but I'm taking you home. You don't need to stay here."

"Please, take me home now."

Luc had people move with a swiftness that saw them settled back at Tautara within the hour. She'd remained silent for the journey in the chopper and hadn't protested when Luc had suggested she go straight to bed when they got back to the house.

"Will you be all right for a few minutes? There's something I need to sort out, but I'll be straight back."

With a weary sigh Belinda leaned against the pillows he'd insisted on propping behind her. "Sure. I'm not going anywhere right now."

As soon as he was gone, she closed her eyes and willed sleep to claim her. Anything would be easier than acknowledging the dreadful memories that now scarred her consciousness.

She'd been the source of the accident that had caused Luc's injuries. She'd been the one to leave him permanently scarred and with a limp he had to live with for the rest of his life. Tears seeped out from beneath her closed lids, and her throat choked up with the enormity of what she'd done. No wonder she hadn't wanted to remember something so dreadful.

But why had it happened? Why had she been behind the wheel of his car? Even now she could recall how desperate she'd felt, how desolate and determined she'd been to get away from what was supposed to have been the happiest day of her life. What could possibly have happened that was so bad that it had made her want to run away from the man she'd just pledged her love to in marriage?

Ten

Dimly, she became aware of the sound of Luc's helicopter spooling up then taking off, the noise of the engine and rotors diminishing as it flew away from the property.

A soft click of the bedroom door was the only warning she had that he was back. The bed depressed as he sat down beside her. She could feel his eyes boring into her, but she couldn't bring herself to face him. How did you look into the eyes of the man you loved more than life itself and admit you'd nearly killed him? Worse, you didn't even know why.

His body shifted on the mattress, then a long, cool finger traced the path of the tears on her cheeks.

"Tears, Belinda? Why?"

She kept her eyes firmly closed and her lips equally so. She couldn't tell him she remembered. Not this. Anything but this. Inside she felt as if her heart was being splintered apart into a thousand shards. Shards that turned inward and struck her anew with the pain of what she now remembered so vividly. Remembered and fervently wished she could shove back into the dark and never know again.

The gentle pressure of his lips on hers was her undoing. She wrenched her head away and pushed her hands against his chest, trying to put some distance between them.

"No, don't," she begged.

"Why not?" His voice held a steely note that demanded an answer. One she was sure he would not be happy to hear.

"Because of what I did."

"What you did? Tell me. What do you remember?"

"I…I nearly killed you. How can you want me with you when I ran you down in your own car?"

"It was an accident."

"Was it? How do you know that? You have to tell me the truth of what happened. Why was I driving your car? Why weren't you in it with me? Why did you bring me back here when you must hate what I did to you—must hate me!"

Her voice had grown in strength and volume as she peppered him with questions. Shudders racked her body over and over. Yet still he didn't turn away from her. Instead he grabbed her hands with his and pulled her forward into his arms, holding her against his chest as she sobbed out her fear and frustration.

"I should never have sent you out with that woman for the whole afternoon. I knew she couldn't be trusted."

Luc cursed under his breath. He'd underestimated Demi, and it would cost him dearly. If Belinda remembered too much too soon, it could set his plans awry. Damn, but he could wring Demi's neck. Hank had obviously sensed the latent anger in him. He'd accepted Luc's suggestion that they leave immediately for Napier, staying at the home of one of Luc's business associates prior to the concert tomorrow night.

He stroked his fingers through Belinda's hair again and again until her sobs began to subside and the shudders that racked her body stilled. Gently he set her away from him, pushing her back against the pillows again. He studied her pale face and wished undone the damage that had been wrought today.

What would she remember next? Would she remember it all, now that large chunks of what had happened were coming back to her? Whether she did or she didn't, didn't matter. She would never leave him again, he'd made certain of that.

"How can you even bear to look at me?"

"Look at you? Why wouldn't I want to look at you? Even if you weren't my wife, you're a beautiful woman. Looking at you, knowing you're mine, gives me the utmost pleasure."

He could see his answer confused her. What had she expected, he wondered. A declaration of undying love? He clenched his teeth together. He didn't do emotion. She'd remember that again soon. How would she react? Would it be like last time, the fight-or-flight reflex taking over? Whatever she did, he had the means to prevent her from running again.

"Luc, I nearly killed you. I know I was trying to get away from you and that you tried to stop me. Why?"

"Why did I try to stop you? That's simple. We'd just gotten married. You heard something that upset you and you tried to run away. I had to stop you. I couldn't let you hurt yourself."

"Instead I hurt you. Was it deliberate?"

Luc had asked himself the very same question but had come to the conclusion that it had been a complete and utter accident. Her unfamiliarity with the six-speed gearbox of the powerful sports car, and her very nature, lent weight to that deduction. Convincing the police not to lay charges against his unconscious wife while he'd been trapped in a hospital bed had been easier said than done.

"No, of course it wasn't deliberate. You were upset, you made a misjudgment. I should never have stepped in front of the car. It was as much my fault as it was yours. Believe me, if you had deliberately tried to run me down, the police would have been at the hospital waiting for the moment you came out of your coma so they could arrest and charge you."

He saw her shoulders drop slightly as she began to relax.

"Then why? What was I doing, what was I thinking? It was our wedding day. We should have been leaving our reception together."

"I can't tell you what you were thinking, Belinda." That much at least was true. He'd had no idea that she would react the way she had, when she'd learned the truth behind their marriage. "But I know if I had to do the same thing again to stop you from leaving me and hurting yourself, I would."

"Even if it meant I'd end up hurting you?"

She looked so confused, so fragile, both mentally and physically as she lay in their bed. Luc took one of her hands in his and lifted it to his lips to press a kiss inside her wrist.

"Even then."

He saw the flare of heat in her eyes at his caress, felt his own answering response. He stroked his tongue gently across the fluttering pulse beneath the pale skin of the inside of her wrist.

"Oh, Luc. How can you still want me after what I did?"

"I will always want you. From the first time I saw you I wanted you. I will never let you go. Never."

He leaned forward and caught her lips in a kiss designed to leave her in no doubt of his intentions, in no doubt of his desire to possess and keep her. She responded like someone who'd been thrown a lifeline in a turbulent sea, her arms linking around his neck and holding him to her as if she was afraid he'd disappear if she let go.

The sweep of her tongue across his lower lip sent a jolt of need through his body. Instantly he wanted her with a desperation he had never thought to feel again. A desperation born of fear of losing her. The fear itself was ridiculous. She would never, could never, leave him again. He knew that as well as he knew each exquisite line of her body. But a small voice deep inside him urged him to admit to wanting more, to needing more than simple possession.

Luc pushed aside the thought with the same ruthless urgency as he cast away his clothing, then divested Belinda of the robe she'd wearily drawn over her body after undressing earlier. His hands shook as he caressed her shoulders and trailed his fingers across the sweep of her collarbone then lower to test the weight and fullness of her breasts.

When she pressed against his hands, silently begging for a harder touch, he obliged—squeezing the globes of flesh with a firmness that saw her nipples harden into tight beads of deepest rose. He bent his head to take the crest of one breast between his teeth, his tongue flicking against its rigid point until she cried out with pleasure, her nails raking his shoulders.

He replaced his tongue with his fingers, pulling and drawing at her nipples as she squirmed against him. He could smell her desire on the air around them and he knew he had to taste her—to drive her to peak after peak of pleasure. To imprint that pleasure that only he could give her on her mind and to effectively obliterate her fears and insecurities. To affirm her place in his life, in his bed.

Her skin quivered as he traced his tongue around her belly button, dipping into its centre and probing the perfect indentation again and again in a teasing mimic of what he planned to do next. When he trailed his tongue lower, to the curve of her inner thigh, her legs fell open, giving him free rein to do with her whatever he wanted. And he wanted. Wanted her so deeply he knew he would never let her go.

He nuzzled against the moist curls at the apex of her thighs, sliding his hands beneath her buttocks, tilting her toward him, opening her further so he had clear and unlimited access.

He dipped his tongue to her centre, stroking deeply, allowing his teeth to graze the shiny nub of flesh that was the key to her release.

She writhed against him, her breath coming in quick pants. His own body burned in response, urging him to rise above her and surge into her—to take him over that edge and into the abyss where only pleasure mattered. Where the past no longer existed. But with a discipline learned from a life of hardship and denial, he held himself back. His first priority was Belinda. First and always.

Beneath his onslaught her body tautened, and he knew, with a rising sense of satisfaction, she was close to orgasm. He eased one finger inside her, smiling as her inner muscles clenched around him instantly. He stroked her deep inside, alternating flicks of his tongue across her swollen bud with the pressure of his finger until her hips rose off the bed and her body bowed and shook as the waves of her climax pounded through her.

Her cheeks were streaked with tears, her eyes glazed as he slid up over her body and positioned himself at her entrance.

Belinda was boneless, floating on a sea of pleasure such as she'd never known before, and yet, as she felt the weight of Luc's body on hers, felt the blunt pressure of his erection probing her core, she was revitalised. She wanted him more than she ever had before. Needed him more. All of him, in every way. She needed to know, more than anything in her life, that the terrible wrong she'd done him was forgiven.

She opened her body to him, lifting her hips and wrapping her legs around his waist. She caught his face between her hands and kissed him, the taste of her own desire on his lips unusual and yet enticing at the same time. As he eased his length inside her body she suckled on his tongue and rocked against him, drawing him deeper within her until she thought she could take no more.

A jolt of ecstasy shot from deep within her, radiating out through her limbs and making her cry out with the sensation, relinquishing his tongue, his mouth, as her head dropped back against the pillows. Pressure built within her body again, faster than before, harder than before, and she moved in rhythm with him as he drove into her with increasing tempo.

She stroked her hands across his chest, over his shoulders and down his back—his muscles marble hard with tension beneath her touch. Lower and lower she trailed her finger tips until she traced the cleft of his buttocks, felt the clench and release of sinew and power beneath her caress.

And then, with a raw shout, he drove deeper than before, his entire body taut as he fought to stave off his climax for just a moment longer. Ripples of pleasure radiated through her in ever-increasing waves until she gave herself over to the sensations. As she did so, felt his body melt into her own, his hips thrusting, straining, as he finally gave in and allowed gratification to dominate him once more.

Tiny pulses of satisfaction, like tiny electric shocks,

vibrated through her body as they lay entwined on the bedcovers. Now that Luc's sensual onslaught had reached an end, she allowed herself to think again about what had happened today. About the shock of remembering what and who had caused his terrible injuries.

Luc's breathing deepened as he lay beside her, his face nestled in the curve of her neck. Belinda stroked her hand down his body, down to his hip and along the path of his scar as it trailed down his thigh.

"I'm sorry," she whispered into his hair. "I'm sorry I hurt you."

"It's in the past," he said, his voice deep and thick with the edges of slumber. "We'll talk more tomorrow. Now, sleep."

"Luc?"

"Hmmm?"

"I love you."

In response his arms closed around her tight, drawing her along the length of his body where she knew she belonged. He pressed his lips against her throat.

"I know." His words were a deep rumble against her skin.

Belinda held her breath, waiting for more. Waiting for him to tell her he loved her, too, but she waited in vain as his body relaxed more deeply into hers and his breathing became more measured, indicating he had fallen deeply asleep.

She stared into the darkness, thoughts and fears pounding at her mind. Did he love her, too, or had she destroyed that when she'd almost destroyed him? That he wanted her, desired her, was obvious. But physical love was only one part of a relationship. What of the rest? Of the melding of minds, the reciprocal emotional bond that came from a union between life mates?

Despite the heat of Luc's body as he slumbered beside her, she felt a chill ripple through her soul. Something hovered on the shadowed periphery of her consciousness, and she fought unsuccessfully to grasp it with her mind even as sleep finally claimed her.

Luc's eyes flicked open, straining to see in the darkened room, the words Belinda had uttered echoing in his mind. Instead of the triumph he'd anticipated, he was consumed with an aching need to respond in kind. But he knew from bitter experience that could only lead to pain. Hadn't his mother's last words been of love for his father—the man who'd ended up destroying them both? No, better that he cap his feelings. Better that Belinda's love not be returned.

Belinda woke the next morning surprisingly rested, and when Luc suggested they have a swim before breakfast she accepted his idea eagerly. The indoor solar-heated pool with its roll-away ceiling, open today to make the most of the late summer sunshine, looked inviting. Luc dived in, cutting cleanly through the water, and for a moment Belinda merely revelled in the beauty of his body as he swam one length after another.

In the water there was no sign of the weakness in his leg, no sign of the limp that marked him as flawed. She knew how much it bothered him to carry such a defect, and it scored her deeply to know she was responsible for that. Yet he'd forgiven her, he'd reiterated that again today when they'd changed for their swim, telling her to leave the past firmly in the past where it belonged.

"Aren't you coming in?" Luc's head, dark and sleek with water popped up in front of her.

"Sure I am."

"What's holding you back, then?"

Belinda let her eyes roam over the corded muscles in his neck, the breadth of his powerful shoulders and chest where they were exposed, slightly out of the water.

"Just enjoying the view, that's all." She injected a teasing note in her voice. Anything was better than admitting the truth that she was even more racked with guilt this morning than she had been last night.

The reality of the long-term effects of his injury sat heavily on her shoulders. The requirements of his position as a host and guide to their overseas guests demanded a certain level of fitness. A fitness that had been sorely damaged due to her actions.

She shook her head slightly to free herself of the lingering sense of dread that still clung on the fringes of her mind.

"I'll race you to the other end," she challenged, diving over his head and neatly into the water.

She struck out firmly across the water as soon as she broke the surface, a thrill of excitement surging through her as she felt his presence close behind. She reached the opposite side, muscles burning at the unaccustomed exercise, a split second before strong fingers wrapped around her ankle and tugged her under. Beneath the water's surface she allowed herself to sink into his waiting arms, her body leaping to life the instant her flesh joined with his.

She could feel the curve of his lips as they kissed beneath the water, sensed the power in his legs as he kicked them back up toward the surface.

"You cheated," he growled against her mouth. "I should punish you for that."

"And if I concede?" She nipped at his lips.

"Then you get to punish me."

"Would that be before or after breakfast?" she teased.

Luc laughed, the sound echoing through the rafters of the pool house and setting light to a deep sense of joy inside Belinda. In the days since they'd come to Tautara, come home, she hadn't heard him give vent to unabashed humor like that. To know she'd been the one to draw it from him made her feel incredibly special. And it made her all the more determined to make him happy like that again and again.

Once out of the pool, they dried each other off, then wrapped themselves in robes. Belinda was fully prepared to forgo breakfast by the time she'd towelled away the moisture from Luc's perfectly proportioned body and, judging by the reaction of one of those proportions, he was, too. Then Manu called through on the intercom to let them know breakfast was ready on the upper deck of the house.

She paused a moment, as they were about to leave the pool house, to wriggle out of her wet bikini bottoms and undo the ties of her top and pull it away from her body.

"What are you doing?" Luc asked, his eyes burning bright with a look she'd come to recognise.

Belinda felt an answering pull at her womb as she chose her words.

"I can't stand wet swimwear against my skin," she said as casually as she could as she walked through the door Luc held open for her.

"And I'm supposed to keep my mind and my hands on breakfast knowing you're naked beneath that robe?"

"Think of it as your punishment."

She smiled and flicked the lapel of his robe to emphasise her point.

"Ah." Luc slid a hand inside the thick toweling to cup her breast, his thumb lightly stroking her nipple. "But I didn't hear you concede."

Her answer caught on the breath that hitched in her throat as, with his body, he pinned her back against the wall. His hair-roughened thigh slid between her legs to rub against her. The contrast of the sudden chill of his damp swim trunks against her heated core made her gasp out loud, the sound swiftly muffled by Luc's lips on hers as he took her mouth in a hungry kiss. He flexed his hips against her, rubbing the ridge of his arousal across her, sending her into an instant flare of burning need.

"Still can't stand wet swimwear against your skin?" he whispered into the shell of her ear.

Luc pulled away from her and straightened her robe before taking her hand and leading her back upstairs to the deck. Belinda could barely think, let alone speak. In a split second he'd turned her on so much she'd have thrown care and propriety to the wind and let him take her against the glass-lined pool house wall. Visible for any of the staff to see as they made their way around the property.

Her wholehearted absorption in him and in everything he aroused in her was daunting. No wonder she'd agreed to marry him. Even in these few short days, with the limited memories she'd regained, he'd become the centre of her world.

So why, then, had she been trying to run away?

Eleven

"What would you like to do today?" Luc asked as he sliced a mushroom on his plate. "I have some work to attend to this morning, but we can do whatever you like for the rest of the day."

"If you're going to work, I'll spend some time in the garden. I've missed getting my hands dirty." She smiled.

"You don't need to get your hands dirty. We have staff for that."

"But, Luc, it's something I enjoy, something I love."

Luc reached across the table and took one of her hands in his. Sunlight caught the blue diamond of her engagement ring, refracting light across the white linen tablecloth like blue fire. For all they were dining al fresco, everything was still five-star. Whatever they promised their clientele, it was obvious that this was a way of life Luc lived, as well. He offered perfection and expected it in return.

He rubbed her fingers between his. "Just make sure you wear gloves. You don't want to ruin your beautiful hands."

There was a note in his voice that set Belinda's spine straight, made her feel prickly and defensive. She pushed the thought aside. He only cared for her welfare, she told herself.

"Sure, if it'll make you happy."

"Having you as my wife makes me happy," he replied, lifting her fingers to his lips and licking lightly between the knuckles.

Again, that frisson of discomfort trickled down her back, raising a question in her mind. Was it having *her*, or having her as *his wife* that made him happy? The question bothered her and she absentmindedly spread marmalade over her toast as she tried to figure out why.

She felt as if she'd truly come home when she entered this part of the gardens. To one side of the shade house stood a shed, lined with shelves filled with terra-cotta pots of all sizes and shapes and with bags of potting mix stacked against one wall. Just outside the shed a pink-veined marble replica of Venus de Milo stood in lonely splendor.

Belinda trailed her hand along the line of the statue's shoulder. She could sympathise with Aphrodite on this score, she thought, as her hand dropped past where the statue's right arm would have finished. It seemed as if nothing was complete in her world right now, either—at least not in her memory. There were still vast tracts of emptiness, gaps splintered by sudden glimpses of the past.

She sighed and looked around her. So much here was familiar, comforting in a way. It would be good to be busy doing something she loved again.

Much later that morning Manu brought her a phone as she worked on repotting some cuttings she'd found in an overgrown mass in a shade house around the side of the herb garden. Obviously, she'd been experimenting with cuttings and grafting prior to their marriage. Those that had taken were strong and healthy, if not a little unruly. Unfortunately, just as many plants had shrivelled up and died. She hoped that wasn't symbolic.

Manu stepped through the doorway with a big smile, and Belinda dusted off her hands on her jeans, having long since discarded the unwieldy gardening gloves she'd donned purely because Luc had requested it.

"Enjoying yourself?" Manu asked, with a twinkle in his deep-set brown eyes.

Laughter bubbled from her throat. "Oh, yes! Definitely."

"That's good. We've missed your smiles around here, you know. Here—" he passed her the cordless phone "—there's a call for you from Auckland. Someone at Pounamu Productions."

"Really, what on earth could they want?"

"Take it and see."

Belinda inspected her hands quickly before accepting the cordless phone and put the phone to her ear.

"Hello? This is Belinda Wal—Tanner." She grimaced comically at Manu at her slip. She'd automatically gone to use her maiden name. Mind you, that wasn't so surprising considering that she still couldn't even remember her wedding.

"Belinda, still not used to being a married woman, eh? Look, it's Jane Sinclair from Pounamu Productions. Do you remember that series we were discussing before your wedding, the half hour per week gardening show? The money men have given us the go-ahead and the powers-that-be love the stills we took of you in your family gardens. They think you're a natural for the job, and the fact you're so gorgeous will widen our audience appeal. When can you come up to Auckland to discuss it further?"

Belinda absorbed Jane's words in stunned silence. Television series? Weekly gardening show? How on earth was she supposed to tell Jane she had absolutely no idea what she was talking about. Disregarding Belinda's lack of response Jane carried on talking about plans for the series, production schedules and all manner of things.

"So, how about next week? Does that suit?" she finished.

"Look, I'll need to get back to you to confirm, but that should be fine," Belinda hedged. "Give me your number."

She scrabbled around on her workbench. She knew she'd seen a marker pen somewhere. A pen and paper appeared in front of her and she flung Manu a grateful look as she rapidly copied down Jane's contact details. By the time she pressed the off button on the phone, she felt as if she'd run a marathon. She looked at Manu in puzzlement, briefly outlining the call.

"Do you know what she was talking about?"

His normally open face assumed a set expression, his eyes giving nothing away. "You'll have to talk to Luc about that. He's still in his office. Do you want me to call him for you?"

"No, that's okay. No need to disturb him. I'll see him at lunchtime. We can talk about it then."

"No worries." He turned to leave, then hesitated in the doorway. "How do you feel about it? That's some opportunity you have there."

"Yeah, it is." She sank onto a stool behind her and met his gaze full-on. "I would have jumped at this opportunity before, I just know it, but something's telling me not to. That it's not right." She shook her head. "I don't know. Seems life would be a whole lot easier if I could just remember everything."

"Ah, well, as my *tipuna* would say, don't trouble trouble until trouble troubles you. Sometimes it's just as well to leave well enough alone."

"Your grandmother was a wise woman. Thanks, Manu."

As he left the shade house, she pondered his words, and the almost cautionary tone in which he'd delivered them. Was it best for her not to keep pushing to remember? She doubted that very much. If her marriage was going to be fulfilling, she had to be able to come to it a whole woman with a whole mind, not, she smiled to herself, one with holes in her mind.

"What's so funny?"

Luc's voice from the doorway made her start.

"Manu said you were still working." She reached up and kissed the cleft in his chin. "Is it time for lunch already?"

Luc picked up her hands in his and gave her a stern look. "Whether it's lunchtime or not, I think it's time you took a break. Look at you."

Belinda ruefully examined her hands. "They'll scrub up okay. Besides, it's not as if I'm on show or anything, is it?" She strived to keep her tone light, but the command in Luc's voice was unmistakeable—and she didn't like it one bit.

"I wouldn't call it 'on show,' exactly, but we're expecting more guests in the next few days and will have near full capacity over the next six weeks. You know I need you by my side, looking beautiful."

Belinda forced a laugh. "You make me sound like an ornament. Surely I'm more important than just that."

"Endlessly." Luc scooped one arm around Belinda's waist and pulled her to him. "You're the most important thing in my world. Is it any wonder I just want to keep you near me as much as I can?"

She was saved from responding as Luc bent his head and kissed her, his tongue stroking her lower lip lightly, coaxing her to open her mouth and allow him entry. Her body flamed to instant aching life. It seemed she couldn't get enough of him—of his taste, his strength— all of him. Whether it had been his intention to thoroughly distract her or not, it worked supremely well and by the time Luc coaxed her from her potting mix and pots, she was looking forward to the afternoon they were to spend together.

Back up in their suite she took a quick shower and changed into clean jeans and a long-sleeved white linen blouse over a soft blue silk chemise. Luc hadn't told her exactly what they'd be doing but had intimated she'd need to dress casual and to bear in mind protection from the sun.

As she picked up her gardening clothes to put them in the laundry hamper, a slip of paper poked out from a pocket. She snagged it between her fingers, looking at the name and number she'd scrawled so hurriedly. She thought about Luc's forewarning that they'd be a full house with guests in the next week. She'd have to check with him when would be a good time to go to Auckland for her meetings.

She stroked the paper between her fingers, staring at the name—willing something, anything, to spring into her mind about the proposed television series. Suddenly a picture burst in her mind, of Jane Sinclair in the gardens at Baxter Wallace's Devonport-based boutique hotel for a wedding. The woman had enthused for ages about the beauty of the old roses, the arbours, the scented plantings Belinda had bordered the property with. When she'd heard Belinda was responsible for that and many of the other Wallace hotel-chain gardens she'd simply gushed with ideas.

Belinda had been hugely excited. Working with her father over the past few years—acting as his right hand as her mother had begun to find the task increasingly wearying—had always been more of a duty than a pleasure. While she did it, as she did everything, with the utmost confidence and competence, gardens were where her heart lay. She loved every part of it. The planning, selecting the plantings, overseeing the work—every stage had its rewards right through to completion.

She'd worked for years, albeit part-time, trying to

build a portfolio from which to grow her fledgling design business and now, finally, she was being given the platform from which to launch—to soar and fly and achieve her dreams.

Belinda shoved the small sheet of paper into the pocket of her jeans and rushed through to the dining room where Luc waited for her. She couldn't wait to tell him about Jane's call—and better yet, that she remembered the reasons why.

It didn't for a minute occur to her that he'd object.

"It's impossible. Give me the Sinclair woman's number and I'll let her know you won't be participating."

Belinda dropped her fork to her plate with a clatter.

"I beg your pardon?" She was incredulous. "Why ever not?"

"I told you. I need you here. This is our livelihood. Our guests expect a host and a hostess, with all the trimmings. It's what you do best, so let's hear no more of this television show."

"What I do best? But, Luc, this is an opportunity I can't turn away. Just think of the commissions I could get for doing gardens like our herb garden. Even Hank wants me to design something for him."

Across the intimately set table in their dining room, Luc stilled. "Hank Walker? No."

"Okay, I agree that working for him would be difficult with Demi and everything. Still, a trip to Texas would've been fun, wouldn't it?"

"That trip is never going to happen, just like you hosting this TV show isn't going to happen, either."

Belinda's spine stiffened as she looked at him. Had he gone completely mad?

"What do you mean, never?"

"Your place is here. By my side."

"By your side? But what of my work, Luc. I have a business to rebuild."

"No, you don't."

Luc watched Belinda carefully from across the table. It had been only a matter of time. His greatest fears were coming to life as her memory returned. He could feel himself losing her already, and the sensation struck dread deep into his heart. Was it so wrong to want to keep her here, by his side? He pushed himself to his feet and walked around to her. He reached for her hand, clenched in a tight fist in her lap, and pulled her up against him. Her eyes looked more grey than blue— cold, defensive—as if he'd suddenly grown horns from his forehead. And maybe to all intents and purposes he had—because the devil would take him before he'd let her go. Under his gaze she paled, her lips fading to the palest of pink, her cheeks totally devoid of colour.

He bent his head to kiss her, to kiss away the anger and fear that reverberated from her like a tangible force, but she turned her head away. Damn, he didn't like the way this was heading, or the sudden sensation of vulnerability that sliced through him.

"We've had this conversation before, haven't we?"

She brushed a hand across her forehead, rubbing across the line of her brow as if to coax something from her mind. Luc remained silent, watchful. He recognised the signs now. She was getting a headache, a precursor to her remembering something that distressed her and that invariably led to a loss of consciousness.

He tightened his hold on her, only to have her pull free and step away from the safety of his arms.

Lord, it was only yesterday that she'd remembered the accident. The memories were coming thicker and faster than before. And he, damnably, had no control over them.

Sudden awareness shot through her features.

"We have." Her voice rose, a thread of anger running like a vein of steel through it. "It was straight after the wedding."

"Go on," he said, fighting to keep his voice level. Fighting back the words of denial that he knew were a lie.

She blinked a few times in quick succession, her brow furrowing as she appeared to sort through the vagaries of her mind. When she lifted her head, her eyes were bright with anger and something else he couldn't immediately identify.

Pain.

It was pain. Pure and simple and wrenching in its presence. Emotional pain of a type he'd never permitted himself to acknowledge. Yet seeing Belinda so stricken sent a piercing arrow of empathy deep inside to the dark place he kept hidden from everyone. Even himself.

Luc reached for her, again but Belinda was quicker. She stepped out of his reach, shaking her head, her voice low.

"Don't touch me."

"Belinda, stop."

"Stop? Stop what, Luc? Stop remembering that you only married me because I was the best applicant for the job? Stop remembering that you deliberately wooed me here to Tautara and then wooed me into your bed?" She slammed her hand on the table beside them, making the plates and cutlery jump. A glass toppled and rolled off the edge and onto the tiled dining-room floor, shattering into pieces. "Tell me, am I on track? Is there anything in particular I might have left out?"

She stared at him, tears welling in her eyes. Inside he felt as if a tenuous link had begun to break apart.

"I never lied to you, Belinda."

"No, you didn't. And you never loved me, either."

The tears finally spilled over her lower lashes, tracking in lines of silver down her cheeks.

"And that's a crime? Love is for fools. What we have is—"

"What we had." She interrupted him with a finality in her voice that froze him where he stood.

"Had?"

"You don't expect me to stay here now I know, do you? I was leaving you the night of the accident. The night we were supposed to be celebrating our marriage. How could you keep that from me and expect me never to remember—never to want to leave you again? I hate you for what you did to me, what you've done to me now."

She spun on her heel and headed for the door.

"Stop. Where do you think you're going?" he demanded, his hands knotted into fists of frustration at his side. No matter what the provocation he would not let go of his anger. He was not like his father, but he would not let Belinda go. Not when she was the centre of his world. He could not.

"I'm leaving. Leaving Tautara and leaving you. You can't stop me."

Her hand was on the doorknob, turning the polished brass and releasing the catch.

"You're right. I can't stop you." He struggled to inject the right note of nonchalance in his tone. As he'd hoped she hesitated and turned at his words.

"Is this some kind of trick?"

"Trick? No, I'm not into games. Never have been." There'd been no games in his childhood. Life had been serious from the get-go, deathly so. He slowly walked toward his wife; noted the way her fingers tightened nervously on the doorknob. "I certainly can't stop you leaving, but you might like to consider the effect of your doing so on your parents."

"On my parents? They wouldn't want me to stay in this…this…'relationship' any longer than I have already. If Dad had any idea of how cold-bloodedly you married me, he'd be helping me out this door as fast as he could."

"Are you so certain of that? Perhaps you should speak to your father before you leave. Make sure you'll be welcome home."

"Why wouldn't I be? I'm their youngest child. I've worked at my father's side for years, helped my mother in every way I can. Of course I'd be welcome home." Twin spots of colour appeared in her cheeks, bright in the porcelain pale of her skin.

"Then perhaps he won't mind so much when I call in my loan. Of course, it'll mean that your mother will have to cease the treatment she's just started in America, and your father's hotels, well, they'll no doubt be sold to defray some of those costs. It's even possible your sisters' husbands will lose their positions managing their hotels. Maybe they'll find other work to sustain the lifestyles they're all accustomed to, maybe not. But it'll all be worth it in the name of love, won't it?"

He stepped past her and opened the door of their suite. "You're free to go anytime you want. Just be sure that you can live with the consequences."

Twelve

Belinda sank to the floor in numbed shock as Luc walked past her and down the corridor to the lodge.

As the echo of his footsteps faded away, her thoughts spun in ever-decreasing circles in the face of his threats.

She remembered it all. The beauty of her wedding day, the excitement she'd felt that she was finally Mrs. Luc Tanner, then the awful sense of displacement when her father had taken her to one side at the reception:

"I'm so happy to see this has turned out to be a love match after all," Baxter Wallace said.

Belinda's joy in her day dimmed slightly at her father's words. Turned out to be a love match? Hadn't it been that all along?

"What do you mean, Dad? Of course we're in love."

Her father coloured up, blustered through his next few words. "Luc Tanner has been after you for years, my dear. He made no bones about how he coveted your skills and the way you complemented everything that Wallace Hotels encompasses. I always stood in his way, but now I've seen you two together, so happy together, I don't feel so bad about it all anymore."

"Bad about what?" *Belinda persisted.*

"Oh, just men's business. Nothing you need to worry your pretty head about, my dear. Suffice it to say your mother and I are very happy."

Her father's patronising manner set her teeth on edge. This was precisely what had held her back in her endeavours to break free of his expectations all her adult life.

"Tell me," *she demanded, meeting her father's worried glance with a firm determination that left him in no doubt that she wasn't going to let the matter go.*

"Well, you know how we were hit with that international credit-card-booking scam, how we were out to the tune of several hundred thousands of dollars."

"Yes, but I thought you said you'd sorted that out with the bank."

"Well, yes, I did. But with your mother's ill health and with waiting to get booked into that special treatment in the States, we needed a little more."

"A little? How much, Dad?"

"Luc Tanner loaned us the money to get out of trouble."

"So you set up a loan. Why do you need to feel bad about that?" *she asked, confused. It wasn't unusual for this sort of thing, surely.*

"Not exactly a loan. Tanner had specific conditions. Actually, one specific condition."

Belinda's heart clenched at her father's words. She knew what he was going to say before he even said it.

"He wanted you. As his wife."

"He bought me?"

How could it be true? Had her father really traded her to offset his debts?

All her life her father had treated her like something to be shown off. Even her showcase gardens had been boastfully spoken of, although he'd never really believed it was more than a hobby for her. He'd paraded her at his side with what she'd hoped was parental pride. But she'd been wrong—terribly, horribly wrong. She'd been nothing more than a chattel in her father's household to be sold to the highest bidder. To another man who regarded her as little more than another acquisition.

"You exaggerate, my dear. You always did. Always so romantic and emotional about things. Besides, it's not as if you're not in love with him, is it? You'll be very happy together—a perfect couple. You'll be such an asset to his business, just the thing to counter any lingering doubts people have about his background. And the best thing is that now your mother can have the treatment her doctor has been recommending in the States. As soon as she's well enough to travel we can be on our way."

Her father's words fell on her like hail stones, each one a stinging strike against her heart. She didn't want to believe it was true, that she'd been sold to the highest bidder. There was only one person who could refute her father's ridiculous claims.

Luc. Only he could tell her the truth. Of course they'd married for love.

Luc appeared at her side in sartorial splendor, his tailored tuxedo giving him an even more powerful presence than usual.

"Are you almost ready to leave? The valet has brought the car around."

Belinda placed a shaking hand on his arm.

"Is it true? Did you buy me?"

"Buy you? Where did you get that idea?"

Luc shot Baxter Wallace a damning look, but it was all Belinda needed to know the truth.

"Luc, tell me you love me. Tell me you married me because you love me."

"Belinda, this is ridiculous. We're married. Come, the car is waiting."

She shook free of his grasp. "Tell me you love me." She enunciated each word carefully so there could be no doubt. "Tell me you didn't just marry me to have a hostess at Tautara Lodge."

"Of course I didn't marry you just to have a hostess at Tautara. I could have employed any one of my competitors' best staff for that role, if that was all I wanted." He lifted a finger to stroke the line of her collarbone, exposed by the scooped décolletage of her wedding gown. Despite the way her world had tilted off its axis, the action sent a shiver of longing, of promise, through her body. "You know we have more, much more than that."

"So you have no objection to me continuing to develop my career in landscape design? Or the television program I'm supposed to start in a few months?" she probed, knowing before he spoke what his answer would be.

"You won't have time for that. You'll be too busy. With me. With the lodge."

Her blood turned to ice in her veins at his words. She truly was no more than an acquisition to him. A perfect complement to the perfect world he'd created. A world that was in high demand with the rich and famous, a world that was envied by those who lacked the resources to provide the luxurious amenities Tautara Lodge boasted. A world in which she was nothing more than a prized possession.

She was a thing. Not a partner.

A lover. Not beloved.

"I can't do it." The words tore from her throat on a sob as all her dreams for the future crumbled into dust. She gathered her skirts in her hands and pushed past the two men. *"It's over. I can't do it. I can't be married to you."*

Her father and Luc stood, frozen, as she all but ran for the side entrance of the crowded ballroom at the lakeside hotel where their wedding had been hailed as the event of the year. Wrapped in the celebrations and the dancing, no one saw her leave the room. She moved as quickly as she could down the corridor to the hotel lobby and then out the front doors to where Luc's gleaming black Porsche Carrera GT stood idling on the forecourt.

She flew around the side of the car to the open driver's door, shoving the voluminous clouds of her gown around her legs as she placed her feet on the pedals. She pulled the door shut and crunched the car into first gear, her foot already pressing down on the accelerator.

Then, out of nowhere, Luc loomed dark and large in front of the car. She pushed her foot down hard on the brake but the slippery soles of her new wedding shoes slid sideways, onto the accelerator. She screamed as the car lurched forward, as she heard the sickening crunch—as she struck the man she loved with every shard of her broken heart, and his body rolled across the hood of the car before falling to the gravelled drive.

Horrified, she wrested the steering wheel to the right, away from Luc's falling form, desperately trying to shift her foot from the accelerator to the brake. But her heel caught in the folds of her gown and the last thing she saw before impact was the solid concrete block wall in front of her.

The numbed shock with which she'd recalled their wedding night soon receded, leaving a throbbing, dull ache in the region of her heart and a nauseating pitch in her stomach. How could she have been so easily duped? All her life she'd believed she would only ever marry for love. And she had. She had loved Luc with every part of her—mind, body and soul. Still did and that was more than half the problem.

That was why she now felt doubly betrayed, not just by his admission that he had never loved her, on the night of the wedding, but by his unemotional determination that their lives should still carry on as they had before. That her discovery of the truth should have no bearing on his grand plan for his world.

She staggered to her feet and closed the door, letting it slam hollowly behind her as she collapsed into one of the large leather couches and curled herself up into a ball of hurt. She remembered it all now. The first time she'd seen Luc, the first time he'd spoken to her. The night he'd asked her to marry him. Every memory was bittersweet, overshadowed by the knowledge that for him she'd been a project. Something to be attained.

No wonder she'd reacted so vehemently at the hospital, and no wonder her father had been so uncomfortable. These past days she'd been living the wrong life.

She'd been betrayed at every turn. By her husband. By her father. And now she was trapped in this castle of her husband's self-made kingdom. There was no way she could walk out now, not with her mother's life in the balance. If it had simply been a matter of her father's losses she was sure she could have done it— walked away from Luc to an uncertain future—but as things stood, she couldn't destroy what chance her mother had at being well again.

She imagined her sisters would tell her to get her act together, to be thankful for the fact she had a wealthy husband and an enviable lifestyle. Things that they'd deemed far more necessary than love. Yet they'd found love with their life partners and their growing families. They were fulfilled.

Family. A shudder ran through Belinda's body. Just prior to their marriage Luc had said he wanted to start a family immediately. She'd pouted and said she wanted him to herself a while before they started trying, and had explained about the long-term birth control she used, something that wasn't subject to the vagaries of time zones in different countries, forgetfulness or illness. So long as she had her shot every twelve weeks she was fine. They'd agreed she'd have one dose prior to the wedding and that they'd review their desire for a family afterward. Now she could only be thankful that there was no way she could be pregnant.

Did she really want to subject a child to a loveless parent? Would that be fair to any of them? The imbalance between herself and Luc would wreak its own toll.

Out of loyalty and responsibility to her family she might not be able to leave Luc, but she could make certain that he wouldn't be able to build his dynasty and inflict on any child the kind of loveless expectations he'd imposed on her.

She dragged in a breath and filled her lungs, wishing she could fill herself with purpose as easily. She was forced to accede to Luc's wishes. To be at his side, to welcome his guests, to ensure that his world was as smoothly run as he deemed necessary. He'd have his perfect bride—the hostess guests from the world over would talk about long after they'd left Tautara Estate. And that was where it began and ended.

Belinda unfolded her legs from underneath her and rose to her feet, her limbs a little unsteady as she walked toward the phone to make the call that would end the beginning of her dreams. By the time she hung up from talking to Jane Sinclair her eyes stung with unshed tears and her throat ached with the words she could never say.

Luc paced the confines of his office. He hadn't wanted to resort to blackmail but he'd been forced to, to keep Belinda where he needed her. Where he'd always wanted her. Where she belonged.

An image of her as he'd left her a few hours ago burned in the back of his mind. He'd caused her immeasurable pain. He understood that. It was all the more reason not to give rein to that abomination people called love. With love came weakness. Luc Tanner was not weak. He'd clawed his way through life in spite of, or because of, his upbringing.

He rubbed absently at his left forearm, the arm his father had broken the night he'd lost complete and utter control. Max Tanner had been a brutal man, who'd ruled his house with alcohol-fuelled fury. That particular night he'd been more angry than usual, with an edge to his drunkenness that was terrifying. Luc could still hear his mother, more than mildly intoxicated herself, goading Max. He still experienced the bitter taste of fear on his tongue, the absolute helplessness that came from knowing what would come next without being able to do a thing to stop it.

When Max had laid into her with fists and boots, Luc, a lanky twelve-year-old yet to grow into his large hands and feet, had tried to intercede. His father had flung Luc aside, breaking his arm. Then he had gathered his injured wife in his arms, sobbing and professing his undying love to her as he'd carried her out to the car to take her to the emergency room. But his judgment had been too impaired and he'd lost control of their vehicle, killing them both. It had taken several hours before the police had come to find Luc. By then he'd convinced himself he'd heard enough of love.

Locking his emotions away had never been a problem after that. Until he saw Belinda and wanted her with a drive that had superseded even his desire to become a success. So he'd acquired her, much as he would a property from a reluctant vendor. And that was that. That was all there was to it. All there ever would be. All he could allow.

They would make a good life together once she accepted all the benefits she would reap. It might take some time to shore up the wall that had crumbled when her memory had returned, but he was a patient man.

Yet he wanted more. He wanted back the woman who'd opened her heart to him as welcomingly as she'd opened her body. He'd come to relish, indeed look forward to, the sudden lift in his spirits when she was near—the sense of rightness in being together. In being man and wife.

Luc ceased pacing and looked out the floor-length window, over the herb garden she'd lovingly created. He could still see her in his mind's eye as she'd directed his garden staff to lay the pavers in the Celtic knot design, could still see her look up here with a smile upon her face, to his office, where she knew he'd be watching her.

She was an obsession with him. Had been from the first moment. He thought that he could have her, hold her, make love to her, yet still remain aloof—his emotions impenetrable.

And he'd succeeded. Until now.

With a curse Luc strode to his door and flung it open, ignoring Manu's query as he stalked past him, through the main section of the lodge and back toward the suite.

The woman who stood up to greet him as he burst through the door was, to all intents and purposes, the same woman he'd left a few hours ago. He let go of the breath he hadn't realised he'd held trapped in his chest, let go of the fear that she would call him on his threat and have already packed and left Tautara.

She'd changed since their earlier altercation. Gone was the casual wear. Instead she wore a sleeveless black dress that crossed over at the front, hugging her perfectly formed breasts like a lover's hands. Blood pooled in his groin. Her feet were showcased in fine strappy heels, and his mind filled with an image of her wearing the absurdly feminine shoes and nothing else. She was perfectly groomed, exquisitely beautiful with not so much as a hair out of place. She was everything he wanted her to be, yet it was as if he beheld a shell of the woman he'd married. And he wanted more than a trophy.

"Finished for the day?" she inquired coolly.

"Yes." He bit the word out. He was finished with the office, at least. The enigma that stood in front of him, that was something else.

"May I pour you a drink?"

"Thanks." Luc shed his jacket and dropped it on the chair beside him.

He watched as she went across the sunken lounge to the minibar built into the corner and deftly removed the foil and cork of a bottle of champagne. Champagne? He'd have laid odds she'd have poured him something else, something raw and burning and on the rocks. She poured two glasses and brought one over to him, clinking their glasses together.

"To our new beginning," she toasted.

Luc eyed her carefully. There was no sign of sarcasm

or anger. In fact, her face was completely expressionless.

"Our new beginning." He heaved a quiet sigh of relief and took a sip of his wine. "I'm glad you decided to stay."

"You didn't give me any other option." She settled herself on the leather sofa and crossed one leg elegantly over the other, the fabric of her dress sliding along the length of her thigh to expose her smooth skin. "But you'll be pleased to know I've been thinking these past few hours, and you're right. Love is for fools. You don't need to worry about me—" she hesitated, as if searching for exactly the right word "—complicating matters between us."

Who was this woman? What had he done? Had he driven the brightness out of her forever? He sat down next to her, tracing one finger across the top of her knee and along the smooth length of her thigh. He saw the flame of desire light her eyes. Slowly she set her glass down on the coffee table beside her, then placed one hand on his chest, pushing him back against the chair while her fingers deftly unbuttoned his shirt before travelling lower, down across his belly to unfasten his belt.

"You want the perfect wife," she whispered against his lips as she slid onto the floor, kneeling between his thighs and reaching out to push his shirt down off his shoulders, tugging it free of his arms before she unzipped the fly on his trousers. "I can do that."

He groaned as she freed his straining erection and fondled him, her fingers sliding lightly along his shaft before tracing his tip. He wanted this, wanted her. That hadn't changed. And yet she had, and somehow it felt wrong—as if a vital piece was missing.

She reached for her glass, taking a mouthful of champagne then bent forward and took him into her mouth. The contrast between her heated lips and the chilled champagne was sheer torture.

And in the split second before his climax robbed him of all cognitive thought, he couldn't help feeling he'd lost something infinitely precious before he'd even realised it had been his all along.

Thirteen

Thirteen

Luc watched as Belinda took a group of their current guests for a horse trek, their single file leaving the stables and heading into the designated track for beginner riders.

She did this as well as she did everything—a consummate rider, a consummate wife—and he couldn't have asked for more. By day she helped ensure their guests, currently a European prince and his family, make the most of the facilities offered at Tautara. By night she stood at his side as they entertained either formally or informally. Repeat bookings had never been higher. Yet still, he was unsatisfied.

Seeing her interact with the prince's children had been an eye-opener and had reminded him of their discussions about children of their own prior to their wedding. After seeing their youngest guest fall asleep in Belinda's arms yet again last night, he was all the more determined for them to start a family of their own. The picture they made was exquisitely beautiful. The child's face relaxed and reposed, totally trusting, and Belinda's wearing a poignant serenity that showed yet another facet to her capabilities.

Maybe that's what was wrong with him these days, he decided as he turned and went back into the house. That sense of being unsettled, as if something was left undone, unfinished. Perhaps a child would cement things for him now. Take away this emptiness he felt, despite having what he wanted.

Most men would have been happy to have what he had, would walk over broken glass to have a wife such as Belinda. A wife who each day made certain everything ran as smoothly as possible and that each night filled their moments before sleep with a fiery passion that left him lying limp and sated, drifting into sleep with a sense of completion he'd rarely known in his life. And still something was missing.

He resolved to talk to Belinda as soon as their obligations to their current group were over. Tonight they were taking their guests into Taupo for a lakeside meal, the restaurant having been booked for them solely to avoid threats to personal security or media intrusion. In the morning they would leave. The next group weren't expected until the following weekend. For the next few days, for first time since the day Belinda had recovered her memory, they would be alone at the lodge.

It was the perfect time and opportunity to bring up the subject of children. He smiled. Their child would be brought into the world as a much-wanted member of his family. He had everything to offer and the resources to guarantee their child lacked for nothing.

The difference between what their child would have and what his own childhood had lacked was gargantuan. Luc's son or daughter would want for nothing and would never have to suffer the pain of two parents who lived their lives to the exclusion of all that was decent and right in a child's world.

With a family of his own he would finally attain every goal he'd painstakingly designed as a way of getting back at his father's influence, of proving he was capable of creating and holding on to his own world. He'd amounted to more than his father had ever dreamed was possible, and every tiny speck of it was his, all his. And there was still so much more he could build on. No matter how difficult his background had been, no matter how painful his childhood, he'd made it. He had it all.

Belinda looked at her reflection in the bathroom mirror and sighed. The strain of living a lie was beginning to show. She could see it in the fine tracery of lines that were evident around her eyes. She hadn't believed it could be so hard to live as she'd always lived. Doing everything she had to, to the very best of her ability—and her ability and experience were vast. Even Manu deferred to her now when it came to planning their guests' menus and activities during their stay at Tautara. Day by day she'd assumed more responsibility, leaving Manu to focus on the heli-fishing, rafting and guided fishing trips, and Luc to do, well, whatever the hell Luc wanted to do.

She gripped the cool marble of the vanity until her fingers ached as she tried to force down the anger she felt every second she thought of her husband and his manipulation of her life.

And the worst of it was she let him.

But it had to be worth it, she consoled herself. She'd heard from her parents that her mother's treatment in the States was proving to be a major success, she was responding to the drugs and therapies far better than anyone had hoped and could look forward to a long and healthy future. That was what it was all about, Belinda told herself. That her mother be well again. That this—every painstaking day, every heartbreaking night—was worth it. She'd had no idea it would be so damnably hard.

In the bedroom she heard Luc shifting around. Her body betrayingly leaped to life as she reacted to his nearness. He'd been extremely attentive this evening. Under different circumstances she would have relaxed and enjoyed his consideration, but she knew without a shadow of a doubt that Luc Tanner didn't do anything in his world without an ulterior motive.

She'd wondered frequently, in the past few weeks, what had made him that way, and, despite the fact Manu had let slip that they'd been boys together, she could get no further information about what had carved her husband into the granite-hard man he was today.

She straightened up and stiffened her spine, the folds of her nightgown falling gently around her body, skimming her breasts and hips like a soft summer breeze. She drew in a deep breath and walked through to the bedroom.

Luc looked up as she entered, a small frown drawing his eyebrows together.

"Tired?" he asked.

"A little, it's been pretty full-on."

"And you've taken on far more than I had a right to expect. I think it's better if you slow down. Delegate back to Manu more."

He stepped forward and cupped her cheek with his palm. She wished, more than anything, that she could rest her head against the dry heat of his skin and take some comfort from him, but she knew that was impossible. Luc had made it clear he didn't do emotion, he didn't do love, and without either of those she wouldn't accept his consolation, either.

The prospect of the next few years stretched out before her like an arid desert.

"I'll be okay. I like to be busy," she attempted to reassure him.

She turned away from his touch catching, as she did so, the look of irritation that crossed his features. So she'd annoyed him. Right now she didn't care and focused instead on turning down the bed and climbing between the crisp cotton sheets.

The evenings were beginning to get cooler with the onset of autumn. As a gardener she knew autumn shouldn't be her favourite season, but there was something about the change of seasons, the hint of slumber coming with winter's inevitable approach, that she'd always loved.

The valley below them was already turning on an amazing colour display of reds through to golds. She should be thinking about bulb plantings for the spring, she reminded herself, and made a mental note to let the grounds staff know where she wanted them. Of course, in an ideal world she'd have been doing the planting herself. Deciding where to set the displays of tulips and irises she'd loved since she was a little girl. But she'd learned it was easier to delegate those tasks than allow herself to be immersed in her love of the garden again.

It had been easier to give herself some distance from all the things she loved best. It would hurt too much to have to let them go again.

She reached over and flipped off her bedside lamp and settled against her pillows, closing her eyes. When Luc reached for her, as he did most nights, she turned and flowed into his arms. At least physical release guaranteed she would sleep. It was better than lying next to him all night and reliving all those moments when she should have seen the warning signs. The signs that should have told her she'd been reaching for a chimera when she'd agreed to marry him. This was her cross to bear and hers alone.

Even as Luc drew her to him he sensed the emptiness inside her. It echoed in his heart like a hollow shout in a vacant room. She always welcomed their lovemaking each night, but every time he felt as if she drew away from him a bit more. And he hated it. He wanted her back. All of her. Heart and soul.

Tonight he took his time to arouse her, to make sure her body was as hungry for him as he always was for hers. Tonight he wanted to touch her heart, to draw her back to him, the way they'd been before—when she'd loved him.

When he shifted above her and positioned himself at her entrance she was already on the brink of climax, lost in the rhythms, the touches and tastes of their love-making. As he eased into her, her fingers clutched at his shoulders and he welcomed the contact. The knowledge that he could bring her to this peak, hold her on the brink of exquisite satisfaction and then drive her over the edge into shattering pleasure was a sharp contrast to the remoteness of their relationship.

Moonlight slanted across the bed. His eyes bored into hers as she felt the tension rise within her, felt her body crest that final wave as he rocked against her. And then, as her body shuddered in release, her eyes squeezed closed and she turned her head on the pillow as if she couldn't bear to acknowledge it was him who had brought her to completion.

He stilled, even as her body continued to pulse around him. He might have her physically, but mentally she was irrevocably lost to him. His heart thudded pain-fully in his chest and his body cried out in protest as he withdrew from hers unfulfilled. He pressed a hot, damp kiss in the hollow of her neck where it met the curve of her shoulders. Beneath his lips a tremor ran through her, but it gave him no pleasure.

He rolled away from her, and even though no more than six inches separated them on the bed, he felt as if a gulf lay between them. As her breathing slowed and she settled into sleep, he rose from the bed, threw on a robe and left the room.

The next morning Belinda made ready to travel to Taupo Airport in the chopper, where their guests would be met by a private jet to take them on their first leg back home again. It was time for her next injection, and she wasn't prepared to take any risks about bringing a child into what was already a dysfunctional relationship, no matter how long she was tied into it herself.

As she swung her bag over her shoulder and went to leave the suite, Luc came through the front door.

"Manu tells me you're going into Taupo."

"Yes. There are some things I need to take care of."

"What sort of things?"

"Some shopping, things like that." She wasn't about to tell Luc about her appointment to see a local doctor. She had no doubt he'd insist she cancel.

"I need you here today."

Belinda sighed. "Luc, I'll be back by lunchtime, really."

"I'll let Jeremy know he'll be one passenger light. We have things to discuss." He reached for the phone clipped to his belt.

Belinda chewed the inside of her mouth. How much should she tell him? "I have an appointment that I really don't want to change. If I forgo the shopping I can be home again in two hours."

Luc's hand stilled as he punched in the pilot's number and he lifted his head, his eyes boring through her.

"An appointment? What type of appointment?"

"A doctor's appointment, actually." She tried to laugh, to make light of the situation.

"You're having headaches again? Why didn't you tell me? You shouldn't be seeing a doctor here. We need to see your neurologist in Auckland."

"No, no. It's nothing as serious as that. Look, it's just a simple checkup. Woman's stuff."

"Woman's stuff," he repeated, his voice a monotone. "Contraception, you mean."

"Yes, well, it's time for my shot again. I know we discussed this before we married and we agreed that when the three months were up we'd start to try for a family, but under the circumstances..." Her voice trailed away.

"Circumstances. Would you care to elaborate on that?"

"Luc, really, is this necessary? Of course we can't even think about having a family. A baby needs a loving home, two parents who love each other. We both know that's not the case here. It would be cruel to have a child." *To all of us,* she added silently. "Besides, I really don't think that now is the time to talk about it. Jeremy's waiting."

Luc said nothing, but lifted his phone again and punched in the numbers. "Jeremy? Mrs Tanner won't be travelling with you today. No, that's right. You can head off whenever you're ready."

"What are you doing?" Belinda demanded. "I have an appointment."

"Which you are not going to make. We are going to discuss this right now."

"There's nothing to discuss. I'm not having your baby. It would be monstrous to even think I would do so."

"Sit down, please."

"I'd rather stand, thank you."

Luc stepped closer to her, taking her by the shoulders. The heat of his fingers as they wrapped around her in direct contrast to the pained chill that held her body captive, captive as she was to his need for her as his wife. He gently pushed her down on the sofa behind her and sat down opposite her. She sat stiffly, her shoulders hunched, her hands bunched in fists in her lap.

"I'm not having your baby. That's final. If you won't let me attend my appointment then I'll just sleep elsewhere, the potting shed if I have to."

Luc's sharp bark of laughter lacked any form of humor.

"You will remain in our room, in our bed."

"You can't make me."

"No, I can't make you, any more than I made you stay. I gave you a choice, remember?"

"A choice? You call holding my mother's health, my father's financial security, the jobs of my entire family hostage, a choice? You bullied me into staying and you know it. If you had tied me down you couldn't have been more effective. What on earth makes you think that I would have your child?

"I don't know who or what made you the way you are, Luc Tanner, but you are not the man I thought I fell in love with. You don't have a single compassionate bone in your body. What makes you think you're cut out to be a parent? How do you expect to raise a child without love? And without that, who's to say it wouldn't turn out to be monster like you?"

Luc stiffened, as if she'd struck him a physical blow. "A monster, you say?"

"You heard me. I made you a promise, that I would stay here, I'd be your wife, I'd be your hostess. That's where it begins and ends. You have no right to demand any more of me and, quite honestly, Luc, I have nothing else left to give you."

Luc watched as she rose and walked gracefully to the bedroom. The "snick" of the door closing echoed emptily through the suite, leaving him alone. Isolated. He replayed her words over and over in his head. *Hostage. Bullied. Monster.* Each one making him no different from the man he hated beyond anything else in the world. Each one transferable to the man he'd sworn he'd be better than.

Each one painfully true.

In the distance he heard the helicopter taking off and heading out over the valley, toward Taupo. To where Belinda had planned to ensure that they would not have a child. A clawlike grip twisted his insides.

How could he have gotten it all so wrong?

It was simple. He had a life plan and he'd stuck to it, every damn step of the way.

Out on the deck he caught a glimpse of his wife, changed into jeans and a T-shirt, as she shot down the stairs toward the garden. Her sanctuary. A shaft of jealousy burned through him that she'd rather face a pile of dirt and manure than be at his side. A short, sharp expletive expelled from his lips.

He was pathetic. She was right. He was nothing but a bully. In forcing her to stay away from her beloved gardens he'd even denied her the simple pleasure that working in there had brought her, not to mention her shot at the television show. He could see now why it had been so important to her—why she'd wanted so desperately to establish her own independence, her own niche. And he'd done his best to suffocate that precious part of her.

His father had been no different. One by one he'd driven away all his mother's friends. Bit by bit he'd undermined her security until she was totally dependent on him, even so far as to what she wore each day and where she went. It had been her one drunken burst of defiance that had signed her death warrant.

Luc drew in a deep breath. He might not be as physically brutal as his father had been, but psychologically he was no different. Was he so insecure that he couldn't even share her with a group of plants? How on earth had he thought to share her with a child?

His insides twisted even tighter, harder. He dropped his head in his hands and groaned.

No wonder Belinda didn't want to bear his child. In fact, how on earth did she bear his touch? By her own admission she would never give him her heart again. He'd taken the gift she'd given him and he'd thrown it back in her face. Not just once, but twice. Life had given him a second chance when she'd lost her memory. He'd had every opportunity to take that chance, to woo her back, to possibly even learn to love himself. But he'd been so hell-bent on what he'd thought he wanted, he'd wasted that window in time.

The solid realisation of what he'd lost settled like a leaden cloak about his shoulders. How could he have been so stupid? He'd had it all and he'd killed it. Had crushed the life out of any chance their marriage had had, of any chance for him to fulfill his dreams—even reach beyond his dreams—and to believe he could be loved and love in return.

There was only one thing left for him to do to fix this, as much as it killed him inside to do it. He had to let her go.

Fourteen

When Belinda finally came in from the garden, she looked shattered. He knew she'd been working all day, stopping only when he'd insisted Manu take her out a tray with cool drinks and something to eat. Looking at her now made him certain his decision had been the right one.

He, too, had been working hard, on the phone and the Internet, wheeling and dealing. Setting his new future in place.

She didn't even speak to him as she walked past and headed for the bedroom. He followed and watched in silence as she grabbed some clothes from the wardrobe before going into the bathroom.

She stopped in the doorway and turned. "What? Why are you watching me like that?"

"Nothing. I'd like to talk with you when you've had your shower."

"I have nothing to say to you, Luc."

"I know. But I have a lot to say to you, so please, when you're done meet me in my office."

Belinda hesitated a moment. Please? He'd said please? In all the time she'd known him she'd never heard him ask. It was his way to demand, to dictate.

"Belinda?" he prompted.

"Yes, all right. I'll be along shortly."

She shut the door behind her and leaned against it. All she really wanted was to crawl into bed and use sleep to escape the reality that had become her world.

She took her time in the shower, letting the water run over her in streaming jets, washing away the grime of the day. Heading off to the garden as she had, had been a frustrated point of retaliation—a strike back at Luc's draconian attitude. She was paying for it now, she realised, as every muscle in her body ached. But it had been worth it. For a while she'd been able to forget.

By the time she headed back through the main house to Luc's office it was nearly an hour since he'd left her. No doubt he'd be steamed about that, but, Belinda decided with a faint shrug of her shoulders, he'd just have to put up with it.

She'd eschewed the clothing she'd taken from the wardrobe before, instead choosing to dress in a black turtle-neck silk sweater and matching trousers. The fabric whispered across her skin, an imitation of the skim of Luc's touch when he made love to her.

Sex. She corrected herself silently. It was sex, not

love. And despite everything, her body still went on full alert at the prospect of being in close proximity with him again. Well, if she had to make the best of a bad thing, at least they had that, she thought cynically. A lot of relationships had less. What kind of person did that make her? She wasn't so sure anymore that she wanted to know.

She knocked once, sharply, on his door and entered his office. Luc rose from behind his desk. He looked pale—the scar on his jawline more prominent than usual, his limp more pronounced as he walked over to the bar installed against one wall to pour two glasses of wine.

"Here, I think we both need this," he said enigmatically.

Belinda took the proffered glass, ignoring the sizzle of electricity that buzzed across her fingers as they brushed against his.

Luc suggested they sit down in the deep leather wing chairs he had positioned near the window overlooking the herb garden. She shot him a surreptitious look as she took a sip of her sauvignon blanc. If anything, he'd grown even paler and his skin appeared to be stretched tightly across his cheekbones and jaw. To her surprise he remained silent.

"So what did you want to discuss, Luc? Our next group of guests?" she prompted, gathering up her nerve for her next comment. "Or perhaps you'd like to browbeat me into bearing your child?"

Luc flinched and pushed himself up from his seat, going to stand at the window, his back to her. When he spoke his voice was low and even, but she could see the

tension that bound every line in his body from the way
his hand gripped the top of his cane through to the set
of his shoulders.

"Neither of those," he eventually replied. "I'm
letting you go."

"Go?" Belinda was confused. Did he mean go to a
new doctor's appointment or leave Tautara completely?

"Yes. I've arranged for Jeremy to take you to
Auckland as soon as we've finished this discussion. A
car will take you directly to your parents' house. Their
housekeeper is expecting you."

"But what about the money, what about the debt my
father owes you?" Panic flooded her. In light of what
Luc had told her about her mother's condition and her
treatment, they couldn't afford to stop now any more
than her father would be able to drum up the funds necessary to repay Luc at such short notice.

He crossed over to his desk and lifted a sheaf of
papers bound by a clip. He handed them to her. "Here's
the legal stuff. I know it's only in copy for now, but two
originals will be couriered to your parents' house for
your attention tomorrow. You'll need to get your own
lawyer to look them over. Make any changes you want.
I won't contest anything. I'll sign whatever you agree to."

Belinda skimmed the document; her blood turned to
ice as she identified a separation agreement. Her fingers
rifled through the pages, halting at the page that
included in her schedule of personal chattels the debt
her father had owed Luc. Her eyes widened as she read
the actual sum Luc had bailed her father out for.

"But this is an enormous sum of money. You can't
afford to simply write it off," she protested.

"Believe me, I can." Luc sank back into the chair opposite her and picked up his wineglass, swirling the pale-gold liquid around the bowl of the glass. "It was never about the money. It was only ever about you. I made a mistake when I thought I could marry you without love. I deceived you, and for that I'm sorry."

Belinda couldn't speak. She gripped her wineglass so tight she feared it might shatter in her fingers, yet she couldn't make herself relinquish the strangling grip.

Luc looked at her again, his eyes now the dull, flat green of the lake on a dismal cloudy day. She felt his gaze as if it was the touch of his fingers as he let his eyes drift over her face, her throat, then back to meet her own eyes, which no doubt reflected her confusion.

"And now it's over." His voice rasped, sounding as if he had an obstruction in his throat. "Manu has packed some of your things—he'll send the rest on. Jeremy is waiting at the helipad."

He stood and took her hand. For a moment she thought he meant to shake it, as if sealing a business deal, but then he lifted it to his lips, pressing a swift kiss against her knuckles before dropping her hand back into her lap.

"Go," he said, and turned back to the window.

Belinda rose on shaking legs and carefully placed her glass on the wine table between the two chairs. Words escaped her. She'd been summarily dismissed, freed to leave. It was what she'd wanted ever since her memory had returned. Without looking back she left the office and walked straight to the front door and out of the lodge toward the helipad, where she could hear the helicopter warming up, ready to take her away from Tautara, away from Luc.

Manu had just finished loading the last of her cases into the luggage compartment of the chopper as she approached. His dark brown eyes were troubled as she hesitated in front of him, unsure of what to say. When he opened his arms and wrapped them around her she welcomed his embrace.

"I'm going to miss you guys," she said woodenly as Manu handed her up into the passenger compartment.

"We'll miss you, too. I never thought he'd let you go, Belinda. He was different with you. More human, you know? He—" Manu broke off and shook his head. "Just don't think of him too harshly, okay? I've known him all my life. Underneath, he's a good man. A strong man. There are just some demons a man can't let go."

"Why wouldn't you tell me about those demons, Manu? It might have made a difference."

"Not my place to tell. I hoped that one day he'd be ready to tell you himself." Manu shrugged hopelessly. "He's stubborn. Always has been—and had to be, to keep on top."

Belinda nodded sadly. There was nothing else she could do. Nothing anyone could do.

As the Eurocopter lifted off the pad and slowly circled over the lodge before descending into the valley to follow the river to the lake, she dropped her head back against the plush headrest of her seat. She realised she still gripped the separation agreement, and let it drop to the floor. Every cell in her body felt as if it had been wrenched from where it belonged, yet she didn't belong there at Tautara anymore. She didn't belong anywhere.

It was still light as the helicopter approached

Auckland's Ardmore Airport to the south of the city. As they set down in the designated area, she could see the sleek dark Mercedes and uniformed driver waiting for her off to one side. She should be thrilled to be free. Free to start again. To start the life she'd always wanted to live until she'd derailed her plans and married Luc.

Her hand shook as she unbuckled her seat belt, and she tried to summon a smile as Jeremy opened the door and held out a hand to help her down from the chopper. He walked with her toward the waiting car.

"I'll send your luggage through behind you. Luc said you'd be eager to get home, so there's no need to wait around for us to unload," Jeremy told her as the chauffeur opened the door to the Mercedes and waited to one side for her to get in.

Belinda halted in her tracks. "No."

"No? You'd rather wait while we unload now?" Jeremy sounded confused.

"No. I don't want you to unload. You're going back now aren't you?"

"After refuelling. But Mrs Tanner, are you sure you don't want your things?"

"Oh, I'm sure I want my things. But I want them to come back with me. You're taking me back."

A huge smile broke across Jeremy's face. "Back to Tautara?"

"Back to Luc."

"What do you mean, he's gone?" Belinda demanded, her head reeling at Manu's news when she arrived back at the estate.

"About half an hour after you left he told me he was

leaving. He said he needed to get away for awhile, to think. He didn't expect to be back for several days— maybe longer."

"Couldn't you have stopped him?"

Manu just raised an eyebrow in response. Belinda shook her head. No, Manu could no more have stopped Luc doing whatever he wanted to do than he could stop the flow of the river racing through the valley floor below. But several days? Maybe longer?

"Would you like me to bring your things inside?" Manu stepped forward to take one of her cases.

"No," she replied quietly. "I'd better leave. There's no point in staying anymore. I'm sorry. I shouldn't have come back."

It was clear to her that Luc had no place for her in his life now he'd made his decision to let her leave, and the knowledge scored her heart like a razor-sharp claw. The journey back to Auckland passed painfully fast and this time she made no objections when Jeremy handed her into the limousine and sent her to her parents' home ahead of her luggage. Right now all she wanted to do was crawl into a deep hole and nurse her wounded soul.

Two weeks later she felt no better. Even working in her parents' extensive grounds offered no solace. Daily calls to Manu hadn't elicited any further information as to Luc's whereabouts. In good news, though, she'd received an e-mail from her father saying that her mother's treatment was nearing its end and her long-term prognosis looked very promising. They'd decided, rather than return immediately to New Zealand, that they'd fulfill a few of their dreams and spend some time touring the U.S.A. together, then doing the same through Europe, before heading home. It brought tears to Belinda's eyes to read that her business-oriented father had realised just how important his marriage was to him. That his wife was more than his right hand—she was his heart, as well, and he wanted to spend as much time with her as they possibly could have together.

If only Luc could have found that denominator in their marriage, Belinda thought as she swiped the tears tracking silently down her cheeks. That balance between love and partnership. If only he'd let her into his heart from the beginning.

Suddenly feeling suffocated by the confines of the house, she went outside into the garden. The sun was lower in the sky as it began to set, casting a golden glow over the foliage and the last of the late-flowering blooms For a moment she regretted sending her parents' housekeeper home for the evening. Right now she'd never felt so desperately alone.

The crunch of a footfall on a fallen leaf made her spin around, her heart racing at the thought of an intruder on the property.

Luc!

Luc's chest tightened as he stopped in his tracks, spellbound at the sight of her. A few weeks ago he'd thought he'd never see her again. His eyes drank in her beauty and he ached to draw her into his arms.

She took a step toward him, her hand outstretched, before she let it drop back to her side.

He cleared his throat before speaking. "You came back to Tautara?"

"Yes."

"Why, when I let you go?"

"You never asked me if I wanted to leave."

Hope began to burn deep inside him. She still wanted him?

"I'd have thought that was obvious. You don't love me anymore. You'd refused to have my child. Of course you didn't want to stay."

"Yet I came back. But you were gone. Why, Luc? Tautara is your home, your dream. Why did you leave?"

"I missed you," he said softly.

Belinda stood, utterly shocked. "Why?"

For a while he couldn't answer, refused to answer and give voice to the words that ached to be spoken.

"Luc?"

"I love you. I didn't want to love you. I didn't want to love anyone. I thought it made a person weak. That it only gave others a chance to hurt you, to make you do things you don't want to do." He reached for her hand. "But you've shown me differently. You've shown me that loving someone and allowing yourself to be loved makes you stronger. And I can't imagine my life without you in it. I want to do things the right way this time. That is, if you'll have me."

"You've always had my heart. But you really hurt me. I felt betrayed when you reduced our marriage to a business deal. You and my father, the two men in the whole world I should have been able to trust, manipulated me. And I've asked myself, over and over, how could I still love you when you used me so badly? There are no easy answers in life, Luc. I think that sometimes we just have to accept things the way they are, but it's important to accept them and then to move on. Not to stay mired in the past. During the past few weeks I thought a lot about love, and a lot about forgiveness. They go hand in hand. I can forgive you for what you did, but only if you can let go of whatever made you react that way, because, you see, it wasn't until we landed at Auckland, the day you sent me home, that I knew I couldn't leave you. If I did I'd be leaving the most important part of me behind—you."

"Are you saying, you'll give me another chance?"

"You love me, Luc. I know that deep in my heart. You could never have let me go if you didn't."

"I do love you. I think I've loved you all along. I let the past keep me from accepting my true feelings for you. I'm asking that you give us another chance. Let's start this marriage over again. Fresh. New. The way we should have started it in the first place. For better or worse, I love you. We can make this work. We can build on what we have as long as we have each other. As long as we can trust each other," he said as he took her hand.

"Yes. We can. We will. Oh, Luc, I love you so much."

Luc pulled her to him, where she belonged. One day he'd share it all with her—his past, his parents, even old Mr. Hensen. But for now the healing had begun, and all thanks to the wondrous human being in his arms.

"I'm only half a man without you. Letting you go was the hardest thing I've ever done in my entire life. I won't make that same mistake again."

And he didn't.

* * * * *

HIGH-STAKES
PASSION

BY
JULIET BURNS

Juliet Burns, having had the good luck to be born in Texas, can't imagine living anywhere else. She's lucky to share her life with a supportive husband, three rambunctious children and a sweet golden retriever. She likes to think her emotional nature – sometimes referred to as *moodiness* by those closest to her – has found the perfect outlet in writing passionate stories late at night after the house gets quiet. She's inspired by the three Cs: country music, cowboys and chocolate. Juliet loves reading romance novels and believes they have the power to change lives with their eternal message of love and hope. She'd love to hear from readers. You can contact her by visiting her website www.julietburns.com.

For my patient hubby, who gave up home-cooked
meals, for my best CP, Pam, who read this book
as much as I, and for Mama, who watched my
kids so I could write.

One

"**I**'ve missed you, darlin'," a deep voice mumbled as a large, masculine body pressed against Audrey's back.

She yelped and tried to move, but his hand stole around her waist. His warm lips nuzzled her neck and sent a tingle down her spine. Audrey was too stunned to move.

The man grabbed her shoulders and spun her around. "I need you tonight, baby." The man's words were slurred, and the smell of beer wafted from his breath, but the yearning in his voice kept her from reacting. He lowered his mouth to hers and captured her lips in a deep and thorough kiss.

His firm mouth moved over hers and he pulled her closer. When his hand slid down to squeeze her bottom, she snapped out of her haze. In one swift move she pulled her lips from his, shoved against his chest and kicked his shin.

She grabbed a knife from the block on the counter behind her as he stumbled backward. She was alone in a strange house. The only person who knew she was here was her editor.

"Damn, woman!" the man bellowed as he leaned against the kitchen island. He grasped his right leg with both hands. Long hair covered half his face, but she saw his eyes squeeze shut and his face twist in a grimace of pain.

"Jeez, you didn't have to do that." His jeans and flannel shirt were rumpled, and his jaw was covered in heavy stubble. Maybe she should rethink this posing-as-a-housekeeper idea. Surely there was a safer way to earn a promotion to staff writer.

Her hands trembled. "You—you grabbed me." Her voice shook and she couldn't catch a breath. This couldn't be the famous rodeo champion she'd come here to interview.

His eyes opened wide and his brows rose. He scowled at the knife. "Put that thing down. I'm not gonna hurt you."

With a jolt of disbelief, she recognized his beautiful blue eyes. Her stomach pitched. It couldn't be.

Mark Malone. *The Lone Cowboy.*

The reclusive cowboy had been thrown from a bull in Cheyenne five months ago. The last anyone had seen of Mark Malone, he was being carried out of the rodeo arena on a stretcher. His press agent had since refused all interviews. Audrey had pictured him in a wheelchair, or worse.

"You're him! I mean…it's you."

"I'm who?" Mark rubbed his aching shin as the woman dropped the knife to the floor. Not that she'd needed any weapon besides her lethal kick. She sure as hell wasn't Jo Beth. He should've known Jo wouldn't show up out here.

After the accident, she'd moved on to the next rodeo star. He hobbled to a chair, pulled it out and dropped into it.

"You're the *Lone Cowboy*."

He sneered. "Not anymore." Mark took in the woman's stained, baggy sweats and disheveled hair. How the hell had she gotten in? Was she a crazy fan? A reporter? Who else would show up at his ranch uninvited? "Who are you?"

Her brows rose and she pointed at herself. "I'm the new housekeeper." The last word rose to a higher octave, as if she were asking him.

"Housekeeper? My foreman never mentioned anything about another housekeeper." He peered at her more closely, taking in the figure her sweatshirt couldn't disguise. Too young, too...

"Maybe you were too drunk to remember the conversation!" She gasped, and clamped both hands over her mouth, eyes widening.

Too interfering! Mark glared through narrowed lids. She was accusing him of being a drunk? Hell, after the news the doctor had given him today, he'd had cause for a few longnecks. "Even if he did hire you, you're fired. I don't want you here." If he was going to live with pain the rest of his life, he wanted to get drunk in peace.

Her eyes enlarged even further. She stooped to retrieve the knife and turned her back to him, dropping it in the sink with a clatter. "John *did* hire me. You can confirm my employment with him. I'm sorry if I hurt you, but—"

"If? Lady, you damn near—" He'd been about to say she'd crippled him. But he was already a cripple. "You're a menace! Just go back to wherever you came from. I don't need a housekeeper."

She rounded on him, hands propped on her curvy hips.

"You need more than a housekeeper. You need a miracle!" The spitfire brushed past him and stomped out of the kitchen.

That took care of that. The last thing he wanted was some busybody snooping around. He grabbed a bottle of whiskey, headed for the den and slumped in his recliner. Might as well finish what he'd started. His damn leg was killing him.

A half hour later, the whiskey had done its work. Feeling no pain, Mark was half watching some late-night talk show. Out of the dark, someone yanked the remote from his hand.

He looked up as John turned off the TV. "The new housekeeper just called. Said you fired her."

"I don't want her here. She's too…snippety." John was more than his foreman. He was the closest thing Mark had to a father.

John sighed. "Mark, when was the last time you ate something decent?"

Mark leaned up and grabbed the remote, snapping the TV back on. "I'm fine."

"Well, I'm not! I can't stand to see you this way!"

Jaw clenched, Mark stared at the television.

John moved between him and the big screen, folding his arms over his chest. "Look, son. I tried being patient. I know life's dealt you some lousy hands. But you never let it beat you before. You gotta cowboy up."

"Let it go, John," Mark said through gritted teeth. The only thing he'd ever been good at, the only thing that made him forget who he really was, had ended. He just wanted to be left the hell alone.

Shaking his head, John cursed under his breath, something Mark had rarely heard him do. "Have it your way. Hide from the world. But if you want me to stay on, the housekeeper stays, too. We've already had two quit, and

FREE BOOKS OFFER

To get you started, we'll send you
2 FREE books and a FREE gift

There's no catch, everything is **FREE**

Accepting your 2 **FREE** books and **FREE** mystery gift
places you under no obligation to buy anything.

Be part of the Mills & Boon® Book Club™ and receive your favourite
Series books up to 2 months before they are in the shops and delivered
straight to your door. Plus, enjoy a wide range of **EXCLUSIVE** benefits!

- Best new women's fiction – delivered right to
  your door with FREE P&P

- Avoid disappointment – get your books up to
  2 months before they are in the shops

- No contract – no obligation to buy

We hope that after receiving your free books you'll
want to remain a member. But the choice is yours.
So why not give us a go? You'll be glad you did!

Visit **millsandboon.co.uk** to stay up to date
with offers and to sign-up for our newsletter

2 **FREE** books
and a
FREE gift

D9JI9

Mrs/Miss/Ms/Mr _____ Initials _____

BLOCK CAPITALS PLEASE

Surname _____

Address _____

_____

Postcode _____

Email _____

NO STAMP NEEDED!

MILLS & BOON®
Book Club

FREE BOOK OFFER
FREEPOST NAT 10298
RICHMOND
TW9 1BR

NO STAMP
NECESSARY
IF POSTED IN
THE U.K. OR N.I.

you need this place cleaned up if you want to sell. We're lucky this one even walked past the front hall." John stared at him a minute, threw up his hands and headed for the door.

Mark scowled. Would John really quit? Mark did want to unload this parcel of pipe dreams. He supposed for two weeks, just until roundup was over…

"John," he called after him. When the foreman turned around, Mark forced himself to meet the look of disappointment in his eyes. "All right. She can stay."

After John called her back, Audrey shed her clothes and fell into bed, only to stare at the ceiling. She'd spent all day scrubbing the kitchen, and every muscle in her body ached. But that's not what kept her awake.

All the fantasies she'd had of her hero had met a quick, painful death. If she hadn't been so desperate to get this story, she'd have turned around and headed back to Dallas.

Disillusionment tightened her throat. She'd arrived at the *Lone Cowboy's* ranch this morning envisioning romantic western decor, but the house had looked more like the scene of a barroom brawl. The odor of stale food, flat beer and cigarette smoke permeated the rooms. The kitchen table had been covered with fast-food trash, overflowing ashtrays and empty beer bottles.

She took a deep breath, turned and bunched her pillow. She couldn't believe that disheveled drunk was the same hero who'd rescued her all those years ago. Closing her eyes, she remembered the night she'd first met him.

She'd been curled up in his stallion's stall to write her article for the school paper…

"Hey, fatso! Aren't you in the wrong building? The hogs are over there!" Raucous laughter followed the taunt.

Audrey flinched and broke the tip off her pencil. Oh, God. Not again. It was the same pack of teenage boys who'd harassed her at the concession stand. She squared her shoulders and stood to face them.

The bullies advanced, making snorting noises.

Audrey clutched her notebook to her chest, forcing herself to hold her ground. "Get lost, losers!"

The leader's eyes flashed and he advanced on her.

"What are y'all doing in here?" a deep voice bellowed from the stall's doorway.

The boys spun around to face a tall, broad-shouldered man.

She caught her breath. It was him. Mark Malone.

His white, long-sleeved western shirt stretched across a strong chest and broad shoulders that only emphasized his slim hips. Leather chaps hugged his long, muscular thighs and drew attention to the very male area covered only by his blue jeans.

Audrey was mesmerized.

"None of your business, man," the boy in the middle retorted.

Mark Malone's gaze traveled past the group of boys, landed on Audrey for a moment, then shot to the one who'd spoken. His eyes narrowed and his jaw clenched.

In a split second he reached out, grabbed the boy's shirtfront and yanked him up, nose to nose. He spoke through clenched teeth. "I make my living riding bulls. You know what that means?"

The boy's eyes bugged out and he shook his head frantically, choking on the tight grip around his throat.

"That means I don't care whether I live or die." Mark punctuated the sentence by jerking on the boy's shirt. "I'll take you out back right now and whip all five of your butts

without a second thought." Mark dropped the ringleader and he stumbled back, glaring, but silent. The boys ex-changed glances and scrambled away.

The scent of soap and subtle, musky cologne followed him as he approached. "Are you all right?" he asked gent-ly. His black Stetson shaded a strong, square jaw covered with five-o'clock shadow.

Her breathing hitched as she looked up into his deep blue eyes.

He swiped off his hat, revealing chestnut hair that curled just above his collar. Her stomach did a strange flip-flop. He held out his hand, beckoning her as he had in her dreams. "It's okay, they're gone now."

She'd learned to accept her plain face and pudgy body a long time ago, but right now she desperately wished she were beautiful and thin like her sisters. A familiar dull ache settled in her chest.

When she gathered her wits and took his large, callused hand, electric currents shot up her arm.

"Come on, I'll walk you back to the Coliseum." The Fort Worth skyline twinkled behind him as they headed for the arena. "How old are you?"

"Sixteen." Way too young for the twenty-year-old ris-ing rodeo star. Audrey looked at the dusty ground and swallowed. "Thank you for what you did back there."

When he didn't answer, she glanced back up at him. The expression in his eyes was old and weary. "That's what us heroes are for, right?"

She stopped and frowned at his sarcastic tone.

Mark brought his hand up to squeeze her arm and kept it there. The heat from his touch raised the hairs on the back of her neck. "Come on, let's get you back."

A shrill voice called from a few feet away, "Mark! It's

getting late, sweetie, and you promised to take me to Billy Bob's."

He dropped his hand from Audrey's arm and glanced behind him at a beautiful brunette. He looked back at Audrey, shrugged and took her hand, giving it a gentle squeeze. *"You'll be all right now?"*

At her nod, he pressed her hand once more, flashed a dazzling smile, turned and sauntered off.

This time, the ending changed. Mark came back, scooped her up in his arms and took her mouth in a deep, passionate kiss.

Audrey raised her arms to draw him closer, but an annoying beeping interrupted her, snatching her out of the sensuous dream. She rolled over to turn off the alarm. Four o'clock. She groaned. Time to start breakfast.

Mark woke up sometime close to dawn, stiff from sleeping in the recliner. Damn it! His calf muscle cramped, and he reached down to knead his right leg. He stumbled down the hall to the bathroom in search of aspirin. Flipping on the light caused spears of pain to shoot through his eyelids. He splashed water on his face, ran his hands through his hair and grimaced at his reflection in the mirror. Water dripped off his beard, and his eyes were so red they looked like miniature road maps.

Easy to see why that woman hadn't recognized the *Lone Cowboy.* Guess he had let himself go the last couple of weeks. No wonder John was disgusted. Hell, he disgusted himself.

Mark swallowed the aspirin and left the bathroom. He flopped on the bed, squinting at the daylight filtering through the blinds. A vague memory of luscious lips, a plump, rounded breast and a clean, citrus smell invaded his mind. He'd never get back to sleep now. He was too restless.

Aw, hell. Had he really groped that poor woman last night? What an ass he'd made of himself. He'd clean up, go find her and then apologize. Rolling over to sit up, he groaned and grabbed his head.

Apologies could wait until the aspirin kicked in.

Audrey descended the stairs carefully, exhausted. As she entered the kitchen, the memory of Mark's kiss washed over her. Even drunk, he'd taken her breath away. The memory of his hard body pressing against her sent a wave of desire through her. Mark Malone certainly hadn't seemed injured.

She shook herself back to reality and set an industrial-size pot of coffee on to brew. Frying sausage in a skillet, she concentrated on her mission. Why had he been drinking last night? She'd never heard of him being a wild party animal. Even in his younger days, he'd had a squeaky-clean image. Several early interviews had told of how he used his personal jet to fly foster children to the national rodeo finals, and made a home on his ranch for retired broncs and bulls.

She kneaded the dough for biscuits and popped them in the oven, then opened the refrigerator. A case of beer sat front and center. She shoved it aside and reached for the carton of eggs. At twenty-nine, he'd had a long career for a bull rider. He could have retired even without the accident. What kind of injuries had he sustained?

She needed to investigate further. And she could start by questioning his employees at breakfast.

"Howdy." An older man with a large, crooked nose stood at the back door. He stuck out his right hand as he removed his hat and carefully scraped his boots on the mud catcher next to the threshold. "Welcome to the Double M. I'm John Walsh, the foreman." He cleared his throat. "Spoke with you last night, I believe?"

"Yes. Good morning." Audrey glanced past him to the men gathered on the porch behind him. "Come in and have a seat. Breakfast is almost ready."

John raised his brows and grinned. Then he hitched up the jeans on his lanky frame and stepped into the kitchen.

Audrey busily scrambled eggs and pulled the biscuits from the oven as the hands filed in. John cleared his throat and motioned to the mud catcher. The men stopped and dutifully scraped their boots before entering, and placed their hats on pegs by the door.

"Let me introduce you." John gestured to the dozen men standing around the table. "Boys, this here's Ms. Audrey Tyson." He pointed to the man beside him. "Ms. Tyson, this here's Jim. You watch yourself around him or he'll pour hot sauce in your pancake batter."

"Mornin', ma'am." Jim gave her a two-finger salute.

Next came Dalt. Whoa. Blond hair, chocolate-brown eyes and dimples. He took her hand in both of his and brought it to his lips. "Very nice to make your acquaintance, Miss Audrey." He spoke with a seductive southern drawl.

"Down, boy!" John barked. "You can charm the lady on your own time."

As the introductions continued, Audrey realized that "boys" wasn't quite an accurate description. Ruth was almost six feet tall, her short, dark curls cut stylishly. She wore makeup, but still looked tough enough to more than pull her weight.

Not a Lefty, Shorty or Slim among them, Audrey thought as the rest were introduced. Just a nice bunch of people who happened to be cow-"boys."

But no Mark Malone this morning.

Audrey placed sausage, eggs, biscuits and gravy onto the long kitchen table as a beautiful Border collie trotted up to her, tail wagging and tongue hanging out.

"Curley!" John admonished the dog. "Get out of the kitchen, boy."

Curley? Guess there was a clichéd cowboy name after all. The black-and-white cow dog leaned against her legs. Audrey hunkered down and whispered, "Don't worry, Curley. I'll save a bite of breakfast for ya."

They all took their seats around the table, and Audrey dodged elbows and filled up coffee mugs. She decided to plunge right in. "So, what's it like working for the famous *Lone Cowboy?*"

An unnatural silence enveloped the kitchen.

Their mouths are full. Just give them a minute.

A minute dragged by. Two. No one looked up.

Okay… Maybe good reporters eased into their questions. "He had quite a career, huh? The Professional Bull Riding Association wants to put him in their Hall of Fame. World championship titles in bareback, saddle bronc and bull riding. And he didn't even start riding bulls until after he graduated high school."

Jim looked at her. "You a rodeo fan?"

Audrey nodded. "My dad was world champion saddle bronc, 1973."

"Really? What's his name?" Dalt asked.

Now she was getting somewhere. This wasn't so difficult. "Ever heard of Glenn Tyson?"

"No," Dalt grinned. "Just wanted to know if Tyson was

your maiden name. Didn't see a wedding ring, but you never can tell. You attached, honey?"

Dalt was coming on to *her?* He must be desperate for female company out here in the boonies. Even on a good day, her looks had never inspired flirting. How to steer the subject back to Mark? "Actually, I'm saving myself for the *Lone Cowboy.* He's not married, is he?" Oh my Lord, had she really said that?

Jim spewed his coffee, and the other hands guffawed and snickered.

Ruth looked at her as if she'd just suggested marrying Hannibal Lecter, her mouth open and her eyebrows raised. "Audrey, honey. Don't waste your time," she warned.

"What do you mean? Has he got a girlfriend?"

Ruth shook her head. "I've been working on the Double M a long time, and Mark's never had a relationship last longer than a few months. He dates 'em, but he don't trust 'em."

"But you're a woman," Audrey reasoned, thrilled she was finally getting some information.

"Yeah, but I'm not interested in his heart, girl. Just his cows." Ruth smiled and stood. "Speaking of which, I think it's time we got to it."

Audrey's smile faded. *I'm not after his heart, either.* Just his life story. She swiveled around and headed for the stove, grabbing the pack lunches she'd made earlier for the men, uh, hands.

Taking the sacks, they filed out the door, crammed them into their saddlebags, mounted and rode off. She waved to them from the back porch, rubbing her arms in the brisk morning air. What had possessed her to think she could do this?

Desperation, that's what.

For two years, she'd bided her time at the magazine, passively waiting to be given a chance. Well, no more! The new Audrey went after what she wanted. She raised her chin and straightened her shoulders, remembering her determination to change her life. She'd sat alone on her twenty-fifth birthday, taken assessment of her stagnant existence and vowed to make some changes.

Tonight at dinner, she'd be more discreet. If she just gave it a little time, the ranch hands might open up more. She had a gut feeling the reclusive rodeo champion was a very complicated man. But if she was to make her story work, she needed to figure out the reasons for his behavior. Maybe he had a history of substance abuse, or violent tempers or marathon orgies.

Though it would make a great story, she really hoped there was nothing like that in his past. Her shining hero was already tarnished around the edges. She'd hate for him to fall off his pedestal completely.

After finishing a seemingly endless stack of breakfast dishes, Audrey decided to take a quick break before tackling the dining room. She poured herself a glass of iced tea and stepped out to the covered back porch. Inhaling the fresh, pine-scented air, she listened to a mockingbird's calls and the wind rustling through the trees. She gazed longingly at a cushioned glider and tried not to think about *him*.

Eyes closed, she sipped her tea. *East Texas is so peaceful.* No smog, no traffic. Maybe living away from the city wouldn't be so bad. And she was only thirty miles from Tyler if she got desperate for a mall or a movie theater.

Listen to yourself. You're only here for two weeks.

Her mind registered a sound coming from the kitchen. She opened the screen door to check it out, and stifled a gasp. Mark stood in the middle of the kitchen, all six feet three inches of him, looking impatient and bewildered. Even so, he was impressive.

His hair was still wet from a shower, and his faded jeans and plaid flannel shirt were clean. He still hadn't shaved, but man, was he sexy. He radiated an overwhelming masculine energy that sent waves of excitement coursing through her. But his eyes—she hated to see them so bloodshot, so full of pain.

Somehow, she summoned a confident smile. "Good morning!"

The first thing Mark saw was the bright morning sun shining on her long, dark blond hair. The slanted light reflected off her crown, giving the illusion of a halo. Was this the same woman from last night? Her full lips curved up in a sensual smile. How long had it been since a woman had smiled at him like that? And there was respect and genuine interest in her beautiful green eyes.

Even after last night.

Mark felt gut-punched…and a stirring of interest south of his buckle. "I wanted to apologize." He cleared his throat. "For last night. I thought you were someone else."

Her smile vanished, and she bit one side of her bottom lip. "I'm sorry about kicking—"

"Forget it. I deserved it."

She licked her full lips and crossed her arms, emphasizing her ample curves. Did she realize what that did to a man?

His new housekeeper was not a great beauty. She had a plain, square-shaped face. But her lips were full and sensuous, and her bright green eyes flashed with intensity. She was short, but voluptuous. The loose-fitting T-shirt couldn't conceal the outline of her full breasts.

He'd always preferred a woman that wasn't all skin and

bones. Here was a woman a man could roll beneath him and not worry he might crush her to death. That thought sparked a vision of his hands filled to overflowing, cupping and squeezing those large, perfectly shaped breasts as he rubbed his face between them.

Damn! He was as hard as the titanium pin in his leg. This was just a sign of how pathetically long it had been since he'd had a woman.

"What? Did I spill gravy on myself?" she snapped. Now her eyes sparkled with indignation.

"Huh? Oh, uh…" *Get yourself together, Malone. Take a deep breath and stop staring at her chest.* "Is there any breakfast left?"

"Oh! Yeah." She frowned, avoiding his gaze, and pushed her hair behind her ears. "I made plenty. Let me get—"

"I can get it myself."

She ignored him and went flying past, pulling plastic containers from the fridge and heating a plate of biscuits, sausage and gravy.

"There aren't any scrambled eggs left, but I can whip some up real quick. Maybe I should make a few more biscuits, too." She began pulling out a skillet, eggs and butter, unloading more food than any one man could eat.

He took a deep breath, inhaling the aroma of homemade biscuits. They sure smelled good! He couldn't remember his last decent meal. He grabbed a chair and sat, studying his new housekeeper. She'd walloped him good last night. He almost smiled.

"Was your leg injured in the fall?"

Mark focused his gaze and realized she was standing before him, staring at his right leg with a worried frown. Damn, he'd been absentmindedly rubbing it! Great. He didn't want anyone's pity.

With a fierce scowl, he barked, "Don't you have a room to clean or something?"

She flinched, a wounded expression on her face. Slamming the skillet on the stove, she walked from the kitchen, chin held high.

"Aw, hell." Now he'd done it. Mark hated it when women played the guilt-trip game. Even so, the expression on her face was going to haunt him. Keith had had the same hurt and accusing look the night Mark had left home. That was the last time he'd seen his kid brother.

With years of practice, Mark pushed the memory back to the farthest corner of his mind. And he wasn't going to think about Ms. Perky either. Damn it, he'd told her he'd get the food himself, and she wouldn't leave well enough alone. Just because she had a beautiful smile and hadn't stared at him in disgust, didn't mean she wasn't like every other woman.

She'd probably summoned that trembling bottom lip just to manipulate him, the way his mom used to. Watching his mother have one affair after another, he'd learned at an early age what women were like. Why should this one be any different?

He looked at the plate of cooling biscuits and gravy and suppressed the urge to slam it against a wall. He needed a beer.

Two

Audrey held the wet washcloth against her heated face and refused to let the tears fall. She must've been delusional to think, even for a brief moment, that she'd seen attraction in Mark's eyes. Why would he be attracted to her? He'd dated some of the most beautiful women in the world. Of course he'd thought she was someone else last night.

But that didn't mean she had to hide in her bathroom like a chastised child. Why was she so upset? Who cared if a hungover, rude cowboy despised her? She was a twenty-five-year-old professional. Not the fat, lonely object of scorn she'd been the first time they'd met. Well, not *as* fat. And she'd stood up to her boss, hadn't she?

When she'd presented him with the idea for this story, Mr. Burke had laughed, his tone condescending as usual. "My mild-mannered little copy editor? You're just not

ready for a story this big, Audrey. If you want to write
something, how about taking over the advice column for
a few months?"

Audrey had known months would turn into years, as
with her current position. The only way she'd been able to
convince him to give her a chance was to go for high stakes.

"Here's the deal, Mr. Burke. If I don't come back with
the scoop on what happened to Mark Malone, I'll edit
copy *and* do the advice column. But—" she'd flattened her
palms on the desk between them, leaned in, and met his
eyes with determination "—when I bring back this article,
I want a staff writer position."

Mr. Burke had finally raised his hands in surrender.
"All right. All right. The magazine needs a good cover
story for the July rodeo issue. If you can get an exclusive
interview with the *Lone Cowboy,* the position's yours."

Remembering that conversation gave her the courage to
return to the kitchen. As she entered, John Walsh was just
coming in the back door. Following him was a slim lady
with thick white hair twisted in a stylish French roll. She
wore pressed jeans and a western shirt. "You must be Audrey!" the woman exclaimed, flashing a big smile with
slightly crooked teeth. "I'm Helen, John's wife."

"Nice to meet you." Audrey offered a friendly smile.
"Do y'all want some iced tea?"

"Does a bull want a heifer?" John asked as he grabbed
a chair and turned it around backward to sit.

"John!" Helen swatted playfully at his arm as John
chuckled under his breath. Helen shook her head and gave
Audrey a rueful grin. "After almost fifty years, I still can't
tame him, and I sure can't shoot him."

John took Helen's hand and raised it to his lips. They
exchanged an affectionate look.

It seemed to Audrey they were still very much in love. After fifty years? She dreamed of a romance like that.

Helen turned to her as Audrey poured the tea.

"We know the house is awful, but…" Helen hesitated and gave John a look charged with unspoken questions. "Mark's recuperation has been slow and, well, you can see why he needs a good housekeeper."

Slow? Now was her chance to get some straight answers. "Were his injuries severe?"

Helen frowned and dropped her gaze to the table. "Well, his right leg was crushed—"

"Crushed!" Was that why he'd been so defensive about his leg? This revelation made her more determined than ever to talk to Mark Malone. She knew this would be the story to launch her career.

"He was in the hospital for six weeks, and then physical therapy. It took another two months for him to walk again. The retirement has been…an adjustment for him."

"Well, if you ladies are through gabbing." John stood, turning his chair and pushing it in. "I've got to get back to work."

"Work?" Helen exclaimed. "I thought you were going to show Audrey around."

His eyes twinkled as he gave her a mischievous grin. "Can't spare the time. I asked Mark to do it."

Audrey heard boot steps behind her and spun to see Mark standing in the doorway, holding a beer. He scowled at John, but stepped in and bent to give Helen a quick kiss on the cheek. "How's your arthritis?"

Helen waved away his concern and stood up. "I'm fine. Got to go." She followed John out but turned on the porch. "Y'all have a good afternoon." She smiled and waved.

Audrey swallowed the lump in her throat and tried to smile back.

Mark glared at her and paced to the fridge. He opened the door, leaned in and reappeared with a fresh bottle of beer. Popping the top, he gestured toward the door. "After you."

"The Double M's over five thousand acres, and there's about twelve hundred head of brindled cattle," Mark said as he passed the corral. He took a long swallow of beer before continuing. "The extra men are here for spring roundup. Usually it's just Jim, Ruth and John."

"And you," Audrey interjected as she quickstepped to keep up with his long-legged stride.

Mark frowned and stuck the fingers of his free hand into the pocket of his jeans. "Not anymore," he muttered. He shook his head and headed for the barn, tipping the bottle to his lips again.

She trailed after him, determined to get some answers. "Why are you selling?"

His stride hitched only slightly before he took another drink and continued as if he hadn't heard her. When he reached the barn doors, he stopped and turned, his eyes sparking with annoyance. "John said you usually work for a disaster-recovery company in Dallas. What are you doing out here in hayseed country?"

Audrey was caught in his intense gaze. She opened her mouth but nothing came out. She'd stick to the truth as much as possible. "My uncle owns the company. I don't actually work there anymore." *Not since college.* "But then I saw the ad for this housekeeping position and…." Her voice trailed off. She dropped her gaze. "And I've always been a big fan."

Mark snorted and angled his head toward the barn. "We keep the hay and feed in here." He pointed his beer bottle toward the other large wooden structure. "Horses and tack in the stable. That's about it." He turned to leave.

But Audrey brushed past him and stepped into the barn. The combined smells of hay and leather reminded her of her dad. With a nostalgic smile, she wandered farther inside. She turned a corner and saw a large metal barrel with a rope tied around it, turned on its side and stuck on a metal post. There was a lever on the wall behind it, and beneath it was a thick pad extending about three feet in each direction.

"Wow. A mechanical bull!"

"It didn't have the pad at first," Mark said quietly behind her. "But when the kids came out here, I added the pad for safety."

Kids? She swiveled to stare at him. "You have children?"

His brows drew together and his mouth pinched into a tight line. "No, I meant the foster kids." Mark headed for the doors. "Coming?"

Audrey reluctantly followed. She'd read of Mark Malone's support for Big Brothers Big Sisters of America, and admired him for making a difference in the world. But she hadn't realized he'd brought the kids to his ranch. That bit of information had never been mentioned in an interview. At last! Something good for her story!

Mark escorted her to the back porch, gave her an insolent salute with his beer bottle and sauntered off toward the front of the house.

An eerie silence descended after he'd gone. Audrey shivered. She hated to deceive him, but she wasn't going to hurt anyone. Just write a little article about what had happened to a famous rodeo champion, earn herself a promotion and, hopefully, get to know a real-life hero.

If she could just put aside this niggling sense of guilt, she'd make it through this just fine.

She rubbed her arms and wandered into the den. Drawn to the wall of picture windows, she gazed wistfully out, past the neglected pool and yard to the barn and corral in the distance. A lush forest of pines, oaks and sweet gums lined the horizon.

Audrey turned to scan the gloomy room. Her heart ached at the wasted potential of the room—and its owner. A pine-paneled wall opened to a dark hallway that led to the master bedroom, and on the other side, a large stone fireplace sat alone, like the house, cold and empty. The only furniture in the room was a tattered recliner and a big-screen TV.

Well, if she were going to carry out this charade, she should start cleaning this pigsty. The cowboys'—and girl's—mud-caked jeans were piled high in the laundry room. As she put on a load to wash, a thought hit her. A real housekeeper would clean Mark's room and change the sheets. She decided to tackle that room first thing tomorrow morning.

That night at dinner, Audrey self-consciously pulled the bottom of her T-shirt down after she set a giant bowl of mashed potatoes in the middle of the table.

Thank goodness for Ruth. All this testosterone in one room left her flustered and overwhelmed. Men definitely didn't eat the way her sisters did. The meal was a loud, boisterous affair.

She learned a lot more than she ever wanted to know about ranching. Discussion of branding, ear tagging, vaccinations, calves, yearlings and castration all figured in the dinner conversation.

One of the youngest hands, Pete, had scrambled for the seat next to her. He leaned close and threw his arm across the back of her chair, caressing her shoulder. Knowing of his nomadic lifestyle, she tried to chalk it up to loneliness, and ignore him. But every time he touched her, she felt a strong urge to bathe.

"Ma'am, these chops are great!" Jim called from the other end of the table. "After working with cows all day, it's nice to not have to eat one." He stuffed a bite into his mouth.

Audrey stopped chewing momentarily as certain images came to mind. She would definitely lose some weight if there wasn't a change of subject.

"They're the best pork chops I've ever tasted," Dalt agreed with his guaranteed-to-melt-hearts smile.

She smiled back. "Thank you. There's a secret ingredient."

"Mark loves pork chops," John muttered from his seat across the table.

Mark was absent from the meal again, and she worried he wasn't eating. Why on earth did she care, anyway? But John had given her the opening she'd been waiting for.

"Mr. Malone seems to have changed a great deal since the accident," she fished.

John frowned and gave his full attention to his plate.

Audrey wouldn't let it go this time. She needed information. "Was his right leg the only injury? What's he going to do after he sells the ranch?"

John glanced up sharply, scowling.

Maybe she should act worried for his health. *Act?* "It's

just that he doesn't seem to eat. I wondered if I should take some dinner in to him."

As if they'd rehearsed it, several guys erupted into laughter at the same time.

Jim, still snickering, said, "Not unless your secret ingredient is whiskey!"

More laughter followed, but Audrey frowned with disapproval. "I don't see what's so funny about a man drinking himself into oblivion every night. You should be encouraging him to join AA or something."

That sobered them up a little, so to speak. Jim finally answered. "Beggin' your pardon, Miss Audrey, but Mark's a grown man and ain't nobody gonna tell him what to do. Besides," he continued with a grin, "I win too much money off him to wanna change things."

Ruth must've caught Audrey's confused expression. "Some of us play poker at night," she explained. "Guess with your room upstairs, you haven't heard anything."

So that explained the mess in the dining room. Poker! She didn't know what else to say, so she mumbled something about being a sound sleeper and started clearing dishes off the table.

Looking slightly guilty, the men and Ruth thanked her for the meal and shuffled out.

As she loaded the dishwasher, a horrifying thought struck her. It would make a sensational story, but if she couldn't stand to see Mark become a laughingstock to his own hired hands, how could she bring herself to write an exposé and tell the whole world about his problems?

Arms loaded with a tray containing pork chops, potatoes, broccoli and a slice of apple pie, Audrey knocked on the master bedroom door.

No answer.

She knocked again, louder.

A deep, slurred voice grumbled, "Go away!"

She rapped again and shouted through the door, "I've brought you some dinner."

Silence.

She took a deep breath for courage and shoved the door open with her shoulder.

The only light came from a metal gooseneck lamp on a small plastic table by the bed. The rest of the room was shrouded in shadow. The hand-carved pine bed and an old-fashioned armoire against one wall was the only other furniture. Empty beer bottles and dirty tumblers littered the table, and clothes were strewn on the floor. How could anyone live like this?

Mark was sitting on the side of the king-size bed, wearing only a pair of white briefs, his elbows on his knees and his forehead in his hands. His broad chest sported a light dusting of chestnut hair, and his arms and left thigh were thick with muscles. Even with the injured leg and a scruffy beard, Mark Malone was sinfully gorgeous.

Stop thinking like that! You're here for one purpose, to get the story of the Lone Cowboy!

Powerless to stop herself, she looked her fill. His right leg was shrunken, with long, jagged scars snaking around from the top of his thigh all the way to his ankle. As she stood there, she wondered where she would find the coverage to ask about his injury?

Mark glanced up and did a double take. What the hell? It was little Ms. Nosy. Couldn't she respect a man's privacy? He grabbed the sheet and threw it over his leg. Had she seen it?

"What do you want?"

She extended a huge tray of food. "Um, I brought you dinner. I thought you should eat something."

"I'm not hungry." His head ached and his leg throbbed and he didn't want her pity.

"Are you sure?" She moved closer, and the aroma of honey and garlic drifted to him. "John said you love pork chops."

Anger flared. Of course—John had put her up to this! "No, thanks." He spied a half-full beer bottle on the nightstand and reached for it.

"You don't really need that, do you? You know, drinking won't solve your problems."

"Look, lady," he sighed, his hand halted halfway to the table. "You don't know anything about my problems."

The bed dipped as she set the tray on the mattress. "My name is Audrey." She strode over to the table and grabbed up an empty beer bottle. "I'll just clear this off while I'm here." The glass bottles clanked as she filled her arms.

Mark winced. His stomach churned. His head pounded as if a bronc had kicked it. He just needed a sip to take the edge off. Before she could take it away, he leaned forward and grabbed the half-full bottle from her hand.

Damn. She had that hurt look again. Her green eyes reproached him. His gaze dropped to her full lips. She licked them and he envied her tongue. He looked back up to her eyes and leaned forward, reaching out a hand to touch her smooth cheek.

For a moment, he thought she felt the same pull he did. Her eyes closed and her mouth opened. But she jerked back and made a little sputtering sound.

Damn it! What the hell was he thinking? He looked away and started to drink.

The beer was almost to his mouth when she latched on to the bottle. "Stop! You have this beautiful ranch, and good friends, yet all you do is sit in here and drown your sorrows. There's so much more to life!"

He glared at her. "Lady, if I want a sermon, I'll go to church." He tugged on the bottle.

She didn't take the hint. "Please. This isn't the man I've admired all these years."

Who the hell does she think she is? "I'm not the *Lone Cowboy* anymore!" As if to prove his words true, his muscle cramped and pain streaked down his leg. "I can barely walk."

"Oh, please!" She let go of the beer and stalked around the room. "The point is you *can* walk. And you've got two strong arms." She grabbed clothes and bottles as she ranted. "You can do whatever you set your mind to."

"Are you through yelling?" he said, grinding out the words. He might take this from John, but he didn't have to listen to some carping housecleaner, even if she did have a cute, round behind.

She turned back to him, one hand on her hip. "No." The woman was relentless. "My brother-in-law has ALS. Lou Gehrig's disease. It attacks his muscles, and every day he loses more ability to move his arms and legs. He's in a wheelchair. He can't talk or move his hands or even swallow. He won't live to see his son grow up!" She stopped in front of him and shook her fistful of clothes at him. "Yet he gets up every morning and thanks God for one more day!"

She glanced at the empty beer bottles and dirty clothes in her arms with a look of disbelief. Her brows drew together and her eyes darted about the room as if she were amazed to find it straightened.

Mark stared at her. Her brother-in-law was dying? What

had she called it? ALS? And the poor guy had a son? What a screwed-up world. His own father had never bothered to be a part of his or Keith's lives.

He realized he still held the beer. *Ah, finally a nice, long swallow.*

She snatched his liquid relief just as he raised the bottle to his mouth again.

"What the hell?"

The interfering little tyrant stalked to the bathroom, and a second later he heard the sound of the precious fluid splashing in the sink, his hopes for a cure flowing down the drain. For a moment he sat frozen by fury until, like a volcano, he erupted, spewing every curse word he knew.

She stomped back out of the bathroom and dumped the clothes and bottles in a heap at his feet. "What a waste of a life!" A smug look of triumph illuminated her face as she sailed out of the room.

Three

A hoarse shout penetrated her sleep. Audrey rolled out of bed, grabbed her robe and scrambled down the stairs, heading toward the origin of the cry. Did her mother need another pain shot?

Audrey stopped and rubbed her eyes as she became more alert. Her mother had died eleven years ago, and she was at the Double M.

Had she dreamed the sound of someone yelling out in pain? She crept to Mark's door and listened. When she heard nothing but silence, she turned to leave.

"No!" a strangled voice called out.

She pushed open the door and raced to his side. With the light from the connecting bathroom, she could see his shadowy figure lying on the bed. He appeared to be asleep. The sheets were tangled around the lower half of his long torso, and his face and chest glistened with sweat. His hair was mussed and he twisted away with a low moan. His expression looked so tortured, he seemed a different man from the belligerent drunk of last night.

Was he reliving that night the bull crushed his leg? Or was there something else in this man's life that prompted this horrible dream?

She reached out a tentative hand to brush a strand of hair off his cheek, but checked her dangerous impulse. Her palm hovered over him for what seemed like minutes.

His arm flashed up and knocked her hand away with a coarse swearword.

Mark bolted up in a cold sweat, shaking uncontrollably. His leg throbbed. Relentless images flashed through his mind.

His mom was screaming. Mark dragged Keith to the safety of the back bedroom. His brother was only three, and didn't understand what was happening. Through the bedroom window he saw the flashing light of the police car. The medic yelled, "She's still alive," while the cops took his father away in handcuffs. Dad would never come back.

And Mark knew it was all his fault.

"Are you okay?" a soft voice asked.

Mark blinked and focused on a blurry figure a few feet away. Audrey. What was *she* doing here? Oh, God. Had he yelled in his sleep?

"Just dandy."

"Anything I can do?"

Great. Florence Nightingale to the rescue.

"No, I'm fine." He closed his eyes and winced, wishing he hadn't thrown out those pain pills the doctor had prescribed. They'd kept him blessedly numb in the hospital.

Beer. He needed a beer and an aspirin.

He threw back the sheet and started to swing his leg to the floor, but she was still there, hovering.

Why didn't she just leave? He couldn't see much, but what he saw had his blood heating up. The lush curves teased him from beneath her robe. His body hardened. At least he wasn't thinking about the nightmare anymore.

"I heard you cry out. It might help to talk about it."

Her melodic voice aroused him more. "You want to help?" He stood and put his hands on his hips, displaying his need. "Come here and kiss my troubles away."

Her gaze darted down, and the whites of her eyes got bigger like a scared filly, before her shadowy silhouette swished out of his room.

He called after her. "What'd ya expect, a hero?"

Ignoring the pain, he stood and carefully slipped on his jeans. He caught a whiff of her lingering, sultry citrus scent as he headed for the stable.

Mark flipped on the light and made his way to his stallion's stall, grabbing a brush and a bucket of oats along the way. It had been a few days since he'd checked on his horse. Lone Star nickered and tossed his head.

"Whoa, there, boy. How ya been?" He ran his hand down the stallion's flank and poured the oats into his trough. Lone Star didn't seem to mind it was three in the morning.

It might help to talk about it. What the hell did she know? Talking wouldn't help. He'd had that nightmare ever since he'd ratted on his mother. And deserting his brother had only made it worse.

Mark ran the brush across Star's back. "We had us some great times, didn't we, Star? For a while there, I could pretend I was somebody else."

He scratched the giant stallion behind the ear. "They been treating you good, boy? You lonely?" Lone Star whinnied and nudged Mark with his nose. "Yeah, me neither." Out of habit, Mark stooped to check Star's hooves. Searing pain shot through his leg. He stumbled forward, catching the horse around its neck for support. "Damn it to hell!"

Lone Star trembled, but remained steady as Mark pulled himself up and rested his forehead against the horse's neck. "I oughta sell you, boy," he whispered. "You're wasted on me."

Mark rubbed his throbbing leg as he headed for the house. Just past the barn doors he caught a whiff of... lemon. Damn it! He turned, and there she was, flattened against the barn wall like a prison escapee.

"What the hell are you doing?"

She stepped forward, clutching the front of her robe together with both hands. "I was worried about you."

"About me?" Women didn't worry about Mark Malone. They either wanted money or their fifteen minutes of fame.

"You find that so hard to believe?"

He crossed his arms. "Yeah, I do. Were you in there?" He nodded toward the barn doors.

She nodded. "I guess we both like to visit Lone Star when we need to sort things out."

"What? Lady, you've been watching too many TV talk shows!" He spun around and walked back to the dark house, putting equal weight on his throbbing leg. He'd be damned if she'd see him limp.

He slammed through the back door and headed straight for the bar. Grabbing a bottle of whiskey, he didn't even bother with a glass. He stopped in midstride, staring at his gold championship buckles on display. Bile rose in his throat, and the rage seething in his veins erupted. He raked his hand across the shelf, sending the belt buckles crashing to the floor.

Audrey awoke with a vague sense of hopelessness. Last night's incident with Mark weighed on her mind. She'd never forget the heart-wrenching pain in Mark's hoarse shout.

It was still pitch-dark when she stumbled to the kitchen to cook breakfast for what seemed like the entire U.S. Army. If she never saw a slice of raw bacon again, she'd be a happy woman. Writing the "Dear Audrey" column was beginning to seem like a dream job. It didn't look as if she'd ever get a story here, anyway. Only propositions from drunks and unsavory ranch hands.

Grumbling to herself, she set the table. Nine years ago, she'd dreamed of Mark whisking her off on his horse and living happily ever after.

How pathetic.

Over the years, the few men who had looked past her plain features and plumpness to ask her out had only wanted one thing. Even if she'd been willing to do *that* on a first date—or even a second—she would've been too embarrassed to get undressed.

She'd been fourteen when her mom died, and until recently, she'd put all her energy into taking care of her dad and two younger sisters. But Miranda had her degree now, and a hunky boyfriend, and Claire had her husband and three-year-old son.

And all Audrey had was a dead-end job.

As the sun rose in a brilliant palette of pinks and lavenders, so did Audrey's spirits. Was she going to give up now? Just because things were a little more difficult than she'd imagined? Slink back to the magazine and be taken for granted the rest of her boring life?

No way.

After breakfast Audrey dragged the vacuum cleaner to the den, intent on conquering the dust and dirt there.

Mark shuffled in with a six-pack and settled into his recliner.

She pursed her lips at the thought of him spending another day lounging in the recliner watching sports news. She glared at him and fired up the vacuum.

Snarling, he grabbed the remote and turned the volume up full blast.

She repressed the urge to seize the remote and chuck it into the pool. Or toss the vacuum at the TV screen.

Mark Malone wasn't the only one who'd had hardships in life. Surviving the loss of her mother hadn't been easy. But she certainly hadn't thrown herself a big pity party.

But she wouldn't lose her temper again. Come to think of it, now would be the perfect time to actually clean his room. She certainly wasn't going to ask him about his past this morning! She left the vacuuming unfinished, gathered her cleaning supplies and headed down the hall.

First, she raised the heavy shades that blocked out the bright morning sun from both windows. What a shame to see such a beautiful pine bed so dry and dusty. A good polish with orange oil brought the wood to a glossy shine. She remade the bed and then began dusting the armoire. On top sat a Matchbox car and an old, tattered, wallet-size picture of a little boy, about eight years old. The boy didn't look like Mark. A brother? A childhood friend? She didn't know anything about his family. And John had acted extremely suspicious when she'd asked.

She caught a movement from the corner of her eye. Jumping back, her heart banged against her chest when she glanced up and found Mark standing in the doorway, glaring.

"What the hell are you doing with that?"

With a shaky breath, she dropped the picture back on the armoire and casually moved past him to the bed, smoothing the comforter over the clean sheets.

Flexing chest muscles and a flat stomach revealed by low-riding jeans distracted Audrey from his question. Hadn't his shirt been buttoned before? It was hard to concentrate with his brown chest hair arrowing down to well-defined abs.

"Just dusting."

He raised one brow in disbelief as he lifted a bottle of beer to his lips. His Adam's apple bobbed as he took a long swallow. From her hands smoothing the comforter, his piercing gaze journeyed slowly to her chest, lingered a moment and continued to scorch over her hips and thighs.

Her facade of poise withered under his scrutiny. There was that look she thought she'd imagined last time. The flare of desire in his eyes made her feel like someone else, someone alluring and sexy.

It was awfully hot in here. Maybe she should have turned down the air conditioner. Changing sheets was hard work.

But that didn't explain the sharp ache between her thighs.

Mark's gaze shifted to the bed, then back to her. "Gonna help me get it all rumpled again?"

Audrey blinked. The romantic haze cleared from her eyes. She crossed her arms and looked pointedly out the bedroom door. "I thought you wanted to watch TV."

He smacked his lips together and wiped his mouth on his shirtsleeve. "Changed my mind."

She rolled her eyes and grimaced, biting her tongue to keep her criticism to herself.

"What? Go ahead and say it, Miss High-and-Mighty. I can see you're dying to give another lecture. You're on your own personal crippled-cowboy crusade? I suppose *you* never drink?"

"Not at ten o'clock in the morning!"

His brows drew together and his scowl blackened. He advanced on her, taking another swig from his bottle, and wiped his mouth on his sleeve again. He closed in until she was nose to chest with him, caught between him and the bed. He was so close she could smell the beer on his breath.

Refusing to be chased away, she stood her ground.

He towered over her with a narrow-eyed glare. "You know, you should've been a missionary or something. I can see you now. Marching for prohibition with all the other Miss Priss, goody-two-shoes, dried-up, old *spinsters!*"

Audrey's stomach heaved, as if someone had socked her. His words echoed in her mind—*dried-up, old spinster.* It was true. That's exactly what she was. Refusing to cry, she forgot about holding her temper. "Well, at least I don't sit around wallowing in self-pity all day!"

He leaned into her and nuzzled her neck. "You know, I kind of like you all riled up. Your eyes spit fire and your…." He stared blatantly at her chest. "I want you, darlin'."

Oh, God. Her nipples peaked of their own accord, as if straining to rub against his chest. Tiny goose bumps rose as his lips nibbled the sensitive skin of her neck. Even with the smell of beer on his breath, she wanted his arms around her and his lips on hers.

No. This drunk was not the man she'd once thought he was. She pushed against his chest. "Move, and I'll leave so you can drink yourself into a stupor in peace."

He set the bottle on the bedside table and abruptly fell forward, pushing her down with him. Arms straight, he held himself above her, his hands spread flat on the bed. Audrey lay perfectly still, trapped between his strong, flannel-clad arms. His lips parted and hovered just above hers.

"Peace is a pipe dream, baby. I'll take passion any day."

Eyes wide, she reined in the urge to grab a hunk of his hair and pull his mouth down to hers. Despite the long hair and heavy stubble, she kept seeing the handsome, smiling hero from that long-ago night at the rodeo.

"Beautiful green eyes," he mumbled. "Give me a kiss, baby." Feverishly, his lips covered hers, moving over her mouth, begging for a response.

No need to beg. Audrey ran her fingers through his hair and kissed him back with all that was in her.

He slowly lowered his body, settling onto her chest with a low groan. His tongue slid in, stroking her lips and tongue.

She shivered and couldn't hide a little moan of pleasure as his lips traveled down her cheek to nuzzle her neck. The evidence of his desire pushed against her thigh, long and hard. He pushed it against her again, and she realized his hand was sliding under her shirt.

She must be insane! A minute ago, he'd called her an old spinster. He only wanted her because he was drunk. She recovered her wits and pushed on his shoulders. "No!"

He rolled away and sat up. "What's the matter?"

Audrey bolted off the bed and flew to the other side of the room, breathing hard. She didn't know which feeling was stronger—humiliation or regret. "You don't even know me."

Grabbing his beer, he took another swig and ran a hand through his hair. "Hell, what's knowin' someone got to do with it? The women who wanted the *Lone Cowboy* didn't know me." He thumped his chest and snarled his famous moniker as if he were speaking of someone else.

Crossing her arms, she dropped her jaw in disbelief. "That doesn't mean— Oh!" Did he think because she was a fat *spinster*, she wouldn't say no?

Mark frowned and crossed his arms over his chest. "I get it. The cripple ain't good enough."

Is that what he thought? As if that would make a difference if she loved— *Don't go there, girl.* "Your injury has nothing to do with—"

"Save it, lady. I know how women are."

Audrey fumed, wishing she could scream. Why bother arguing with him? "Think what you want. *Do* what you want. But leave me alone. And I'll leave you alone, okay?" She spun on her heel, snatched up her cleaning supplies and left the room.

Mark cursed, and pitched his empty bottle on the floor. Now his room was quiet. But he could hear the vacuum whirring out in the den.

Yeah. Alone. That's what he wanted. Wasn't it? No one judging him? Or expecting more? Then why did his chest ache when she left? Why had he wanted to reach out and apologize and promise her anything if she'd stay? What the hell was wrong with him?

He straightened his spine. Nothing another beer wouldn't cure.

Audrey spent the rest of the day grumbling under her breath as she cleaned. She couldn't stop thinking about how much Mark Malone had changed. Some hero. Maybe the Double M stood for "Mad Malone." She pictured the headline, with her name underneath.

Madman Malone Massacres Meddling Magazine Journalist. She giggled, delving deep for more alliterative headlines.

Lone Cowboy Loser at Life.

Or how about: *Callous Cowboy Casts Off Comfort—* Comfort? Since when did she want to comfort him?

Audrey sighed. Since she'd seen the pain in his eyes.

Ugh! There was a full spittoon under the card table. How disgusting. What the heck was she supposed to do with that? And the carpet? She didn't want to think about it. She made a mental note to rent a carpet cleaner in Quitman, the closest town to the Double M.

Cleaning this mess was her job, but did they have to spit and smoke and drink in here? Couldn't they go out to the bunkhouse? She was tempted to discuss it with John. They wanted to sell the place, didn't they?

But maybe she'd better let it go for now. In just three days, she'd kicked her employer in his bad leg, threatened him with a knife and lectured him about his drinking.

She heaved a frustrated sigh. Besides, she'd be gone in less than a couple of weeks. She could stand anything for that long. Even rude, ex-rodeo stars.

As she snatched empty beer bottles off the floor, she glanced across the foyer to the formal living room, bare except for a wet bar with a half-full wine rack and a pile of trophies and gold belt buckles scattered across the floor. *His* championship buckles.

Now that her temper was spent, the memory of Mark's kiss caused a pang of desire. He'd actually kissed her! And called her beautiful. The beer must have blurred his vision. There was no mistaking his aroused state though. He'd admitted that knowing someone had nothing to do with wanting someone. And it must not.

Because she'd wanted him, too.

He was her employer. But the thought of suing for sexual harassment never entered her head. Then again, he hadn't fired her for pouring his beer down the sink, either.

She cringed thinking about that. And how she'd talked to him. Maybe she'd taken her new "assertive" attitude too far. If he fired her now, she'd never know the whole story. But she just couldn't stay in this house and watch him drink himself to death.

He'd obviously let the injury ruin his life. She should have mentioned professional help. She knew it was none of her business, but someone had to care enough to—

Care?

What are you doing, girl, planning his rehabilitation? Where's your precious objectivity? You're a journalist, not a social worker. Get over it!

Unfortunately, that was easier said than done, and hero or not, Mark Malone was more than just a story to her. He always had been and always would be. And this whole business had the potential to ruin her new career.

Four

The next afternoon, as Audrey headed to the bunkhouse carrying neatly folded stacks of laundry, she heard hooting and laughter coming from the barn. Curley, usually at her heels, barked and rushed inside.

Audrey couldn't resist changing course to check out the commotion. Maybe in this more relaxed atmosphere they'd let something slip about Mark. She had to get to the bottom of this mystery. There must be more to this story than his injury. What could have made him change so much? Had all his endorsement opportunities dried up after the accident?

She followed the sounds back to the far corner of the barn. Dalt twisted and turned on the bucking mechanical bull, while Jim operated the lever.

After a couple of seconds, Dalt flew off and landed on his backside. When he saw Audrey watching, he jumped up, gingerly rubbing his behind. He sauntered over to her with his most charming grin. "Hey, Audrey. You wanna give it a try? I'll make sure we take it real slow." Dalt raised his brows, then actually winked—at her! Was he playing a cruel joke?

Someone taunted, "Come on, Pete, show your sack!" Pete leered at her, blew her a kiss and then climbed on the barrel.

"They were just tellin' him to, uh, to have some, uh, you know, courage," Dalt explained.

"My dad's a rodeo man, Dalt. I'm familiar with the expression."

"So, you gonna be next?" He slipped an arm around her waist, pulled her close and whispered in her ear, "I'll help you hold on, if you want."

"Oh, no. I—" A small voice buzzed through her brain, tempting her. *Why not?* it whispered. *You wanted to experience more of life, didn't you?*

"Okay." She plunked the laundry into Dalt's unsuspecting arms. "I'll need a step stool, though."

A huge grin spread over Dalt's face. "Sure, sweetheart. Whatever you want. Come on in here and we'll get you all fixed up."

Pete jumped off, and before she had time to reconsider her foolishness, she climbed on, coaxed by Dalt in his soothing southern drawl. The barrel began to rock in gentle, rhythmic motions. Audrey clenched her fists tightly around the rope. Her legs hugged the barrel so hard she could feel her thigh muscles straining.

After a few seconds, with Dalt and the other guys cheering her on, the rocking motion sped up. She concentrated on not falling off, matching her body's wits against the "bull." A powerful energy surged through her. Her heart pumped faster. This must be what Mark felt when he rode. Excited. Challenged. Unconquerable. She stuck her right arm in the air and laughed.

"Don't you have dinner to cook?" a deep voice barked.

The shouting and hooting silenced. The barrel stilled. Audrey caught her breath and jerked around to find Mark scowling at her. Her face heated as blood pounded in her temples. She knew her thighs must look even fatter, spread around the barrel. Shame and embarrassment washed over her. Why did he affect her this way?

Dalt stepped over to Mark. "I was keeping her from getting back. It's my fault."

Mark glared at her, ignoring Dalt. His breathing was ragged and his blue eyes flashed with heat.

Audrey wriggled off the barrel, conscious of his gaze following her every move. Her awkward dismount couldn't be helped, but she was determined not to be intimidated.

She strode up to him and smelled the beer on his breath. He had some nerve acting as if she was shirking her duties! "Dinner, Mr. Malone, is warming in the oven. I was just about to call everyone in to eat. But you smell like you already drank yours!" She picked up the laundry Dalt had deposited on a hay bale and stalked off toward the house.

All the men except Dalt hurried for the bunkhouse, leaving Mark to stare after her retreating figure.

And what a figure it was. He couldn't decide if he wanted to wring her neck or throw her on the ground, strip her naked and take her right there in the yard. She wouldn't give him the time of day, yet here she was, flirting with every cowhand in sight.

"You're making a big mistake, Malone."

Mark glanced at Dalt. "What the hell do you know about it?"

Dalt put his hands on his hips and shook his head. "When you want a woman, you sweet-talk her, you don't growl at her."

Mark narrowed his eyes, warning him with a look.

Dalt shrugged and walked away.

Was Audrey sleeping with Dalt? He'd only been here a few weeks, but according to the guys at the poker table, his exploits with women were legendary. Why would Audrey be immune?

Except, all week he'd watched her smile and hum while she cleaned. He'd seen her sneak leftovers to Curley, and even hug John. Stupid to feel a spark of envy toward John. She'd seemed so innocent. She'd transformed the house from a dark, gloomy wreck to a warm, glowing haven. As if all was right with the world.

He wanted that feeling. He wanted her to smile at him as she had that morning in the kitchen.

He wanted her.

"Are you sure you won't come with us?" Ruth asked Audrey one more time. It was Friday night, and all the hands were going into Quitman for dancing.

"I'm sure. I don't know how you do it. I'm exhausted. Besides, I've got a good book I want to finish." Audrey loved to dance, but it'd been a long time since she'd been to a club. And in the past, she always ended up standing around watching everyone else dance.

Ruth hesitated, leaning against the door frame with her arms folded. "A bit of advice, girl to girl." She turned and waved at Dalt to go on, then looked back at Audrey. "Stay away from—"

"You know, I was just kidding about saving myself for Mark," Audrey cut her off.

A crease appeared between Ruth's brows.

Audrey cringed. She'd just made a monumental idiot of herself.

Pushing off the door frame, Ruth finger-combed her bangs back and put on her tan cowboy hat. "I was talking about Pete. He's slime. Don't let him get you alone."

Audrey's skin chilled. "Why do you say that? Did he hurt you?"

"Hah!" Ruth laughed. "Don't worry about me. Pete won't bother me anymore. Just wanted to warn you while we had a minute alone. Be careful."

With a sick stomach, Audrey nodded and waved her off. Was Pete really dangerous? She went to the kitchen and opened a window, breathing deeply to calm her shaken nerves. A cool breeze carried the sweet smell of grass, pine and wildflowers. The fresh air soothed her.

She turned on the radio while she washed the dinner dishes. As she dried the last pot, one of her favorite songs came on. The words always made her a little misty-eyed, but it had a perfect two-step beat. She cranked up the volume and danced around the kitchen.

How her heart ached to have a man who loved her so much he'd do anything just to see her smile. The way her sister, Claire, had with her husband, Danny. Someone to dance with and hold at night. They'd have a few babies and grow old together.

She remembered the beautiful smile Mark had flashed that long-ago night at Cowtown Coliseum. He never smiled now. It was as if that smile had vanished with his rodeo career. What would it take to make him smile again?

* * *

Mark heard the music and found himself drawn to the kitchen. He thought Audrey had gone dancing with everyone else. But here she was, dancing around the kitchen, adorable in her jeans and bare feet. Her blond ponytail swayed back and forth, and her arms were held out, embracing a phantom partner.

Damn his useless leg! He couldn't even take her in his arms and whirl her around the floor. Why hadn't she gone with everyone else tonight? Even as he thought the question, he stepped closer to her.

"Oomph!" He grimaced as she bumped into him. Her eyes were closed and she obviously hadn't seen him. What was his excuse?

She grabbed his arms and steadied herself. "Oh, I'm sorry! I wasn't watching where I—"

He suppressed a shiver as she ran her hands down his arms. His sleeveless sweatshirt offered no protection against the soft caress of her hands on his flesh.

She dragged in a ragged breath, bolted to the sink and stood gazing out the window.

Had he seen tears in her eyes? Without thinking, he followed her. *Wait a minute, Malone. She's already rejected you once.*

Still, he was tired of her disdain and their angry truce.

He lowered his face to her hair and inhaled the scent of lemons. He longed to place his lips on the back of her neck. No. He fisted his hands. He wouldn't touch her. "What's wrong?" he whispered in her ear.

Now she'd say, "Nothing," as all women did. Then she'd slyly mention what she really wanted. Probably money.

She turned around, eyes on the floor as she wiped at her cheeks. "It was just that song." Her lips trembled as she tried to smile. "It's stupid to cry over a song, isn't it?" With a choked laugh, she started sobbing.

No, don't...don't cry. Don't lean into me. Don't you know I can't help you?

With a frustrated growl, he wrapped his arms around her and let her weep into his shirt. Whispering soothing words, he brushed his hand down the crown of her head and across her shoulders. She was so soft and rounded. Her breasts pressed against his chest, and he wanted to feel them in his palms. But she needed comfort now, not lust. He concentrated on keeping his hands on her back and continued murmuring soothing noises.

This wasn't so bad. This was something he could do, even with a bum leg. She trusted him. Needed him.

When her sobs had run their course, she raised her head and stared at him, her lashes still wet with tears. The contempt usually sparking in her eyes was gone. Only pain and longing softened them now. He leaned down and gently kissed them dry. Hesitant, he pulled back to check her reaction.

Her eyes were wide and her lips were parted in a questioning look.

A fierce desire swept through him, stronger than the need for the fiery liquid he poured down his throat. He lowered his mouth to hers, kissing her with all the hunger he'd pent up since she'd first smiled at him. She tasted like strawberries and innocence, and he wanted more. With a low moan, he drew her lips even deeper into his mouth.

She shivered and opened her mouth, and he pushed his tongue in, swirling it around hers and across the inside of her lips. Her arms came around his neck, and she pressed her body close against him. Damn it all to hell! The feel of her soft curves against him was more than he could handle. He lost control.

He swung her around and pushed her against the island, squeezing her soft, generous bottom and grinding his hips against hers.

Oh God, he'd missed a woman's body! Every night this week, through a drunken haze, he'd dreamed of her in his arms like this. Still kissing her fiercely, he brought his hand up to one beautiful breast.

She jerked her lips from his, flattened her palms against his chest and shoved him away.

He lost his balance and had to take a step back with his good leg, throwing his arm behind him to grab the edge of the sink. Before he could reach for her, she raced from the kitchen and up the stairs.

What the hell had he been thinking? *Get it into your thick head, Malone. You're not the Lone Cowboy anymore.* All the *buckle bunnies* have moved on to the next big rodeo star. No woman was gonna be interested in plain old Mark Malone. A white-trash guy with a mutilated leg, a guy who had betrayed his own family.

Guilt had a way of sucking the passion right out of a person. Audrey paced in her room and berated herself. She was on the same evolutionary scale as pond scum for lying to Mark Malone.

But when Mark had kissed her, she'd responded with an intensity she'd never experienced before. His lips had sparked a trail of fire that had inflamed her entire body. His kisses had awakened her, as if she was finally alive instead of wandering numbly through a sham of a life. His strong arms surrounding her, he'd tenderly kissed her tears away. The concern in his eyes had made her knees weak.

Tonight she'd caught a glimpse of a different man. There had been passion, yes. But there'd also been compassion.

Here was the man who had braved five rowdy rednecks to rescue her. She'd not been wrong to hope he was still that man.

Audrey finally went through the motions of preparing for bed, squeezing toothpaste on her brush. *Let's get real here.* It was a pity kiss. Poor little fat girl staying at home because no one asks her to dance. Ooh, it hurt to be so honest. And she hated that he'd seen her so vulnerable.

But hadn't she seen him writhing in the throes of a nightmare, tormented and in deep pain? She'd suspected that underneath the drinking and belligerence, he hid a secret. Something besides the crushed leg had made him give up on life.

That *something* was what she needed to find out. And the only way she would was by getting him to talk. The hands probably didn't know, and though John and Helen might, they were too loyal to share Mark's private demons with her.

But could she betray him now?

She wanted this promotion to staff writer. She was determined to be more assertive, to go after her dreams. The emptiness, the loneliness, of the past few years loomed in her future.

She got into bed. Sleeping was impossible. She was restless. Edgy. Thoughts whirled through her mind. Her emotions were in turmoil. She'd been here almost a week. What was she going to do? Give up on her ambitions just because a handsome cowboy kissed her in a moment of sympathy?

She heard raucous laughter coming from downstairs. Guess the guys were back from town.

Men! It still infuriated her that they smoked and spit and threw their trash all over the place. If they had to play poker why couldn't they—

Poker! Of course. This way, it would be less of a betrayal and more like a challenge. Mark would have a choice. A simple, winner-take-all game. All she had to do was wait for a winning hand and the right moment, and force him to bet an exclusive interview. It would be a relief to be honest about why she was really there.

She showered and dressed, purposely wearing the one blouse she owned with a low neckline.

Audrey figured she'd need all those acting skills she hadn't used since her tenth-grade drama class to pull this scheme off. When the men turned to stare at her as she walked into the dining room, she almost lost her nerve. She tried to stop her voice from shaking when she said, "I couldn't sleep. Mind if I watch?"

A chorus of male voices answered, "Sure!" and, "Yeah!" at the same time. Dalt jumped up to get her a chair from the kitchen.

Mark's usual scowl grew even darker. Gone was the compassionate man from a few hours ago.

"Oh, thank you." She sat across from Mark, folded her arms on the table and leaned forward. Her father had taught her that an important tool in winning a poker game was distraction. Might as well use the only asset she had. She was out to win.

She felt the men's gazes drop to her chest. "I used to play cards with my family when we were younger, and it was really fun."

With a small sigh of relief, she could tell her ploy was working with predictable ease. Both Dalt and Jim tried to coax her into playing "just a couple of hands." Pete hadn't raised his eyes from her chest yet. The lecher.

Thank goodness Ruth wasn't playing tonight. Audrey

knew another woman would have seen straight through her act.

Mark didn't say a word. He narrowed his eyes and raised a beer bottle to his mouth for a long swallow.

"Well, you'd have to tell me what beats what and all that stuff. Sure you don't mind?" *Don't overdo it, girl!*

Several noes were drowned out by a bellowing "Hell, yes!" Mark slowly lowered his scorching gaze to her chest.

A tense silence hung over the table before Dalt challenged his boss. "Come on, Malone, let her play. What's the harm?"

Glowering at Dalt, Mark finished his beer and twisted the top off another. Finally, he gave a disgusted snort. "I can't believe y'all are gonna fall for this Little-Miss-Innocent act." He shifted his eyes to her and said, "Fine. Join us if you must."

Audrey pretended to listen intently as Jim explained about two pair and three of a kind. She even went so far as to get a pad from the kitchen and take notes.

Dalt shuffled the deck, slid it over to Mark to cut and then dealt everyone five cards. Audrey picked hers up and kept her face blank as she fanned them out. Two jacks, an ace and two sevens!

Mark opened with five dollars, and everyone stayed except Jim, who folded. Mark then raised five dollars and everyone stayed.

Audrey let go of the ace, hoping for a full house. When she got back a seven, she purposely let her excitement show. Pulling a twenty-dollar bill from her pocket, she raised the stakes and everyone folded.

She played it low-key for a while, and kept them guessing by folding with a fairly good hand or blundering a bluff.

Several hours later, Audrey had a considerable stack of

cash sitting in front of her. It was difficult to conceal a triumphant gleam behind a look of innocent amazement at
her beginner's luck. Of course, it helped that all her oppo-
nents had been guzzling beer all night.

"Well, that does it for me." Dalt stood and stretched,
throwing in his cards.

One by one, the other men left the table. Jim had said
he had to be up early and left around one-thirty. Pete had
drifted off soon after that when he ran out of money.

Audrey glanced at the clock. It was after three in the
morning and she and Mark were the only players left.

Mark dealt the next hand, and Audrey picked up three
queens and two fives. This was the hand she'd been waiting for. As the bidding started, she continually raised the
stakes until she knew Mark had bet all the cash he had. Perfect. The time was right.

"I'll see your ten dollars and raise you, let's see, um,
oh, what the heck, I'm feeling wild. I'll just throw in this
whole big stack of money." She looked at Mark and gave
him her best smile.

Mark leaned forward and glared at her. "I don't have
that much money left."

No IOUs were allowed. Probably because, Audrey
guessed, it would give Mark an unfair advantage.

She took a sip of her iced tea, to wet her suddenly dry
throat, and said a little prayer. With a casual wave of her
hand, she said, "Well, I guess if you don't want to fold, you
could bet something besides money."

Audrey saw Mark's jaw muscle working as he gritted
his teeth. His scowl grew menacing. "What do you want?"

She stopped smiling and looked directly into those tormented blue eyes. "I want…" Her gaze slid away, falter-
ing under the guilt.

Say it, Audrey! An exclusive interview. Your life story.

She couldn't. She couldn't force the words out. She couldn't bear to see the look of betrayal in his eyes. He suspected something. But that was just it. He acted like he always expected the worst of people, and she didn't want to be another person who let him down.

"I want..." she forced her gaze back to his "...you to...stop drinking." Of course! That's what she really wanted. For him to be the man he once was. That's the story she'd write.

His eyes widened. "What?"

She braced herself for the storm. "And shave that god-awful beard!"

Mark slammed his cards on the table and hollered, "What the hell kind of bet is that?"

"Well, if you don't think you can do it...."

"I can quit drinkin' any time I want!"

Remembering that day in the barn with the mechanical bull, Audrey took a deep breath, lowered her chin and looked at him with an evil grin. "Come on, Mark. Show your sack!"

She knew what part of the male anatomy this term referred to, and it took all her willpower not to run to her room and lock the door. For one terrifying moment, she thought he might reach across the table and grab her throat with his bare hands. His eyes narrowed to slits and his upper lip curled in a snarl.

He took a deep breath as he slowly composed his expression. Keeping eye contact with her, he leaned back in his chair and one side of his mouth rose in a dangerous imitation of a smile.

That frightened her more than the thought of being found out.

He grabbed his beer and took a long, deliberate swallow before he said quietly, "Let's see…" He studied the money in the middle of the table. "I calculate you got about seventy-five dollars there. That may be worth taking a razor to my throat, but not giving up my beer. If you want to play for high stakes, you'll have to offer me something more."

"W-what do you mean?"

Mark clasped his hands behind his head. He looked smug, as if he sensed her uncertainty. "I'll see your bet by shaving my beard. And I raise you by pouring out the booze. Now you can see my raise with something I want, or fold."

"Uh, maybe we shouldn't…."

"Oh no," he cut in. "This game just got real interesting." He narrowed his eyes and jerked his chin. "You started it, you can finish it."

She was trapped. Surely he didn't want…. "You, um, want me to go on a diet?"

His eyes smoldered as he slowly shook his head. "I think you know what I want, Audrey. I want you in my bed. Tonight. Now, do you fold? Or play?"

The room began to spin and she couldn't breathe. She closed her eyes to escape those piercing blue ones. She'd come this far. She couldn't quit now. She had her pride, too.

She opened her eyes and looked at her cards. He couldn't possibly beat her full house, could he? She straightened her spine, stuck her chin out and looked at him. "Okay." Her voice wobbled and she cleared her throat. "I call. If I lose, I'll sleep with you."

Five

Damn, the woman had spunk! Mark should've felt triumphant. He knew his straight flush was practically unbeatable. But she was acting like some sacrificial virgin standing at the edge of a volcano. *Is this the only way you can get a woman, Malone? Do you really want her this way?* His stomach burned.

What did she really want? Was this because of the kiss in the kitchen? Would she really risk her precious virtue to get him to stop drinking?

He'd wanted her since she'd smiled at him that first morning, her beautiful emerald eyes shining with excitement. But not like this. He had no doubt she'd pay up if she lost. That stubborn tilt to her chin would see her through. But there were tight lines around her mouth, and her eyes were filled with apprehension.

Maybe if he became the *Lone Cowboy* again, she'd

come to him willingly. He wanted her excited, her eyes flaming with passion. His chances of that happening to-night were less than the chances of him ever getting an-other straight flush.   .

Who was this force of nature who'd found a way to make him care? He realized he didn't know anything about her. Not even her last name.

He leaned forward. "What've ya got?"

Audrey's face wavered between smug and worried as she spread her cards. "Full house, queens high."

Aw, hell. Before he had time to change his mind, he tossed his cards across the table, scattering them. He scowled at Audrey and threatened, "Don't expect to win the next one, darlin'."

A week later, Mark was cursing that poker game. Mut-tering a string of obscenities, he glided the razor up his neck. He'd planned on growing the beard once he sold the ranch. His face was too recognizable without it, and he'd wanted no reminders of his past. Damn it! He threw the razor into the sink and bent over, leaning on one hand. Why had he thrown that game? He'd had her right where he'd wanted her. Jeez, he wanted a beer. No, he wanted *her.* But a drink would have to do.

Mark strode to the living room, hoping Audrey would see him, daring her to say something. But no one stopped him. He stepped behind the bar, grabbed a bottle of whis-key, and unscrewed the lid. Closing his eyes, he raised it to his lips. A pair of green eyes filled with contempt and loathing swam before his closed lids. *Gonna add welsh-ing on bets to your list of sins, Malone?*

To hell with this! He slammed the bottle on the bar and

stalked back to his room. Why did he care what she thought of him?

He'd avoided her intense eyes and voluptuous body all week. He barely managed a civil conversation with John, and he refused to alienate Audrey by snarling at her. Thinking of her passion-sated body lying in his rumpled bed was the only thing that made it worth this trouble.

The past week, he'd drunk enough iced tea to piss out a west Texas grass fire. He'd also done a lot of thinking. Looking back on his behavior over the last few weeks was worse than climbing in the chute with a rank bull. Shame filled his throat with bile at the thought of facing everyone. But John was right. He needed to cowboy up and get on with it.

He'd survived worse than a lost career, hadn't he?

He owed John an apology. He owed John and Helen a lot more than that, but he could never repay them. Just two more on the list of people he'd let down. Mark grabbed the razor from the sink and finished shaving as best he could. He'd go see John now. Before he left his room, he rummaged around in his closet and pulled out his Stetson.

The *Lone Cowboy* was back.

When Helen opened the door of her small house, Mark could smell bacon frying. He stood a moment before he remembered and took off his hat.

"Mark! Come on in." Though she recovered quickly, Mark had noticed her eyes widen in shock when she first saw him. "What are you doing here so early? Is everything okay?" Helen motioned him in, linking her arm through his as they walked toward the kitchen. He glimpsed a faint smile of approval.

"Fine. Is John busy?"

Helen squeezed his arm and beamed at him. "He's in the kitchen. Come on back and I'll get you some coffee."

John sat at the small kitchen table reading the paper, sipping from a steaming cup. Glancing up, he did a quick double take, but erased his shocked expression immediately. Before Mark asked, John stood and said, "Let's go into the study."

"I'll have breakfast ready when y'all are done," Helen said. "And I'll cut your hair for you after you eat, if you want." She handed Mark his coffee and winked.

John entered his study and motioned for Mark to sit. He folded his arms across his chest and sat on a corner of his big, scarred oak desk, but didn't speak.

Mark stood for a moment, sipping his coffee, remembering John's study in the Walsh's old house back in Fort Worth. As a kid, Mark had always loved going in there with John. This one looked exactly the same.

He looked around the room, examining the books that filled the shelves on two walls. There were the same red leather chairs with the brass buttons around the edges, the same old-fashioned globe in the brass stand in the corner and the same feeling of refuge and peace.

It smelled the same, too. Like old leather and furniture polish and a hint of fine cigar.

On the wall behind the desk was a large framed picture of Mark taken astride a bucking bull. The bull's back legs kicked up six feet in the air, with a cloud of dust behind it. Mark's left arm was raised behind him, and his right hand, in a thick leather glove, gripped the rope tied around the bull's body. He'd worn the same black cowboy hat he carried now, and had his chin tucked into his chest in a look of steely determination.

He hadn't seen that picture in a long time. Looking at it made his chest hurt. His rodeo days were over. Could he recapture the grit of that man on the bull? He looked away and sat down.

John broke the silence. "What's going on?"

Mark looked at him and shifted in his chair. "First of all, I owe you an apology for being such an ass these last couple of weeks." He lowered his gaze to his hat, shifting the brim round and round in front of him. "I can't believe you put up with my crap for this long."

John's eyes were suspiciously moist when Mark finally looked up. John cleared his throat. "I don't quit on the people I love. Apology accepted."

John had never told Mark he loved him. That was probably the closest he'd ever come to it. But it was enough. Mark had never told John he loved him, either. Come to think of it, he'd never said those words to anyone. Probably never would. "I've decided I want to keep the Double M. Will you stay on?"

John walked over to look out the window as the faint light of dawn crawled over the land. "No more booze? You gonna work the ranch?"

Fair questions, all things considered. But Mark hated being doubted. "You have my word."

John turned and offered his right hand. "Then I'll stay. Good to have you back."

After he left John and Helen's, Mark parked his truck in the garage and went straight to the stables. He hadn't ridden Lone Star since the accident. Hadn't even considered whether he could. What if he fell flat on his face? How the hell had he gotten in this predicament?

Oh, yeah. Audrey.

He saddled up Lone Star and led him out of the stable. The stallion was frisky after months of being corralled. Mounting was tricky, but after a few false starts, Mark felt steady enough in the saddle to walk around the paddock.

His hands trembled and his stomach clenched. God, his leg was so damn weak. And it hurt like hell. But if he wanted Audrey in his bed, he'd have to be the rodeo champion she thought he was. When he imagined making love with her, his need for a beer evaporated like the water in a stock tank in July.

He gripped the reins tighter and kicked Star to a trot. Soon he was racing across the pastures trying to outrun the demons that had chased him for two decades. He'd missed the wind in his face and the smell of horse. And there was a hint of rain in the air. Was it April now? The bluebonnets would be in bloom. He caught sight of a separated calf and roped him on the third try. Maybe he could do this.

Is this what the love of a good woman did to a man?

He checked that thought. Love? Hell, Audrey didn't love him. She just wanted the *Lone Cowboy.* His new housekeeper was no saint. She'd gotten what she wanted. He was clean-shaven and sober. Now that he was, he'd persuade her to come to his bed freely—not because of a bet. She'd responded to his kisses, melting and burning all at once. That wasn't something you could fake.

The Lone Cowboy would get back in the saddle in more ways than one. He wanted to crush her in his arms, bury himself inside her and take her again and again, until they were both spent. Then wake beside her in the morning and have her again. Just thinking about that was enough to start his blood racing south.

What was she doing now? He had to see her. He tugged the reins around and galloped Lone Star home.

* * *

It was time to leave. Audrey's bags were packed and sitting in the foyer. If she left now, she could arrive in Fort Worth in time to have lunch with her dad at the Cattleman's Club. Then Sunday could be spent writing up her piece for the magazine.

She was due back at work Monday with story in hand. And she had one. Not an in-depth interview, but a story nonetheless. The story of a man who struggled to walk again after months of surgeries and physical therapy.

As far as she could tell, Mark had honored their bet. Mark had avoided her all week, denying her the chance to explain about her promotion and the need for a story. But she wasn't sure she would have had the nerve to confess, anyway.

The hands had just headed for the fields when Helen walked in. "Good morning, dear."

"Good morning." Audrey reached into the cabinet for two mugs and motioned for Helen to sit. "I'm glad you're here. I wanted to say goodbye." She poured them both some coffee, feeling more lonely than when she'd arrived.

Helen looked up from her coffee, frowning. "Must you leave today?"

Audrey stared down into hers. "I should get back. I have another…" She hated lying to Helen. But neither could she admit the truth.

"Mark stopped by this morning," Helen saved her from having to choose. "I haven't seen him out of bed at that time of day in weeks. Not to mention sober." Helen rushed on, excitement lighting her eyes. "He told John he's keeping the ranch!"

Mark wasn't selling? A spark of hope lit in her heart. He was going to be okay. This ranch was a part of him. He belonged here.

"Are you sure you couldn't—"

"No." Audrey cut her off and stood to pace across the kitchen, hating to see the joyful expression on Helen's face disappear. "This was always meant to be a temporary job."

Helen stirred her coffee, gazing into her mug. "You know, when you first came here, I had a feeling you were just what this place needed. You don't know how worried John and I have been. Mark changed so much after the accident. It was like he'd given up on life."

Audrey turned and leaned on the counter. "Yes, but why? Rodeo's a dangerous sport. Dozens of cowboys get injured, some permanently. Yet they remain positive. A few even stay involved in the circuit."

Why had Mark started drinking? Was it only the loss of his career? Or was there, as she suspected, something more, something to do with his nightmare and that picture on his armoire.

Helen frowned. "Mark is quiet, reserved. I always thought his nickname had more to do with his preference for being alone than a play on his name. He never let anyone close. Never let anyone help." She looked at Audrey with admiration in her eyes. "I don't know what's going on between the two of you, but I know this—he's back among the living. And I think it has something to do with you."

Audrey dropped her gaze to the counter. Shame dug in and clutched at her heart. She'd lied to Helen. And now the dear lady thought she was some sort of saint. But she was a fraud.

"Oh, dear, has Mark ruined his chance with you?"

Audrey felt the tears on her cheeks and swiped them away. How on earth could she tell this sweet woman the truth? She shook her head. "No, no, it's nothing like that." Grabbing the empty mugs from the table, she took them to the sink and turned on the water. "Helen, how long have you known Mark?"

"Since he was just a kid. His family lived next door to us. Why?"

"There's something else you're not telling me, isn't there? I mean, I know he can't ride anymore, and that's got to be frustrating, but..." Audrey gazed out the window, thinking aloud. "He had product endorsements, the charities and this place. He was probably close to retiring, anyway. And it's not like he's in a wheelchair. He doesn't even use a cane."

Audrey turned and Helen lowered her eyes, tracing the tablecloth pattern with her finger.

"You know, don't you?" Audrey said quietly.

When Helen looked up, there were tears in her eyes. "You'll have to ask Mark."

Audrey's shoulders drooped, weighted with dread. "It was something awful, wasn't it?"

"Only Mark can tell you, dear."

"Like he'd tell me," she muttered. She whirled back around to the sink, washing the mugs to distract her from ominous thoughts. Looking up, she glanced out the window and saw one of the ranch hands riding up. She did a swift double take when she got a good look at the man.

It was Mark on Lone Star!

"H-he's riding!" Audrey whispered, clutching the counter for support before her knees gave out.

Helen stood and came to put her arm around Audrey's shoulders, flashing a grin. "Miracles do happen. Maybe you shouldn't give up so easily, dear."

Six

Audrey watched Mark slow his stallion to a walk. God, she loved watching the man ride a horse. The way his hips moved in the saddle and his thigh muscles bunched to control his mount. He halted at the back porch and dismounted slowly, easing his right leg over and down with a grimace, and then tied the reins at the railing.

When he stepped into the house, her stomach did a little flip. She couldn't speak.

Mark scowled. "Hell, I nearly killed myself shaving this morning." He pointed at himself. "Isn't this what you wanted?"

He looked so different with his clean-shaven jaw and short haircut. He was still a little pale, but determined, strong and sexy as hell in that black Stetson and those tight Wranglers.

Luckily, Helen filled in the silence. "Well, there's a

proper greeting. Where'd you learn your manners, boy, in a barn?"

Mark yanked his hat off and turned to Helen. "Sorry. Guess I need some practice in that department." His serious gaze traveled back to Audrey. He took a deep breath and cleared his throat. "I was just on my way to the north pasture. Thought I'd get somethin' to drink. Uh, water, I mean."

But he didn't move.

Helen pushed away from the table and stood. "I just remembered I've got a pie to bake." She headed for the door, but turned back. "Mark, see if you can convince Audrey to stay a while. She's planning on leaving today."

"Helen!" Audrey glared at Helen. If looks could kill, the foreman's wife would be in ICU right about now.

"Leaving?" Mark scowled again.

Helen grinned and winked at Audrey behind Mark's back. "Y'all have a good morning. I'll talk to you later."

How could Helen do that to her? What did Audrey do now? What a moron she was, just standing there, staring at him. She wanted to confess, to tell him her real reason for being there, but she couldn't.

In two strides he was at her side, his eyes locked on hers. "You're not going to leave before the party tonight, are you?"

Hmm. That cologne. It was the same musky scent he'd worn the night he'd rescued her. She couldn't catch her breath. "The party's tonight?"

He leaned closer. "The temporary hands are leavin'."

"Oh, yeah. That's right." *And so am I.*

"We need to talk."

Talk? Did he know why she was really here? He couldn't, or he'd have thrown her out.

"About what?"

He brought his hand up and caressed her cheek with his knuckles. "Us," he whispered.

She closed her eyes and swallowed. *Us?* She imagined for a moment all the possibilities in that word. Mark and Audrey. A couple. Dating. Meeting each other's families. The fantasy was absurd, but deep inside exhilaration, anticipation thrummed through her body. His hand traveled down her throat. "Jim's bringing barbecue from town."

Audrey raised her face. "That's…good," she whispered. Her skin tingled where he touched. Maybe just for tonight…

He stepped away. "So, I'll see you tonight."

Her eyes snapped open, and she almost pitched forward.

He'd put his hat on and turned to leave. Then he stopped and turned back. Grabbing her around the waist, he pulled her against his length and brought his mouth over hers for a deep kiss.

Before she could catch her breath, he let her go and left the kitchen.

He forgot his water, Audrey thought in a daze. But Mark had already mounted his stallion and ridden away.

Helen came back that afternoon and, to Audrey's surprise, had two pies with her. She smiled and raised her brows. "So you decided to stay?"

"Just for the party. I'll leave in the morning."

Helen accepted her answer with a nod. "I knew he could convince you to stay," she mumbled under her breath.

Let Helen believe what she would, but Audrey had to discover what Mark wanted to talk about. Maybe she could find the courage to tell him she worked for a magazine, and ask for an interview. She refused to run off like a coward and not finish what she'd started.

Audrey and Helen made gallons of iced tea, and set up tables in the backyard. Someone set a CD player and speakers on the porch, Jim brought the barbecue and John set a keg of beer out by the pool.

The party was in full swing when Ruth approached Audrey and handed her a beer. Audrey took a big sip just as Ruth said, "Hey, girl. I heard you and Mark were the only ones left at that poker game the other night. What happened?"

Ruth slapped her on the back a couple of times as Audrey choked. To Audrey's horror, Ruth broke into a deep laugh and looked over to where Mark stood. "I don't blame you for wantin' to check out his, uh, 'breeding methods.' Just remember my warning."

Audrey considered the odds of God granting her a favor and making a hole appear to swallow her up. She had to distract the cowgirl—quick. Looking over Ruth's shoulder, she spied another interesting source of bunkhouse gossip. "So, what's the deal with you and Dalt? Anything serious?"

Ruth took a quick look behind her. "With Dalt? Mr. Haven't-met-a-woman-I-couldn't-seduce? He's definitely not into serious. But horses ain't the only thing he knows how to handle." Ruth turned knowing eyes on Audrey.

Dalt sauntered over and pulled Ruth into a two-step. Audrey remembered all the school dances she'd stood around waiting and waiting for some boy to ask her out on the floor. Her throat tightened.

Her emotions were out of control. Guilt assaulted her conscience. She'd lied to all these nice people. And what did Mark want to talk about? It couldn't be anything good.

From the corner of her eye, she saw him. Mark held a plastic cup of iced tea, and was talking to Bill Kingston, the owner of the feed store in Quitman. He had one thumb hooked in the pocket of his jeans and his hat pushed back on his head. His blue western shirt matched his eyes, and he was so handsome it hurt. As if he sensed her stare, he turned to look at her.

Somehow, things were turned around. Tonight, Mark was the upstanding citizen and she was the self-pitying jerk.

She couldn't stay in this crowd one more second. She looked away and slowly made her way past the barn and bunkhouse.

It was a clear night with a waning moon and a blanket of twinkling stars overhead. You didn't see stars like these in the city, with all the lights and pollution. She became aware of crickets chirping and frogs croaking, and the sound of the breeze rustling through the trees. The serenity of the pine trees beckoned her like arms waiting to embrace her troubled soul. Audrey kept walking, losing herself in the beauty of the country.

She came to a stop at a creek bank. The gurgling of water over stones and the sweet smell of new grass calmed her. Nature had a way of putting things in perspective. She sat and wound her arms around her upraised knees.

She knew what was really bothering her—she didn't want to leave. Maybe if she'd finished that beer, she'd have had the guts to tell Mark the truth. What if she told him now and he threw her out in front of everyone at the party?

Leaves and twigs rustled and a shadow moved from behind a tree to her right as a figure approached. Fear immobilized her.

"You all alone out here, Audrey?" Pete came closer, stopping only a couple of feet away.

Too late she realized she'd been an idiot to come out here alone. Hadn't Ruth warned her? "Uh, well, I was just about to head back. Ruth is waiting for me to, uh…" She put her hand down and started to stand.

Before she could get fully to her feet, he lurched closer and grabbed her shoulders. "Why'd you come out here? You wanted me to follow, didn't you?" She struggled to escape his hands, but he slid one arm around her back and pulled her against him with a wiry strength. His foul breath hit her cheek as he dipped his head and planted a sloppy kiss on half her mouth.

"Pete, no." She shoved with all her strength, but he didn't budge. Her heartbeat raced as he growled and swooped down again. This time she barely avoided his mouth.

"You aren't serious about saving yourself for that crippled old has-been, are ya?" He spat out the words as he fought to kiss her. "He's been holed up here for so long he'd screw the first thing that held still long enough."

A wave of nausea hit her. Struggling was getting her nowhere. Time for extreme measures. Position the knee, aim for the groin….

"What are you doin' out here? Everything all right?"

Oh, that deep, husky voice. Audrey had never been so glad to hear it.

Pete dropped his hands and backed away. "Just talking, man. Everything's cool."

She needed a moment to compose herself. She stayed where she was, gazing at the creek.

Pete turned his head and spit into the grass. "See ya later, Audrey." He strolled back toward the party.

She heard Mark move closer and straightened her dress. There was a minute of tense silence. Had he seen her fighting Pete off? Did he think she'd been a willing participant in that?

"Was he botherin' you?" Mark's voice shook. He stalked past her, heading after Pete. "I'm gonna knock that punk from here to next Sunday."

She grabbed the back of his shirt. "No!" Pete would be leaving tomorrow. No sense in Mark making a scene at the party.

Mark swiveled to face her. "You sure you're okay?"

"I'm fine. Just tired. Had a busy day." She hoped her voice sounded normal. She tried to step away, put some distance between them. Big mistake. She didn't watch where she was going. She tripped over her own feet and started to pitch backward.

"Whoa, there." He caught her in his arms and didn't let go.

His big hands held her shoulders just as Pete's had, but she wasn't afraid. Beneath her dress, her skin burned. She ached. Audrey looked into his eyes. They seemed black in the moonlight, and still sparked with temper. Her gaze traveled down to his close-shaven jaw, and over to his chiseled, masculine lips. They parted, and she became aware of his ragged breathing. The breeze shifted, and she smelled the musky, clean scent of his cologne. Barely aware of her actions, she rose on tiptoe and buried her nose in his neck, inhaling until she was dizzy.

Mark moaned under his breath, turning his face to nuzzle against her cheek. He stepped closer, spread his legs and wrapped his arms around her waist, hugging her tight. He brought his palms up to cradle her face and crushed his mouth to hers for a long, hard kiss.

His lips were warm, strong and soft at the same time. Her arms stole around his neck and she angled her head to deepen the kiss. This was so right. No hidden motives or games, only a soul-deep longing for him.

Too soon, he pulled away and looked her in the eyes. "I called your company today and let them know you're stayin' here."

"What?" Did workers' comp cover panic attacks?

He shrugged. "The place needs a housekeeper. And you and I have some unfinished business."

What unfinished business? He must know! As upset as she was, she couldn't begin to sort through all the implications of his announcement. Would Mr. Burke think she had quit? And who did Mark think he was, calling Uncle Bill without asking her? He had no right.

But hadn't she been depressed at the thought of leaving and never seeing him again? Did she want to stay?

Stay? Her heart dropped to her stomach at the thought. Suddenly a lifetime of waking before dawn, cooking and cleaning for a dozen hungry ranch hands didn't sound that bad if it meant being with Mark Malone every day.

Was she in love with Mark?

Hah! It would be ridiculous if it weren't so…true. Love? No, no, no. This was just a response to his attentions. He'd kissed her and made her feel desirable. No one had ever done that before. She was just flattered and grateful.

He was a grouchy, overbearing—handsome, tender and sexy…. Enough! So he was all that. So what? Was she seriously considering giving up a career as a journalist— okay, copy editor—in Dallas just to scrub pots and pans in the middle of nowhere? Besides, she was living a lie. She couldn't do that.

"I can't do that," she said, pushing away from him.

He let her go. "Your uncle says you can. I doubled your salary, and he accepted a finder's fee."

She looked back up, her mind spinning. "But I, I have to be in Dallas on Monday for, uh, another job."

"He said to tell you not to worry, he'd take care of your other assignment."

What the heck did that mean? Had Uncle Bill talked to Mr. Burke? Was their deal off? Was she fired? Why did Mark want her to stay? Was he impressed with her spectacular housekeeping skills? She thought not.

It didn't matter why. She just couldn't do it. Even if she were willing to alter her life, she couldn't stay here without telling him the truth. The thought of telling him why she was really here made her short of breath. He'd hate her for deceiving him.

"No." She backed away. "There must be some mistake. I can't stay here. I just can't!" She half stumbled, half ran toward the house.

Mark wanted to roar his frustration to the sliver of moon just breaking the tree line. Or better yet, jump in the creek and cool his heated flesh.

He'd watched Audrey at the party, standing on the fringes of the yard, talking to Ruth. The sight of her in that green cotton dress, with her soft hair curling around her face and those full, red lips had had him painfully aroused all night.

He felt like he was back in eighth grade, when a glimpse of one of the cheerleaders in her skimpy little skirt forced him to step into the bathroom and make a few adjustments.

When he'd caught Audrey in his arms, fire had rushed through his veins. When she'd started snuggling into his neck, he'd gone beyond the call of duty not taking her right there in the grass.

And Audrey had wanted him, too, the way she'd leaned in and opened her mouth, asking for more. What kind of game was she playing now? And what the hell had she been doing out here with Pete? Had she arranged to meet him out here and then changed her mind? The kid was barely shaving.

Of course, that had never stopped Mark's mom. She'd paraded so many men through their house, it's a wonder he'd ever gotten any sleep.

A vivid memory flashed through him. It was winter and he was small, around five. He remembered her stubbing out her cigarette and leaving him alone in the back seat of the car.

He'd asked her where she was going, and she'd told him to shut up and stay there. He was cold and scared, but he'd known better than to complain. They were supposed to be at the grocery store, but he'd seen his mama kissing a man as she went inside the small house.

What the hell? He was shaking like a rookie on his first bull. Mark wiped the sweat off his upper lip with his sleeve. Audrey had better not be sneaking around with Pete. If she were, it'd kill him. He didn't want to think about why. But a small voice said it was because he had started to trust her.

The hell he had! He'd never trust any woman.

Good thing the scrawny kid was leaving tomorrow. He'd have a little talk with the punk and make sure he left tonight. And if he knew what was good for him, he'd never come back.

And tomorrow morning, Mark would put the rest of his plan into action.

Seven

Mark got up early Sunday morning and cornered John and Dalt in the stables, feeding the horses. "Hey, John. Thought maybe we'd have a picnic today."

John's mouth hung open as he dropped the scoop of oats and stared at Mark.

Mark scowled. "What?"

"You're catching flies, John," Dalt said.

John closed his mouth. "You wanna go on a picnic?"

"Roundup's over." Mark shrugged. "Thought we'd take a break. Could you invite Helen? I'll bring the food."

"Uh, sure."

"Thanks." Mark slapped him on the back and headed toward the house.

* * *

"Good morning, Audrey."

Audrey stumbled, and grabbed the banister to stop a potentially dangerous fall down the stairs.

Mark raced up the stairs to catch her. "Be careful!" he snapped as he slid his arm around her waist, holding her snugly against him.

For the past two weeks she'd made her way downstairs at this ungodly hour without one misstep. Even the shock of being addressed by Mark at this time of the morning didn't account for her clumsiness. It was the sexy, seductive tone oozing from those little words. He may have said, "Good morning," but to Audrey it had sounded more like, "I want you."

No, she must be imagining things. She was still half asleep, hearing what she wanted to hear, the words she heard in her dreams.

Turning to look at him was a mistake. He'd lowered his head close to hers, and their mouths were only inches apart. He'd already shaved, and his musky cologne filled her nostrils, sending waves of heat through her body to pool between her thighs. How was she supposed to be careful when his hand on her waist made her incapable of logical thought?

"Thank you," she whispered when they reached the bottom.

Mark's gaze lingered on her lips. She wanted to lean close and press them to his.

"We're goin' on a picnic. Be ready to leave by noon," he said in a raspy voice.

Audrey's heart filled with dread. She should leave now, call Mr. Burke and straighten things out.

She could turn in her story, get her promotion and get

on with her life. Mark couldn't possibly be interested in someone like her. He probably knew who she was, and was playing some cruel game. If she stayed she'd only get hurt. "I can't. Y'all go on."

"Of course you can. It's all been arranged."

He looked so earnest, a hint of something in his eyes. Imploring? Well, why not?

You know why not, Audrey. The longer you stay, the greater the chance he'll discover why you came here. And the harder it will be to leave, her heart whispered.

But the thought tempted her. One more day. One day to pretend. She'd treasure this last day with him. As long as she remembered it was only make-believe.

She exhaled loudly. "All right."

At exactly twelve o'clock, John and Helen rode up to the back porch. Mark rode behind them on Lone Star, leading a dappled gray mare. Wearing the usual jeans and boots, his black cowboy hat pulled low over his forehead, Mark made a commanding and compelling figure.

"Oh, she's beautiful." Audrey approached the gray, crooning soothing words. She held her hand out slowly, and then stroked the mare's nose. "Isn't anybody else coming?" she asked Helen.

"Most of them left this morning. Jim took Ruth into Tyler, and I don't know where Dalt went. Guess it's just us," Helen answered with a wink.

Audrey took the reins to lead the mare to the mounting block by the corral, but Mark came up behind her and leaned close, extending his arm to rub the mare's neck.

His chest brushed against Audrey's shoulder as he whispered in her ear. "Her name's Starlight. She's gentle as a lamb." Grabbing Audrey around the waist, he lifted her up to the saddle. "Swing your right leg over."

"Oh, you don't have to do that!" Audrey protested. She struggled to be let down, but she might as well have been fighting a machine.

"Damn it, swing your leg over!"

After she'd complied and settled into the saddle, she looked down.

Mark glared at her, his hands on his hips. "What the hell was that about?"

"I'm, um, I've always been… I'm too heavy."

"Too heavy for a cripple like me, you mean."

How could he even think that? "No! I mean too heavy for anyone!" She looked away. "I'm fat, okay? I just didn't want you to strain your back."

Mark stepped back. "Darlin', don't you know you're just perfect?"

He sounded so sincere. Did he honestly not see how big her butt and thighs looked in her jeans?

She shouldn't have come today. Her heart ached just being near Mark. This was her last day with him, and now she'd insulted him.

"We're burnin' daylight, folks," John broke in.

Mark shot her a glance before mounting Lone Star, and they set out across the west field.

The warm sun combined with the cool breeze to produce perfect weather. Mark was right about Starlight. The mare responded beautifully and had a smooth gait. Audrey had always loved horses. Her father had made sure all his girls could ride.

Mark cantered up next to Audrey. "I'm gonna have to buy you some boots, woman." He grimaced at her sneakers.

"Mark, I told you—I'm not staying. Thank you for the offer, but I—"

"If you think," he began, his voice lowered, his tone threatening but promising, too, "I'll let you go now, you'd better think again, darlin'."

She had to stop herself from calling to Helen and John, who had ridden ahead.

She desperately searched for something, anything, to divert the conversation. "So, you've probably traveled everywhere on the rodeo circuit. What's your favorite place to visit? I've always wanted to see the Rocky Mountains."

He held her gaze captive, controlling his stallion with the ease of an expert. He was quiet for so long she didn't think he would answer. Finally, he shrugged and looked thoughtful as he said, "Yeah, the Rockies are beautiful, especially in Canada. But I guess my favorite place is the Grand Canyon. You just can't imagine how big it is until you're standing on the edge and looking out. You feel so insignificant. Like you're only a drop of rain in the whole big ocean, you know? And what you do on this earth doesn't really matter."

She had a hard time concealing her astonishment. She'd expected a sightseeing conversation, not philosophy. Intrigued, she asked, "Do you really think what you do doesn't matter?"

He shot her a brief, panic-stricken look, and sidestepped the question with one of his own. "What about you? Have you always lived in Dallas?"

She blinked and paused before answering. She could take a hint. There'd be no soul sharing today—or any day.

"I grew up in Fort Worth. My dad owns a horse farm. Mom used to take us downtown for lunch, and we'd play at the Water Gardens. You've been there before, haven't you?"

"No."

Again, she was shocked. He'd grown up in Fort Worth and never been to the Water Gardens? She longed to ask him about his childhood, but she knew he'd avoid any personal questions.

So she told him all about her family: her mother dying of breast cancer at thirty-nine, leaving Audrey at fourteen to help care for her two younger sisters, Claire and Miranda; her brother-in-law's illness; and her nephew, Devon, who was three. And finally she talked of her daddy, the champion bronc rider.

"My God! You're Glenn Tyson's daughter?"

He was frowning. Why should that bother him? "Do you know him?"

Mark nodded, then looked away, silent.

They finally came to the creek, and Audrey gazed in awe at what had to be one of the most beautiful sights in the world. The vast meadow in front of them was covered with a dense blanket of bluebonnets. The color reminded her of the deep sapphire blue of Mark's eyes. Audrey sat reverently, stunned and speechless at the splendor before her.

John broke the spell. "Well, I don't know about y'all, but my stomach thinks my throat's been cut!"

Helen chuckled and rolled her eyes. "Leave it to John to think of food at a time like this."

John helped Helen dismount, and with a face of stone, Mark helped Audrey. The men took care of the horses while Audrey helped Helen unpack the food and spread the blankets under an old, gnarled oak tree close to the creek.

Audrey tried to ignore Mark as he lowered himself to the ground with a grimace. He and John discussed the beef market while Helen told Audrey about her son and grandkids, who lived in California.

After the meal, John stood, held his hand out to Helen and asked, "Helen, my love, would you care to take a stroll with me along the banks?"

In an exaggerated southern accent, Helen replied, "Why suh. Ah thought you'd nevah ask!" John pulled her to her feet and they walked hand in hand toward the creek.

Mark cursed silently and vowed to kill John for leaving him alone with Audrey. Earlier, he'd have given John a raise for thinking of such a ploy, but he'd just discovered that she wasn't just Audrey, she was Glenn Tyson's daughter.

The afternoon had been torturous bliss. Spending time with Audrey, watching the sunlight play in her hair as the breeze blew wisps of it across her cheek. The way her face lit up when she smiled at him, and hearing her infectious laughter when she described her nephew's antics. He'd admired the love and concern in her voice when she talked of her family, especially her brother-in-law.

Every time he glanced at her shapely legs spread around the horse, he pictured them wrapped around his hips as he plunged into her. But how could he seduce his hero's daughter?

He decided to stand up to put some distance between him and temptation. But getting to his feet was easier said than done. Aware of how awkward he would look trying to stand, he put plan B into action. He lay down, pulled his hat over his eyes, and stuck his hands behind his head.

Irritated at Mark's rudeness, Audrey barely resisted the urge to dump a glass of iced tea on his chest. Of course, if his cotton shirt was wet, it would only make it harder to resist staring at all those hard planes and slopes. He'd rolled up his sleeves, and his biceps bulged as he stretched his arms above his head. She lost her fight with temptation as her gaze traveled down to his concave stomach, and even farther to the other bulge beneath his zippered jeans.

Mercy! It sure was hot for April. Audrey had to pull her blouse away at the neckline and use it to fan her heated face.

She must've sighed out loud. Mark removed his hat and trained his blue eyes on her. She expected a comment, but he only looked at her in stony silence.

It was times like these she wished she was more witty. But he had the power to render her speechless.

He rose up on one elbow to face her. "You ever been to the Grand Canyon?" he asked.

This time, she didn't bother to hide her surprise. She'd thought they'd spend the rest of the afternoon in silence. "No. But I'd love to see it someday. I guess it would probably make me feel insignificant, too."

"Not you." His gaze bored into her.

"Why do you say that? I'm nobody. You've done so much with your life. Think of all the children you've helped with your Stay in School campaign, and all the happy memories you gave to kids who wouldn't normally get to go to the rodeo and meet a celebrity like you." The words gushed from her mouth before she could stop them.

His lip curled in a sneer. "I'm no hero. I needed the tax deductions."

"I don't believe that. I used to dre—"

When she didn't continue, he glanced up sharply and prodded, "You used to dream what?"

She couldn't believe she'd almost told him about her youthful crush. Since she couldn't make herself magically disappear, she decided her best bet was to make something up. "I used to dream of, um, flying on an airplane to anywhere. Tell me more about traveling."

He stared at her a moment. She could tell he debated

whether to believe her or not. Finally, he looked past her into the distance, as if he were seeing a different vista.

He talked of Calgary and Vegas, Tucson and Tulsa. He described the mountains and the deep banks of snow in Canada, the endangered tundra of Alaska and the tall red-woods of California. He lay back as he spoke, waving his arms and using his hands to depict certain images.

Lost in his beautiful portrayal of the places she'd always wanted to see, Audrey lay down, too. Getting comfortable, she rolled over to lie on her side, bending one elbow to hold her head in her hand. Her other hand sifted through the new spring grass and dry pine needles past the blanket's edge.

As his voice died away, she became conscious of how close they were. She lay beside him, only a few inches sep-arating their upper bodies. Their gazes locked and held. His breathing grew heavy. His eyes darkened. He looked like a starving man peering through the window at a feast.

Without thinking, she brought her hand to his cheek and caressed the rough texture with her fingertips.

Mark closed his eyes and turned his face into her hand.

Encouraged to risk more, she smoothed his brow and raked her fingers through the hair at his temple.

He let out a low groan and turned to face her again. Opening his eyes, he whispered, "Audrey."

Tentatively, he reached up and tucked a strand of hair behind her ear. His hand dropped to her shoulder and pulled her to him. Gripping the back of her head, he brought her lips to his. A brief touch, a gentle pressure, then he pulled her closer for a deeper joining. When she didn't resist, he wrapped his arms around her, crushing her chest to his.

While he plundered her mouth, he ran his hands down her back to her bottom, to squeeze and caress. She moaned, and combed her fingers through his hair, releasing the passion she'd saved all these years for him. Her other hand slid down to find his racing heartbeat.

He rolled her beneath him, flattening his body against hers. Deepening the kiss, he pushed his tongue in and out, playing hide-and-seek with hers. He groaned into her mouth, palming her breast, unbuttoning her blouse.

"Audrey," he whispered as he kissed down her neck. "I want you."

"Yes," she whispered back, pulling his shirt from his jeans. She wouldn't stop him this time.

Gathering her breasts in his hands, he nuzzled his face between them, kissing to the edge of her bra. His fingers tugged her bra down, and he covered a nipple with his mouth.

She gasped and he jerked back. But she grasped the back of his head to bring his mouth back. He groaned louder and sucked. She shuddered at the intimate contact, and he moved his mouth over and gave equal attention to the other nipple.

"You feel so good," he said in a strangled voice, bringing his mouth up to hers again. His kiss was fierce and hard. Hands trembling, he raised them to either side of her face. He pulled back, breathing hard, and looked into her eyes.

"Tonight…" Mark rolled off her, leaving the rest of his sentence unsaid. He sat up, turned away and, breathing heavily, ran a hand over his mouth and through his hair.

Audrey bit off a whimper of frustration. She wanted to reach up and pull him back to her. For a moment, she lay dazed and confused, until she heard the sound of grass rustling, and Helen and John carrying on a loud conversation a dozen yards away. Reality came crashing back. She stood and stumbled a few steps away to adjust her clothing.

Thank goodness they were still hidden by the trees, she

thought, brushing grass and pine needles from her hair and clothes. Once her heart rate and breathing slowed, she was absolutely mortified, not to mention amazed, that she, Audrey Tyson, had lain outside, half-undressed, almost making love to Mark Malone. And he'd said, "Tonight."

But she knew there would be no tonight.

Eight

Mark accompanied Audrey to the back porch in silence, helped her dismount and then took their horses to the stables. His fiery look promised pleasures she wouldn't be here to experience.

Audrey dashed up to her room. She grabbed her cell phone from her purse to call Mr. Burke. Two voice mails, one from him and another from her sister.

"Audrey," her boss had said in the message. "What the hell is this about you staying on as a housekeeper? Have you got the story or not? Call me."

She ignored it for now. She'd call him from the road.

The message from her sister was more frantic. Worried for her brother-in-law, Audrey quickly punched in her sister's number.

"Claire, what's the matter? Is it Danny?"

"He's sick, Audrey. He's got a fever and he won't let

me take him to the hospital. He's so stubborn! But he's going whether he wants to or not. Miranda's out of town and Dad has the flu. I don't want Devon sitting around the hospital all night."

Audrey's nephew was only three. The hospital was definitely not the place for him in the middle of the night. "Of course I'll stay with him. I—I'm still at the ranch. I'll explain later. But I'm leaving now. I'll be there in two hours."

Audrey grabbed her suitcase and overnight bag from the closet and threw them on the bed. She was still mostly packed, but snatched up a few things lying around the room.

As she flew down the stairs, Mark stepped into the entryway, directly in her path.

He folded his arms and scowled. "Where do you think you're going?"

Guilt and worry brought a sting of tears to her eyes. She quickly looked down and squeezed them back. This wasn't about her petty problems anymore. "My brother-in-law is sick. I'm afraid it might be pneumonia. I'm going to take care of my nephew while he's in the hospital."

Before she'd even finished the last sentence, Mark had unfolded his arms and stepped closer, pulling her against him. She could smell the scent of new grass and pine from the heat of his body. "They're in Dallas?"

She nodded against his chest. "Arlington. I—"

"We'll take my jet. Have you there in thirty minutes." He stepped back, still caressing her shoulders. "Leave it to me. I'll get you home." Then he turned and strode to his study.

His jet? After a few seconds, Audrey became aware she still stood in the entryway with her mouth hanging open.

Mark was glad he hadn't gotten around to selling the airplane now. He called his buddy, Jake, who agreed to the last-minute flight and met them at the airstrip along the back forty acres of the ranch. Within ten minutes, they were in the air.

Audrey was quiet. She fidgeted in her seat, but he saw nothing in her eyes except worry. Had a part of him hoped to impress her with his jet? How shallow could he get? Besides, hadn't she proven several times she wasn't interested in his money?

There was a municipal airport in Arlington that turned out to be only a few miles from Audrey's sister's home. Mark had arranged for a limo to pick them up.

At the house, the door was opened by a beautiful woman with long blond hair, a flawless complexion and penetrating violet-blue eyes. He'd never seen blue eyes quite that shade before. She was tall, too thin and sported circles under her eyes darker than some football players. He removed his hat and finger-combed his hair.

She looked at him in confusion until Audrey stepped in and hugged her. "Is Danny all right? I wasn't thinking. We could have met you at the hospital."

Audrey's sister hugged her back, her brows creased. "I didn't want Devon there. You're early. What'd you do, fly?"

Audrey stepped back and gestured to Mark. "Oh, Claire, this is, um…the new job I told you about, he offered to…"

Mark stuck out his right hand. "Mark Malone. Nice to meet you, Claire. And yes, we flew."

Claire's gaze darted to Audrey, but she didn't ask any more questions.

A man in an electric wheelchair rolled up. He couldn't have been older than thirty, and had the look of an athlete who'd stopped working out. But Mark knew this guy had had no choice. His face was pale and his eyes were glassy.

As her sister retreated into the house, Audrey bent down and gave him a big hug and a kiss on the cheek. She put her hands on her hips and flashed an exasperated look. "Are you giving my sister a hard time?"

The brother-in-law nodded and grinned.

Audrey pointed her finger at him. "You better take care of yourself. Us Tyson girls stick together, you know."

Again, her brother-in-law nodded and smiled.

"You don't have to hog every conversation," Audrey teased. "You could let me get a word in every once in a while."

The man slid his eyes over to Mark and raised his brows.

"Oh, I'm sorry. Danny, this is Mark Malone, he gave me a ride." She finally looked at Mark. "Mark, this is my brother-in-law, Danny Grant."

Danny turned his head, grabbed a stick with his mouth and pushed a few buttons on the screen of a machine attached to his chair. A stilted male voice said flatly, "Nice—to—meet—you."

Audrey's sister came back carrying a small boy who was a miniature version of the man in the wheelchair. He had big brown eyes and dark curly hair. Audrey swooped the boy into her arms and raised him above her head. "Devon! Give me a kiss."

He gave her a big smooch on the cheek.

The boy wiggled down and moved to stand before Mark. He fingered Mark's hat and said, "Cowboy?"

Claire chuckled. "Devon loves Cowboys and Indians, Mr. Malone. You, uh, still have your horse?"

"Horsies," the kid squealed.

Mark wanted to squat down to the boy, but knew his leg wouldn't hold him. So he bent at the waist and placed his hat on the kid's head. Man, this kid reminded him of Keith. Then an idea hit him. "I've got lots of horses on my ranch. Would you like to ride one?"

The kid's eyes got wide as he nodded.

Audrey gasped. "That's nice of you to offer. But he'll do better in his own home." Out of the corner of his eye he could see her shaking her head and waving her hands at her sister.

Mark ignored her and appealed to the kid's mom. "He could stay for a few days. Get to see a real ranch, ride a pony…."

Claire said, "So, Audrey's staying on for a while longer?"

"No."

"Yes," Mark said at the same time Audrey denied it. Mark clenched his fists. She wasn't getting away from him that easily.

Claire grinned at him. "Are you sure he wouldn't be an imposition?"

Silently, Audrey glared at her younger sibling.

Man, she was cute when she was mad.

Mark looked Audrey right in the eye and said to her sister, "I wouldn't mind at all. We'd love to have him."

Audrey moved in front of her sister and bent down to Devon with her hands on her knees. "Wouldn't you rather stay here with Aunt Audrey and make popcorn and watch a movie?"

"No! Horsies!" the kid exclaimed.

A rush of triumphant adrenaline hit Mark's veins. Just as when he'd had a good ride. He knew he'd won. "He'll have a good time and I'll keep him safe."

Claire looked down at Audrey and back up at him. "Well, I think it's a great idea." She put her hand on Danny's shoulder. "Devon needs to get away for a few days. I'll go pack him a bag. Danny, take Devon to get his toothbrush, will you?"

The man and the boy wheeled out of the room, and Audrey turned on Mark. "I can't go back!"

"Why not?"

She frowned and looked at the floor. "Well, I— Because I—" she stuttered.

Maybe he should let her go. But there was too much passion between them. Too much left undone. "It's too late. Your nephew's got his heart set on riding a horse."

"Mark!" She grabbed his arm when he turned to leave. His skin burned at her touch.

He stopped and turned back to her.

"I know you can find another housekeeper."

He raised a brow and lifted her cold, trembling hand from his arm, taking it in both of his. "Remember what I said, Audrey. You started this. You wanted me sober." He leaned in, lowered his head. "Now I want you." His lips lingered just above hers.

Her eyes fluttered closed.

"And I'm not letting you go," he breathed into her parted lips. "Not yet."

Mark opened his bleary eyes Monday morning and found a pair of dark eyes peering at him as if he were a strange specimen in a petri dish. What the hell had he been thinking bringing this kid to his ranch? He couldn't be any kid's hero anymore.

"Are we going to ride a pony today?" asked the little boy.

"Uh…not right now." Mark sat up, rubbed his face and ran a hand through his hair. "Go find your aunt Audrey."

The boy stared at him with sad brown eyes. "Yes, sir." He turned to go, his chin lowered, his bottom lip trembling.

Mark felt as if someone had reached inside his chest and squeezed his heart. He remembered Keith looking like that all the time. Aw, hell. "Kid. Wait."

The little boy stopped and turned, his expression still bleak, as if he expected more bad news. "Let's go get you a pony."

The boy lifted his face to Mark. "Really?"

"Yeah, let's see. First, you need the right equipment."

The boy's—Devon's—eyes widened. "Can I have a hat, Mr. Lone?"

"Uh, yeah. And call me Mark."

Three hours later, Mark walked into the kitchen with a new little cowboy. Devon was outfitted in Wranglers, a western shirt, boots and a black hat. He swaggered in like a miniature John Wayne, then ruined the effect when he scampered to Audrey. "Audey! Mark got me a pony! I'm a real cowboy!"

Mark was worn out, but it was worth it to see Audrey smiling at him as if he just roped the moon and stars and laid them at her feet. The way he'd longed for her to smile at him since they'd first met.

Audrey instructed Devon to give Mark a hug and tell him thank-you.

"Thank you," the little boy mumbled, wrapping his arms around Mark's bad leg. What he really wanted was a hug from the kid's aunt.

Before he'd finished the thought, Audrey was in his arms and squeezing him tight, her cheek pressed hard to his chest.

This is where she belonged—in his arms. Yesterday's picnic had been a revelation. He'd never talked so freely about himself with anyone. Or lost control. He'd snapped like stressed barbed wire.

This was becoming more than a game. She'd gotten under his skin. When he saw her hugging her sister and brother-in-law with tears in her eyes, how caring she was with her nephew, it made him think about families. Made him dare to dream about having one.

And that was dangerous.

With a beautiful smile, she looked at him, worship in her eyes, and whispered, "Thank you."

Heaven help him.

Mark's throat tightened. He'd never been the recipient of such gratitude for so little. Unable to stop himself, he swooped down and kissed her, starved for the taste of her soft lips. He kissed her possessively, longing for more.

Audrey pushed away sharply, and he felt as if he'd been doused with ice water. The sound of the kid's high-pitched giggling finally penetrated his passion-numbed consciousness. Confused and uncertain, he stood there as she ushered her nephew upstairs, instructing him to let Mark rest, but rest was the furthest thing from his mind.

He took himself out to the corral to saddle the pony, contemplating the days to come. John rode up just as he was tightening the cinch of the child's saddle. The older man dismounted and ambled over to the corral, hooked a booted foot on the bottom rung of the fence and hung his arms over the top rail. "That nephew of Audrey's sure is a cute little rascal," he called across the corral to Mark. "Gonna teach him to ride?"

Mark cocked a brow. "You might say I was roped into it."

John threw his head back and laughed.

* * *

Audrey made Devon a sandwich for lunch and berated herself for oversleeping. When she hadn't found Devon in his room, she'd feared he was bothering Mark. She'd been amazed when she'd found the note stuck to the refrigerator with a magnet. "Kid and I've gone to town. Mark."

She smiled to herself. She couldn't believe he'd bought Devon a pony. But why was she surprised? He'd always been good to children.

Except he'd looked ill at ease when he'd first come home with Devon, standing by the door, hands in his pockets and hat pushed back. If she hadn't known he'd once brought foster children to his ranch, she would have sworn he was uncomfortable around the little boy.

But when Devon had hugged Mark's bad leg, and he'd put his hand on Devon's shoulder, Audrey's heart had turned a somersault. In that moment she'd known she couldn't pretend it was a leftover crush any longer.

She was madly and deeply in love with Mark Malone.

Nine

Trapped.

With no escape. Audrey rolled her shoulders, trying to ease the tension lodged there.

Mark had taken Devon out to the corral for a lesson, and Audrey spied on them from the kitchen window. Watching Mark hold her nephew on the little pony, she fell more deeply in love with the man. She allowed herself to fantasize that they were married, and Devon was theirs and this was her house.

And that she'd never deceived him.

How pathetic was that?

The phone rang, jarring her from her dismal musings. Claire was calling from the hospital. Danny had a circulatory infection, not pneumonia, thank goodness. Still, he wouldn't be discharged for two or three more days. Until then, Audrey was caught in a hell of her own making.

That night after dinner, she hauled a few kitchen chairs into the den and helped Devon stretch blankets across them. Her nephew wanted to "camp out" in front of the fireplace, as the ranch hands sometimes did. Audrey crawled inside the makeshift tent and refilled the bowl with the last of the popcorn. "After you finish this, it's time for bed."

"Aw, I don't wanna go to bed."

A deep voice answered, "You heard your aunt Audrey. No arguing." Mark bent down, grasped Devon under his arms, tossed him in the air and caught him.

Audrey was mesmerized. Wearing that sleeveless sweatshirt, his biceps were displayed to perfection. What was it about the man's arm muscles that literally weakened her knees? Okay, so it was his muscles, and his lips and his eyes....

And the caring way he treated her nephew.

The boy squealed and giggled. A tender look softened Mark's face as he lowered Devon and ruffled his hair. "Got any popcorn for me?" He tugged on the heavy recliner until it faced the fire, and settled into it as if for a long, cozy stay.

"Tell me a story?" Devon asked, handing Mark the bowl of popcorn.

"All right, but you gotta crawl in your tent and lie down."

Devon scrambled to comply and Mark began. "The first time I saw Lone Star, he was bucking and neighing in a big, fancy corral."

As captivated as the boy, Audrey sat on the floor listening to Mark tell how he'd outbid everyone at the auction with his first-prize money to buy the horse.

When Mark stopped speaking, she looked over at Devon. He was fast asleep. "Guess I better put him to bed."

"He's all right for now. Want some coffee?"

Oh, yes, she thought. And you. For the rest of my life. He started to rise, but she shot up from the floor. "I'll get it," she mumbled as she slipped past him. She needed to put some distance between them.

When Audrey returned, she handed Mark a mug and sank back to the floor beside the tent.

"Thanks." Mark accepted his mug, but didn't drink. He sat on the edge of his chair, watching her, his gaze intense.

Distracted and nervous, she took a sip of her coffee. The hot liquid burned her mouth and she hissed her pain.

Mark bent forward, laid his palm on her cheek and lifted her chin. "You all right?" Gazing at her lips, he ran his thumb gently across them. He lowered his head and touched his lips to hers.

Thoughts of the picnic swirled in her head as his mouth opened and he pressed closer. It would be disastrous to succumb to his seduction. How could she when she'd lied to him? She pulled away and scooted out of reach. "Claire says Danny will be home in a few days, so I'll be taking Devon home first thing Thursday morning."

Mark leaned back with a loud sigh. "We'll take him in the jet."

She made herself meet his gaze. "That's not necessary. But thank you for letting him stay here. He's had such a wonderful time."

Mark gazed at the toddler as she spoke, but his mind seemed far away. "He was really good on the pony. Reminds me of my brother."

A piece of the puzzle snapped into place. The boy in the picture. "You have a brother? What's his name?"

Mark gazed into space, lost in thought. His mouth turned down and his eyes took on a haunted look. "Keith."

She wanted so desperately to know everything about Mark. Would he finally talk about his past? Audrey waited.

He continued, "He'll be twenty-two this month. I remember the time Helen made a cake for his seventh birthday. And after we ate it, John took us to the Stockyards and we got to ride a horse. I was fourteen, and John said I was a natural. That was the day I decided I wanted to own a horse someday."

Helen and John? What about his parents?

"Does Keith live close?"

His jaw clenched tight. "Last I heard." He stood, reached for the poker by the fireplace and started jabbing the solitary log.

Last he heard? About his brother? "What about your mom and dad?"

He spun around abruptly. "They're dead," he said fiercely.

Audrey flinched. "Oh, I'm sorry." It was lame, but she knew from experience there was nothing else to say. She wondered how old he'd been when they died.

Breaking into her thoughts, he turned toward her nephew, his face now an unreadable mask. "We should get him in bed."

Mark picked up Devon, and Audrey tried to take him, but he wouldn't let her. She followed them up the stairs, worried as she watched him slowly climb the steep steps, wondering if it caused him pain.

After getting Devon tucked into bed, she quietly said good-night.

Mark stared at her a minute as they stood in the doorway. She could hear his ragged breathing, but he didn't speak or even attempt a kiss. He just turned and headed back down the stairs.

It scared her to realize she'd wanted him to touch her, had yearned to feel his lips on hers again. With a trembling intake of breath, she knew that when she left on Thursday, she might as well tear out her heart and leave it here at the ranch, crushed on the floor.

Mark grabbed the back of his shirt, pulled it over his head and tossed it on the floor. Why the hell had he mentioned Keith? What had possessed him?

He sat on his bed to tug off his boots. He never talked about his past. Never. But it seemed from the moment she'd arrived, Audrey had bewitched him. He thought about her constantly.

His hands trembled as he stood and carefully unzipped his jeans. Since when had he lost control? Even as he'd carried the kid, and his leg had throbbed, he'd wanted to lean down and kiss her. He shucked off the jeans and stalked to the shower, turning the faucet to cold.

When John and Helen had come wandering back from their walk at the picnic, he thought he'd explode. If he'd been thinking straight, he'd never have started something in the open like that, knowing there wasn't enough time to finish it.

But that was just it—he wasn't thinking straight. He was supposed to be seducing her. Not the other way around, damn it. He'd better be careful, or she'd have him pouring out his whole miserable life story, like some pitiful jerk on one of those stupid talk shows.

He shook his head. Like hell, she would.

When she first heard the phone ringing Tuesday morning, Audrey thought maybe it was Claire calling. She rushed from the laundry room to answer it, hoping it wasn't her boss. She'd left him a voice mail, but hadn't heard back from him.

By the time she got to the kitchen, she heard Helen say into the phone, "Yes, I'll tell her."

As Audrey stood in the doorway, Helen hung up the phone and turned to her. "What's going on, Audrey? That man said he was your boss."

The world turned black at the edges of her vision, and she grabbed the door frame. She just couldn't do this anymore. The strain of living a lie, betraying Mark, had taken its toll. She could never expose Mark behind his back. His adoring fans would just have to keep wondering about his mysterious disappearance from the public eye.

How could she feel so strongly about this place, and its people, in such a short time? And why the heck hadn't she considered that possibility before she'd cooked up this harebrained scheme?

For as long as she could remember, she'd always wanted to be a journalist. But, until recently, she'd never believed in her abilities enough to try and make her dream come true. And now, she wasn't sure she wanted to if this was the price she had to pay. She just didn't have the killer instinct to do this job.

Finally, with a sigh, Audrey said, "He is. He's the editor for *Dallas Today*." She pulled out a chair and plopped down, deciding to come clean with Helen. She was relieved that she could share her burden, like a sinner confessing to a priest, asking forgiveness, hoping for mercy.

She told Helen everything. When she finished, she searched Helen's face for a clue to her fate.

Helen was quiet a moment, but she didn't seem upset. "So you've decided not to write the article? You'll lose your chance for a promotion?"

"I swear, Helen, I couldn't betray Mark. Not now. I'll figure out some other way to become a staff writer."

"Well, then, all we have to do now is tell Mark." She waved a hand as if the whole thing were swept away like the piles of empty beer bottles Audrey had found her first day there.

Audrey cringed at the thought of telling Mark the truth. "I just can't. He'd hate me."

"He'll be madder than a cattle-prodded bull at first, but I bet he could be persuaded to get over it." Helen raised her brows and widened her eyes. "And Jim tells me you're a betting woman."

Audrey could feel her face heat at the memory of that poker game. How had she ever gotten the nerve to do such a thing? Helen couldn't possibly know the whole story.

Helen stood and hugged her. "Tell him, Audrey. You and Mark are overdue for a long talk." She headed for the back door and turned. "I miss being around little ones. Why don't John and I take Devon to the zoo tomorrow?" Her mouth turned up in a secretive smile. "I'll ask him if he wants to come over after dinner and spend the night so we can get an early start."

After lunch, Audrey heard the doorbell and opened the door to a fresh-faced man in his early twenties dressed in jeans and a T-shirt. He had blond hair and wore small, wire-framed glasses.

"Yes?"

He hesitated, brows furrowed in uncertainty. "I'm here to see Mark." He looked past her shoulder, as if she were hiding Mark behind her back.

"He won't be back till this afternoon."

"Yeah, Helen told me. I'll wait. You must be the new housekeeper. Audrey?" He ran a hand through his hair. The gesture was disturbingly familiar.

"Yes. Audrey Tyson. Are you a friend of Mr. Malone's?"

He stood a moment in silence, folded his arms and sighed. "Mark's never mentioned me? I'm Keith Malone, his brother."

Under camouflage of pouring him a glass of tea, Audrey hid her curiosity. Keith looked nothing like his brother. He was shorter, slighter and had lighter hair.

He accepted her offer of a drink and sat at the kitchen table. Keith frowned and looked at the glass of tea he clutched in both hands. "After Mark's accident, I realized I needed to see my brother. But Mark wouldn't let anybody into his hospital room. He wouldn't return my calls. So when Helen told me he'd sobered up, I thought I'd take a chance and just show up."

Audrey didn't know what to say to that, so she remained silent.

He looked through the doorway toward the den. "Helen says you've done wonders for the house. But she didn't mention kids."

Devon was watching cartoons. "No, my nephew just arrived yesterday. Mark was kind enough to let him visit."

Keith looked impressed and surprised at the same time. "She said you've made a big difference around here." He began to tell how John and Helen had been their next-door neighbors in Fort Worth. About how they would play catch with John, and eat Helen's homemade cookies. "I've kept in touch over the years. I talk to Helen every week."

By the time they'd finished a couple of glasses of tea, Keith was so open and friendly, Audrey ventured a question about his parents. "It must have been hard not having a mother or a father." She thought of her own mother dying when she was so young. "How old were you when they died?"

Keith's jaw dropped and his brows rose. "Did Mark tell you that? Our parents aren't dead, Audrey."

Ten

Keith refused to say any more on the subject, except that he needed to talk to Mark. "It's past time. I haven't seen him in years."

Audrey could hardly contain her shock. Keith had only been a kid the last time he'd seen Mark. What would Mark do when he saw Keith here?

Audrey had barely finished the thought when she heard boot steps on the porch, and Mark opened the door, calling for Devon to meet him at the corral for more riding lessons.

He stopped midstride and stared at Keith.

Before anyone could speak, Mark turned and strode out. But not before Audrey saw his face. What little tan he'd acquired this week had paled, and his eyes had widened in—what? It was more than shock. It was the look of a tortured man.

Keith shoved his chair back and raced out the back door

after Mark. Audrey shut her eyes and prayed. She grabbed a brownie and sat at the table, using all her willpower not to go watch what happened from the window. All she could think about was the look of agony on Mark's face.

After several more minutes, Keith stepped into the kitchen, hands in the pockets of his jeans, head hanging. Audrey hesitated, and the silence became awkward. "Would you like a brownie?"

"No, thanks." He paced to the sink and looked out the window. "Would you convince him to talk to me, Audrey?"

Audrey gave an unladylike snort. "You'd be better off asking John or Helen."

Keith turned and leaned against the counter. After a long, considering stare, he shrugged. "Helen seemed to think Mark would listen to you."

She shook her head. "I'm just a housekeeper."

"That's not what Helen says. I'd appreciate it if you'd try. Please?" Keith implored.

How could she say no to that?

She found Mark in the barn, in a stall toward the back, saddling the pony. For a few gutless moments, Audrey considered leaving him to his solitude. Where was that assertiveness she'd been cultivating? What the heck was she supposed to say? Obviously a subtle approach was needed. She stepped forward and grabbed the top of the stall door for courage.

"Why won't you talk to your brother?" Okay, so subtlety wasn't her strong point.

Mark whipped around to gape at her, fury sparking in his eyes. "None of your damned business," he snapped. He went back to buckling the bridle.

Audrey shrugged and lowered her head. "I know. But, he's your brother and he cares about you."

Mark grunted.

"He does! You should hear the way he talked about you." She stepped closer. "Everyone deserves a chance to apologize. Life's too short to hold grudges."

Mark turned and narrowed his eyes at her. "You don't know what you're talking about, Audrey. Just let it go."

She raised her chin and glared at him. "I can't. I think family is important. No matter what he did, he was only a kid, and he wants to work things out now, so—"

"He didn't do anything! I'm the one who let *him* down. I left him there alone to fend for himself." He swung around and pitched his brush against the wall at the far end of the stable. "Damn it! You're worse than a fly at a picnic." He stalked toward her. "Just stay the hell out of it!" He pushed his way past her, marching toward the outer doors.

Late that afternoon, Mark was trying to free a cow from a sinkhole when Keith came loping up on Shadow. Aw, hell. Guess he'd just helped himself to the bay gelding. The frightened cow fought and squirmed, bawling loudly, and Mark returned his attention to the job at hand. He lassoed the cow's neck and tied the other end of the rope around his saddle horn. Shoving his hat down hard on his head, he pulled back on Lone Star's reins. The rope stretched taut as Mark backed up, but the cow slipped on the incline and slid back down.

With a messy splat, Keith jumped knee-deep into the mud hole and pushed on the cow's flank. Without his glasses, and sporting that innocent grin, he looked like the kid Mark remembered from a lifetime ago.

"Damn it, Keith!" He dismounted, jumped into the mud and shoved his little brother away from the cow. "One hard kick could kill you!"

Keith clamped his mouth shut, trudged toward Mark and shoved him hard in the chest. "What do you care?"

Mark landed on his backside. He pushed up from the sticky muck. Keith thought he didn't care? All the emotions from his childhood swept through Mark's body, pulsing in his blood. He charged on Keith, bent and grabbed him around the waist, trying to force him out of the mud. White-hot anger and pure adrenaline surged, giving him the strength to lift Keith and wrestle him to the hard ground. They both landed in a heap at the edge of the hole. Mark raised himself to his hands and knees. He hung his head and squeezed his eyes shut. "I always cared."

Keith rolled to the balls of his feet and grabbed him by the collar. He yanked tight and pressed his nose against Mark's. "I'm okay now. It's over."

Mark stared into his kid brother's solemn eyes. He couldn't believe this self-assured man was the same kid he'd deserted. It felt as if a burden had been lifted from him. Keith was okay. He'd survived, better than Mark had. He wanted to say something to his younger brother, but words escaped him.

Keith scrambled up and extended his hand to Mark, reminding Mark of all the times he'd helped Keith off the ground after a backyard tussle. He'd locked that part of his life away for so long, never admitting how much he missed his little brother. He cleared his throat to dislodge the lump that had formed there, wanting to refuse the hand held out to him. He didn't need it.

But maybe his brother did. He slapped his gloved palm into Keith's.

Keith looked down at himself, covered in sludge, and burst into laughter.

Mark tried to smile, but couldn't seem to make the corners of his mouth turn up.

Smacking the mud off his jeans, Keith turned and grabbed Shadow's reins. "You had a great career."

Mark headed for his horse, which still held the rope taut. He was surprised the mention of those rodeo days didn't bother him. "Let's take care of this cow and head in. I'm starved. Maybe there's some chicken and dumplings from last night."

Keith raised his eyebrows and whistled. "Did Audrey make it? I wonder if she's seeing someone."

Mark spun around and glared at his brother. "She's taken. Find your own."

Keith grinned. "Interesting."

The red haze lifted and Mark blinked a couple of times. He drew in a deep breath and allowed half his mouth to lift in a smirk. "What's your degree in? Psychology?"

That night after dinner, Audrey brewed a fresh pot of coffee and then busied herself with laundry.

Tired from the emotional strain of the past couple of days, she poured herself a cup and went out to the back porch to curl up on the glider and watch the sunset. With Devon spending the night at Helen's, Audrey was alone. The long night stretched before her.

Keith was heading back to Denton tonight. This afternoon, as they'd stepped into the kitchen, Audrey had glimpsed Mark slapping Keith on the back. Keith had grinned from ear to ear. It looked as if they'd worked things out.

She wished it were that easy for her. She'd be leaving

in a couple of days, too. That thought caused a physical ache in her chest. A part of her wanted to confess and throw herself into Mark's arms, begging forgiveness, another part knew he wouldn't grant absolution that easily. It had taken him eleven years to talk with his brother.

The small portion of his past he'd given away yesterday gnawed at her. Why had he been estranged from his brother? And why had he lied about his parents being dead? She didn't care about the article anymore. She just wanted to know.

Keith appeared in the doorway, a mug of coffee in one hand. "I hear you're a pretty good poker player."

Audrey choked on her coffee. "Who told you that?" she asked after she quit gasping.

He made a gesture with his free hand that asked, "Mind if I sit down?" At her nod, he made himself comfortable next to her. After he drained his cup, he continued. "Mark says you distracted him with your, um, your—you had an unfair advantage." Bright patches of red appeared on Keith's cheeks, and he tried in vain to avoid glancing at her chest.

She bit her top lip, trying to keep a straight face. They must have had quite a talk. Finally, she gave in to her laughter. "It didn't help that he was drunk. Anyway, I'd do it again in a heartbeat."

Keith took off his glasses, pulled a perfectly pressed handkerchief from the pocket of his jeans and began cleaning the lenses. "You don't have to justify your actions to me. As far as I'm concerned, anyone who could get Mark to stop drinking and work the ranch again deserves a medal." He leaned over and kissed her gently on the cheek. "Or at least a kiss," he said quietly, his eyes full of admiration and gratitude.

Audrey smiled at him and put her hand on his arm,

wishing she'd had a brother like him. If only he knew how she'd deceived them all, she thought guiltily.

"Well, now, isn't this a cozy little scene?" sneered that deep voice from the doorway.

Eleven

Audrey froze, but Keith slowly stood and put his glasses back on. He either didn't feel the waves of fury coming from Mark, or he chose to ignore them.

"Guess I better be going. I played hooky from my classes today."

"Don't break up the party on my account. First Dalt, then Pete and now you?" Mark said, practically spitting out the words.

"What do you mean, 'First Dalt, then Pete'?" Audrey seethed. "Are you implying that I've—"

"I was just telling Audrey goodbye, fool!" Keith jumped in. "Besides, I don't see any ring on her finger!"

"Hell, a ring never stopped Mom!" Mark roared.

Audrey was stunned. She couldn't speak.

Keith shook his head. "I can tell you right now, Audrey is *not* like Mom!" He relaxed his shoulders, took a step back and grinned. "You've got it bad, don't you? You're jealous as hell!" He laughed. "Lucky for you, I've got a fiancée in Denton." He glanced at his watch. "And if I don't leave now, I won't get to see her tonight."

Mark's features slowly eased from rage to bafflement. "You're getting married? When? Why didn't you tell me before?"

"I should have mentioned it. But I figured you'd try to talk me out of it. Why don't you come up to Denton soon? I want you to meet her." Keith moved to open the back door, but he turned and gave Audrey a quick hug. "Goodbye, Audrey. Sure was nice to meet you."

Mark still looked confused as Keith shoved his shoulder and the brothers disappeared into the kitchen. Audrey heard Keith chuckle, "Boy, you should've seen your face! Women sure can twist up your guts, can't they?"

Mark waved to Keith as he drove off, branding himself an idiot as he headed back to the house. When he'd seen Keith kiss Audrey, his vision had blurred and his heart had started pumping a mile a minute. He'd wanted to throw his own brother out on his butt. Was Keith right? Was he jealous? He'd never been possessive of a woman before.

She wasn't in the kitchen or the living room, and all the lights were out. Well, hell. She must've already gone to bed for the night. Audrey in her bed, writhing in the sheets. The image hardened him instantly.

Climbing the stairs was torture on his leg. It ached worse at night. But this couldn't wait until tomorrow. He'd never get any sleep remembering the hurt he'd caused in her eyes. He had enough guilt on his shoulders.

He knocked decisively on her door.

No answer.

He knocked again, longer and more forcefully.

Still no answer.

"Audrey, can we talk for a minute, please?" he asked in a calm and reasonable voice.

"Go. Away."

"We need to discuss this. Open the door," he commanded.

"Just go away. I don't want to talk to you."

"If you don't open this door, I'm gonna kick it in!"

The door jerked open and Audrey spoke through gritted teeth. "What?"

Mark was speechless as his gaze swept over her.

She must've just brushed her long hair. It fell in soft waves past her shoulders, glossy and golden. Seeing her in a plain, white cotton gown started an ache in his gut. And this was no ulcer. The sleeveless gown buttoned down the front from neck to hem, with a modest round neckline. But with her arms crossed, her breasts were pushed together. He wanted to cup his palms around them.

He was ready and at attention.

Audrey looked ready, too. Ready to kill. She glared at him through narrowed eyes. Her beautiful lips were drawn in a tight line.

"Well? I'm listening," she said.

For the life of him he couldn't remember what he'd wanted to say. *Think, Malone!* "I, uh…" He ran his hand over his mouth and down his jaw. "I'm sorry." He swallowed hard and tried to look appropriately ashamed.

If possible, she looked even madder. "Apology not accepted." She shut the door in his face.

Mark stopped the door with the flat of his hand and pushed his way into her room. "Damn it, Audrey, you've gotta listen to me. I know I was an ass, but—"

"Glad we can agree on something. Now get out!" Her

voice was wobbly and stringent at the same time. She pointed at the hallway, and he could see the shadow of her dark nipples through the thin cotton gown.

He couldn't think. He couldn't counterattack. With those weapons at her disposal, he might as well concede defeat. Although, he could handle a lifetime of losing arguments if she always wore that gown when they fought.

Wait a minute, Malone. Lifetime?

Mark was, once again, temporarily speechless. All he wanted right now was to wrap her in his arms and kiss her until all that anger turned to passion. He stepped up to her, slipped his arms around her back and pulled her to him.

Audrey wished she'd never opened that damn door. She resisted, pushing her fists against his chest.

He let out a deep breath and looked into her eyes. "Keith was right. I was a stupid fool tonight."

She twisted away. "Even if your assumptions were true, it's none of your business."

Mark's usual scowl returned as he crossed his arms. "But they aren't true, are they?"

She tilted her head. "Maybe. Maybe not."

In the blink of an eye, he moved in and grabbed her shoulders. "You're not like that. Tell me you're not!"

The misery in his eyes melted the last of her indignation. She sighed. "I'm not sleeping with anyone, okay? I don't know why you would think that, anyway."

Mark raised his head, looking away. "Women aren't generally a real faithful breed."

Audrey stepped away. "You can't lump all women into the same category. Can you imagine Helen ever cheating on John?"

He shrugged. "She's the exception that proves the rule." His eyes flared as if a new thought had just struck him. He looked back down at her. "And you." His gaze fled hers again. "But most women? They like variety. My mother couldn't have stuck to one man if she'd been super-glued to his butt."

The bitterness in his tone made her wince. "Your mother cheated on your dad? Is that why you lied about your parents being dead? They're divorced?"

He didn't answer, and an expression she'd never seen on him crossed his face. Uncertainty.

Shaking his head, he gazed over her shoulder. "I...don't know. They're dead to me."

How could he not know? What had happened to his family? But her questions were drowned out by the thumping of her heart as Mark leaned down and gently kissed her, his lips lingering as if he couldn't bear to break away. Tightening his arms around her, he lowered his head and whispered into her ear, "Let me stay tonight, Audrey."

She hesitated, her mind in turmoil. *He doesn't love you. You've got to stop torturing yourself, go home and get over it.*

But what about all those lonely nights she'd spent at home, wishing...?

How many more lonely nights would she lie awake and regret not making love with Mark Malone? Her cowardice would haunt her forever. She had to risk herself.

Burying her nose in his chest, she said, "Okay."

Mark caught her chin in his hand and tilted her face up. "You're sure?" The hesitancy in his voice made her sure.

She raised her eyes to his and smiled. "Yes."

His blue eyes darkened. He circled his arms under her bottom and lifted her against his chest. "Kiss me, Audrey."

She wrapped her arms around his neck, held captive by the heat in his gaze. Waves of desire coursed through her so powerfully she forgot to worry about her weight as she parted her lips over his.

With a low moan, he consumed her with the strength of a man possessed. One hand slid under her hair, caressing the back of her neck as he angled her head to deepen the kiss. Licks of fire blazed between her thighs as he drove his tongue in and swirled it around the cavern of her mouth.

Pulling back, he hitched her higher and buried his face between her breasts. "God, I love the way you smell."

Her nipples hardened and ached as he nuzzled each breast, leaving damp patches on her gown. "I want to see you, Audrey."

Before she realized his intent, he let her body slide down, raising her gown along the way. He reached for the hem and began to lift.

No! She snatched it from him.

Mark stilled. His hands remained in midair before he gradually straightened and brought them to his sides.

Oh, God. Couldn't they just crawl under the covers? Or at least turn out the light? Audrey hugged her body and focused on the floor between them.

"Should I leave?"

"No!" She looked up.

Mark's jaw muscle twitched and his eyes had hardened to chips of blue ice.

She frowned. "It's just…you know. I'm not…thin."

His shoulders relaxed, his features softened. He took a step closer, bringing two fingers up to tuck a curl behind her ear. "You're perfect." He lowered his lips to her cheek, pressing gentle kisses down her jaw and throat.

Audrey closed her eyes and breathed in his musky scent. Relief swept through her. He was going to stay.

Before she could do more than whimper, he stepped

back, brought toe to heel and pushed off his boots. He kicked them aside, pulled his shirt from his jeans and un-snapped the front.

Then he waited.

A thrill shot through her as she realized he was hers to touch and caress. She brought her trembling fingers to touch his hard chest, running her hands through his soft, chestnut curls. There was a long, vertical scar across his collarbone, and a small, crescent-shaped scar several inches below his right nipple. He must have had a couple other dangerous encounters with bulls over the years. When she leaned in and kissed them, he shivered. She reached to tug his shirt off his shoulders, and he helped her pull his arms from the sleeves. He tossed it on the carpet and said, "Now you."

Oh, Lord. He was so beautiful, so chiseled. There wasn't an ounce of fat on him. Could she do this? As if in slow motion, she forced her hands to unbutton her gown.

His heated gaze followed each tiny button, while his hands clenched at his sides.

She stopped at the fifth button, just below her breasts, her fingers hovering at the edges.

Mark reached for her bodice and spread it wide to gaze hungrily at her breasts. He reached inside and lifted her breasts in his palms, kneading them reverently, his thumbs grazing her puckered nipples, tightening them into aching peaks.

"So beautiful." A growl rumbled in his throat as he low-ered his head and drew one into his mouth. His tongue flicked, and a sharp ache surged between her legs, so in-tense it was painful. She clutched at his hair and moaned. Catching her around the waist, he opened his mouth over her breasts, nibbling and then devouring.

Her knees gave way, and he lifted her in his arms and carried her to the bed. A vague thought formed that she was too heavy and should protest, but she was beyond coherent speech.

Lying beside her, he slid her gown off her shoulders and hugged her to him, kissing her while he rubbed his chest across her lush breasts. He took her hand and pressed it to the long length beneath his zipper. "Touch me. Feel what you do to me."

Hesitantly, Audrey slid her palm up and down his straining hardness. She gazed at his shape, enthralled with the feel of him. When he didn't stop her, she began to explore farther down, and then back up to squeeze the tip.

He growled. "That's enough." He rolled and braced himself above her, crushing her mouth with his. Audrey tensed when he pushed his knee between her legs. "It's all right." He slipped his callused hand under her gown and spread her thighs. His touch burned along her thigh, and then pleasured her where she ached the most.

Audrey squirmed beneath him, pushing into his hand, needing more, striving for something she couldn't quite describe.

He deepened the kiss, entwining his tongue with hers. His fingers seemed to know exactly what she wanted. Blood pounded in her temples and the room spun. Her muscles tightened, and she gasped and clutched him around his waist. "Mark!"

Mark pressed his hard length into her hip, willing himself to be patient. A woman's enjoyment was usually a matter of pride to him, but with Audrey, her pleasure increased his own. He enjoyed watching her uninhibited response as her eyes squeezed shut and her back arched. He cupped her face and softly raked his fingers through her golden tresses.

When her lids fluttered open, he reveled in the fire he'd ignited in her green eyes.

"That was…amazing," she whispered.

He took possession of her mouth, wanting to taste her joy. She tore her lips from his and pulled back to breathe deeply. "I want you inside me. Now. Please, Mark."

"Oh, yes," he breathed into the hollow between her shoulder and neck. She whimpered, and wiggled her luscious body, driving him to the brink. He rose to his forearms and looked into her eyes. "I can't go slow now."

She smiled. "It's all right."

He grappled for an old packet from his wallet and yanked his jeans open. Then he remembered. His damn leg! He couldn't pull his jeans off without some awkward maneuvering. Besides, seeing that grotesque mass of scars would send her running for the door.

Frustrated beyond endurance, he shoved his jeans and underwear to his knees and pushed into her with one long, driving force.

She yelped in pain and stiffened under him, her eyes wide. He stilled.

Clenching his teeth, he forced himself not to move. This was her first time? Why the hell hadn't she said something? No woman her age was still a virgin.

Except Audrey.

Fighting for control, Mark gently pushed her bangs off her forehead. "I'm sorry. Are you okay?"

"I'm all right." She lifted her head and gently kissed his lips and cheeks and eyes. Spreading soft kisses down his jaw and over to his ear, she tugged on the lobe with a gentle bite.

He pulled out and thrust again and again. The feel of

her tight heat surrounding him shattered his control. Sliding his arm beneath her hips, he pushed her into the mattress, groaning as he plunged in to the hilt one last time. His body tightened, and he set his jaw, but a strangled cry escaped as intense pleasure overtook him.

Breathing heavily, he collapsed, burying his face in her neck. Lemon, mixed with the scent of their lovemaking, filled his nostrils. He shivered, exhaling. He knew he should move, but he couldn't make himself leave just yet. He wanted to stay inside her, cushioned on her soft body just a little longer.

Sated, he slid his hips over and drifted into a deep, lethargic sleep. Just as oblivion claimed him, he heard her whisper, "I love you."

Audrey lay awake, holding Mark and reliving every sensual moment. The fingers of one hand combed through the silky curls at his nape, and the other gently stroked the now relaxed muscles of his back. Even her most romantic fantasies couldn't compare to the reality of tonight.

She committed to memory the taste of his salty skin as she'd kissed his beard-roughened jaw. The feel of his muscles tensing, his back slick with sweat as she ran her hands over him. His tongue teasing her nipples. She loved the feeling of being filled by him, of holding him inside her. Of hearing his hoarse groan and seeing that vein in his neck stand out as he'd pushed into her one last time.

Mark snored softly into her neck, still holding her breast. Glancing lower, she grinned. His jeans were gathered around his knees. She stifled the urge to giggle. Maybe she should wake him to remove them. Her eyelids grew heavy, and she, too, drifted into a contented sleep.

She was awakened by a movement at the bottom of the bed. Why had she left the bedside lamp on? She blinked.

Her legs were gently pushed apart by big, warm hands. Mark! She rose onto her elbows. "What are you doing?"

"Shhh, just relax." He licked the inside of her thigh, kissing and nibbling his way higher. "You should've told me this was your first time, darlin'." Stroking her with his thumb, he ran his fingers through her blond curls. He drew back and whispered, "A true blonde, huh?"

Mark had removed his clothes. Gloriously naked, he crawled up, still under the sheet, trailing kisses along the way. He grabbed the bottom of her gown and pulled it over her head, ignoring her gasp of protest.

Audrey crossed her arms over her body and turned away, staring at the nightstand beside them.

"Move your arms, Audrey." He grabbed her wrists and held them to her sides.

She squeezed her eyes shut and held her breath. Oh, God. If he said something about losing weight, she'd die.

Agonizing seconds later, her eyes shot open as she felt his stubbled cheek rub back and forth over her less-than-flat stomach.

"Your little belly turns me on, babe." He eased up the rest of the way and lowered himself on his forearms above her, cupping her face in his palms. "Audrey, look at me."

She forced herself to raise her eyes to his.

"You're beautiful just the way you are, darlin'," he said.

She looked at the ceiling, and couldn't stop the tears that welled up and rolled down her cheeks.

He gently wiped them away with his thumbs. "Why don't you realize how beautiful you are?"

"Beautiful?" She shook her head. "My sisters are beautiful. I'm the plain one. I guess growing up around Claire and Miranda, I learned to rely on my *personality*."

He picked up a strand of her hair, rubbed it under his

nose and kissed it. "Your eyes are a gorgeous green that remind me of pastures in spring." He kissed her. "Sexy lips." His hand traveled down to caress her hip, moved up to her waist and stopped at her breast to squeeze. "And you're soft and full, not all bony and sharp like some anorexic model."

No one had ever spoken to her this way. His eyes pleaded with her to believe him, desire smoldering in their cobalt depths. She was almost convinced he actually thought her beautiful. Unable to help herself, she'd whispered her love after she was sure he'd fallen asleep. But this time the urge to say she loved him out loud was so strong she ached with it. She could just picture the look of pity—or worse, amusement—on his face. It was less risky to show him her love.

Audrey wanted to explore *his* body. She pushed at his chest.

He frowned. "What are you doin'?"

"Roll over. It's my turn to kiss you everywhere," she said with more determination than she felt.

Then it happened. His face broke into that glorious smile Audrey had seen that long-ago night when he'd rescued her. For a moment, she couldn't breathe.

Still smiling, he flipped obediently onto his back and put his hands behind his head. "Kiss away, darlin'."

She rose to her knees, forgetting her nakedness, and began with his lips. She opened her mouth and kissed him deeply, smiling at his groan. Despite his protest, she moved her lips to his eyes and the tip of his nose. She nibbled down the line of his jaw to his throat, and ran her hands through his curly chest hair as she kissed his nipples. He gripped the sides of her head.

Moving lower, she kissed his flat, taut stomach, pausing to dip her tongue playfully into his belly button. He moaned again, this time deep in his throat. She traveled farther down and explored with her lips and hands down each muscled thigh to the edge of the sheet.

He tensed, grabbed her hand and guided it to his rigid shaft.

She glanced at his face, afraid she'd hurt his leg, but he only smiled and pressed her fingers tighter. Captivated, she gladly encircled him. She'd never felt anything like it before, so soft and warm, yet so solid and alive. She kissed and licked just the tip of him before he gave a strangled choke and reared up to roll her beneath him.

"No more, Audrey!" he gasped.

He kissed her soundly and then raised his head, looking into her eyes. "I need you again, baby." He grinned. "Let's see if I can last longer than eight seconds this time." He brought his lips back to hers and pushed into her with one long, sensuous stroke.

Audrey felt the pressure building inside her with each thrust. The sharp ache between her legs intensified until his rhythmic pressure pushed her over the edge.

Mark watched with pure male pride as her whole body tightened and she practically bucked him off. But he held on tight and thrust one more time. Burying his face in her neck, he stiffened and stilled, enjoying the lingering sensations. He whispered her name before relaxing against her, exhaling a long sigh.

Before Mark fell asleep, he waited to hear her say that she loved him again. A teardrop hit his forehead. He lifted his head. "Did I hurt you?"

She smiled and tightened her arms around his neck. "No. It's just that, you *smiled!*"

He shook his head, puzzled. "You say that like it was some miraculous event. My smilin' makes you cry?"

She chuckled, and rolled her eyes at him, pushing his head back onto her shoulder. "Oh, never mind." She gave a big sigh as he pulled her close to snuggle.

He laid his head on her chest and drifted off to sleep.

Twelve

The sun was just creeping past the horizon when Audrey slowly opened her eyes. She knew she should get up, shower and start breakfast, but she wasn't ready to step back into reality yet. She wanted this dream to last just a few more minutes. To relish all the details in her mind.

Waking up wrapped in Mark's warm, strong arms, hearing his heartbeat as she lay with her head on his chest, smelling his unique odor, her naked skin touching his from head to toe, was true bliss. She'd remember last night forever. And Mark's beautiful smile.

He stirred beside her and kissed the top of her head. "Mmm, I haven't slept this good since I quit drinkin'," he mumbled.

I guess that was kind of romantic.

"I wish I didn't have to get up. I love lyin' in your arms, darlin'." He rolled her over and kissed her thoroughly.

Now, that was more like it! She met his tongue with her own and heard him moan softly. His male scent, his hard body, even the rough scratch of his morning stubble, intensified the ache of all her lonely mornings to come.

"I want you," he whispered into her throat.

"Mmm, I really should get breakfast started." But she said it halfheartedly, even as she wrapped her legs over his. A twinge of pain shot through her thigh muscles. She was sore in places this morning she didn't know a person could be sore in, but it didn't stop her from wanting him again. Did Mark's bad leg ache, too?

Mark groaned and slipped inside her.

One more time, then he really would have to get going. He'd loved waking up with her draped across his chest, her breasts pressed against him. He could spend all day with her in his arms, even if his leg was cramping up. She ran her fingers through his hair and down his back, and he had to suppress the urge to push into her hand like a cat craving a rub.

"Mark, is this hurting your leg?"

Mark stilled in midthrust. Why had she asked him that? Had he favored his injured leg last night and not realized it? Was she feeling sorry for the poor crip? Trying to get a glimpse of the freak's mutilated leg? No. Audrey wouldn't do that to him.

"Mark?" She sounded worried. "I'm sorry. You don't have to talk about it, okay?"

"Uh, yeah. I mean, no. I—you're right. It's getting late. I've got chores to see to." He refused to look at her as he rolled off and scooted to the edge of the bed. He reached for his underwear and jeans and slipped them on.

He'd completely forgotten about his leg after he'd made love with Audrey. All he'd cared about was tasting her and pleasuring her. Feeling her skin against his. What was the matter with him?

Muttering to himself, he located his shirt and grabbed his boots. As he reached the door, the silence hit him. He turned around and glanced at her.

She looked so beautiful with her hair falling over her shoulders and the sheet outlining her magnificent breasts. He expected anger, screaming, accusations. She was scowling—or trying to. But what he saw in her eyes was pain and embarrassment.

What the hell could he say? *I don't want your pity?* He didn't want to bring it up. Not with Audrey.

"I…uh…"

He cleared his throat and tried again. "I—"

"It's getting late. We've both got a lot to do today." She smiled, but it was a pretty dismal attempt. "So, if you wouldn't mind?" She actually made a little shooing motion with her hand.

She was shooing him out?

He knew she was only trying to save her pride. And who could blame her? He didn't want to leave it like this, but he had no idea what to say. This may have started as a physical need, a mutual attraction, but…she'd said she loved him.

He swallowed. "Audrey, last night was…"

"Yeah, um, me, too. I really need a shower before breakfast."

"Damn it, Audrey!" She was going to hear him out if he had to tape her mouth shut! He strode over to the bed, leaned down and took her face between his hands, forcing her to look at him.

"Just listen a minute! Last night was damn good and— aw, hell!" He grabbed her shoulders, pulled her up to her knees and took her mouth in a deep, passionate kiss.

Straightening slowly, he headed for the door. "I'll see you this afternoon."

When he turned back to look at her, she stared at him, her brow creased in confusion.

Mark's leg throbbed all day. Driving the tractor probably didn't help, but, as with riding Lone Star, he had something to prove. And his leg wasn't the only thing throbbing.

Right after dinner, he'd get things straight with Audrey. He couldn't keep his mind on work. Visions of last night brought phantom twinges of pleasure coursing through his body. Just thinking about her made his heart speed up. How perfect they'd been together. He'd never had a woman fill his thoughts so completely. He smiled as he remembered her whispered confession.

She'd said he didn't have to talk about his leg. So he wouldn't. He had some paperwork he really ought to finish, but to hell with that. He'd take Audrey to his room and make sure she was too occupied to think about anything but pleasure.

He ached to be with her right now. He didn't know when or how she'd become so important to him. She was interfering and stubborn and, damn it, he liked her that way! He grinned remembering how she'd poured his beer down the sink. And he'd been her first lover! His throat tightened up. He should feel guilty that she'd wasted her virginity on him. But he didn't. He reveled in the fact that she hadn't slept around.

Yet.

The thought of Audrey being with another man made him feel sick. But it was inevitable. The best he could hope for was a couple of weeks. Maybe a month. Would she stay that long?

He hoped so.

If someone had told him a couple of weeks ago that he'd want more than a good time with a woman, he'd have thought they'd landed on their head once too often. But now, he longed for it. Someone who wanted him, thought she loved him. Course, she didn't really love him, Mark Malone. She loved the *Lone Cowboy*. The legend. The hero. But he might as well enjoy it while it lasted.

"Mark! Watch out!" Jim shouted from his horse. He waved his hat in Mark's face as if he was hazing a calf.

Mark braked with his left foot, pulled his bandanna from his pocket and wiped his face. He'd almost run into Jim.

"You looked like you were in another world for a minute there. Still worried about the drought?"

"Uh, yeah." What else could he say? *No, I was dreaming of how Audrey's beautiful breasts overflow my palms.*

"Want me to finish up here?" Jim offered.

Mark realized he was rubbing his leg. He straightened and adjusted his hat. "No. See you back at the house."

"Nice meeting your brother yesterday." Jim turned his horse to ride away.

Mark nodded. Was it only yesterday he'd quarreled with Keith? Only last night he'd made Audrey his? Each incident seemed like a lifetime ago.

He shook himself. What was he doing sitting here mooning over the woman like a lovesick fool? The blazing afternoon sun must have given him heatstroke. He put the tractor in gear and tried to concentrate on planting grass seed.

With Devon gone for the day Audrey completed her tasks by rote, her mind lost in sensual memories and her heart crumbling like the top on the Dutch apple pie she'd prepared that day.

You will not cry, Audrey Alyse Tyson! You knew how it would be when you made your decision. You wanted the "experience," remember? And what an experience it had been.

She snapped green beans and heaved a big sigh. Making love with Mark was worth it. Even if the pain did equal the pleasure. For a little while, he'd been her magic mirror, reflecting a beautiful, alluring woman.

And she had made him smile!

No, she would never regret last night. She'd known all along that this was just a physical release for him. He probably made every woman he slept with feel special.

Why had she asked him about his leg? That was obviously a touchy subject. But after feeling so close to him last night, she'd longed to know all of him. His past, his dreams, his childhood... What had he said yesterday? Something about leaving Keith to fend for himself? Against whom? His mother? Well, she'd never know. Certainly Mark would never tell her.

That was the painful part—knowing he would never let her get really close to him. Lovers didn't just have sex; they shared the deepest part of themselves with each other. Or at least that's what Audrey thought they should do. But whenever she'd asked personal questions, he'd pushed her away.

Audrey was leaning into the fridge for lettuce when footsteps sounded behind her. She barely had time to turn before a masculine arm stole around her waist.

It wasn't Mark's arm.

Pete brought his other arm around her back and squeezed the breath from her lungs as he pressed her to him. "I'll show that damn crip he can't scare me off." His fetid breath offended Audrey's nostrils as he leaned over her and forced his mouth over hers. Struggling made no difference. She was cornered against the refrigerator, its door between her and the block of knives.

Finally, he came up for air. "I've been dreamin' of gettin' you naked ever since I saw you."

Audrey sucked in a short breath and turned her head, avoiding his persistent lips. "Pete, I can't breathe."

The minute he loosened his grip behind her back, she shoved hard.

Pete fell back and knocked into the table. His face contorted in rage. "You witch!" he roared, lunging for her throat.

Audrey made a dive to the right, hoping to reach the drawer containing the ice pick.

He captured her arms and pinned them behind her back.

Audrey kicked out behind her, hitting his shin, but Pete only tightened his arm around her waist. He grabbed her hair, yanked her head back and planted his wet lips on her neck. "Don't fight me, Audrey. You won't win."

Mark was still smiling when he drove the tractor into the shed and saw John heading his way.

John greeted him with a nod. "I'm glad you and Keith worked things out."

"Me, too. Hey, did you know he's getting married? I can't believe my little brother's fool enough to ask for that kind of grief." Mark held his hands up and smirked. "Uh, no offense to Helen."

Mark expected John to commiserate, but he gave him a serious look. "Marrying Helen was the best thing I ever did."

Mark shrugged. "I just hope he knows what he's gettin' himself into, that's all."

"What about you? You ever think about taking the bull by the horns?"

"Me? Hell, no!" John might as well have proposed he strip naked and run through the streets of Quitman.

John shook his head. "Well, I'm eatin' with my wife tonight. See you tomorrow."

And Mark was eating dinner with Audrey tonight.

After washing up at the bunkhouse, Mark headed for the kitchen, trying to tamp down his potent anticipation by reminding himself this was only temporary.

As he stepped in the back door, his heart stopped and all thoughts of seduction vanished.

Pete had Audrey cornered between the stove and refrigerator. He had one hand around her throat, the other behind her head, forcing his mouth on hers.

Audrey fought him, yanking on his hair, terror etched on her face.

Rage clouded his vision. He swung Pete around by the shoulder, reared back and punched him in the jaw.

Pete landed hard, several feet away, with a satisfying thud.

Mark wanted to wrap his hands around Pete's scrawny neck! "Get up, you bastard."

Pete stayed on the floor, his palms up. "She asked for it, man."

Mark blinked, clenching his fists to keep from dragging the punk up by his shirt and beating him to a bloody pulp. "I'll give you thirty seconds to get your butt off my property before I call the sheriff. You set foot on this ranch again, I'll make you wish you were dead."

Pete scrambled up, swiping the blood from his nose. He sneered as he kicked open the back door and strode off.

Mark turned to Audrey and she flew into his arms. "Did he hurt you, darlin'?" he whispered, pulling her close and stroking her tangled hair.

She buried her face in his chest. "N-no," she croaked.

Damn, she was shaking. He should have killed the son of a bitch. "I'm sorry, baby. I thought I'd made sure he wouldn't bother you. I'm calling Sheriff Townsend."

She clung to him tighter. "Don't let go!"

Despite his fear and rage, he smiled and moved his arms down her back, caressing, comforting. "I won't." He liked this feeling. Rescuer, protector, lover. She was his, and he'd do anything for her.

Pressed against him, he could feel her trembling breaths and the moisture on his shirt. "You sure you're okay? Where's Devon?"

She nodded, and the movement rubbed his shirt. "He's at the zoo with Helen."

He took her shoulders and leaned back to look into her eyes. "Pete won't bother you again, I promise."

Audrey gave him a wobbly smile and stepped from his arms. "I'm all right now." She moved to the stove, avoiding his gaze. Grabbing a towel, she opened the oven, pulled out a pie and put it on the counter.

Mark put his arms around her waist, brushing her cheek with his lips.

Audrey melted into his embrace. In his arms she was safe. If only she could stay this way forever.

She'd never been attacked before, never felt so threatened. Pete had been so strong. She'd like to think she'd have fought him off eventually, but the truth was, if Mark hadn't shown up, she wasn't sure.

All she knew was Mark had rescued her again, and she loved him, and she'd make love with him right here on the kitchen table if Jim and Dalt weren't due to show up for dinner any minute.

What was she thinking? She had to calm down and remember this morning's resolve. One night was a special memory. Anything more and her hard won self-respect would be chipped away a little each day. He'd tire of her, or find out who she was. She couldn't go there. She moved to start setting the table.

Desire radiated from him as he stalked her across the kitchen. His eyes held a determined glint and his hands flexed at his sides.

She held her hands in front of her in a feeble attempt to ward him off. They met his hard chest, and she could feel his heart beating double-time. He captured her hands and kept them pressed to his chest while he lowered his mouth to hers.

No! She turned her head at the last moment. She'd never let him go if she started kissing him now. "Don't you want to eat?"

"Yeah, I'm starving." He gave her a wicked grin.

His grin immobilized her. She still wasn't used to seeing him smile. She leaned her forehead against his chest. Even his sweat smelled sexy.

He raised his hand to her cheek and lifted her face. "Embarrassed? After last night?" Enfolding her in his powerful arms, he kissed her tenderly. "I know Pete frightened you, but I would never hurt you," he mumbled against her lips.

"Mark."

The next kiss was deeper, possessive. "I've wanted you all day, darlin'."

She pushed against his chest and he loosened his hold. "I don't think this is a good idea."

He stiffened and dropped his arms. "What are you talking about? What's the matter?"

She mustered up her courage and looked him in the eye. That muscle in his jaw was working overtime. She sighed heavily. "Sit down, okay? I need you to listen."

"I don't need to sit down. I am listening."

The sound of the hands' boots stomping on the back porch promptly ended any discussion. Dinnertime. Audrey was relieved, but Mark cursed under his breath as she rushed to put plates and silverware on the table.

Mark crossed his arms in front of his chest. "This isn't over."

After dinner, Mark decided he'd had enough. Audrey acted as if he had mad cow disease. Had Pete scared her that much? She had to know *he'd* never force her.

Mark stalked into the kitchen and grabbed a towel. The sooner the dishes were done, the sooner they could…talk.

But while he was drying the last pot, she slipped past him and out of the kitchen. He followed her and caught her halfway up the stairs. He grabbed her hand and stopped her on the stairs. "Not so fast. You want to explain what you meant earlier?"

"No, not particularly. Devon's waiting for me to tuck him in." She tugged at her hand, but he hauled her to him and held her close.

"I already did. He's fast asleep." He liked her standing a step above him. He didn't have to lean down to capture her mouth. Closing his eyes, he breathed in her lemony scent. "Talk to me, Audrey. Tell me why you don't want this." His lips lingered on hers.

She pushed away from him. "Please, Mark. I can't think when you're this close."

"Good. Don't think." He tightened his arms and brushed his lips over the sexy little spot below her ear.

"Mark, I can't do this."

"Why not?"

"I'm leaving in two days. Let's just forget it."

"Forget, hell!" He took a couple of deep breaths to calm himself.

He was determined to persuade her. After sleeping in her arms last night, his bed would seem lonely without her. He'd meant what he'd said that morning. Peace had filled his soul, and he hadn't slept so deeply since—well, never. He knew he'd rushed things the first time, but he'd made sure she had her pleasure. So what was the problem?

Leaning down, he spoke softly in her ear. "Are you gonna forget how it feels when I'm inside you? How I made you shiver and beg for more? 'Cause I sure as hell can't forget the way your nipples tighten when I kiss you, and the feel of your hands all over me. Just be with me to-night, honey, and quit thinkin' things to death." He licked her lobe and spread gentle kisses down her jaw to her throat, persuading with his lips and tongue.

Audrey lost her breath and her resolve with his sensu-ous murmurings. His hands pushed her hips into his, and his mouth captured hers. His tongue swept in and out, raising little chill bumps on her arms and behind her neck. She succumbed to Mark's overpowering persuasion. In-stead of pushing him away, she whimpered and ran her hands down his chest and around his waist.

He groaned and covered her breast with his palm.

That action brought her back to reality. Somehow, she summoned the strength to tear her mouth away. If she could just resist for one more day, Danny would be home from the hospital.

"No, I can't do this." Pushing away, she headed up the stairs. "Good night, Mark."

He caught up to her on the landing and grabbed her wrist. "What kind of game are you playin'?"

Audrey twisted from his grasp. "This was all a mistake. I'm not who you think I am." She clamped her hands over her mouth.

Tense silence hung in the air. Amazingly, Mark looked more bewildered than suspicious. "What do you mean?"

How could she tell him the truth after last night? What would he think of her? She chickened out, looked at the floor. "Never mind."

"What do you mean, never mind? What the hell are you sayin'?"

She panicked. Her mind scrambled for something to tell him that would scare him off, make him drop it. A half-truth. "Mark, I just can't have an affair. I would want more. I want a home of my own and kids and everything. And you don't want that." Then, piteously hopeful, she added, "Do you?"

Mark looked appalled. "Kids? Hell, no!"

Audrey flinched at his outburst. Had she even dared to hope he would want something permanent with her? He could have the most beautiful women in Texas at his fingertips, probably already had. The humiliation was unbearable, the rejection excruciating. This time he didn't prevent her from retreating to her bedroom...alone.

Thirteen

Audrey leaned against a leafy oak and quietly observed Mark and Devon in the corral. The famous cowboy coached the small boy with calm words and infinite patience. Along with her special night, she folded this precious memory and stored it in her heart to pull out in the years to come.

His large hand gently stroked the pony's nose, and she remembered how it felt sliding over her skin, cupping her breast. She shivered.

Devon laughed and brought her mind back to the present. The little boy held the reins tightly, as Mark taught him how to control the pony with verbal commands.

"Whoa, Little Star," Devon called to the black pony he'd been allowed to name.

"Ready for cookies and lemonade?" Audrey called from the yard. Not that she expected Mark to come in. After last night, things could only be awkward between them. He'd probably avoid her now. She'd known he didn't love her, but that cruel reality didn't stop her heart from breaking.

She hurried back into the house, though she knew they'd be another fifteen minutes or more. Mark would make sure Devon helped rub down and feed Little Star. "A cowboy always takes care of his horse." Devon had solemnly quoted Mark's words to her with a grown-up expression on his small face.

She removed the jug of lemonade from the refrigerator and took some cups from the cabinet. Pulling the tray from the oven, she transferred cookies to a ceramic platter. She heard Mark on the back porch, quietly instructing Devon to wipe his boots. Her stomach did a somersault. Would he join them?

"Aunt Audey, did you see me riding?" Devon shouted as he clambered onto a kitchen chair.

Mark stayed by the door, taking in the beautiful sight of Audrey in a green-checkered apron, pouring glasses of lemonade.

Homemade oatmeal cookies. They smelled good. Seeing the little boy reach for a cookie reminded him of when he and Keith were kids and their Mom would lock them outside. Helen would ask them in and feed them cookies and chocolate milk. He could still picture the terrified look on Keith's face when their mom yelled at them from across the yard to get their butts home.

His stomach ached, but he didn't think eating would help. God, he'd missed Audrey last night. Couldn't sleep for thinking about what she'd said. He'd pictured her with a big, rounded stomach, or nursing a baby. Pictured himself holding a little blond-haired girl who called him "Daddy." For the first time in his life, he'd actually allowed himself to consider the possibility.

But then he'd remembered him and Keith hiding from their mother's wrath, and the belt she used when she caught them. That stopped him cold. No way would he bring a kid into this world. No woman was that trustworthy. Audrey was pretty good with her nephew, but he was temporary. How would she handle a permanent responsibility? More importantly, how would he?

You can't have that, Malone. You can't risk it. A sharp pain sliced through his midsection.

He took off his hat, hung it on a wall peg and wiped his forehead on his sleeve. Then he stepped up to the table and grabbed a cookie from the platter. What was he doing? He should turn around and get the hell out of there. *It's over. You knew that last night. Quit torturing yourself like this.*

But his legs wouldn't move. And he couldn't take his eyes off her.

When Audrey looked at him, he mumbled, "Oatmeal's my favorite."

Her eyes burned into his from across the table. "I know." She dropped her gaze and smoothed her apron over her hips. "Helen told me."

He stood, mesmerized, yearning for her touch, craving a dream. Remembering.

Devon pulled the platter close to him to grab another cookie. It tipped over the edge and crashed to the floor.

"Oh, Devon! No!" Audrey reached for the little boy.

Before she could get to him, Mark scooped him up and held him away from her. "Don't you dare touch him!" he yelled, rage pumping through his veins. "It was just an accident!"

A tense silence hung over the room like a ghostly presence spreading cold and gloom.

Mark blinked as the haze cleared from his eyes. Oh, God. What had he done?

Devon was shaking, his eyes wide and trained on him.

Audrey's brows were crinkled, her eyes filled with bewilderment…and pity. Finally, she said quietly, "I only wanted to get him away from the glass so he wouldn't cut himself."

Mark choked and dragged in a ragged breath, trying to control the trembling that had taken over his body. He set the boy down and turned his back on her, cursing as his mind reeled. He'd made a damn fool of himself. She'd never look at him without pity again.

She was soothing the boy and sending him to the den to watch television. A moment later, she touched Mark's arm.

"Mark, I hope you know I would never, ever, hurt a child."

"Yeah." He couldn't say any more or she'd hear his voice shaking. And he refused to turn around and look at her. Without a backward glance, he slammed out the back door.

Mark didn't return that evening. With a certainty beyond her understanding, Audrey knew she must find him, and she knew exactly what she would say.

After dinner, Audrey sought out Ruth in the bunkhouse. Jim was just coming in. "Can either of you tell me where I might find Mark?"

Ruth shrugged. "Well, there's only two bars—er…" She looked at Jim.

Jim stuck his hands in his jeans pockets and shrugged. "Try the Texas Rose first."

"Will you two watch Devon this evening? I—I need to talk to him."

"Sure." Jim's mischievous grin returned. "I'll teach him to play Go Fish!"

Audrey looked back at Ruth. "Where's Dalt?"

Ruth shrugged. "We were both ready for greener pastures."

Before she left, Audrey settled Devon at the card table in the dining room with Ruth and Jim and then headed out for Helen and John's place. At the last minute, she came back and grabbed Mark's Stetson off the peg in the kitchen.

He wasn't with John and Helen, so she got back in her hatchback and drove into Quitman. It was a small enough town. Hopefully, he hadn't gone into Tyler.

He wasn't at the Texas Rose, either. She found his truck parked in front of Sam's. The place was empty except for a couple of grungy-looking older men in the back. The stench of cigarettes and booze hung thickly in the air, and a television blared from one corner of the ceiling.

She stepped farther in and saw Mark leaning against the bar, hands clenched around a tumbler of golden liquid. A dark lock of hair curled down his forehead. He stared into his glass as if contemplating drowning in it.

Audrey closed her eyes and took a deep breath, then focused her gaze. As she walked toward him, time slowed, her surroundings blurred, her heartbeat thrummed in her ears.

"You forgot your hat." She set his black Stetson on the bar in front of her.

He turned on her, teeth bared like a rabid dog. "Get that out of here."

Audrey forced a swallow past the lump in her throat. She straightened her back and squared her shoulders. "Why?"

Mark shoved the full tumbler across the counter, splashing the alcohol. "I haven't taken a drink, if that's what you're worried about. Save your preaching for someone else."

How long had he been staring at that glass? He must have wanted to drink so badly. But he hadn't. Her eyes stung with tears but she blinked them away. "If you're not drinking anyway, come home with me. I mean...come back to the Double M."

His eyes flared wide and then squinted in menace. "Get the hell out of here before I do something we'll both regret. You better run on back to Dallas, little Miss Innocent."

Audrey smiled and shook her head. "You would never hurt me, or any woman."

His menacing snarl faded into a miserable frown. "What makes you so sure?"

Drawing a deep breath for courage, Audrey said, "Come with me, and I'll tell you."

Agonizing minutes went by while he stared at her. He dropped his gaze and then closed his eyes. "Go away, Audrey." He didn't move or open his eyes. "Please." He spoke the last word on a deep sigh.

"I'm not leaving without you. If you come with me, I'll tell you a secret about me."

His head jerked up and he narrowed his eyes at her. "What? You got a ticket for jaywalking? You voted for Ross Perot?"

She heaved a sigh, pulled up a stool and sat down. "You rescued a young girl once. Do you remember?"

Mark's gaze traveled down her body and back to her eyes. "What?"

Audrey stared at the scarred wooden counter, that long-ago night as vivid as this moment. "You'd just won your first championship. You came into Lone Star's stall. There was a fat girl, cornered by some drunken bullies."

Mark went still. "That was you," he whispered.

She looked into his eyes. "Yes."

"Damn." He lurched away and left the bar, his face creased in bewildered pain.

Tears stung her eyes as she jumped off the stool and followed. She'd hoped to make him see that he wasn't the only one with a painful past. Had she said the wrong thing...again? She pushed out the door.

It was still light, but the sun was almost down and the building cast dark shadows. She could barely see him as he strode down the gravel parking lot. She caught his arm. "Where are you going?"

He yanked away. "Go back to the ranch, Audrey. Don't waste your time. I'm not worth it." He turned and headed for the field behind the bar.

She might not have had the red hair of her father and younger sister, but she had just as much Tyson stubbornness. Setting her jaw, she ran back for his hat and then set out after him.

Even at a brisk pace, it took her a few minutes to catch up to his long stride. When she did, he rounded on her, grabbed her upper arms and shook her.

"I don't need your pity," he said through gritted teeth.

Audrey set her hands at her waist. "Pity? I just told you about the most embarrassing moment in my life, and you walked away. I was trying to tell you how much I admire you. To remind you of all the wonderful—"

Mark cursed, dropped his hands and stalked off across the field.

It was getting dark. Audrey raced after him, grabbed him around the waist from behind and held on tight. "Don't leave."

His chest expanded and Audrey almost lost her grip.

Then he gave a heavy sigh and turned in her arms. He reached behind himself, grabbed the hat from her fingers and flung it across the grassy meadow. As he looked back at her, he grasped her shoulders and gently pushed her away. "It wasn't me that saved you that night."

Shock coursed through her body. "What are you talking about?"

"That was the *Lone Cowboy*. I'd just come off the high of riding that bull and winning that buckle. I could do anything, be anything when I was rodeoing. But that's not who I really am. I tried. I put that hat back on and tried to be him again these last couple of weeks, but I was bound to mess up eventually."

Audrey raised her eyes to the stars sparkling in the night sky, and knew she must take the ultimate risk. She stepped close and put her hands on his chest. "Mark, I don't love the *Lone Cowboy*. I love you."

He gripped her wrists and yanked them away. "You don't know me. I'm no hero."

Audrey framed his face and rose on tiptoe to gently kiss his stubbled cheek, wanting to soothe the anguish she saw blazing in his eyes. "Tell me, then, why I shouldn't love you."

She could feel his jaw clench beneath her palms, and his temples were damp with sweat under her fingertips.

"You're one stubborn woman!" He pulled away and turned his back to her.

She stepped in front of him, but he turned his head and squeezed his eyes shut. "You don't understand. You don't know."

She swallowed. "Then help me understand."

Mark drew in a shuddering breath, his whole body trembling.

Audrey couldn't stand to see him like this. But she remained silent.

"I don't remember my father ever being drunk. So we never had any warning. He was stone-cold sober and, wham, out of the blue, he'd let Mom have it. And then she'd take it out on us. But I had my revenge.

"I was ten when I'd finally had enough. I knew Mom had boyfriends, 'cause she used to take me with her to use as her alibi. Then, I told Dad about Mom's little secret—that he wasn't Keith's real father." Mark stopped and wiped his sleeve across his eyes. He made a choking sound and his hand shook as he rubbed the back of it across his mouth.

"He beat her so bad she was in the hospital for weeks. He went to prison, and I never saw him again."

Oh, Mark. Audrey closed the distance between them and placed her hand on his back. "Mark, you were just a kid. You were too young to understand the consequences."

Audrey gathered him into her arms, but he remained stiff.

"Some hero, huh? You still think you love me?"

Though she couldn't stop the tears that ran down her cheeks, she looked into his eyes with a calm certainty. "Yes, Mark. I love you."

"No." He shook his head.

"I love the man who would never raise his hand to a woman, even when he's got a raging hangover and she pours his beer down the sink.

"I love the man who throws a poker game so a scared virgin won't have to have sex because of a bet."

"How did—"

"I love the man who used his jet to help his housekeeper's sister."

He crushed her to him and kissed the top of her head.

"I love the tender man who bought a little boy a pony and taught him to ride."

Mark groaned as he fell to one knee and pushed her down to the soft bed of grass, ravishing her mouth with a harsh kiss. He couldn't get her shirt off fast enough.

Audrey let him undress her. He needed someone right now. Someone to hold him tight and love him, no matter what.

And she needed him.

He palmed her breasts and sucked each nipple in turn before kissing his way back to her mouth. His lips journeyed frantically down her neck to her breasts again, but soon returned to devour her mouth with a low groan.

With her help, he pulled her jeans off. Audrey held him close and returned his kisses.

Mark freed his rigid member and pushed into her. He couldn't begin to fathom the depths of the longing that threatened to swallow him. He simply let it wash over him as he buried his face in her neck, pumped into her and whispered her name over and over.

With her legs wrapped around him, her hand running through his hair and her scent permeating his nostrils, he was surrounded by Audrey and her love. Keeping the world at bay, he was safe for one moment. For one moment, as his body tightened and his passion spilled out, he couldn't think. He could only feel…soft, safe, free, good, whole, loved.

Fourteen

She loved him. Audrey had said she loved him, Mark Malone. The thought consumed him. She knew the worst of it, and she loved him anyway. She had cried. No woman had ever cried for him.

He rode out to the north pasture, but he knew he wouldn't get any work done today. Devon was leaving, and Mark wished he'd taken the day off and gone with Audrey to take him home. That way, he'd have her all to himself on the plane ride home.

If he hurried, he could still make it. He turned Lone Star around and galloped him home.

When he came into the kitchen, she wasn't there. He stopped in the dining room and saw her standing at the open front door, surrounded by suitcases. Too many just for Devon.

She hugged her nephew and sent him off with Dalt to say goodbye to the pony.

As Mark watched her, his scarred heart took a tumble off a bucking bronc, and the hard shell he'd built around it cracked like the bones he'd broken in his rodeo days. She couldn't leave him now.

He wanted to hold her. After only a few hours, he missed the feel of her in his arms. But he wanted more. He wanted to hear her say she loved him again. Every day. And he wanted to tell her he loved her, too.

Where had that come from? He loved her?

Did he?

Yes, a tiny voice whispered. And he knew it was true.

He watched Audrey wave her nephew off and step away from the front door. "Mr. Burke! What are you doing here?"

Mr. Burke? Who the hell was Mr. Burke?

A hefty man in an expensive suit pushed his way past Audrey and strutted in, looking around. "So this is the *Lone Cowboy*'s house, huh? You better have a good story for the magazine after all this time."

The word *magazine* echoed and pounded into Mark's brain. Something snapped inside him. His chest constricted and he couldn't breathe. She was a reporter? *All she'd ever wanted was a story?* What a fool he'd been, thinking Audrey was different! His stomach cramped. He couldn't see. Must be sweat—it sure as hell wasn't tears—in his eyes.

How she must've been laughing her butt off these past weeks. The pitiful drunk who fell for the little schemer.

"About the article," Audrey began as she closed the front door. She turned to face the pompous man, looked past his shoulder and met Mark's eyes. "Oh, no!"

If she didn't get out of here right now, Mark was going to wrap his hands around her lying neck and strangle her. "Get out!" he yelled. "Both of you! Now!"

Audrey came toward him, her hand outstretched. "Oh, Mark. It's not what you think. Please let me explain. I...I never meant to hurt anyone."

She lifted her hand as if she might touch his arm.

He flinched and jerked away. "Don't."

She was so convincing in her apologetic role. She'd probably rehearsed in case she got caught.

He crossed his arms, making sure he stared at her full-figured hips. "We both got what we wanted."

Audrey recoiled as if she'd been physically slapped, and all the color drained from her face. She swayed as if she might faint, staggering to catch herself.

"Now get out!" Mark yelled.

She didn't even look to see if the man followed her when she raced out the front door, choking on a sob.

Burke—Audrey's boss, he assumed—stared at him.

Mark's fist curled and he took a step toward him.

The man snapped into motion and followed Audrey out.

Mark slammed the door, wiped his eyes and staggered to the recliner. Everything hurt. He dropped to the edge of the chair, doubled over with the pain. He couldn't catch a breath.

Just thinking about his private life being plastered all over the front page of some tabloid made him want a drink. Mark had to warn his brother. And, hell, he'd have to talk to his mother, too. Once the story broke, more reporters would come snooping around.

His mother would enjoy that. She and Audrey ought to get together and compare notes. Start a consulting business on how to be a deceitful shrew.

Maybe he'd sell this ranch, after all. Move to a different state. But first, he had to do what he'd sworn he would never do.

Go home.

* * *

Danny was home, and over the infection. He and Claire were glad to see Devon again, and there were hugs of greeting all around. But Audrey didn't stay long. Telling them she was exhausted, she kissed them all goodbye and drove to her apartment.

She was resigned to whatever her fate might be with the magazine. Her heart was breaking. What was her career compared to that?

Though she'd known it would end eventually, she'd savored the fantasy. Her last night at the Double M had been the sweetest torment. Being in Mark's arms, loving him one last time. They'd clung to each other for a while and then gotten dressed. He'd walked her to her car and driven her back to the ranch, all without saying a word.

She hadn't expected him to return her love. But she hated that he'd discovered her deceit. Now he'd never believe she loved him. A stab of pain hit her heart at that thought.

The next morning, she began her new job dispensing advice to troubled lovers. What a joke. For the first time in her life, Audrey lost her appetite. As diets go, this had to be the most excruciating way to lose weight. Over the next couple of weeks, she had to force herself to eat. Not even chocolate could coax her into caring about her life.

It took all her emotional strength just to wake up and face each day. All she wanted to do was curl up on her couch and stay blessedly numb. She'd come so close to a dream she'd never hoped to live, and deceived a man who had been betrayed once too often.

"Come on, Aud," Miranda cajoled, sitting next to her sister on the couch. "Let's go shopping. Claire's in-laws are in town to watch Devon, and I need a new suit."

After two weeks of her moping around, Audrey's sisters had shown up, determined to coax her out of the blues.

"Audrey, you're pale, you have dark circles under your eyes and your hair looks like a rat's nest. Now get off your butt and take a shower. You're coming with us!"

Three hours and three makeovers later, the sisters sat down in the mall for some frozen yogurt.

"Now." Claire looked determined as she scooped up her yogurt. "Tell us what happened. What happened with the story? Did you get it or not?"

Audrey opened her mouth, but no words would come. How to explain? She realized she'd never shared her feelings with her sisters, believing it was her job to listen and advise, not burden them with her insecurities. Perhaps she wouldn't be in this mess if she'd gone to them in the first place. In that moment, her perception shifted and so did their relationship. She wasn't alone.

"Come on, Audrey. Spill it," Miranda said.

Claire grasped her shoulder, her brows furrowed in concern. "We're really worried about you."

Audrey shook her head. She was so ashamed. "I've ruined everything!" The look on her sisters' faces changed from concern to disbelief as she told them what she'd done.

Claire put her hand over Audrey's. "You love the cowboy?"

Audrey nodded.

Miranda spoke up. "You should be glad you're rid of that redneck. He'd only end up hurting you. Believe me!"

Audrey exchanged a shocked look with Claire. She turned to Miranda, frowning. "Randa, has something happened between you and Ron?"

Miranda sat back in her chair. "Never mind, Aud. I just don't like seeing you so upset. If you're so miserable, you should at least print the story you wrote and get something from the experience."

Audrey let the subject of Miranda's boyfriend go for now. She nodded, thinking about what she'd written. "I should apologize." She straightened in her chair. "I wonder if he'd see it...." she mumbled. She'd send a copy to John and Helen.

"What?" Claire asked.

"The story of how I deceived a good man," she answered, warming to the idea. It beat lying around feeling sorry for herself.

Mr. Burke might just go for a story about her experience undercover.

Miranda protested, "Audrey, you don't have to do that. Don't humiliate yourself that way."

Much as she appreciated Randa's concern, her sister didn't understand. This was not a pathetic attempt to gain a man's attention. "I'm not doing it for him. I'm doing it for me. I need to regain my honor. I was so desperate for...I don't know, something significant in my life, I convinced myself that the end justified the means." For the first time in two weeks, Audrey smiled, feeling a paradigm shift in her self-esteem. "I'm going to do what I should have done all along." She swallowed a bite of frozen yogurt. "Be myself."

When Audrey talked to Mr. Burke the next day, he gladly agreed. As a publicity stunt, it couldn't be beat.

The following week, Audrey hunched over her laptop around the clock. If she hadn't been writing on a PC, her bedroom would have been filled with thousands of crumpled pieces of paper. Considering she aspired to be a writer, one would think a story this personal would be child's play. But every attempt was deleted. Somehow, the words didn't sound right. They just weren't magic enough to convey her feelings.

Maybe mere words couldn't. Maybe she needed action.

"You seen this month's copy of *Dallas Today?*" John shoved the magazine under Mark's nose.

Mark was eating cold soup from a can while he watched the late news. It was after ten, and he'd just gotten in from the barn, where he'd been checking tack.

How many weeks, or months even, would it take for him to forget her? In every room in the house, Mark saw her. He woke in the middle of the night hot and hard, missing Audrey's soft breasts cushioning his head, aching for her touch—if he managed to sleep at all. He lay for hours envisioning the love in her eyes and the heat in her kisses. How could she have faked that kind of passion? It had felt so real, so strong.

What he should do was find another woman. A brunette. Maybe then he could forget.

His mood reflected the lack of sleep, and the hours of frustration. He impatiently barked out orders, working later and later each day. He knew he'd put off seeing his mom. He should've gone weeks ago, but just thinking about it made his stomach ache. He shoved the magazine back without looking. "How bad is it?"

"Oh, I think you'll wanna read this for yourself." John tossed the magazine in Mark's lap.

Well, damn. Had he really hoped she might have a scrap of principle? He should've been surprised it'd taken this long for the story to come out.

Mark forced his eyes open and read the caption: *Big Brothers to Benefit from Reporter's Blunder.*

"What the hell? What is this, John?"

John had a smug smirk on his face. "Read it."

"This would-be journalist made a horrible mistake. To get the scoop on a reclusive rodeo legend, I posed as a housekeeper on his ranch, the Double M.

I thought I'd meet a legend, write his story and ride off into the sunset. But Mark Malone is more than just a handsome cowboy with a bunch of gold buckles.

For two weeks, I had the privilege of getting to know the real *Lone Cowboy.* He's an honorable, generous man who's overcome obstacles that would make most men give up. But I was there under false pretenses and I regret betraying his trust.

As a gesture of my sincerity, I will be helping to raise money for Big Brothers and Big Sisters of America, the association Mark Malone spent so much of his time and money sponsoring over the years.

A fund-raiser will be held next Saturday, and I, personally, will be sitting on the platform at the dunking booth. So, come help a worthy cause…."

The article went on to give information on the date, place and time of the benefit.

Mark sat in stunned silence, disgusted with himself because all he could do at first was picture Audrey in a wet T-shirt, her nipples hard from the cold water. He was gonna need another cold shower tonight. "Damn it, she probably planned it that way."

"Of course she did. The question is, what are you going do about it?"

Mark jerked his gaze to John. "Nothing! She's not going to make a fool of me twice."

"Fool? She's tryin' to apologize."

Mark frowned at the magazine in his lap. "She's probably hoping I'll show up so she can have another story."

"You *are* a fool if you think that. She told Helen right before Keith came that she'd decided not to write a story about you, even if it meant losing her job."

Mark stood, ignoring the spark of hope those words had ignited and concentrating on John's betrayal. "You knew who she was? Why didn't you tell me?"

"Don't get your balls in a brace. Helen just told me last week. She thought it best not to interfere. She hoped, in time— Well, it doesn't matter now."

"I can understand how Audrey had you two suckered. It's myself I'm disgusted with. I knew better than to believe any woman could lo—" He stopped.

John finished his sentence. "Could love you? Don't you think it's possible she really does?"

Mark remembered Audrey whispering her love for him that first time, boldly proclaiming it the next. His chest constricted, and fury welled up in him.

He fought to keep his features blank. "I can do without her kind of love."

"Not all women are like your mother, Mark," John persisted.

Mark looked at the floor and hooked his thumbs in his pockets. "Maybe."

John folded his arms across his chest. "You've survived bulls and broncs, broken bones, a busted leg and booze. Don't you think you could handle the love of a good woman?"

Mark snorted. "There's no such thing. Not nowadays."

Fifteen

The drab little house on the north side of Fort Worth was even shabbier than Mark remembered. Keith had offered to go with him, but this was something he needed to do alone.

He parked his truck across the street and sat there for almost an hour, contemplating what he was about to do. He gripped the steering wheel like a lifeline, praying for the strength to get through this meeting with his mother.

She opened the door after the first knock—as if she'd been expecting someone. Her face was heavily made up, but he could still see the deep lines around her mouth, drooping bags under her eyes and sallow skin that declared a life of hard living. Her pantsuit was skintight on her still slim but sagging body, and she wore the same type of large, dangling earrings and bleached-blond hairdo he remembered from his childhood.

"If you're lookin' for Dudley, he ain't here," she snapped, a lit cigarette hanging from her bright red lips.

Mark swallowed hard. "Hello, Mama."

She leaned forward, squinted and peered closely for a few seconds. With her first and middle finger, she grabbed the cigarette from her mouth, leaned that same hand in the doorway and smiled, revealing yellowed smoker's teeth.

"I knew you'd come crawling back someday."

Mark's jaw hardened, his hands in tight fists at his side. "Can I come in?"

"Sure, sure. Come on in." She led him back to the small, dirty kitchen, waved him to a chair and grabbed two beer bottles from the fridge. Setting one on the table in front of him, she stubbed out her cigarette and said, "Sit down and have a cold one."

Mark took off his hat and sat down. He moved the beer away and put his hat on the table in front of him. The stench of stale beer, cigarettes and cheap perfume flooded his senses and unearthed long-repressed childhood memories. His throat was as dry as trail dust, and he couldn't seem to force any words past his lips.

"So? Whaddaya want? You ain't cuttin' me off, are ya? 'Cause I need that money." She plopped in a chair and lit another cigarette.

"No. You'll still get your money."

"Well? What is it then? Keith send you over here?" she sneered, and took a drag on her cigarette.

A small smile curved his lips. "In a way."

"Well, you can just tell him to keep his damn psycho-babble to himself! Thinks he's better than everybody 'cause he's getting some fancy-ass degree!" She took another drag.

Keith had warned him, but still, Mark shook his head in disgust. "You oughta feel lucky somebody cares enough to worry about you! Don't you ever think about anybody but yourself?"

She jumped from her chair and leaned across the table, hand raised, ready to strike. "Don't you talk to me that way, boy. I'm still your mother!"

Mark remembered when fear of her temper would make him stiffen in terror. But he'd learned to hide that terror with the same mask of indifference he hoped he displayed right now. He didn't move a muscle except to narrow his eyes. He wasn't scared, he wasn't even angry anymore. All he felt was a profound pity. What had Audrey said? *What a waste of a life.*

Like lightning in a summer storm, the truth hit him. It wasn't his fault. Audrey was right. He'd just been a young kid whose mother beat the crap out of him until one night he'd had enough. At ten years old, he couldn't have predicted the horrible consequences of his actions.

All these years he'd believed if he'd been smarter, or stronger, or worked harder, his parents wouldn't have gotten mad, would have loved him and Keith. If he hadn't told on his mom, they could have been a real family. But he saw now, it didn't matter.

It was like he'd been walking through life carrying a saddle on each shoulder. And now he tossed them off. He was free and the past no longer had power over him.

When she got no reaction from him, his mother sat down, breathing heavily and trembling, wariness in her eyes. "Dudley's gonna be home any minute! You better get out of here."

Mark leaned back. "I came to ask a favor. Some reporters might show up, askin' about me. I don't want you talkin' to 'em."

Her eyes widened in surprise. "Reporters? I don't

know," she said slyly. "What if they make me an offer I can't refuse?"

Mark took the hint. "How much?"

She smiled. "A couple of thousand oughta do me."

Mark slid his wallet from his back pocket and pulled out two hundred-dollar bills. "Here's a down payment. I'll have my business manager write you a check for the rest. If they offer you more, I'll double it."

She sneered and stubbed out her cigarette. "Think you can buy whatever you want now that you're so famous and all?"

Mark smiled sadly. He'd been wrong all these years. He'd been wrong about Audrey, too.

"What I needed, I got for free." He grabbed his hat and headed for his truck.

Audrey dipped her fingers in the tank of cold water, and a chill shot up her spine. She stood behind the dunking booth, tugging down the hem of the oversize Big Brothers T-shirt that covered her from neck to knees—for now, at least.

Underneath she wore only her one-piece swimsuit. It helped that her father and Miranda were there to show their support, but all she could think about was that once the T-shirt was off and the suit was wet, she might as well be naked.

All they needed was a patron to hand over his five dollars for three baseballs. Audrey was going to throw up. Her palms were sweaty, and her heart pounded in her chest.

But she had no regrets. Though she was nervous, she was also proud. A few months ago, she would never have been able to do something like this. Being with Mark might have cost her heart, but she was a stronger person for it. He'd seen her body and thought her beautiful, desirable. Never again would she sit on the sidelines while life passed her by. She had taken control.

Grudgingly, she acknowledged the irony of her situation. She hadn't taken a test yet, but she suspected she might be pregnant. She'd wanted to change her life, and that goal had certainly been accomplished.

Though she had moments of sheer terror, the thought of having a little chestnut-haired, blue-eyed boy or girl thrilled her. What would it be like to have a new life growing inside her?

"Hey, Toby! Here's that magazine woman. Let's dunk her!" The teenager, in baggy jeans and backward cap, handed the attendant five dollars and reached for his first baseball.

She reluctantly took off her T-shirt and stepped onto the dunking platform, shivering more from the humiliation of being so exposed than from the fear of being dunked.

"Aim good, Kyle!" the other teenager called.

"Piece of cake." The boy named Kyle raised his arm behind him.

Audrey squeezed her eyes shut. *This is a mistake. I can't do this. Everyone's staring at me!*

She heard a loud bang, but she didn't fall.

He'd missed! But he still had two more tries.

Another bang, another miss. This was too good to be true. Dare she hope?

"Hold it, son."

Audrey's eyes flew open. She froze like a marble statue, unable to speak or even breathe. He'd come. The black hat, the white shirt, the tight Wranglers. He looked like her hero from long ago.

"I'll donate five thousand dollars for a kiss from the lady."

Only now he was her tormentor.

The volunteer attendant whipped around to look at her, eyebrows raised, questioning. He did a double take at Mark. "Wait a minute. You're the *Lone Cowboy!* Can I have your autograph?"

Her father and Miranda shoved past the attendant, attempting to talk Mark out of his outrageous offer. Guess they thought she'd been humiliated enough. Both had the tempers to match their red hair. Miranda poked Mark in the chest, and her father raised his voice. Mark only stared at her saying nothing. The attendant and Kyle were yelling, and more people crowded around to see what the commotion was about.

Chaos ensued.

It was as if Audrey had been transported into some bizarre TV sitcom with no script. Fed up, she put her pinky fingers on either side of her mouth and whistled.

Instantly, silence reigned.

Audrey glared at Mark and climbed down from the platform. If he wanted a little extra revenge, so be it. She held his gaze as she approached. "Let's see the five thousand."

Mark reached into his jeans pocket, pulled out a wad of bills and slammed them on the booth's table. "Now, for my kiss."

Audrey scowled. Why was he doing this? Who cared? She threw her arms around his neck and smothered his mouth with hers.

Mark started to kiss her back, but pulled away, looking surprised.

Hah! She glared back at him. Did he think she'd cower and simper like a scared virgin? She wasn't that timid girl anymore. And she was through playing games. "I thought you wanted a kiss."

He stared at her a moment until a slow smile curved his lips. Then he took her face in his hands, bent close and kissed her back, long and deep.

Audrey heated and tingled under his sensual assault. His lips were firm and warm, and she drank him in like a tall glass of cool water after a day in the hot sun.

She opened her eyes when Mark slipped a hand under her knees and swung her up into his arms. She clutched his neck. "What are you doing?" she hissed.

"You're through for the day," he answered, his voice raspy. "The dunking booth made its quota." He headed toward the outer doors.

"Put me down." She wiggled and pushed against him, but he held her in an iron grip.

"For crying out loud. You're not heavy!"

"I didn't say I was. But I'm not—" she smacked his chest and continued fighting "—going with you."

Mark squeezed her closer and narrowed his eyes. "Yes, you are. Now quit squirmin'."

She stilled. The heat from his body inflamed her. She was tempted to run her hands down his muscled arms and up to his broad shoulders. But she forced herself to look at him. "Where are we going?"

Mark lowered his gaze to her chest. His jaw clenched and his eyes narrowed. "Cover up, or I won't be responsible for my actions." He gestured with his head to her T-shirt he'd picked up along the way.

Of all the nerve! She didn't know which to respond to first, being kidnapped or being ridiculed. But she gratefully grabbed the shirt off his shoulder and draped it across her chest.

Mark stepped through the outer door of the Dallas Convention Center, stopped and turned around. "Smile and wave at your dad. Tell him you're fine and you'll see him later."

"But where are we going?"

"Just do it, damn it!"

Audrey reluctantly did as he bid.

At least her dad had quit following them, and even smiled at her. She caught a glimpse of John leading him away.

Mark whisked her into a waiting limo, maneuvered himself in beside her and the chauffeur took off. Snatching off his hat, Mark tossed it on the opposite seat and ran a hand through his hair. He didn't speak or look at her.

His hair was a little longer, and dark circles shadowed his eyes. But he was clean shaven, and smelled of his unique musky scent. His arm held her tight against him.

She swallowed past the lump in her throat. "So? What do you want?"

Mark turned to her, and she thought she glimpsed a flicker of passion in his eyes. But the next moment it was gone. What more could he want? Audrey raised her arms and began putting her head through the T-shirt's neck opening.

Mark reached over and stopped her.

"I thought you wanted me to cover up?"

His eyes swept over her breasts and he took a deep breath. "Changed my mind."

She twisted away from his grasp and continued dressing, daring him to stop her. Just because she felt badly about deceiving him didn't mean she'd revert to being a doormat.

Though she struggled, Mark easily wrenched the shirt from her hands. He grabbed her wrists, held them over her head and pushed her down to the plush leather seat.

The full weight of his body pressed her down, his

breathing as ragged as hers. She looked into his oh-so-beautiful blue eyes, striving for composure, determined not to let him guess she was aroused.

"Look, I know I lied to you. But I never printed your secrets, and I apologized publicly. What more do you want? Isn't this taking things a bit far?"

"Not far enough, darlin'." He captured her lips with his, kissing her until she whimpered.

She wished he'd let go of her hands so she could run them through his hair and reacquaint herself with the feel of him. She soon got her wish, but he only released one.

His free hand glided down her hair to her shoulder, lowering her suit strap and landing firmly on her breast to squeeze and caress.

If he meant to punish her, he was succeeding. She ached for him. "Let me up."

He ignored her plea, kissing down the line of her throat.

She pushed against his shoulder with her free hand. "Please. Don't do this."

"Why not?" he grumbled, lifting his head to look at her with narrowed eyes. "Didn't you mean what you said in the field that night?"

She bit back the resounding "yes" on the tip of her tongue. Was he serious, or playing some cruel game? Maybe it would be better to let him think she'd lied. He already had several advantages in this situation—her guilt and his strength. Why give him one more? Besides, the last thing she needed was more humiliation or pity.

Mark let out a sigh. Was that disappointment she'd seen in his face before he'd shuttered his expression? "All right. Guess we'll do this the hard way." Slowly, he let her go and sat up.

Audrey scooted away, sat up and pulled her bathing suit

strap over her shoulder. She gathered the T-shirt in front of her. "What do you want?"

Mark slid close and put his arm across the back of the seat. He turned to her and grinned. "One more high-stakes game, darlin'."

The force of that gorgeous smile hit her like a wind-storm, chasing away her caution. High stakes? For a moment, she envisioned wedding bells and happy ever after.

If only.

He was so handsome it made her stomach clench. But that only strengthened her belief that he was way beyond her reach. He was limousines and private jets, beauty queens and television ads.

She was hatchbacks, plus sizes and macaroni and cheese.

She had three choices. She could bluff her way out—threaten to press charges and demand to be let go. But he'd probably call her bluff. Or she could plead for leniency. Or she could simply wait, and face her fate with what dignity she had left.

She chose dignity.

She looked away, out the tinted window. "Fine. Let's get it over with."

His fingers caught her chin, forcing her to turn toward him. No longer smiling, his eyes burned into her. "It'll be a long time before it's over, darlin'."

Abruptly, he leaned forward and tapped on the glass. The chauffeur lowered the barrier. "Yes, sir?"

"Where's the deck of cards in this thing?"

"In the right side compartment, sir."

"Thank you."

As the glass rose, Audrey racked her brain to guess his intentions. He wanted to play poker now?

He reached over her to grab the cards, and she scooted a little farther away, clutching the T-shirt like a shield. If only she had her clothes on, she wouldn't feel quite so vulnerable.

"One game." He shuffled the cards. "You cut. I'll deal. Five-card draw, nothing wild, winner takes all." He placed the deck on the seat between them. "Cut."

To Audrey, the deck might as well have been a rattler about to strike. "But, I don't have any money with me. What are the stakes?"

"Stakes?" Mark smiled again—a dangerous smile. "I told you. The stakes are high, darlin'."

Sixteen

A surge of triumph filled Mark's chest. Her eyes widened, and she gripped that damn shirt as if it was the only thing standing between her and complete ravishment.

Maybe she was right.

He couldn't take his eyes off of her. A deep pink flush spread down her cheeks. Her hair was twisted on top of her head, a few curly tendrils hanging around her face. She was beautiful. When she'd planted that kiss on him, her back ramrod straight and her green eyes sparked with challenge, the blood had rushed to his groin so fast he'd actually felt light-headed.

He had to remind himself to stay focused on the plan. Hiring that kid to throw and miss had been sheer inspiration. But it was a good thing the traffic on I-30 was bumper-to-bumper from Dallas to Fort Worth. She was being stubborn. Or did she really not love him? He'd never understand women. That night in the meadow, he couldn't keep her from saying she loved him. Now, he needed to hear her admit it. Only the fire in her sea-green eyes gave him hope.

"S-so, what are these high stakes?" Her voice trembled.

He wanted to hold her and tell her it would be all right. And he would…eventually. "Come on, Audrey. Show your sack." He flashed her the same evil grin she'd given him.

She played right into his hands. Gone was the cowering girl, and in her place was the strong woman he admired. Her spine straightened, and her chin came up. She even dropped the shirt.

"All right. I assume you had something in mind? You want my job? I'll quit, but I'm a good writer. I'll find something else. You want sex? I don't see why. You said you'd gotten what you want—"

"Hold it!" Mark said. "Let's get one thing straight right now. That was never the—" *Spit it out, Malone.* "Aw, hell, Audrey. You know it was good. Better than good."

She became intensely interested in the limo's upholstery. But at least he'd shut her up. "Now, as to the stakes. We'll play one game. If you win, you get the Double M."

"Your ranch?" Audrey gripped his arm. "You can't do that! I haven't got anything that valuable."

The way she leaned over afforded him a fantastic view of two very valuable assets. But he didn't think she'd appreciate his sentiments. He forced his gaze to her eyes. "The Double M is worthless without you there, Audrey." It was true. He'd sell the place if he couldn't have her with him.

She shook her head. "Me? But you hate me. I lied to you."

If she only knew how much he loved her. But he had to know she really loved him first. "If I win, I get you. In the limo. Right now. Without the suit."

"Here? But, everyone can see in. What about the driver?"

"He can't see anything. It's one-way glass. All the windows are."

For once, Mark couldn't tell what thoughts were whirling around in Audrey's usually expressive face. Finally, she took a deep breath and said, "All right. But I can't take your ranch. I just want to hear you say you forgive me."

"Done." It didn't matter what he bet. Either way, he won.

Mark dealt them each five cards.

As Audrey picked hers up, it took all her self-control not to smile. Eight of hearts, seven of hearts, six of hearts, five of hearts and a three of clubs. What were the odds? Was he dealing straight or was this a setup?

No way. Besides, why go to all this trouble?

He caught her studying him and grinned. "Cards?"

She looked him in the eye but kept her face unreadable. "One, please." She slid her three of clubs over the seat.

The smug curve of his lips said he wasn't impressed as he dealt her one card. "Dealer takes one, also." His face remained blank as he looked at his new card.

Audrey steeled herself to remain expressionless as she glanced quickly at her new card. She almost gave it away when she saw the four of hearts. A straight flush! No way could he possibly beat that. It would be too unbelievable. She'd won! Oh, it was hard not to grin triumphantly. "Well, Mr. Malone. What've you got?"

Without hesitation, Mark laid down his hand: three aces and two jacks. A full house. Normally a winning hand.

She pictured his face when she showed him her cards, imagined hearing his grudging words of forgiveness. But just because he said the words didn't mean that, deep in his heart, he had actually forgiven her.

It would be an empty victory. A sham. No bet could give her what she really wanted—his love.

Maybe if she lost and he got his revenge, he would at least be free to get on with his life. What was a little humiliation compared to that? She knew he wouldn't hurt her. She loved him. She wanted him happy. If that's what it took, that's what she'd do.

With her decision made, her worries vanished. Might as well enjoy this last time with him. One more memory for those lonely nights.

She reached for her window button and lowered the glass a few inches. Holding his gaze, she lifted her arm behind her and let her cards fly out the window. She raised the window and brought her hand to the strap of her bathing suit, lowering it slowly. "You win." She smiled.

Mark sat there a moment, stunned at the realization that she was finally his. Well, that and the fact that she smiled as if *she* was the one who had won as she willingly stripped off her bathing suit.

She pulled out one arm and lowered the other strap. Mark swallowed, twice.

Last time, he'd refused to make love with her on a bet. But that was before she'd told him she loved him. The stakes were too high now. She must love him if she could smile that way as she gradually lowered the suit to her waist. Her nipples were already tight and pointed, begging for his mouth. He licked his lips in anticipation. He wanted his mouth on her now, but he forced himself to wait and enjoy the show she so freely offered. Besides, there was one more thing to do first.

She briefly glanced at the driver, and for a split second Mark saw her confidence slip, but she quickly masked her uncertainty. What a woman.

And from this moment on, she was all his.

Audrey couldn't believe she was doing this. Kind of hard to remove a bathing suit seductively in the seat of a car, even if it was a limousine. Well, maybe some women could do it, but not her.

Still, faster than she wished, here she sat in all her naked, chubby glory. She kept her arms at her sides and boldly dared him to look his fill.

His eyes roamed over her body, leisurely exploring her from top to bottom with obvious approval. Not knowing what to expect, she flinched when he began unbuttoning his shirt.

His chest muscles rippled as he pulled his sleeves off and threw the shirt on the floor. She caught a whiff of masculine sweat and musky cologne, and breathed in deeply.

He unbuckled his belt and unzipped his jeans. As he watched her watching him, he pushed his jeans down, taking his briefs with them until he reached his boots. He swung his legs onto her lap, silently asking her to tug off his boots and jeans.

Dazed, she complied, her eyes roving from his strong, hairy chest, to his flat stomach, to his long, muscular thighs and finally coming to rest on his potent male organ.

Enthralled with his nakedness, she jumped when he finally spoke. "You're the only woman besides hospital nurses who's seen me like this." He narrowed his eyes and jerked his chin at his leg. "Take a good look, Audrey. Disgusting, isn't it?"

She looked.

Where the left leg had a light dusting of brown hair, the right was covered only in scars. In addition to the long, thick one that snaked around from thigh to ankle, there were dozens of tiny white scars scattered around. The knee was sunken and the calf malformed. It wasn't a pretty sight. To her, it was a miracle he could walk at all, much less ride. Thinking of his persistence and determination to recover overwhelmed her.

She met his eyes. If he was anxious about her opinion, he didn't show it. Looking down, she ran her hand over his leg as she spoke. "I think it's a miracle. A testament to your strength and your indomitable will."

When he grabbed her hand and squeezed it, she raised her gaze to his again. She hoped he could read the truth of her heart in her eyes.

His were filled with unshed tears, brimming over, threatening to spill down his cheeks. He pushed her down, taking full possession of her mouth. After kissing her senseless, he pulled away and scowled. "Why did you lie to me, Audrey?"

This isn't exactly how she'd pictured herself explaining to him. She only hoped she could make him understand. "I spent my twenty-fifth birthday alone." She laughed, a short, humorless sound. "I don't even have a dog. I thought a more challenging career would fill the emptiness in my life. I needed something more."

He brushed his lips over her eyes, cheeks and forehead. "But you gave that up, lost your promotion, for me?"

"Once I got to know you, I couldn't betray your trust. Not even for the good of my career. I wouldn't have been able to face myself in the mirror. Besides, I got my promotion. I'm going to write more articles on charity events like this one."

He ran his hands through her hair, down her throat, over her breast and stomach. "And do you still need more?"

When she could breathe again, she answered, "Yes."

"What do you need?" He lifted himself over her, his magic fingers delving between her thighs.

This, she thought, closing her eyes. Oh yes, this. And so much more. "I—I need for you to understand, and to forgive me."

His fingers dug into her arms and she opened her eyes. He looked menacing. "Don't ever lie to me again."

She shook her head. "Never."

"Okay." He smiled. "Then, I forgive you."

She threw her arms around his neck and hugged him. "Thank you."

"After you left, I almost started drinking again. I hated you."

Audrey held her breath. She couldn't live knowing he despised her. "But, you don't anymore?"

"John told me you confessed to Helen. And even if you'd lied about who you were, you couldn't have faked it all. Your passion, your belief in me, not as the *Lone Cowboy,* but as Mark, just plain Mark. You made me believe in myself." He opened his mouth over hers and kissed her again. "Was it just an act?"

Hadn't he heard anything she'd said? Didn't he know? She lifted her head to return his kiss.

He took control of the kiss, plunging in his tongue. Abruptly, he pulled back. "Say it, Audrey. Tell me."

She had no reason not to tell him now. "I love you, Mark."

"Yes." He growled the word as he entered her, and said it again and again as he moved in her. He took her hard and swift, and they both spiraled swiftly to completion.

She could feel his heart racing even when he raised himself on his elbows and put his palm on her cheek, forcing her to look at him. "Say it again."

"I love you, Mark."

He smiled. "I want to hear you say it every day. And I don't want you doin' all the cleanin' and cookin' anymore. We'll hire someone to help."

"Wait a minute."

"Especially if you get pregnant. We can have the wedding here in Fort Worth if you want. I figure you'll want your family—"

She put her hand over his mouth. "Mark! What are you talking about?"

He looked at her as if she were a little slow. "Us. The ranch. Everything."

"You want me to live at the ranch?"

"You want to live in Dallas? I guess we can buy a house here. But I need to be on the Double M most of the time."

"But—"

"What? You're worried about your career? I'm sure you could still write for the magazine, but I kinda hoped you'd wanna stay home with the babies, too."

"Mark." She shook his shoulders. "What babies?"

Now he looked exasperated. "Our babies. The ones we're gonna have some day. Maybe you could work from home. We—"

She smacked her hand over his mouth again, but took it away before she spoke. "Did you mention the word wedding?"

"Yeah."

"But you haven't asked me."

"Woman, you're gonna marry me—"

"I'd like to be asked." She smiled.

Mark narrowed his eyes and let out a long, suffering sigh. "Ms. Tyson, would you do me the honor of becoming my wife?"

"No."

"What? Why not? You said you loved me."

Audrey looked away. Would she have to force him to say it? "But you haven't," she barely whispered.

Mark broke into a wide grin. "I love you, Audrey. I love your beautiful eyes, your smile, your—" he squeezed her breast "—your spirit. Now, are you going to marry me, or do you want to be dragged back to the Double M to live in sin?"

Oh, how she loved hearing those four words. She knew she would never feel empty again. Still, she hesitated. One more thing should be discussed.

As she thought about how to tell him, his grin faded into a mask of indifference. "If you really don't want to marry me...." he whispered.

Oh, she'd hesitated too long. "No! That's not it at all. It's just that—" Should she tell him when she wasn't sure? "Our first baby might be here in about eight months."

His eyes widened and his whole body went rigid, but he remained silent.

"Mark? Do you understand? Are you upset?"

A slow smile spread across his face. "Upset, darlin'? How could I be upset?" He wrapped his arms beneath her and squeezed her to him. "I'm gonna be the best damn father, I swear!"

"I know you will. And, if you're sure, I'll marry you."

"You bet you're gonna marry me, woman, if I have to lasso you and tie you to a church pew."

Audrey giggled. "I think we've had enough bets for a while. Would you really have given me the ranch if I'd won?"

"Honey, no stakes are too high for you." Mark grinned. He swooped down for another kiss.

Audrey whispered against his lips, "As long as the stakes are love, Mark."

Epilogue

Cowboy Christmas. The Fourth of July weekend had taken on a whole new meaning.

This year, instead of traveling from city to city, riding in two or sometimes three rodeos for prize money, Mark was flipping burgers on a backyard grill and watching his four-month-old daughter play in her bouncy chair on the porch. Alyse Helen Malone had her daddy's blue eyes and her mama's blond hair.

Mark gazed around the yard that had changed almost as much as its owner. Instead of choking weeds and a scum-laden pool, the back of his house now hosted the first annual Big Brothers and Big Sisters Dude Ranch Weekend. Dozens of fatherless boys and girls ran around playing baseball, squirting water guns, riding ponies and splashing in the pool.

"Is she doing okay?" his wife called as she shouldered her way out the back door carrying a large bowl of chips.

His wife. He still couldn't believe he'd found this kind of love. Though, last month they'd celebrated their first wedding anniversary.

"My little angel?" Mark smiled as he set down the spatula and picked up his daughter. He brought his forefinger to Alyse's nose and wiggled it. She gave him a grin, showing off her first tooth.

"Angel! Little hellion is more like it." Audrey smiled at her baby girl, belying her words. Audrey looked around the yard. "I never would have thought I'd end up married to the *Lone Cowboy*." She looked at him with the same wonder and joy in her eyes that he imagined showed in his.

Audrey put a hand on his shoulder and bounced up on her tiptoes to give him a kiss. "Thank you, Mr. Malone."

Just her touch had the power to undo him. Mark swallowed the lump in his throat. He couldn't afford to get all mushy in front of these kids. But, wait until tonight. "You don't have to thank me. I love having the kids here. It was a great idea, Audrey."

"Not for this. For trusting me with your heart after what I did."

Mark raised Alyse onto his shoulder. "Oh, that. Well, it was just a scarred, shriveled up lump of horse dung before you came along. I'd take that ride again in a heartbeat, darlin'. The best ride of my life. I fell hard and landed right in your arms." He grinned and bent to kiss her beautiful lips, smiling down at her emerald eyes.

Oh, what the hell. Who cared whether he had an audience. He gently set Alyse in her carrier and swept Audrey into his arms. Bending her backward, he closed his lips over hers, pouring all his passion and promise for tonight into his kiss.

* * * * *